CHAIN
of *mercy*

Brenda S. Anderson

Marjorie,
His mercies
never fail!

Blessings,
Brenda S Anderson

WINSLET
P R E S S

WINSLET PRESS

Chain of Mercy
Copyright © 2014
Brenda S. Anderson

ISBN-10: 0985723572
ISBN-13: 978-0985723576

This novel is a work of fiction. Names, characters, places, and inci-
dents either are the product of the author's imagination or are used
fictitiously. Any resemblance to actual events, locales, organizations,
or persons living or dead is entirely coincidental and beyond the
intent of either the author or the publisher.

Cover & Interior Design by Tekeme Studios

Printed in the United States of America

First Edition: April 2014
14   12   11   10   9   8   7   6   5   4   3   2   1

TO:

My husband Marvin who loves all my stories!
Thank you for believing in me before I believed in
myself. I could never do this without your
love and encouragement.

"I denied myself nothing my eyes desired; I refused my heart no pleasure. My heart took delight in all my work; and this was the reward for all my labor. Yet when I surveyed all that my hands had done and what I had toiled to achieve, everything was meaningless, a chasing after the wind; nothing was gained under the sun."
Ecclesiastes 2:10-11

"Some sat in darkness and the deepest gloom, prisoners suffering in iron chains, for they had rebelled against the words of God and despised the counsel of the Most High."
Psalm 107:10-11

CHAPTER *one*

"The good news is that the company only lost a million this quarter." Richard Brooks smirked at his assistant and slapped the quarterly report down on her desk.

"That's the good news?" Verna stopped typing and turned to him, propping a hand on her hip, her Southern accent always a welcome sound in this sea of nasal New Yorkers. "Young man, in my day people didn't make a million dollars, much less lose it. Now, tell me, if that's the good news, what's the bad?"

He stared at the Picasso print above Verna's desk. Reminded him of his life. "It looks like we're going to have no choice but to close the Phoenix plant." How had he missed the unmistakable signs of its mismanagement? Now, because of his lack of foresight, hundreds of people would lose their jobs. In all his years in New York City, he'd never made such a costly blunder.

"Goodness. And you're blaming yourself. I can see it in those beautiful blues of yours."

"I should have seen it coming months ago. All the signs were there."

"It just so happens you've had a few other things on your mind lately."

The muscles in his cheeks tightened. "I'm not paid to think of other things."

"You stop putting yourself down. It's time I see that gorgeous smile again."

He chuckled. "Happy?" Only Verna could make him smile under these circumstances.

"That's more like it. Now for my good news." She handed him several pink message slips. "Your wonderful family is sending you love and birthday greetings. There were two very disappointed little ladies by the names of Katydid and Lillykins who couldn't wait to talk to you."

"I missed their call?" He peeked at his watch. Not enough time to call them back now, but definitely later. They always brightened his day, and today he could use some sunshine.

"They called about ten minutes ago and told me to make sure I gave you this." Verna reached beneath her desk and pulled out a shoe-sized box covered in Little Mermaid wrapping paper and what looked like an entire roll of tape.

His Katydid's work most likely. He accepted the box and shook it. A slight rattling. They probably used an overabundance of tissue paper too. He tore at the paper, revealing a shoebox. He lifted the cover and grinned. Just what he expected. Nestled among balled tissue paper were several plastic toys from kid's meals. He pulled out a Spiderman figurine and moved its arms. This one he'd center on his desk.

"Those darling girls love you, you know."

"Not as much as I love them." He replaced the toy and covered the box. They'd be perfect additions to his shelves back home. He'd keep his favorites on his desk here at work. His colleagues could scoff all they wanted.

"Then when are you going to take a weekend off and go see them?"

Oh boy. Here it comes. "I saw them at Thanksgiving."

"Which was seven weeks ago"

He massaged the back of his neck. "It's not like Minnesota is right next door."

Verna poised her hands on her hips. "And it's not like your bank account doesn't have a few dollars, not to mention frequent flier miles to spare for plane tickets."

"And when do I have spare time to fly out there?"

"I'm very glad you asked." She struck a key on her keyboard, and turned the monitor toward him. With a pen, she pointed at the screen.

His schedule. Crafty woman. She aimed her pen toward

three open days in the coming week. "And you're booked on Delta's six a.m. flight."

"Fine. I should know better than to argue with you." He shook his head. What a blessing this woman had been to him. If not for her mothering, his life would be in even worse shape than it was now. "Verna, you're something else."

"You just remember that."

"You won't let me forget."

She resumed typing on her keyboard. "Speaking of not forgetting, the board meeting's about to begin, and you have the privilege of explaining that little million dollar loss."

Yeah. He scratched his head. Not something he looked forward to. Especially since that loss never should have happened. He carried the shoebox into his office, set it on his desk, then walked to his wall-sized window and stared out at Manhattan's skyline. If only he could turn back the clock. Make the right choice this time. Then he wouldn't have been distracted from doing his job. None of this should have happened.

One reckless decision devastated so many lives.

With a sigh, he snatched his Versace suit coat from the back of his leather chair, slipped it on, grabbed his briefcase, and headed for the conference room. He had fifteen short minutes to come up with a viable explanation for the company's doldrums.

Keeping his head down, avoiding eye contact, he walked down ACM Technologies' carpeted aisle. He'd heard enough of his co-workers' sneers these past seven plus months to last until the next century. And now, this company loss heaped on top of all his other problems. Just what his life needed.

He rounded a corner and strode past his CEO's assistant, praying she wouldn't notice him. Only a few more steps to the safety of conference room.

"Hey, Richie."

He stopped and pinched the bridge of his nose before looking back at her. "Patrice."

She tucked a bra strap back into a skin-tight sweater that dipped way too low to be professional. "You got a minute, darlin'?"

"Sorry." Not for her. Hard to believe he once dated the

woman. His standards once dipped as low as her sweater, but not anymore. Never again.

He nodded toward the conference room. "I've got a meeting."

"Oh, well it's busy." She waved fingers with half-inch long red nails. "They're not ready for—"

"They? Who's they?" He looked down the hall at the room reserved for board members only. The doors were closed. His heart rate accelerated as he glanced at his watch. Still ten minutes early. "What's going on, Patrice?"

"A board meeting. Mr. Entenza asked that you wait here." She pointed to a visitor's chair. "Can I get you some coffee?"

"Whoa. Back up. A board meeting? I'm a member of the board."

"I know, Richie, they—"

"It's Richard." He stared at the room's closed door and panic tingled through his body. This couldn't be happening. He was too valuable to the company. The failings of these past seven months were his first blip in four years as a vice president. No one could match his record for saving the company money.

He wiped perspiration from his forehead and squinted at Patrice. "How long did they say they'd be?"

"Oh, a few more minutes."

Good. Enough time to gather his wits and steel himself against the accusations he knew were coming. To prove they needed him.

"I haven't seen Marissa around lately."

His jaw tightened, and he glanced at his watch again. The board's accusations would be more pleasant than Patrice's inquiry.

"Did she quit or something?"

Or something. "She's at the White Plains office."

"You break up? I mean, if you did, I just broke it off with—"

He glared at the assistant, praying daggers would shoot from his eyes. "Yeah. We broke up." Marissa had single-handedly destroyed his personal life. Now, it looked like he was about to lose his career. All because of her.

"You don't need to get testy about it."

Testy? Patrice was lucky he didn't hit women. He glanced

toward the conference room and dragged his arm across his forehead. No more waiting. He'd barge in there and show them he wouldn't be walked on.

He strode down the hallway and tugged open the heavy wood door. Eight other men sat around the mahogany table, relaxing in their plush seats. Each one looked up at him, surprise written on some of their faces, but scorn on the others. Or, was it gloating?

"Gentlemen." He rolled out his padded leather chair and laid his briefcase on the table. "I apologize for being late. My memo told me two o'clock."

The CEO, Montegue Entenza, leaned back in his chair and rested hands on his ample stomach. "Actually, Richard, your memo was correct."

Richard's stomach twisted, but he tried to hold his poker face. Don't let these men see his fear. He sat, folded his hands on the table, and looked around trying to connect with each man, but most looked away. Cowards. He glared at Entenza. "Please enlighten me."

"The facts are right there in your quarterly report. I don't take kindly to losing money."

"Come on, every business on Wall Street is losing money right now. Besides, most of that loss comes from the Phoenix plant. Once we close that, our losses will be negligible, and with the new manager in Atlanta, I foresee profits coming from them in—"

"Mr. Brooks." Mr. Entenza leaned forward. "The fact is, someone has to pay for the loss."

"So you're scapegoating me? Over the past four years, I've been your top performer." He pointed to the man seated kitty-corner from him. "What about Edwards? Wasn't he responsible for a three million—?"

"Quiet." Entenza raised his voice and sat up straight. "This isn't about Edwards, or Constapoulas, or anyone else. It's about the image you present of ACM Technologies."

Richard laughed. "So this has nothing to do with my performance."

"Our shareholders don't take kindly to having a member of

our board with a police record."

"Ahh, I see." Just as he thought. How could he win a battle against the truth? "Let me save you and the shareholders a little trouble." He pushed away from the table, grabbed his briefcase, and stood. Neither a demotion nor an outright firing was unacceptable. "I'll have my office cleared in an hour. Other companies have been begging for my expertise. I guess it's time I answer them."

"So be it." Entenza pushed a button on the conference phone. "Patrice, will you send in Cowell?"

"Cowell?" Could this possibly get any worse? "A security escort?"

"Protocol, son. I'm sure you understand."

Richard pinched the bridge of his nose. "Perfectly, sir." He gave Entenza a mock salute and strode from the room, slamming the door behind him.

Happy unbelievable birthday.

Cowell, dressed in a complete security officer's uniform, glanced warily at him and shook his head. "Sorry about this, Richard. Entenza has no clue you're one of the good guys."

"Right. Good guys don't get themselves thrown in jail, now, do they?"

"You paid your dues." Cowell slapped his back.

"I'll be paying for the rest of my life." He muttered under his breath. As well he should. If he were still a drinking man, tonight would have been a perfect time to drown his sorrows with a few Coronas.

With Cowell at his side, Richard hurried through the hallways, keeping his head down. The snickers he heard from passing co-workers told him they already knew of his dismissal. He flew past Verna's desk without acknowledging her. She was the one person he was going to miss.

"I'll wait outside for you." Cowell reached into Richard's office—make that his former office—and closed the door.

Richard fisted his hands. How could he have thrown away everything? One lousy night ... One moronic choice.

Well, standing here feeling sorry for himself wouldn't solve anything. It was time to move on. Maybe Chicago. Close enough to drive to Minnesota. Far enough to make those drives rare. And with all his connections, he shouldn't have a problem linking up with a Fortune 500 company. Out there, his tarnished reputation wouldn't be slapping him in the face at every turn. Yes, Chicago was a good choice.

After stuffing his laptop in his briefcase, he pulled a copy paper box from his closet and packed the few personal possessions he kept in his office. Some novels, the gift from his girls, pictures of his family, his nephews. What would they all say now? Would his brother laugh that the high and mighty Richard Brooks had been laid low? Again?

No. Not even Marcus would be that small.

He covered the box and took one last look around the office. He wasn't forty yet, and other corporations had frequently sent headhunters his way. This setback wasn't going to stop him. He'd prove to Entenza, and all those finger-pointing shareholders, they'd fired the wrong man.

With a grunt, he picked up his briefcase and the box and carried them out the door.

Verna sat at her desk, sniffling. Tissues overflowed her garbage can. "Richard, I am so sorry. It just breaks my heart to see you go."

"It's been a good run, Verna, and you've been like a mom to me."

She dabbed a tissue at her eyes. "Before you leave, I do have one little smidgen of good news for you. Something I know will bless your heart."

"I could sure use some good news." He propped the box on her desk and managed a smile. "You have another grandchild on the way?"

"That would certainly brighten my day, but I'm afraid all my children are done having babies for now."

"So, what have you got?"

She handed him a pink message slip. "Some much needed mercy."

He read it through once, and his heart dipped. He read it through a second time. The message stayed the same. No. No. No! He balled up the paper and hurled it against his former office door.

Forget New York City.

Forget Chicago.

Much needed mercy? Mercy was the last thing he deserved, and God knew it too.

God couldn't have exacted a more perfect revenge.

TREMBLING, SHEILA PETERSON GRABBED JOE'S hand as he pushed away from the restaurant table. "Please, let me explain."

He jerked his hand from hers, disgust darkening his milk chocolate eyes. His silence said more than words as he snatched the velvet box off the table, grabbed his leather jacket, and strode through the dimly lit room toward the exit, weaving around diners with the grace of a natural athlete.

"I had no choice," she whispered, perhaps only to convince herself, and clutched a hand to her chest. Her heart pounded like waves against the shore of a storm-tossed lake.

Joe stopped by the arched exit and turned his head her way.

Her breath stilled. The contempt in his eyes wasn't visible from here, but she knew it was there. He'd made it clear that her offense against him was unforgivable. If he would only listen, understand her perspective, perhaps his ache would ease.

She curved her hands on the edge of the table, about to push back and go to him, but he heaved the box into a planter decorating the door's entrance.

She gasped and covered her mouth.

A second later, he disappeared out the door.

Eyes stinging, she slumped into her chair.

Abandoned. Again.

Joe was just like her parents.

She closed her burning eyes and drew in a trembling breath. Grilled sirloin. Joe's favorite. It sat uneaten. She couldn't blame him.

I will not cry. She opened her eyes and scanned the dining room, a setting groomed for a romantic proposal. Window shades were purposely drawn. An amber glow emanated from candles set at the center of tables draped in burgundy linens. Nearly all the seats held customers, mostly with couples seeking intimacy in a public setting, talking in whispers that created a low buzz throughout the room. Shadows highlighted faces, hiding imperfections.

Joe had no physical imperfections to hide.

Sheila no longer had anything to hide.

How many other couples would end their evening apart? It was too dark to tell. But, it didn't matter. What mattered was that there was no one familiar, no one glancing her way, no one gloating over her humiliation.

He'd embarrassed her.

In public.

Anger tensed her body. How dare he?

Abandoned. Yes. But no longer a victim. Not this time.

She snatched her Kenneth Cole clutch off the table. A link on her bracelet snagged and tugged the tablecloth, knocking over an untouched goblet, and red wine gushed toward her silk sheath. She jumped up, her bracelet pulled free, and she released a grateful sigh. Her new Vera Wang was safe.

Even if her heart wasn't.

Steadying her breath, she laid her mulberry pea coat across her arm, and with her chin raised, she walked toward the exit intending to glide right past the planter.

But, she couldn't.

Blowing out a breath, she scowled at her professionally manicured nails then squatted and dug into the soil. "Aha," she said softly as her fingers found the box and pulled it out. She wiped residue from its velvet exterior and checked to see if anyone watched before focusing on Joe's unanticipated gift. Her chin quivered, and her eyes moistened as she raised the indigo cover.

She stroked the marquis for only a moment then closed the lid to the box, effectively sealing off her heart.

The ring would never circle her finger. She'd have a courier return the diamond along with a note expressing her apologies, but she couldn't be sorry for what she'd done. It was the only thing that made sense. She didn't regret her actions even if it meant losing Joe.

SHIVERING IN JANUARY'S THIRTY-ONE DEGREE temperatures, Richard zipped up his leather jacket and pulled on gloves. He rested against the U-Haul that stored his surprisingly few meaningful possessions. It had taken him all of one week to pack and sell his Brooklyn Heights condominium, with a nice little profit even. A sure sign he was meant to flee New York.

He stared out beyond the Louis Valentine, Jr. Pier. This would be his final journey here, a rare place of tranquility in this unsleeping city. He pulled the truck's door handle, making sure it was locked, then walked across Coffey Street's cobblestone, down the sidewalk that split snow-coated parkland, and onto a pier quieted by cold. Once upon eight months ago, he'd dreamed of fishing side by side with a son off this pier. Now, that would never happen.

Winter's wind gusted off the water as he leaned into the railing and gazed out over New York Harbor, at the Statue of Liberty rising above it. The country's symbol of freedom.

Freedom, huh! He kicked at a guardrail, and it made a clinking sound. He glanced down. A chain necklace, coated with snow, circled the post.

He squatted and loosened the chain, then stood and ran his thumb over its filthy oval links. This must be a gift from God himself to remind Richard of mercy's shackle. He stared out at the Statue, the chains of tyranny lying broken at her feet, and tugged at the necklace's cold links. They held firm. Unbroken. Perfect.

He shook snow and dirt from the chain, removed his gloves, then pulled a tissue from his pocket and polished it. It had been exposed to the elements too long for it to have a burnished shine. All the better. He retrieved his keychain and removed the key he should have left alone eight months ago. If he had …

No. Not going there.

He unclasped the grimy chain, slipped the key onto it, and then fastened it back together. His palms clammy despite the cold, he grasped the chain in both hands, hefted it over his head, and anchored it around his neck, tucking the key inside his sweatshirt.

In moving back to Minnesota, he would no longer encounter the stabbing reminders that living in New York brought him. But, with this chain forever circling his neck, he'd certainly never forget.

CHAPTER *two*

This new "dungeon" was darker than the jail cell that once encased him, and that suited Richard just fine. He nodded his gratitude to the scowling co-worker standing silent and specter-like only feet away. These underground shadows would provide the anonymity Richard deserved.

And the bowels of this Minneapolis business was the perfect place to start his new life, a mere three months after his exodus from Manhattan. He walked in a slow circle, surveying the room, ducking his tall frame beneath 60-watt bulbs that hung naked above him. Endless arms of vents and pipes spider webbed the concrete walls and the unfinished ceiling. An ancient furnace slouched in the corner huffing a labored breath as if it had smoked too many years. Its tarred lungs couldn't survive another Minnesota winter.

That beast would be the first thing he'd take care of.

Sunlight infused with dust motes shone from a single window set below street level. More dust motes crowded in layers on all the basement surfaces.

He'd fix that next.

He gazed over at his co-worker, Wharton Sports' Human Resources Director, a colleague from before Richard's life swerved and crashed.

"I don't get it." Ethan Johnson loosened his tie and leaned against a gray metal desk.

"What's there to get?" Richard stuffed his hands in his jean pockets. "I asked you for a job. You found me one. I'm grateful."

"And you're sure this is what you want?"

"Want?" Richard laughed dryly. "Hardly. It's what I need. This is where I belong."

"I'm just glad you're here. Wharton Sports is lucky to have you, even if it's down here." Ethan picked up a manila folder from the desk, the folder guarding the truth about who Richard was. "But, if you ever change your mind—" Ethan nodded upward. "—you know where to find me."

"I appreciate the thought." Ethan's offer was one he could never accept.

"Man, I hate to see you like this. In New York, you didn't let troubles get to you. I always thought 'Here's a guy who knows how to live.'"

"Don't you see, Ethan? That's the problem, I …" He cleared his throat. "I … lived."

"Whoa, buddy." Ethan clasped his hand on Richard's shoulder. "You're not thinking …"

Richard shrugged off Ethan's hand and backed away.

"We've got counselors on staff—"

"I don't need counseling." Richard clenched his jaw.

Ethan raised his palms and stood silent.

Richard looked down, but still felt Ethan's studied gaze. His friend didn't have to worry. Suicide wasn't on his mind. He'd already wasted several months telling a therapist things not even his family knew and never would. If this past year had taught him anything, it was how precious life really was.

And that maybe his family had been right all along. He needed God back in his life.

Right. The ultimate form of surrender.

It was time to resurrect his life, on his own, and there was no better place to start than here at the bottom. He tugged open his locker, it's squeaky hinges protesting. An easy fix. He strode to the metal shelves lining a wall and grabbed a can of WD-40. He sprayed the hinges then opened and closed the locker several times. No hint of a squeal anymore. One task already accomplished.

Behind the lockers, a dehumidifier exhaled an incessant wheeze, but a musty stench still clung to the air. He'd fix that too. Today, even. Really, was this job any different from his Manhattan career? So what if repairing dehumidifiers didn't hold the same glamour as fixing businesses?

And now, it was time to mend his life.

Bending down, he zipped open the sports bag he'd dropped by the locker and pulled out his motivation. A smile tugged at his lips as he opened the frame's easel. He angled his nephews' portrait on the locker's metal shelf. They needed their uncle. He pulled another picture from the bag. Gazing at his girls, his smile broke free. They needed him too.

He needed them even more.

Grinning, he set that frame on the shelf and added three plastic figurines from a kids' meal.

"Your family?" Ethan cuffed a hand over Richard's shoulder.

Richard nodded. "I'll get to see them more now." The best perk of this new job.

"I'm glad for you." Ethan slapped Richard on the back. "You taught me the importance of family."

How had that happened when Richard had never appreciated their importance? Until now, anyway. "So, you and Linny are doing well?"

"Better than well. I have you to thank for saving my marriage."

"I just pointed you in the right direction. You did all the work." And effective today, he was aiming in a new direction. The right direction for once.

Ethan reached toward the desk and picked up a custodian uniform that blended in with the desk's drab tone. He handed the outfit to Richard. "Sorry. It's not exactly what you're used to."

Richard ran his hand over the fabric. Stiff, starchy cotton. Cheap. Perfect. "You don't suppose this'll keep the women away?"

"Sorry." Ethan grinned. "You could walk through the building in bib overalls and a straw hat, and the women would faint."

"Then I'll just have to keep my head down." His last months in New York had trained him to do that well. He folded the uniform into his sports bag and closed the locker door.

"Still living like a monk, I see."

"And basking in its freedom." This way, no double-crossing vixen would ever bring him down again.

Ethan slapped Richard's back. "I'm here for you, buddy."

They shook hands, and Ethan walked from the room.

Richard flinched as the heavy metal door closed with a familiar echoing clang. Darkness cloaked the room, but a strip of light squinted from beneath the door. A miniscule ray of hope.

He glanced over at the gasping dehumidifier. It was time to breathe life into that old machine and begin the process of reviving his own life.

WALKING THROUGH THE CARPETED HALLWAYS of Wharton Sports' upper floor, Sheila pulled her iPhone from her purse and scrolled through the contacts. There had to be someone to break up the solitude of her evening.

She gasped as Joe's name popped up. Still there, three months after their break-up. It was past time to let him go.

"Sheila, wait up."

Oh, wonderful. Inwardly rolling her eyes, Sheila dropped the phone into her purse and lengthened her stride. Joe would be deleted later when she could properly celebrate his complete expulsion from her life.

"How are you?" Heels scuffling over carpet accompanied the nasal voice. Soon Karla, the company gossip, walked at Sheila's side, taking two steps to Sheila's one. "I haven't seen the ballplayer around in months. Did you two break up?"

Sheila glanced at her watch and quickened her pace.

"You know …" Karla huffed to remain even with Sheila. "What about the hunky new janitor?"

Janitor? Sheila stifled a laugh. Me, a company executive, date a janitor? Not on your life. Slowing herself, she glared down at the woman. "If you don't mind, I've got a meeting." It was a lie, but the caustic words achieved their purpose as Sheila hurried through the hallway alone.

Unfortunately, Karla's words didn't retreat as well. Thoughts of Sheila's last evening with Joe swarmed through her head and soured in her stomach. Why did it make her so uneasy? The breakup didn't bother her. It had threatened for months. His religion played too big a role in his life for her to get serious about him. After all, religion was for hypocrites.

Truth be told, it's what she did to cause the breakup that still seethed in her gut. Joe hated her for it, but given a second chance, her choice would be no different.

She rounded a corner and braked just in time to avoid a collision with a ladder straddling the hallway. "What in the—"

"Sorry about the ladder, ma'am." A deep voice spoke from above. "I just need to finish putting together this fixture. I'll be out of your way in a moment."

Ma'am? How old does he think I am? She glanced up, her mouth opened to throw a snide remark, but eyes the shade of a moonlit sky met hers, leaving her mouth agape.

Those eyes, framed by a sculpted face darkened with an evening shadow, stared down on her. He nodded, smiling, his lips tilting slightly higher to the right. Deep crevices lined his cheeks, and the skin by his eyes crinkled just enough to add a distinguished touch. Only on men. Just as quickly, he looked away.

Pursing her lips, she watched him twist the final screw. *So, this must be the janitor Karla mentioned. No wonder she salivated over him.*

She held the ladder as he climbed down, temporarily wrinkling a steel gray uniform that was unusually clean and pressed. A pleat that looked sharp enough to slice through wood, lined the front of his slacks. A dirt-streaked rag hanging from his back pocket almost seemed out of place. Even in his janitor grays, the man was breathtaking.

"Is there something I could help you with?" He combed a hand through dark brown hair that was lightly salted at the temples. Another distinguishing touch. For men only. Life was truly unfair.

Yet, a sly smile curved her lips. This could be the distraction she desperately needed. "Yes, actually there is." Although she stood near five-foot-ten and wore two-inch heals, she still had to glance up to connect with those gorgeous eyes. "My desk drawer sticks, and I can't seem to fix it. Do you have a moment to look at it?"

"Sure thing. Show me the way." He folded the ladder, tucked it beneath an arm, and picked up his toolbox with his open hand.

"Follow me." She lifted her chin and squared her shoulders, reclaiming her superiority as she strode toward her office through halls papered in commercial beige. "By the way, I don't believe we've met." She briefly turned while walking. "I'm Sheila Peterson."

"Richard Brooks." He nodded, his face devoid of expression, and followed like a proper subordinate.

Within minutes, they entered her office. Colleagues had often described her domain as sterile. But white walls and taupe carpeting suited her. Visitors and clients frequently stared blankly at her one piece of artwork that she'd commissioned from an Uptown artist, with the white canvas split by a singular three-inch-wide black stripe. It was the stripe she found most intriguing, wondering what secrets hid beneath its darkness.

Even now, the janitor studied it, his eyes narrowed in obvious confusion. What else should she expect from a maintenance man?

"You wouldn't understand," she mumbled and walked toward her desk positioned in front of a window framing in Minneapolis' blue-glass towers. An exposition of power. That's what she truly wanted people to see.

"Pardon me?"

"Oh, nothing." She waved her hand dismissively. What had she been thinking, asking him here? Her love life wasn't that pathetic, was it?

"It's over here." She knelt by her desk, tugged open the broken drawer, and grimaced. Bottles of fruit-flavored water and a sleeve of Fig Newtons bobbed among waves of crumpled paper containing unusable sales ideas. "Just give me a moment, please."

"Take your time." Amusement flickered across his face as he rounded the desk.

His opinion doesn't matter. Clenching her teeth, she removed the clutter and hid it beneath her desk. The mess shouldn't matter, really. The outside was what most people saw. Her desk's lacquered oak top was always visible, the paperwork neat and organized. A black insulated coffee mug, imprinted with Wharton Sports' company logo, sat right where she wanted it, on the left next to her phone. The computer monitor to her right. Everything was in its proper, orderly place.

Her drawers were another matter, although she knew exactly where everything was. Still, the mess was a constant reminder for her to keep things simple.

With the drawer empty, she stood and caught the janitor eyeing the company's quarterly report centered on her desk. "This wouldn't interest you." She snatched up the document and motioned toward the drawer.

He didn't move.

With an exasperated sigh, she looked up at him. His face was taut, drawing his lips into a tight rope, and his eyes had lost their moonlit glow.

Just like her final memory of Joe.

Her shoulders sagged. Why did she insist on hurting people? This man had done nothing to earn her derision. She laid the report back on her desk. "Listen, I'm sorry. I'm having a lousy day, and you just happen to be a convenient target."

His cheeks straining, he crouched by her desk.

She studied him as he worked, the tension ebbing from his face. The man was definitely easy on the eyes. His only obvious imperfection was a narrow scar, still red with newness, that jagged up his muscled bicep and disappeared into precisely rolled-up sleeves. It only added to his appeal.

Would dating a janitor simplify her love life? She walked around her desk, and a knock sounded on her open door.

Ethan stepped in and held up a stack of manila folders. "Here are the finalists for your new ..." His gaze went to Richard. "Oh, I'm sorry. I didn't realize you were busy."

"Don't worry." Sheila waved her hand and accepted the files from Ethan. "It's just the janitor."

The drawer banged behind her, making her jump. Her eyes wide, she turned toward the custodian.

He shrugged, his eyes darker yet. "It slipped."

She clamped her mouth shut, preventing more derogatory words from tumbling out, and thumbed through the files. Her eyes narrowing, she pulled out a Girl Scout cookie order form and stared at Ethan. "Lose something?"

He scratched his head. "Hmmm. Wonder how that got in

there."

"I'm sure you do." Sheila plucked a pen off her desk and glanced over the form. "No Fig Newtons, I see."

"What can I say?"

Pursing her lips to prevent a smile, she marked a one below each column. "Then I guess your daughter will have to donate these cookies to the food bank." She handed the form back to Ethan, picked her purse off the desk and pulled out two twenties. "Keep the change."

"You're a peach, Sheila."

"Don't let the word get out."

"Your secret's safe with me." He winked and looked past Sheila. "Richard, what can I get you?"

"Just mark me down for one of each. No, Make that three each of the mints and those caramel coconut cookies."

Sheila raised her eyebrows.

Grinning, Richard patted his stomach. "Gotta keep up this figure."

Her gaze floated from a clearly flat stomach to muscular arms. The man was indeed a specimen.

Wrapped in a janitor's uniform.

Shaking her head, she directed her attention to Ethan. "Thank you." She waved the files. "I'll get back to you tomorrow."

"I'd appreciate it." With a wink, he walked from the room.

Too bad Ethan was married. Now, there was a man who could hold his own in a conversation, and his Jersey accent gave him an air of sophistication Minnesotans lacked.

To think she even considered asking the custodian out. Sure, beneath the dull gray uniform was one fine-looking man, but when had she ever chosen her dates based solely on appearance? Spending an evening with someone not her intellectual equal would be a nightmare. Clasping Ethan's files, she stifled a laugh. No, she would not stoop that low.

"What's your opinion regarding Wharton's proposed plan to expand to the East Coast?"

The folders slipped from her fingers, and papers cascaded onto the floor. She stared at the kneeling man and rubbed her ear. "Excuse me?" It was time to have her hearing checked.

He peered up, and his confident eyes drew her in. Maybe a drink with the man wouldn't hurt.

Get a grip, Sheila. She clutched her hands on her hips. "You're aware of the company's plans?"

He slid the drawer in and out twice and stood, looking down at her. His eyes narrowed, and his mouth curved up to the right. Oh, the man had a sexy smile. "I make it my job to understand the company I work for."

"I'm surprised you'd even care." She knelt to straighten Ethan's documents, removing herself from Richard's penetrating vision. What would this guy possibly know about business? He was obviously trying to make a move on her.

"Why not?" His voice bounced over the desk. "This proposed expansion will affect my future with the company the same as yours."

True. But most employees didn't usually care beyond their own little world. What made him different? Gathering the folders in what resembled an organized bundle, she stood and faced him.

He crossed his arms, looking way too assured for a man of his position. "Personally, I believe the company is looking in the wrong direction. There are countless solutions available to relieve Wharton of its financial predicament without encroaching on an area that currently has a glut of indistinguishable industries."

What? She caught herself staring. No, this wasn't a corporate meeting. He was a custodian, for Pete's sake. But what custodian had that kind of vocabulary? Much less knew about business. And he'd even echoed her exact opinion. What was up with this guy? Nothing about him made any sense.

She positioned the files on her desk and crossed her arms, mimicking his pose. It was imperative to maintain an edge in this absurd conversation. "How are you aware of the company's financial situation?"

He flattened his hands on the document he'd eyed earlier and leaned forward. "You think you're the only one who reads quarterly reports?"

She found herself wanting to back away, but held her ground and listened, wanting to hear his explanation. Certainly, up until this point it was all an act. Someone at Wharton's, probably Ethan, had to have put him up to this. Was probably even filming it.

"This last fiscal year has seen the profits level off and even dip." He tapped the report. "I believe the proposed expansion will spread the corporation too thin. At present, a tightened focus would serve Wharton much better." He squatted, gathered his tools, and stood again. "It's the wrong direction for the company." Certainty rang in his voice.

He's dead right. This guy understood the corporate world better than half the board. Why? How?

Intriguing.

Perhaps he was worth getting to know better. Give her a mystery to solve … along with a little romance. She relaxed her arms at her side and even smiled. "I expressed the same opinion at the last board meeting. They've elected to study it further before going ahead."

"Good." A shine relit his midnight eyes. "Let's hope they keep listening to you."

Her smile broadened, then the reality of the conversation set in. *Girl, he's a janitor.*

"Your drawer is rolling smoothly now." His voice interrupted her confused musing as he walked toward the door.

Her gaze honed in on his left hand before he stepped into the hallway. Naked. Not even a hint of a ring ever circling his finger. Karla was right. There couldn't be anything less complicated than dating a janitor. The relationship could never go anywhere, which was precisely what she needed.

She hurried after him, exiting her office as he picked up the ladder propped next to her door. "Could you wait one moment?"

The man rested the ladder and peered back with those piercing eyes.

She pulled up within a foot of him, purposely invading his space, drawn even closer by the subtle scent of musk. He didn't back away, clearly not threatened. She lifted a foot to retreat but stopped herself. No, she would not be intimidated. Instead, she tilted her head up and smiled her most alluring smile, the one no man could say "no" to. "Perhaps I could take you out for a drink to say thank you for your help."

A smile flashed across his face then vanished. "No, thank

you, Ms. Peterson. I prefer to leave work at work." He hefted the ladder and walked away, disappearing around a corner.

Sheila stood still, biting the insides of her warming cheeks. Her eyes widened and narrowed before she realized she was holding her breath.

No one ever turned her down.

She crossed her arms and smiled.

Next time, she wouldn't accept "no."

RICHARD TRUDGED THROUGH THE HALLWAY, his clomping footsteps echoing in its emptiness. What had he been thinking? Flirting with Wharton's executive sales manager? Oh, he knew her all right, but hadn't let on. Even exiled in maintenance, it was crucial to keep up with the company's fiscal situation and to be aware of who the main players were. But, more so, Sheila Peterson was not one who could walk through the building unnoticed.

Richard allowed a half smile as he recalled following her, watching the natural sway of curvy hips and the light bounce of acorn-colored hair. A linked silver bracelet loosely circled her right wrist accenting slender hands. The floral fragrance of her perfume had trailed his way, stimulating senses he couldn't chance exciting.

With fists clenched, he rounded a corner and aimed for the elevator. He punched the down arrow and the doors opened immediately. It was empty, thank goodness. The last thing he wanted was more conversation. He dragged the ladder in, reclined it against the back wall, and pressed B for basement. There, he would find a quiet refuge. The doors slid together as he leaned against the carpet covering the elevator wall, and he closed his eyes.

A vision of Sheila imposed on the darkness. He should have kept his mouth shut. But, he so longed for provocative conversation, and company finances was not a topic that came up with his maintenance colleagues.

Oh, the debate he could have had with the spirited executive. His blood heated just thinking about it. If their conversation had been held a year ago, he'd have followed up the discussion with an invitation to dinner, a walk, maybe a nightcap, probably breakfast.

The elevator's bell dinged. His eyes opened as the doors parted. He stepped into a concrete hallway and breathed in. The musty odor was disappearing. One small victory. He walked toward the boiler room, inspecting the pipes running along the ceiling. No leaks or beading sweat. Not anymore.

Of course, company executives would never know there had been a problem in the first place. Such a matter was trivial for them. They never mingled with the custodial staff. It would be beneath them.

So why wouldn't dating him be beneath Sheila? He imagined having breakfast with her. What that actually meant. It had been a long time …

With a grunt, he muscled open the metal door leading to his dungeon and returned the ladder to its new home.

Beautiful women had always been his Achilles heel. Obviously, that hadn't changed. Turning her down had been the right thing to do, but would he be able to do the right thing if there was a next time? If only he could see into the future.

He flipped the light switch, shrouding the room in blackness, and stepped into the hallway. He'd just have to avoid her. It shouldn't be too hard. By tomorrow, Sheila Peterson will have forgotten all about her flirtation with a lowly janitor. He didn't need to see the future to know that.

CHAPTER *three*

Phantom-like silhouettes confronted Richard as he strode to his car in the downtown Minneapolis parking ramp. Exhaust fumes, cemented into the concrete, exposed the garage's old age when ramps were built without the public's safety in mind. Sometime in the past decade, it had been updated with lighting and security cameras. Still, there were too many places evil could hide.

His size was a natural deterrent to crime, but wouldn't intimidate everyone. Living in Manhattan taught him that. He scanned the support beams and their shadows as he walked noiselessly, his ears trained to the sounds around him: traffic buzzing on the streets outside, the slam of a car door nearby, the click of high-heeled shoes, and a muttered curse.

Quickening his steps, he glanced up the ramp. His gaze settled on a well-dressed woman, hands on hips, standing next to a highly-shined Lexus sports sedan. Alone and safe, but he wouldn't leave until she drove out of danger's reach.

Hoping to remain unnoticed, he leaned against a beam and watched her shoulders droop and her head bow. An expletive flew from her mouth, and she kicked at a tire that looked like it had melted onto the floor.

No wonder she was upset. Good thing he stayed late tonight. Earlier in the evening, he had considered going home and firing up the grill, but the empty house would have been too lonely, too quiet. His physical job helped cover the solitude, but hadn't erased the guilt. Nothing would take that away. He didn't want it to. At least being a Good Samaritan would steal him a few moments of joy.

He approached the woman from behind, but maintained a couple yards distance, hoping not to frighten her. "I'll give you a hand."

Her body stiffened and keys sprouted between each knuckle on her right hand as she spun around.

Sheila Peterson. He groaned, and his shoulders sagged.

Her eyes widened, clearly recognizing him, but her body remained rigid. "I can do this myself." She displayed her key-filled hand.

Holding his palms up, he walked toward her. "I don't doubt it. I just thought I could lend a hand." He stood still, her eyes piercing his.

After a few long seconds, her body relaxed. "Fine. You get the tire." She clicked her remote, popping the trunk open. "I'll jack it up."

He opened his mouth to protest, then clamped it shut. Arguing would probably offend the self-sufficient executive. When it came time to raise the car, he'd convince her to surrender the jack. He glanced in the open trunk and grinned. Somewhere beneath the reams of paper, empty water bottles, and Fig Newton wrappers, there must be a tire.

As he picked up a ream, she pushed him aside. "Excuse me." She shoved the clutter to the back of the trunk and lifted the thin carpet unveiling the spare and the jack. With a grunt, she picked up the jack.

Okay, maybe she wouldn't be easily convinced.

He removed the spare and the tire iron then knelt next to the wheel. "Give me a moment to get it ready." The hubcap slid off easily, but unscrewing the lug nuts required extra elbow-grease. Good thing he was here to help.

Now it was her turn. He stood and backed away, allowing her plenty of space. He suppressed a smile as she held the jack away from her suit, compressing her lips, while staring down at hands already stained with grease.

Just what he anticipated.

He pulled the rag from his back pocket and offered the cloth. "Listen, I'm dressed for this work, and you're obviously not. Why not let me help?"

She scanned his eyes before exchanging the jack for the rag. Moments later, he raised the car enough to enable a quick tire change. Richard swore he felt Sheila's eyes on him while he worked. What was she thinking? He wouldn't ask her out, but if she made the request, could he turn her down again? Did he want to? *Work, Richard.* Focus.

In a matter of minutes, he had the spare on the car and the lug nuts secure. He gently lowered the sedan and gave the lug nuts a tightening turn. "Now, this tire is only temporary." Standing, he concentrated on her black leather, stiletto-heeled pumps, avoiding her eyes, trying to submerge his interest in her. "It's not meant to go fast or travel long distances. I recommend driving straight to a repair shop to have your tire fixed or replaced." He set the tools in her trunk along with the flat and the hubcap.

A smile curved on her lips as she handed back the rag.

"Thanks." He wiped his hands and closed the trunk. "Matter of fact, it doesn't hurt to have a quality tire for your spare. It could offer you some peace of mind."

"I appreciate the advice." Her eyes locked with his.

He couldn't stop his smile. Maybe it was time to consider dating again.

Right, and there would go his anonymity.

Still … He glanced at her shoes again, her narrow ankles, her toned calves … Stop it! He plunged his hands into hip pockets and redirected his gaze to the spare tire. That should be safe. "If something like this happens again, please find someone to help you. I see you feel as insecure in parking ramps as I do."

"Point taken." She looked to the ground and raised a hand to her face, wiping below her eyes before looking back at him. "I've been unfair to you, and I apologize. You've treated me with kindness, though I haven't deserved it." She raised her head and nodded to her car. "And you've protected me from whatever predator might be out here. I do appreciate it, even if I'm bad at showing it."

The peek at her vulnerability surprised him and made her all the more attractive. "Glad I could help you out."

"This is the second time you've helped me in two days. Certainly you wouldn't object to another offer."

He held his mouth shut. Don't listen. Go home immediately. But he couldn't resist studying her. Her eyes, the shade of warm maple syrup, were large and bright. Youthful dimples dotted her cheeks when she smiled, and that smile was enticing with full, kissable lips. Longing stirred in his gut. It had been far too long since he'd kissed a woman.

"I don't get turned down often." She took one step toward him. "What's your story? Married? Engaged?"

"Never." There was only one person he'd ever considered making that kind of commitment to, but he'd blown that opportunity years ago.

Her nose wrinkled. "Gay?"

His gaze swept over her curves and stopped at her eyes. "What do you think?"

A rosy pink tinged her cheeks. Whoa. Talk about sexy.

She took another step toward him. The floral scent of her perfume invaded his air space. "I have this feeling there's more to you than you show here at work. You've got me curious, Mr. Brooks, and I don't leave my curiosity alone."

He crossed his arms, needing to erect some barrier between them. "What is it you want from me, Ms. Peterson?"

"Sheila." She stepped closer.

If he tried, he could easily reach out and draw her close. His heart rate increased, and it took every ounce of his strength to restrain from kissing her. Swallowing hard, he took a step back from her danger zone and wiped the perspiration from his forehead.

She narrowed the distance between them again. "You turned down the drink yesterday, but can you say no to a baseball game? We face the Yankees tomorrow, and I have seats right behind the home dugout."

Now, she wasn't playing fair. How could any red-blooded male turn down a date with a beautiful woman who not only knew how to wield a lug wrench, but also enjoyed baseball? Okay, maybe her motives were suspect. There was only one reason an executive dated someone beneath them, a reason he knew intimately. Still, he longed to have the company of a woman again.

And Sheila Peterson was not just any woman. Beautiful. Intelligent. A soft spot for kids. And even a tinge of vulnerability.

Nearly one year of his dateless purgatory was long enough,

wasn't it?

He relaxed his arms by his side. "Fine, but allow me to pick you up."

She cringed.

That's right. Janitors drive rusted out beaters. At least that's what the stereotype claimed. Not too long ago, he would have arrived at the same conclusion. He should have known better. "My car's over there." He pointed up the ramp at his black Audi Cabriolet hardtop.

Her gaze followed where his arm directed, and her eyebrows rose.

Idiot! He was showing off, flirting again. Normally, he didn't drive the Audi to work—his one extravagant purchase since moving home, a flimsy tether to his former life. The convertible attracted unwanted attention, but the warm April morning encouraged the wrong decision. His four-by-four pickup would have been just fine, and it wouldn't have raised suspicions.

She cocked her head. "I prefer to walk. Meet me at my place. I live in the North Loop, only about seven blocks from Target Field. We have to walk through the warehouse district, but I'll protect you."

He chuckled. "I'm sure you will." Maybe it was time to stop hiding behind his job and add a little danger back into his life.

CHAPTER *four*

Richard climbed the steps to Sheila's condominium, eyeballing the Mississippi River flowing east of her home. He pushed the doorbell then looked up at the glass buildings scraping the clouds to the southwest. She couldn't have found a location better than this.

The lock clicked, and the door opened. He couldn't help but grin. Blue jeans and an oversized team jersey looked as good on her as a fitted suit.

She smiled back. "Find the place okay?"

"Not a problem." He stepped inside refraining from kissing her cheek. The old Richard would have done that.

She closed the door and walked to her kitchen. "I need to grab a water, then I'll be ready. You care for one?"

"Yes. Please." It would give him a second to study her home, get a feel for who this woman was apart from work.

The living room angled to his right. A patio door, leading to a deck hemmed in by wrought iron rails, was sided by windows framing the Mississippi and its tree-lined river walk. *Nature is important to her.* A definite plus.

The room was decorated with a contemporary flair: black and white with occasional splashes of color. No clutter, few knick-knacks, nothing exposing a particular hobby, interest, or even family.

Wouldn't it be nice not to have relatives complicating his life?

Crossing his arms, he focused on a robin perched on the deck railing. A sure sign of spring. A time for new beginnings. No thinking of his family today. Nothing was going to spoil his evening.

Sheila walked from the kitchen and handed him a water bottle. "Ready?"

"Very." He followed her out the door and down the steps. Tonight was all about starting over, and who better to make that start with than this beautiful executive?

The sun hovered ahead of them as they walked side by side, passing warehouse buildings nearly as old as the city itself, many of which had only recently been given new life, housing night-clubs, art galleries, and an eclectic collection of shops.

And now, even more life was being breathed into the area because of the new baseball stadium.

They arrived at the ballfield and walked through Gate 29. Richard breathed in the heavenly scent of popcorn and hot dogs permeating the bustling concourse. It smelled like baseball. Sharing his love for the game with Sheila somehow made it better.

"Scorecards! Programs!" A vendor shouted above the din of fans loitering in the concourse, waiting for food, or filing to their seats.

"Scorecard?" He touched Sheila's arm. A date never accepted before, but he always asked, hoping.

"Please."

He raised his eyebrows. Another plus for his date. He purchased two scorecards and was handed two pencils. Could the evening get any better?

She led them down concrete steps to their cushioned seats, arriving just in time to see the last players take batting practice. "Look at Max." With her pencil, Sheila pointed at the player in the batting cage who pulled a slow grounder to third. "No wonder the guy's in a slump. He's stepping out of the box way too early, getting ahead of the pitch."

Richard studied the batter's swing. What do you know? She had Max pegged. Max and the rest of the team, it seemed, as she repeatedly pointed out flaws in their stance or swing. Talking baseball seemed natural as talking business. A rare and intriguing quality.

"Where'd you learn so much about baseball?" He watched a ball clear the wall in right field. "Most women I know come here to gab. They've no interest in the game."

"Like you should have no interest in Wharton's bottom line." Eyebrows raised, she glanced at him.

He smiled his answer. Inadvertently, his last statement became an excellent cover.

Sheila looked back at the batting cage. "I played softball in high school and college. Even coached some in college. Besides, it's my job to know sports. I bring clients to baseball, basketball, football, hockey—"

"Beer! Cold beer!" A vendor advanced down the steps hauling a crate of amber bottles.

Sheila turned toward Richard. "Care for one?"

He squinted at the vendor, eyeing the golden-brown beverage. Nothing would taste better. How long had it been? *Ten months? No, almost eleven. Not nearly long enough.* He shook his head. "Nah. I'll grab a Coke later."

Sheila shrugged and ordered one for herself.

Richard gave her a ten.

"Thank you." She handed the money to the vendor in exchange for her drink and change then returned her attention to the batting cage. "Being a woman in a male-dominated business, it's imperative I know the games inside and out. We're more likely to make a sale if I can demonstrate that I know what I'm talking about." She smiled. "Besides, I love sports and, I'm warning you, I can get rather vocal."

"I'm looking forward to it." And he was. If the date continued in this direction, maybe he could get Sheila to see beyond their perceived occupational differences and treat him as an equal, not a conquest. He had no delusions about her true intentions.

Part of him wished he could tell her the truth and break the barrier between them, but his practical self knew such a confession would bring devastating results. She'd have to accept him as the man his current profession defined him to be, or not at all.

Batting practice ended and the home team jogged to the dugout. Several players spotted Sheila in the stands and greeted her with familiarity. She responded back, joking with and teasing them, accepting good-natured ribbing in return. The carefree banter didn't surprise him. If she'd held season tickets for any length of time, the players would naturally take note of the beautiful and outgoing fan.

In the process, though, he'd become invisible. No surprise

there, either. Wasn't that why he sought the custodial position in the first place? He shouldn't feel offended. So why did he? He studied his scorecard, memorizing the opponents' batting averages, and realized Sheila had grown quiet.

Her fingers hovered beneath her eyes, wiping. He rested a hand on her arm. "Sheila, what's—"

She shrugged his hand away and nodded toward the field. Peering up to where the players stood only moments before, he connected eyes with veteran outfielder Joe Maitland. The scowling player shook his head then stepped down, disappearing into the dugout.

Richard felt Sheila's seat rock upright.

She stood on the steps and nodded upward, a tear trickling over her cheek. "I'm going to grab a hot dog. You want one?"

"Are you all right?"

"Of course. Why wouldn't I be?"

He sighed and stood just enough to reach his billfold and pull out a twenty. "I'll take a dog and a Coke."

"It's on me." She shoved his hand away and bounded up the stairs.

Okay, what just happened here? He shrugged it off. Not his business. Whatever bothered her was in the past and not his concern. After all, this was just one evening out. There was little chance of it going any further.

Sheila returned just before the first pitch.

At least with having the food, he didn't need to make conversation. He'd let Sheila set the tone. They sat silent for a few minutes, anticipating each pitch, letting the game become priority, her emotional outburst filed away.

She watched the game with intensity, energetically vocalizing observations only a keen student of baseball would catch.

Richard reclined in his seat, watching and listening, frequently agreeing with her spirited comments, letting her boisterous voice speak for them both.

Still, her avoidance of Maitland, in each repeated appearance on the field, made Richard curious. Clearly, a relationship between Sheila and the player wasn't limited to adoring fan and flattered athlete. No doubt, the invitation to this game was not spontaneous as Richard first believed.

At the beginning of the seventh-inning stretch, the players jogged off the field, and he prepared to stand for the singing of *Take Me Out To The Ballgame*. Before he rose, Sheila's hand rested on his knee. Spontaneous invite or not, her touch felt warm. Good. Wearing a contented smile, he glanced at the field. Maitland neared the dugout, and Sheila's other hand coaxed Richard's head toward her and she pressed her lips onto his.

With the muscles in his face flexing, he gently, but firmly, peeled her hand from his cheek. She tried to dip her head, but he forced her chin back up. This needed to be stressed to her face. "The game is over, Sheila." His voice was low and unwavering.

Chin quivering, she peered down.

When her head rose, she looked toward the playing field. "Joe and I …" Her gaze fell toward her lap. With her pencil, she colored in looped letters on her scorecard. "It was a bad breakup. I wanted to get back at him. But, that wasn't my intent in asking you to join me tonight."

"Right," he said with a disbelieving chuckle. Why had he allowed himself to become comfortable with her? He placed both hands on the back of his neck, massaging it, stroking the skin beneath his chain. How many people had he treated in the same manner before he ran from New York?

He deserved the treatment, all right.

"Richard." Her voice became soft and enticing, her game resuming. "My behavior has been shameful and, I'll admit, somewhat planned. If you'll forgive me, I promise to make it up to you later."

Funny how the offer held no appeal. Maybe he had changed over the past year. "I'm done playing, Sheila. Let's watch the ball game, then I'll walk you home." *We'll go our separate ways so I can settle back into obscurity.*

Right where he belonged.

SHEILA TURNED HER HEAD JUST ENOUGH TO examine the silent man walking beside her. In the dark, his eyes were unreadable, but the firm lock of his jaw spoke everything. It shouldn't bother her that he was upset. She'd fulfilled her purpose for the evening by exacting her revenge on Joe. The Wharton custodian was to be collateral damage and nothing more.

Miles seemed to separate them as they walked side by side down Third Avenue toward the Mississippi. The renovated and repurposed structures surrounding them proved restoration was possible even when inevitable destruction loomed. Third Avenue spilled out onto a river walk devoid of people. Few drivers knew of the parkway meandering alongside the Mississippi. With stars dotting the sky and the crescent moon smiling on them, it should be a romantic setting. It could have been if she hadn't …

She closed her eyes and breathed in fresh April air that predicted spring's colorful and fragrant life would soon be here, renewing what winter destroyed.

This evening could still be restored.

As they stepped onto the walkway, Sheila grasped Richard's hand and breathed a sigh of thanks that he didn't pull away. He certainly had every reason to. "I am sorry."

Richard returned a gentle squeeze, but held on. "Forget about it."

She nodded, enjoying the feel of his callused hand warming hers. "I had a good time."

"Yeah, me too." Ahh, a hint of a smile coated his voice.

A cool breeze, carrying a remnant of winter, blew off the river. Sheila shuddered, wishing she had the forethought to bring a jacket, but Richard snaked his arm around her shoulders warming her in a much better way. Her gait easily matched his. They fit together well, like two pieces of a complex puzzle joining for the first time. Maybe there was hope for this evening after all.

The remaining blocks passed quickly with conversation surrounding the game and even business. Why this intelligent man hid in Wharton's basement was a mystery. One she firmly intended to solve.

He escorted her up the steps leading to her condo before his arm left her shoulders.

Why did she feel as if a part of her was missing? Her attraction to this man made no sense. Steeling herself, she unlocked and opened the door then turned to find his eyes. Moisture clouded her own. It was past time to make up for her unladylike behavior, especially when Richard had been nothing but a gentleman. "I really am sorry. Seeing Joe again made me crazy. I thought I could handle seeing him again. Apparently not."

"That's okay." He kicked at her steps.

"No, it's not." She reclaimed his hand and pulled gently, nodding toward her open door. "Won't you come in?" she said in a breathy whisper. "I'll make it up to you."

His Adam's apple fluctuated. "I can't." But, the squeak in his voice said he wanted to.

Victory was unavoidable.

Taking advantage of his uncertainty, she circled her arms around his neck. Her fingers wove through his thick hair. She pulled him in and pressed her lips onto his.

A millisecond later his arms enveloped her body, drawing her into a tight but matching fit, with his mouth answering hers.

Victory was complete.

His lips and arms sprang away as if bitten by a rattlesnake, and he strode down the steps before looking back.

What? Sheila raised her palms and shoulders but found no words to accompany the gesture.

He shook his head. "I can't."

A smile slithered to her lips. So, the janitor was not only intelligent, but a Boy Scout too. Even more appealing. And judging by the way he'd kissed her moments ago, "can't" wasn't a problem. It wasn't the kiss of inexperience. Obviously, something else held him back. One more mystery for her to solve. "Well, then." She sashayed forward. "Perhaps we need a second date."

He stared at the sky.

"Please?" Next time, she'd make sure he couldn't say no.

Rubbing the back of his neck, he retreated a few more feet. "How about a show this Saturday? I have main floor seats at the Orpheum."

Expensive main floor? She tapped a finger on her thigh. *So, the Boy Scout enjoys theater too.* She pressed a finger to her lips. What other surprises did he hide? "Agreed. But, just to let you know, I don't take 'no' so easily on the second date." She turned and swaggered inside without another look back. Make him sweat it out until then.

Next time, she'd be fully ready for him.

CHAPTER *five*

After the long workday, Sheila withdrew to her balcony with a vanilla latte warming her hands. She leaned against her wrought iron railing and watched the steady current of the Mississippi recently freed from the freeze of winter. Sparkling lights speckled an indigo sky with no clouds blocking their view.

It was quiet tonight, no speedboats or other watercraft yet, just a quiet lapping of water. The peaceful evening helped block the thoughts of work. Why couldn't she erase Richard from her mind?

She sipped her coffee, letting it awaken her senses. If she had any intelligence at all, she'd call off tomorrow's date, but nothing about him was logical. Tickets to the theater? Expensive main floor seats? With the company janitor? Was she truly that desperate?

She sat in a wicker chair, rested her feet on a matching ottoman and closed her eyes. A vision of Richard climbing down the ladder played in her thoughts. A gorgeous man oozing quiet confidence and wisdom. Why would he settle for a custodial position? Did he lack ambition? That didn't seem to fit him either.

She sat up straight and pushed the foot rest away. Yes, going out with him again, getting to know this mysterious man better was the best option. Really, the only intelligent decision. She did want to see him again, and this new setting would hopefully provide answers to her questions.

RICHARD STOOD BEFORE HIS FULL-LENGTH MIRROR and grinned. He'd been a fool on Wednesday. His arms had surrounded the beautiful executive, locked in a sweet embrace, and he told her no. All the noble reasons he pondered that night now clanged like foolish excuses. But, she gave him a second chance, and tonight, he wouldn't blow it.

He combed his hair, added a touch of gel, and smoothed on a hint of aftershave, just enough to entice. The fitted Italian suit draped like silk against his skin compared to the chafing janitor uniform. It helped him achieve the look he desired, filling him with renewed determination. Tonight he didn't care if he drew attention to himself. He'd shed the custodian image, recreating the look that once made so many women swoon. Sheila would be no less affected.

He reached inside his coat pocket, pulled out a black leather wallet, opened it, and grinned. What he needed was there. Waiting. Had been for too long. Tonight, he planned to break the vow of abstinence he had made and upheld for nearly a year. That it had been so long was nothing short of a miracle. Tonight she'd want him, not as an evening conquest, but for the man he was: intelligent and handsome.

The future would choose when, or if, he should disclose the complete truth of who he was.

THE DOORBELL RANG AS SHEILA GLANCED IN the full-length mirror hung on her front door. She tugged on the hem of her black satin sheath, pulling the V-neck down a pinch more, just enough to add mystery without disclosing the whole plot. That would be revealed later tonight. In this curve-caressing dress, victory was inevitable.

Smiling, she opened her door. Her mouth hung open in silence.

The debonair man standing there was not who she expected. No way. This man's black suit was designer quality and, definitely, not purchased in Minneapolis. Even his hair was meticulously styled.

Wearing his killer, crooked smile, Richard reached out, took her hand in his, and kept his other arm braced behind his back. "You look stunning tonight." His eyes captured hers, and he raised her hand to his lips, kissing it without relinquishing eye contact.

"As do you," she finally managed to squeak out, trying to numb the current electrifying her hand and tingling up her arm.

This man was not supposed to make her feel like this. The man standing in her doorway couldn't possibly be the company custodian. He had clearly stepped out of the pages of a fashion magazine or Hollywood movie. No, that wasn't right either. Those men were too plastic with Botoxed faces and bleached smiles. They lacked any sense of character, as if their lives were dedicated to standing there smiling or pretending to smile. Perhaps they were.

But, this man's smile was slightly crooked. His eyes held mysteries she desired to solve. This man clearly had lived a life beyond what she saw of him at work. He was no more a janitor than she was. So why was he there now?

He drew his arm from behind his back, delivering a single stemmed, orange rose.

She accepted it without speaking, afraid her voice would betray the unwanted feelings he summoned in her.

"Do you have a vase?"

It was a simple question, but her cheeks burned all the same realizing he was inviting himself in. "I'm sorry." The words whispered across her lips as she gestured for him to enter. "Please come in."

She led him to her kitchen and pointed upward. "Center cupboard, top shelf." She could have reached it herself but found it far more gratifying to stand back and observe.

The man glided through her kitchen with the practiced precision of someone who'd been there before. He was obviously comfortable in his own skin, or any surrounding, for that matter. Not chameleon-like. No, this man could not blend in if he wanted to. How had he eluded her eyes for so long?

He set the single bud in a vase he'd filled with water and centered it on her dining table. He was right in choosing a solitary flower. Its simplicity matched her home, and he clearly knew that, probably remembering her understated decor from the brief moment he stepped inside the other night.

"Orange?" She fingered a silky petal, certain he chose the

specific color for a reason.

He smiled the adorably crooked smile again, his eyes detaining hers.

She couldn't have looked away if she wanted to. She didn't want to.

"Single stem for simplicity, although I doubt there is much that is simple about you. Orange for fascination. I find you fascinating and complicated, Ms. Peterson, and your interest in me has whetted my curiosity."

Her heart rate accelerated. *He finds me fascinating? Complicated?* Certainly, he had their roles reversed.

"Shall we go?" He offered his hand.

Still unwilling to speak, she nodded and accepted his hand.

She led him out of her home, turned and locked the door behind them, using the moment to gather her wits.

"May I?" He rested his hand in the small of her back, lightly pressing her forward, drawing her off-balance again.

She didn't reply, but didn't resist either, enjoying the feel of his firm, yet gentle guidance. His masculine cologne beseeched her to come closer, and she obeyed as he directed her toward his Audi.

He opened the passenger door, took her hand and assisted her in before shutting it gently behind her. It had been a long time since a man had shown this consideration and care, if it happened at all. This sophisticated gentleman couldn't possibly be the same man she discovered in janitor's clothing.

As he slid behind the wheel, she breathed in the intoxicating combination of cologne mingling with leather. To be honest, did it matter who he really was?

CHAPTER *six*

Sheila hated letting go of Richard's hand, but the actors' performances warranted a standing ovation. The evening ahead held great promise. Judging by his continued affection, it was what he planned for. She wouldn't let him down.

But, first she needed to freshen up—make sure her makeup, hair, dress, perfume were all perfect—like he had been.

GUIDING SHEILA THROUGH THE ORPHEUM'S carpeted hallways, with his arm draped comfortably around her waist, Richard couldn't contain his smile. When she had asked to go the powder room, he gladly escorted her there, knowing full well what was on her mind. She'd seemingly forgotten where they met and what he did for a living, and her attraction for him was obviously strong as his was for her. Tonight he'd break his vow and not regret a moment of it. What had happened a year ago was an anomaly. Tonight, he was prepared so it wouldn't happen again.

"Sheila!" A familiar voice called out ahead of them, stealing Richard from his dreams. Ethan Johnson strolled from the direction of the men's room. He greeted Sheila and then, with a raised eyebrow, offered his hand to Richard.

"Evening, Ethan."

"Excuse me, gentlemen." Sheila's arm deserted his waist and she hurried to the ladies' room.

Richard's smile flattened, and he refrained from rolling his eyes. So, she'd been seen with him, the lowly janitor. How would she explain it when the grapevine carried this information throughout the company? It would tarnish her carefully polished image.

How could he redirect Sheila's perceptions and resurrect those feelings they both had only moments ago?

Ethan braced his hand on Richard's shoulder and nodded toward the restroom. "No more monk lifestyle, eh?"

Richard couldn't prevent a chuckle. "Not if I can help it."

"Not exactly low profile, either." Ethan's tone became serious.

Richard's good humor evaporated, and he glared at Ethan. "What are you saying?"

"No offense, buddy, but a few months back you came to me wanting to hide. With Sheila, that's not happening."

Richard rubbed the back of his neck. "Tell me about it, but ..." He glanced at the restroom door. "There's something different about her. She doesn't need to hang on my arm to make herself look important. She's already there. Maybe she likes me just because."

"Maybe ..." Ethan rubbed his chin, and hope sparked in his eyes. "Under different circumstances I could see the two of you together. The question is, when are those circumstances going to change? If you're planning to return to the corporate world, where you belong by the way, there's always room at the top for you. Right now, with this economy, Wharton could really use your expertise. Don't you think it's time to move up from the basement?"

Richard eyed the restroom, fingers tapping impatiently against his leg. What would returning to the business world have to do with her? *Everything.* Everything, if tonight ended well and they continued to see each other, which was what he truly wanted. Sheila would want to know the truth, and would deserve to hear it. But, taking an executive position would only feed her curiosity, and he couldn't tell her yet.

For the time being, it was best to stay put in his monotonous job. Setting his jaw, he stared at the ground. "I've been thinking about it. I'm just not quite ready."

"What's keeping you? Do you have something else to prove?"

"No." He pressed his hand to his chest and traced the chain's outline with his thumb. "Until I learn to deal with this …" This choking guilt. "I don't belong in corporate."

"Then you don't belong with Sheila, either." Ethan slapped Richard's back.

He's right. Richard massaged his neck as Ethan laced through the crowd, returning to his wife. Keeping his gaze on the restroom door, Richard slumped against the wall, letting sequined and tuxedoed patrons flock past.

His breath caught when Sheila emerged from the ladies' room and wove toward him. The woman was stunning, and he very much wanted to be with her … to serve her breakfast in bed. But, judging by Sheila's reaction to him moments ago, they wouldn't even share a nightcap.

She approached him, her eyes darting. "Is Ethan gone?"

"Long gone." He was right. The barriers of position were fully rebuilt. She still considered herself superior to him and not his equal. The run-in with Ethan solidified the bias. "You know, you don't have to be embarrassed to be seen with me, especially with Ethan." Richard tried to cover the defeat in his voice. "We go way back. He won't say anything."

Her darting eyes stilled, and she took his hands. "I'm sorry, Richard. I didn't mean to hurt you. Again." She drew his arms around her back. The woman was so hard to resist. His body screamed, "Don't resist," especially when she whispered in his ear. "I would like to see more of you."

It was the response he planned for, longed for.

You don't belong with Sheila. Ethan's comment whispered in Richard's conscience.

He pulled out of her arms. A full retreat was necessary. Ethan was right. Sheila still viewed him as a conquest and not her equal, and he wouldn't settle for less than equality in a relationship.

Something he and Sheila could have had if he'd known her a year ago. But, excavating the past was too high a price to pay. And, if she knew the whole truth, she wouldn't want him anyway.

"I'VE GOT A *PINOT NOIR* CHILLING." SHEILA

opened her condo door and gripped Richard's hand. She couldn't recall an evening she enjoyed so much. From the moment he picked her up, he had made her feel special: the distinctive rose, the invigorating conversation, the protective warmth of her hand in his. Inviting him in was the ideal way to cap off the perfect evening. If she was lucky, they might begin a torrid romance that would permanently expel Joe from her thoughts.

"I'm sorry." He pulled his hand away.

"What?" This couldn't be happening. Again. Her pulse quickened. "I thought you wanted to …" *Stay the night.* Every signal Richard had given off all evening screamed those words. Until …

Her breath stilled. No. This was all her fault. Everything was superb until they saw Ethan. At that moment she'd personally reconstructed the barriers Richard let down. Her reaction to Ethan's presence must have felt like a swift kick in the gut.

Well, she couldn't retract those actions, but at least she could try to make it up to him, let him know she didn't want it to be over.

"I understand." Her eyes rose to his, hoping to convince him of her sincerity.

"I have to go." His lips smiled, but the curve of his mouth didn't match those dark, impenetrable eyes, pleading with her not to push.

"Call me?"

His smile deepened, this time lighting the spark in his eyes as he nodded.

Relief filled her as he walked away. She wasn't about to give up on this mystery man.

RICHARD SLAMMED THE CAR DOOR BEHIND HIM and glared through the windshield. "Okay, God. Happy now?"

Where did that come from? He was talking to God? Why did God keep nudging in on his life?

He gripped the steering wheel. Had he ever turned down an offer like Sheila's? Hardly. Even now, the lingering bouquet of her perfume insisted he change his mind. He glanced at her condo door with its inviting light illuminating the landing. She would welcome him in.

Keeping his hands locked on the wheel, his gaze moved to the starlit sky, and an unfamiliar peace snuck up on him.

He had done the right thing.

Maybe God was right all along.

He chuckled. "Wouldn't my family love to hear that?" *That*—He turned the key in the ignition until the engine gave off a soothing purr—*will* not *happen*. Nevertheless, he'd actually done the right thing, and it felt good.

Better yet, Sheila asked him to call her. It wasn't over, nor did he want it to be, in spite of what Ethan said.

He steered his car onto the street. Maybe for the first time in years, his life was heading in the right direction.

THE FLORIST STEPPED FROM THE BACK ROOM OF her shop and held up a flower.

Richard grinned. The Dawn Chorus rose, its petals tipped with a hue vivid as an orange peel and faded to yellow at the base, was the perfect selection for the dawn of their relationship.

He thanked the clerk and handed her his debit card. *Relationship*. The term rolled through his thoughts. A month ago, he wouldn't have dreamed it possible, but four weeks of seeing Sheila proved otherwise.

He fingered the silky petal. It was the fifth rose. Sheila had come to expect it on their Saturdays together. Picnics by the Mississippi watching groups on Segway tours. Slow jogs around the Minneapolis Chain of Lakes. Climbing rocky bluffs by Minnehaha Falls.

Evenings spent discussing stocks and public corporations confirmed her to be his intellectual equal. She no longer seemed offended by his expertise and even encouraged his ideas.

The clerk returned his card.

He picked the flower up from the counter and brought it to his nose as he walked to the exit. Its fragrance was discreet.

Sheila was anything but subtle when she probed through his past. If she knew what he'd done, she'd never forgive him. So what if his family offered forgiveness. His former employer hadn't. Much less himself. How could he expect her to? Disclosing his past would terminate any future they might possibly have. Besides, he and Sheila would never last—his relationships never did—so why not enjoy their time together and not trouble her with his history?

A bell jingled as he pulled the door open. He stepped out into warming sunshine and checked his watch. The day had dawned nearly four hours ago leaving a good nine hours of sunlight to spend with Sheila.

Today, he wasn't going to worry about sunsets.

WHO ARE YOU, RICHARD? SHEILA PERCHED ON THE edge of her home office chair and pressed the power button on her computer. In this electronic age, the answer shouldn't be difficult to uncover.

Ethan sure hadn't been any help. When Richard admitted he knew Ethan before coming to Wharton, she thought she'd made the connection that would reveal his past. Ethan only told her to ask Richard. Oh, she had. Dozens of times, in many different ways. The man was the master of evasion.

When the screen lit up, she clicked on the Web browser icon and glanced at the time in the corner of her monitor. He'd be here soon. Two minutes. No more. No less. The man was punctual as he was neat. She typed *Google.com*. What she did know was that Ethan came from New York, so it was logical to assume they knew each other there. When Google popped up, she keyed: "Richard Brooks" + "New York."

With the doorbell chiming, she rocked back in her chair and stared at the ceiling.

109,231 hits.

CHAPTER *seven*

White Plains, New York

Meghan steadied the mortarboard on top of her head while waiting on the temporary outdoor stage to hear her name announced. The academic cap wasn't level, as the school suggested. One final, if small, rebellious act before she escaped this school. This town.

A mere year ago, her brother had worn his mortarboard flat, just like he was supposed to. Justin always did what he was supposed to do, but she wasn't Justin. She resisted scratching her upper arm that still itched from the tattoo she'd gotten two days ago. The forget-me-nots that now circled her arm would never let her forget her brother. She could almost envision Justin grinning, although her parents were none too happy.

The principal finally announced her name. She stepped briskly across the stage. Accepting the diploma in her left hand, she shook the principal's clammy palm with her right, and smiled through her grimace.

She walked down the metal steps, taking care to do it noiselessly, as the next graduate was announced. *High school is over.* A smile touched her lips. And on to college, a thousand-some miles from White Plains, New York. Half a country away from her parents. She glanced at the bleachers, and scanned the jumble of faces.

They were out there somewhere. Would she miss them when she left home? Probably. But she wouldn't miss her church and the people she thought were her friends. She'd be far from their judgment and pity. Mostly, she'd be far from the memories of her brother.

Pacing her steps, she walked down the aisle keeping the recommended distance from her classmate. Just a year ago, Justin made the same walk—one of the last times she had seen him. He'd still be alive if she hadn't ...

She raised her hand to her eyes and fingered away the tears. Hopefully, her classmates would interpret the emotion as joy. But, how could she be joyful when all she could think of was her brother?

She shuffled between the rows of folding chairs and stood by her assigned seat, clutching the red folder in her hands, channeling the sadness and anger away from her face. She needed to appear happy.

Perhaps the feelings of loss would go away when she entered the University of Wisconsin-Madison in the fall. A place where memories of her brother wouldn't haunt her.

Naturally, her parents were unhappy with her choice of schools with the East Coast having more than its share of superb universities. Well, too bad. Someday, she'd have to locate and thank the anonymous benefactor who started her college fund after Justin died. Thanks to them, she'd been granted absolute freedom.

The usher at the end of her row raised his hand, palm up, giving her row the signal they waited for. She reached up and raised the tassel, moving it from one side to the other, before sitting. A smile even tugged at her face. It was now official.

The trust fund had paved a new path, allowing her to break free from this town, free from the reminders of that night, hopefully free from her guilt.

CHAPTER *eight*

Richard opened his living room window, allowing a tropical June breeze to cross through. Installing a central air system would be his next project, now that the bookshelves were completed. Walking past them, he ran a hand over the smooth surface. Maybe his brother would even choke out a compliment. The phone rang as he considered the rare likelihood of that happening.

He hurried to the kitchen, lifted the phone from its cradle, and grinned when he read the caller ID. *Sheila.* "Hey there."

"Hi, Richard."

Keeping the phone at his ear, he returned to his living room and settled into the leather couch. The daily phone call had become habit—a welcome habit. These past two months of dating her had been two of his most enjoyable months in years. That alone set Sheila apart from any other woman he'd known. "You caught me heading out the door."

"You're going somewhere?"

What do I say? He didn't want to tell her, but lying wasn't a palatable option. "To the farm. I've got a family thing today—my nephew's birthday."

Brief silence answered before she said, "You didn't tell me." Disappointment clung to her words.

"I didn't think you'd be interested." The lie oozed out too easily and tasted bitter on his tongue. But, he knew she'd jump at the chance to meet his family, which was precisely why he hadn't mentioned the Sunday trip in the first place.

"Of course I'm interested. You rarely mention your family."

He sank lower into the couch and rubbed his temples. "I have my reasons." Good reasons. If she came with him today, he'd be assaulted with questions about her, and assumptions would be made about their relationship. Those assumptions would be wrong, though earned.

"Come on, Richard. This would be a good chance to get to know each other better."

That's just it. I don't want you to know me better. Already, she knew him better than any other woman he'd dated. That scared him to death because, really, she didn't know him at all. "Maybe another time." Probably never.

"You don't talk about us, do you?"

Us? He stared up at the popcorn ceiling, his open hand resting on his forehead. Didn't an us reference mean they were getting too close, too familiar? How had he allowed that to happen? Why hadn't he listened to Ethan?

"There must be a girl back home you're going to see. You don't want me to find out about her."

It was obviously a tease, but he answered brusquely anyway. "It's not like that, Sheila." He sat up, planted his feet on the floor and combed his fingers through his hair. "You don't know my family. They're Christian. Evangelical. You go up there, you're gonna be saved by the end of the day."

"Christian." She spat the word. "Oh, I can hold my own, believe me." An icy certitude rang in her voice, chilling his tropical room. Clearly, sometime in her life, religion had donned its deceitful head. One more thing they had in common. No doubt she could do more than hold her own.

"I'm sure you can, but …"

"Listen, Richard, if you can't give me a solid reason to leave me behind, I'm certain to come up with one for myself and I guarantee, you won't like it."

"Do you really think we're ready to meet family? Doesn't that mean—"

"Ahh, I see. Apparently I'm taking this relationship a bit more serious than you are. Well, please forgive me. Perhaps you're right. It's time to move on to someone who will appreciate me."

"No." He shot off the couch, surprised by the fear pumping his heart at the thought of losing Sheila. "You're right. Blame it on cold feet. Come on up. I'd be proud to introduce you to my family." That was even the truth. There'd only been one other woman he'd been proud to bring home, but she'd been stolen from him eons ago.

"I'm ready right now." She sounded way too eager. "I'll set my GPS and be up shortly."

After hanging up, he walked through his house making sure there were no hints of where he'd come from. There shouldn't be. He left nearly everything behind. A glance in his bedroom assured him his closet doors were closed. He shut the bedroom door as an extra precaution.

Covering the past with closed doors was the easy part. He didn't want to visit his family as it was. With Sheila along, there would be insinuations. Even worse, the trip would add to her growing list of questions. Questions he was still unprepared to answer.

SHEILA NEARLY MISSED THE GRAVEL DRIVEWAY tucked between lines of pine trees. The house was completely hidden from the road. The home itself was a small rambler, probably forty or fifty years old, although the siding and roofing appeared new. The lot was secluded and private but well maintained. *Not unlike its owner.* With a smile, she parked her Lexus next to his convertible and walked to the house, eager to see Richard on his own turf.

He responded quickly to her knock, and his mouth curved into that lopsided smile.

"Are you going to invite me in?"

"Sorry. Even on short notice, you look great." He gestured stiffly for her to enter.

"Thank you so much." Sarcasm rang in her voice. Did he really think she'd be seen in public looking less than perfect?

"Sorry." Richard winced.

So much for the lack of tension. "You can make it up to me later." She put a finger to his lips then slipped past him into his living room.

No kiss. Not even a hug.

All he did was point to a leather recliner. "Have a seat. I'll grab the veggie tray, then we can go."

She remained standing as he disappeared into the kitchen. Finally, the opportunity she'd hoped for. She glanced around the room, looking for some hint of where he'd come from. But, the room was typical for a bachelor's pad. The carpet was tan and threadbare and begged to be replaced. A brown leather sofa and recliner were both situated to maximize TV viewing. A television hung on the wall like a blank piece of artwork. It was the only "artwork" hung on dingy white walls.

Directly beneath the TV sat a wood burning fireplace artistically framed with stone. Built in bookshelves—it looked like cherry wood—flanked the fireplace. She ran her fingers over the tomes lining the shelves: mystery, espionage, history. A handful of framed pictures were showcased between the books. Portraits of happy families and giggling children.

She picked up a figurine set next to one of the pictures and inspected it. A plastic cartoon figure with moving arms—a toy from a kid's meal. More toys were interspersed among the books. Intriguing. Yes, some adults collected kids' toys, but the Richard she knew didn't seem to be the type. That man was far too serious. *The Wall Street Journal, Sports Illustrated*, and daily paper, arranged neatly on an end table by the couch, attested to that.

Nothing she saw answered her many questions. The kid's collection only added to her list. Otherwise, the room said he was typical, when he was anything but.

Richard walked from the kitchen carrying a vegetable platter wrapped in plastic, with the price and nutrition label still attached. An envelope with "Happy Birthday, Josh" written on it lay on top. In his other hand, he carried several plastic souvenir cups from Target Field. Those, he handed to her.

"Well, thank you." She frowned. "They will match my decor perfectly."

Finally. A smile. "They're for my mom. She collects them."

"These?" She wrinkled her nose.

He nodded, and his smile grew.

Must have an interesting mother. "I see you put a lot of work into your veggie tray." She eyed the platter.

"Believe me, everyone's grateful that this is the trouble I go through. At least they'll eat it. I don't do food well, unless it's on a grill."

"We've got something else in common."

He chuckled and nodded toward the fireplace wall. "Like it?"

Her fingers slid down the shelf's smooth finish. "It's beautiful. This stone and the shelves are done exquisitely, but it seems out of place in this room."

"It's all I've had a chance to do so far."

"You did this?" Was there anything this man couldn't do well?

"With some help from my mom. She's got the eye for design. I've got the skill to put it up."

"My compliments to your mother. I especially like the toys. They're a unique touch. Play with them much?" Yes. Another smile.

"They're presents from my girls."

Her eyes widened and nausea roiled in her gut. "Your girls?" He was a father? No wonder the man was elusive. Children weren't a complication she needed.

His smile lifted to a full toothy grin. "Yeah. My nieces."

Oh, she could strangle him for teasing her like that.

"My sister convinced them that's what I want for birthdays and Christmas. Debbie's happy because she gets rid of the toys. The girls are happy because they get fast food once in a while. I'm happy because they're given with love. And, yeah, I do play with them."

"I'd like to see that." A new look lit Richard's face. She'd never seen that smile before, the full grin with twinkling eyes. No matter how the rest of the day went, her self-invitation was worth it just to see this reaction. Now, if she could only keep it going.

With Richard standing by her side, she examined the pictures on the shelving. She studied one with two brown-haired girls playing with red tractors and yellow Tonka trucks in a sand pile. Boards with chipping red paint colored the background. Sheila placed the plastic cups on the floor and picked up the frame. "Is this them?"

"Yeah. This is Kaitlynn." He pointed to the older girl pushing a tractor. "My Katydid. Only I can call her that. She just turned seven." His finger moved to the smaller child. "This is Lilly. She's three and a half."

"They're beautiful." She studied the girls' faces. Happy. What would it have been like to be a happy child? She looked closer at Lilly, at the girl's broad nose, pudgy cheeks, and tear-dropped shaped eyes. "Does Lilly have Down syndrome?"

He nodded. "Never knew I could love a child so much." He put the picture back, placed the vegetable platter on the floor and picked up another portrait. "Here's their whole family. My little sister Spock and her—"

"Spock?"

He laughed, a glorious, carefree laugh. "Otherwise known as Debbie. Don't tell her I said that. She doesn't exactly appreciate the nickname. But, she earned it. Always on an even keel, looks at every situation logically."

Sheila shook her head. "I suppose she had to be, what with you for a bigger brother."

"You have no clue how right you are. She worked as a counselor up until they had Kaitlynn. I think I drove her to the job."

"I don't doubt it." Sheila pointed to Debbie's husband. "And this is …"

"Jerry. Jerry Verhoeven. He's a principal at a small school up north. I'm probably closer to him than I am to my own brother."

Interesting. She scrutinized the family picture. Like Richard, Debbie appeared to be above average height, but was slightly on the plump side. The girls got their hair color from their mom. The dad didn't have any hair left to determine color. "Your sister? She doesn't look at all like you."

"I know. Debbie's frequently told me how grateful she is."

"I think I'm going to like her."

"You probably will." He set the picture exactly in its original position then picked up another five by seven. "This is Mom and Dad, Marlene and Bernie Brooks. Married forty-three years now."

Love and respect glowed in Richard's face when he talked about his family. So, why hadn't he mentioned them?

He took down one final photograph, and the smile deserted

his eyes. The man in the picture was clearly Richard's brother. They shared the same hair color, physique, and crooked smile. "This is my younger brother's family." He pointed to each person. "Marcus; his wife, Janet. Their boys Nathan—gosh, he's fifteen—almost sixteen. Almost driving. There's a scary thought. Doesn't seem that long ago when he was born. This is Joshua. Eleven today, and their 'oops,' three-year-old Jaclyn. She and Lilly were born just seven weeks apart. Mom was in Grandma Heaven. You've never seen people so excited about an 'oops.'"

"I was an 'oops' myself, but my parents made it clear to me, throughout my childhood, that I was a mistake. Soon as I could, I got out of there." Sheila clamped her mouth, horrified that she'd exposed more of herself than she cared to, more than she ever told anyone. She ignored Richard's inquisitive look. "Tell me about Marcus."

Through her peripheral vision, she saw him staring at her. *Don't ask.* Refusing to look his way, she concentrated on breathing. *Please don't ask.* She pretended to admire the family picture. Thank goodness, he said nothing. Maybe his own reluctance to open up secured her privacy.

"Marcus." He blew out a breath, and his voice lost its upbeat tone. "He's almost two years younger than me. We've always been fairly competitive. I was the rebel—he was the saint. Things haven't changed much."

She raised an eyebrow. "You, Mr. Boy Scout, a rebel? That's setting the bar a little high for the rest of us."

"Believe me, I'm no Boy Scout." Gravel coated his voice, and his fingers tightened against the picture frame.

"Okay, so you're no Scout." What could he possibly have done to get upset over her compliment?

"Sorry." Richard rubbed the back of his neck. "I didn't mean to snap."

"That's okay." If she avoided an argument, maybe he'd open up more.

"Marcus was the Scout. Earned his Eagle, of course. As a matter of fact, dinner's on him today. A technique he learned camping. He's cooking a turkey in the ground."

"In the ground?" She wrinkled her nose, picturing a dirt-covered turkey.

"But, it's the best turkey you'll ever eat, just wait. I'll even give Marc credit for doing that well. When he's not cooking, he's a building contractor in the Brainerd area—builds some of the million dollar 'cabins' you read about. His wife, Janet, is a sweetheart. Don't ask me how she ended up with him. She's way too good for him."

The comment was made in jest, but Richard's jealousy rang out clear. She'd ask about it later, when he wasn't so touchy.

He stared at the picture for a moment before placing it on the shelf. "Janet's the brains of his business."

"Your family sounds typically all-American. I'm eager to meet them."

"And they'll be surprised to meet you."

"They don't know about us?"

He shook his head.

Why would he keep their relationship a secret? Maybe there was someone else. Or maybe he was using her like she'd started out using him. Her stomach soured at the thought.

He laid a hand on her arm. His first touch since she arrived. "It has nothing to do with you. I just don't talk to them much. I've mentioned you to Deb, but don't know if she's talked to anyone else. We'll find out soon enough, I guess." He crossed his arms. "What about you? Do you keep in touch with your family? Have things improved since you left?"

She picked up the plastic cups and squeezed them. "That's a subject for another day."

"Okay, I can take the hint."

Thank you. "You don't know how fortunate you are. I've often wondered what a family like yours would be like." With parents who didn't abandon their only child.

"You say that now. Wait till you meet them."

"I'm looking forward to it."

An unintelligible response grunted from his throat, and he looked at his watch. "Time to go." He bent down, picked up the vegetables, and led her outside. After locking the door, he nodded to his car. "Top up or down?"

"Leave it up so we can talk."

"Fine."

Startled by his change of voice, she glanced over at him. Tension oozed from his clamped jaw and balled fists. Obviously there was more going on with him than being afraid to introduce her. What kind of situation had she just insinuated herself into? Had she just signed the death warrant to their relationship before it barely had time to start?

CHAPTER *nine*

We're here."

Sheila blinked her eyes open and peered over at Richard.

His fingers white-knuckling the steering wheel, he slowed and turned onto a sloping gravel driveway framed by pines. A black dog charged toward them baring pointy teeth.

"Richard, careful!" She clutched her purse as the bear-sized dog reached the car then ran along the driver's side. "Is he safe?"

Richard laughed.

What a heavenly sound, even if it was at her expense.

"That's Prince, purebred German Shepherd." He nodded at the animal. "The best farm dog you could ask for." The car climbed toward a red barn topped with a gambrel roof. "And a great burglar alarm. No one comes on the farm without Prince announcing it and, frankly, strangers don't get out of their car if he's looking in their window."

"Like me."

"Exactly."

Okay, maybe he was enjoying her fear a bit too much.

"He's an old softy. Wouldn't hurt a flea, unless I told him to, of course."

"Oh, real comforting."

Grinning, Richard backed his Audi against a line of lilac bushes, parking between a Suburban and a Chrysler minivan. He shut off the motor and covered her hand with his. "Don't worry. He won't hurt you."

Staring at the beast peering in Richard's window, she wasn't convinced.

The dog let out a single bark as Richard opened the door. Prince stuck his nose in the crack, nudging the door open, and thumped massive paws on Richard's lap. "Prince, down." Richard turned his face, preventing the dog from licking it. "Down, boy."

The dog obeyed, ran around the car, and stood by her window looking down upon her, panting and displaying his fangs.

Thank goodness, the top was up. "I'm not getting out till you get over here and call this dog off."

"I promise, he won't hurt you."

"Richard Brooks." Venom laced her voice.

"All right." Chuckling, he stepped out of the car and cupped his hands beside his mouth. "Hey, Nathan."

A lanky young man, standing by a white farmhouse with black shutters, tossed a football to a smaller boy then jogged toward the car. "Hey, Uncle Ricky."

Ricky?

"Would you mind calling off Prince? My friend's a little nervous."

"No problem." The curly-haired blond bent over, peeked into the car, and grinned before slapping his leg. "Come on, buddy."

The dog bounded toward the boys, thankfully forgetting about her. Too many people were enjoying her fear. Well, by the end of the day, she and Prince would be best friends. Who was she to avoid a challenge?

Richard walked around the front of the car, opened her door, and offered his hand. "Care to join me?"

"Any more surprises?" She put her hand in his, and he helped her stand.

"Just a warning that I'll probably be accosted by three dazzlingly gorgeous ladies any minute now."

"Oh really? All under five feet, I presume."

"You presume correctly." He closed the door, and made a sweeping motion with his arm, pointing to the farmstead. "This is where I grew up."

Her gaze swept over the house, its base trimmed with colorful perennials, and the barn whose red was just beginning to crack and fade, but the roof's spine held strong. "It's lovely."

Unlike so many of the farms they passed along the way, that were weathered and decaying with neglect, this one seemed to age gracefully.

"Mom and Dad have worked hard to keep it up."

"They've done well." She closed her eyes and breathed in. *Ahh, fresh air.*

"It does smell good, doesn't it? Especially since Dad got rid of the cattle. Nothing better to clean out your sinuses than shoveling manure."

"Oh, please." She swatted his arm. "There's an image I really didn't need."

With a laugh, he leaned over and kissed her. "Make up for it?"

Oh, the man knew how to kiss. Even the lightest brushing of his lips against hers sent tingles through her body. "It's a start."

He leaned in for another kiss and a door slammed in back of them followed by a chorus of three cherubic voices.

"Uncle Ricky! Uncle Ricky!"

With raised eyebrows, Sheila glanced up at him. "Ricky, huh?"

He narrowed his eyes and whispered. "Don't."

Ahh, the name was off-limits. Too bad for him. "I rather like the way it sounds." It didn't fit the man she knew before today. But, a man who collected kid's meal toys? Perhaps.

"We'll talk about this later." He knelt, opened his arms, and the tallest girl bowled into him, knocking him on his behind. "Whoa, Katydid. Nathan's been teaching you to tackle, huh?"

"No, he hasn't. That's silly."

Sheila raised a hand to her mouth, suppressing a chuckle.

"That is pretty silly, isn't it?" Keeping Kaitlyn in his arms, he pushed into a squat. Seconds later, a girl with a mop of brown curls hugged his back. He patted her arm. "How's my Jaclyn?"

"I miss you." Jaclyn clung tighter.

The smallest girl lagged behind, chugging hard, wearing a toothy smile. Richard reached for her. "Hey Lillykins."

She circled her arms around his neck, but didn't say anything.

Kaitlynn pulled her head back and, keeping her arms on his shoulders, glanced over at Sheila then back at him. "Mommy got me a Hula-Hoop, and I'm really good at it. Can I show you?"

Hula-Hoop? Sheila knelt next to Richard. *I used to be good once.*

"Maybe in a bit, okay sweetie? I need to say hi to everyone else first."

"You promise?"

"We promise." Sheila laid a hand on Kaitlynn's arm. "Do you think I could give it a try?" She'd love to try it again.

Richard looked at Sheila, grinning.

"Hm, hmmm. Mommy says I need to share better. She says I don't share good with Lilly, but Lilly's little yet. She's three and I'm seven. She's not big like me."

"Would my big girl mind if you shared your uncle for a bit?" Richard kissed her cheek. Keeping a grip on Lilly, he reached for Jaclyn and gave her a one-armed hug. He nodded toward Sheila. "This is my, uh … friend, Auntie Sheila." As he said "Auntie," his eyes met hers, apparently seeking approval of the title.

She nodded, blinking away a tear. Where did that come from? Kaitlynn spread her arms out toward Sheila. *She wants a hug from me?* Sheila stared at the waiting arms, and then enveloped the little girl, burying her nose in the child's hair and breathing in. Berries. She blinked away more tears.

"Glad you could make it, Ricky."

Sheila startled at the deep male voice. She released Kaitlynn and looked up at an older man who shared Richard's crooked smile. The man's body was strong and lean, and his slightly graying hair was just beginning to thin. Hopefully, Richard inherited those genes.

"Dad." Richard nodded upward.

"Please introduce me to your lovely lady friend."

And the man was a definite charmer. Another attribute inherited by his son.

Keeping the three-year-olds wrapped in his arms, Richard stood.

Sheila stood alongside him and Kaitlynn ran toward the boys still tossing a football. Sheila might have to join them later.

"This is Sheila Peterson. She works with me at Wharton."

His dad's arms surrounded her and she stiffened. Her own father had never held her like that. He released her and showed the smile Richard had inherited. "It's very nice to meet you, Sheila."

"You too, Mr. Brooks."

"Just call me Bernie."

"Bernie." She smiled, squelching a sniffle.

"We'll have to have a chat later." He patted her hand. "Ricky, we're all out at the fire pit. Why don't you come join us?"

The smile deserted Richard's face. "After I say hi to Mom."

Bernie winked and walked off, past the house, onto a dirt path paved between a copse of trees.

"I love your family," she whispered and wiped a stray tear from her cheek.

Richard circled a tense arm around her waist. "You haven't met everyone yet."

In answer, the screen door on the house slammed, and Richard's arm sprang from her waist. A dark-haired man stood on the deck and looked their way, his jaw working back and forth. The man wasn't as tall as Richard, and his belly stretched the front of his shirt slightly, but it was obvious the two were brothers.

With crossed arms, Richard's brother stared at them, but didn't smile. He shook his head and continued past the row of lilac bushes, following their father.

LOVE YOU TOO, MARCUS. RICHARD HOPED HIS brother would have the decency to cover his contempt. Now, Sheila's curiosity had been fed more ammunition, and he'd have more questions to answer. But, the inquiry would wait. He wanted Sheila to meet his mom. At least that would be a pleasant introduction.

He retrieved the vegetable tray and the plastic cups from his car. While balancing the tray in one hand, he handed the cups to Sheila. Clasping Sheila's hand, he aimed for the house.

"You said you and Marcus were competitive?" She leaned into him. "There's more to it, isn't there?"

"There is, but you don't want to hear about it now." And he didn't want to talk about it. "Let's find Mom. She'll be eager to meet you."

His mom stepped out of the house before they reached the weathered deck leading to the home's enclosed porch. Her dark, curled hair was just showing signs of grey—each one of those grey strands put there by him personally, he was sure. She wiped her hands on a rooster-print apron tied around her waist. The apron covered well-worn jeans.

Her smiling face glowed when she looked at him. Now there was unconditional love. After all he'd done, in all the ways he hurt her, she still loved him. She didn't find it necessary to endlessly remind him of his failings, unlike his dad or Marcus.

"Sorry it took me so long to come out, Ricky." She embraced him in a long hug before turning her attention to Sheila.

"Hello, Mrs. Brooks. I'm Ricky's friend, Sheila."

He rolled his eyes. *Figures.*

"It's nice to meet you, Sheila. Ricky didn't tell me he was bringing a friend today."

"I invited myself. I hope that's okay."

"Absolutely, dear. We love company."

"Oh, and apparently, these are for you." Sheila innocently handed the souvenir cups to his mom.

He grinned, and his mom's lips puckered.

"Fer gosh sakes, Ricky, you know I hate these things!"

He shrugged. "I keep forgetting."

"Hm, hmmm." She clamped her lips and shook her head. "Sheila, why don't you come on in with me? Let me show you around, introduce you to the girls. Ricky, you can go help the men with the turkey."

His smile collapsed. His own mother was sending him to the wolves, and Sheila wouldn't be alongside deflecting their bite.

Taking his time, he walked past the barn, through a patch of woods and into a clearing. Marcus, Jerry, and his dad sat on homemade log benches surrounding a smoking mound of dirt. The smoke carried the flavor into the air. Richard could almost taste the turkey already.

"Without getting a decent quarterback, the Vikings have no chance." Marcus flipped open the cooler next to his bench.

Football. Now there was a conversation he'd enjoy. Maybe, for once, he could join in the debate and avoid the sermons that seeped out in his presence.

Marcus underhanded a Miller Lite in Richard's direction,

eliminating any hope of casual conversation.

Richard snagged the can out of the air. "You know I don't drink anymore." He heaved the can back at Marcus' feet, praying for an explosion.

Another unanswered prayer.

"Oh, so sorry." Marcus slapped a hand over his heart. "I thought maybe all these changes you've made in your life were a thing of the past. I see you've got yourself another trophy."

Trophy? Richard's eyes widened. If his nephews weren't so close, Marcus would be nursing a black eye. Boy, would that have felt good. Someday. For now, words would have to do. "Don't you dare start on Sheila. She's nothing like the women I used to date."

Jerry turned away, shaking his head. His father just sat there, smiling. *Go ahead, take Marcus' side again.*

"So, I'm assuming she knows all about you." Marcus stirred the coals with a tree branch.

Not on your life. Richard turned around and stalked away, clenching and unclenching his fists, wanting badly to pummel something with them. Marcus always knew how to inflame him, although the flames were usually fed with the truth. Perhaps that's what made Richard so angry. Marcus was usually dead on in his accusations. No sense letting him know that, though.

Holding back his anger, Richard turned to his family. "I'll tell her, in my own time, when I'm ready."

"Forgiveness can go a long way." His father braced hands on his knees.

Richard closed his eyes and tightened his jaw. *Here it comes …*

"You're wound so tight from keeping this all in. Everyone's forgiven you. You need to forgive yourself. It's time to be honest with yourself—"

"Sheesh! I've been more than honest with myself!" He cursed under his breath. Why couldn't they understand that was the problem? "I'd feel so much better if people hated me for what I've done. At least I deserve that. You insisted I come out today? It took you all of twenty minutes to begin lecturing." What he wouldn't give now to take the beer back from Marcus.

He stepped toward the fire pit and kicked at the smoking mound, sending orange embers into the air. "I didn't come here to listen to a bunch of preaching. Why do you think I don't visit? I don't want to listen to your sermons, and I certainly don't want your forgiveness or God's forgiveness or anyone else's." He stuffed his hands into his pockets and glared at Marcus. "Can we enjoy the afternoon and not fight?"

Frowning, Marcus stood and offered his hand. "Truce."

Richard grabbed it, glowering back. When would his family accept him again?

He released Marcus' hand and grabbed a Pepsi from the cooler before sitting next to Jerry. That was the safest place. At least Jerry accepted him. Richard popped the tab, took a long swig, and the carbonation burned down his throat. A beer would have tasted much better, but he wasn't ready yet, especially in front of his family. He wiped his mouth with the back of his hand, hoping to redirect the conversation. "What do you think of the Vikings' draft?"

"Personally, I think they would have been better off drafting the linebacker out of Columbus instead," Sheila said, and he jumped, as did the other men. Apparently, no one had seen her enter the clearing.

What did she hear? She strolled toward them and Richard perused her face. Her warm smile showed no hint that she heard their argument.

He stood as she neared. The other men followed suit, and he introduced her to Jerry and Marcus.

"It smells wonderful." Sheila stood next to Richard and flashed a smile at Marcus. "Richard tells me it's the best ever. How do you make it?"

"This is the best turkey you'll ever eat." Even Marcus fell prey to her dangerous dimples as he explained, in detail, how to cook the turkey. "It takes about eight hours, but it's well worth the wait."

"I'll second that." Richard grasped Sheila's arm and stood. "But, until it's ready, let me show you the farm." Clinging to Sheila's hand, they walked away from the pit. How ironic it was that, even as a janitor, he was good enough for the executive, but not the Christian.

CHAPTER *ten*

After walking several hundred feet, Richard glanced back toward the turkey pit. The easygoing conversation had resumed. They were probably as grateful for his departure as he was.

He and Sheila entered another wooded area, taking them further away from the house, and his muscles loosened. Winding dirt paths carved between trees showed his nephews spent a lot of time out here, carrying on a Brooks' tradition. There was a time when he, Marcus, and Debbie raced their bikes on the paths they created. Skinned knees and elbows were commonplace and a badge of honor.

"Thanks for rescuing me," he finally said, his tension easing away.

"Bad, huh?"

"Actually, it was normal. I can't seem to come out here without getting into a fight." She didn't need to know she was the subject of the dispute.

"Tell me about the farm."

He loved Sheila's ability to know when to drop an issue. One more thing to set her apart from any other woman he'd dated.

"Does your Dad still work it?"

And that was a subject he'd gladly talk about. "Mom and Dad retired about ten years ago. None of us kids had any interest in farming so they sold off most of the cropland, keeping twenty acres for the homestead. It's enough for Dad to have a couple acres to garden plus the acreage bordering the lake."

"A lake?"

"Lake. Pond. Swimming hole. We call it Lake Albin, named for my great-grandpa who first farmed the land. It's too small for motor craft, but it's perfect for swimming. I'm sure the kids will all go out after lunch. In the winter, it makes a great skating and hockey rink." He sighed, picturing himself as a teenager, actually getting along with Marcus. They plowed snow off the lake with a tractor and teamed up for hockey games against area kids. At that time, he, Marcus, and Debbie made a strong team. What he'd give to go back and recapture those innocent moments.

"Will you show me?"

"I'd love to." Keeping his fingers entwined with hers, he steered toward the lake, leading her through a field of chest high corn stalks. Just the tenderness of her touch helped ease his anxiety. Years ago, the lake served as his private getaway, a place to calm him. Farmland encompassed it, offering no public access. The only intrusion was the occasional tractor or combine. Perhaps if he'd found such a place in New York, his life wouldn't have taken its drastic turn. "I could always go there to clear my head, so this is probably a very good idea."

She squeezed his hand. "Why don't you like to be called Ricky?"

He laughed softly and turned around to walk backward through the rows of corn, wanting to observe her expression. "I always hated it. Thought it was immature. So, once I went to college, I became Richard. To me, it was more adult. More professional. Unfortunately, the family knows me as Ricky, so I'm stuck with the name when I'm around them. But, don't you get any ideas."

"You'll always be Richard to me, unless I really want to irritate you."

He wasn't going to let her know he liked the way it sounded when she said it.

"Where'd you go to college?"

What he didn't like was the new direction her line of questioning headed.

"The U." That much was safe, but how much information could he divulge? At what point would he stop? And what would he tell her then?

"Minnesota?" She wrinkled her nose.

"Something wrong with that?"

"You're my arch enemy."

"Oh, so you're a Wisconsin Badger?"

"Is there anything else?"

"You know, it's almost sacrilegious for a Gopher to date a Badger." Good, the conversation had taken a detour. He could hopefully avoid further exposure.

Sheila pulled his hand, stopping him, and put a finger to his mouth. "I've never knowingly kissed a Gopher."

A teasing smile broke free as he recalled his college days.

"I see you can't say the same about a Badger."

He scratched his chin. "I think it was a freshman dare."

"And what else did you do on that freshman dare?"

"That's personal." Wishing for more mature stalks, he pulled Sheila close, and kissed her. "There, now. Much better than those Badger boys, don't you think?"

"I don't know. I need to try it again, just to make sure." Her arms circled his waist, and she leaned in for another kiss.

He pulled back, keeping his hands on her hips, unable to cover his grin. "Please don't tell me you're a Packer fan."

"If I am?"

"I can kiss a Badger, but a cheesehead? That's asking a bit much, don't you think?"

She drew a finger down the front of his chest stopping at his heart. "Have no fear. I bleed Viking purple, just like you."

"Thank God."

She locked her fingers behind his neck and kissed him long and sweet.

Way too sweet and far too tantalizing. His heart pumping, he backed away. "It's been a long time since I've made out with a girl in the corn field." *And look where that got you.*

Rustling leaves alerted him. He scanned the field, seeing nothing, but that didn't mean they weren't alone. His nephews probably excelled at covert operations. "Let's keep going. Sometimes these stalks have eyes." Again, he slipped his hand into hers and led her through the field.

He smiled freely now, enjoying her company and the quiet walk and even their moment of teasing. He almost felt like a teenager again, his heart skipping, experiencing love for the first time. Maybe having Sheila along today wasn't so bad after all.

It wasn't long before they exited the field and stood at the top of a hill. It sloped sharply downward providing a panoramic view of the lake and the farmland surrounding it, with miles of rolling hills, trees, and fields colored by their ripening crops. Tops of silos, from adjacent farms, periodically peeked above nature.

No people. No arguments. Only peace.

Sheila followed him down the steep embankment, toward the water, on a well-worn path. The three-acre lake was artfully landscaped with perennials, trees, and rocks. A small sand beach, with homemade benches and a changing shack, fronted the lake.

They removed their shoes and sat side by side in the sand, inching their toes into the lukewarm water.

"This is the same type of stone in your fireplace, isn't it?" Sheila picked up a stone bordering a hosta garden and rolled it over in her hands. "Where does it come from?"

He laughed. "The field. It's genuine, inexpensive field rock. When you prep fields for planting, you have to walk them first to remove the larger rocks that work their way to the surface so you don't wreck the machinery. Picking rock is hot, dirty work. Figures, Mom would find a way to turn drudgery into something beautiful. Most farmers make a rock pile. Mom turns them into artwork."

And her artwork blended well with nature that insisted on being heard. Heeding nature's voice, Richard closed his eyes and listened to her symphony. Crickets and frogs sang in contrapuntal harmony. Mourning doves underscored the melody with their haunting coo, and ducks' wings flapping on the water provided steady percussion. Wondrously absent was the ceaseless buzz of traffic, horns, and voices.

Apparently, Sheila heard the music too and allowed his silence. That fact alone drew him to her. Unlike most of the women he'd dated, his attentions didn't always have to center on her.

She rested her head on his shoulder. "Your family really loves you, you know."

Tension slinked up his back. Oh, he knew all right.

"I get the feeling, though, you see yourself as the black sheep. From what I know of you, it doesn't make sense."

From what she knew … well, she knew enough, for now. He shrugged. "It's partly because I didn't stick with the faith I was raised in. I grew out of the passion for God the rest of my family clings to. They're always worrying about my salvation and …" And maybe he should tell her the rest.

He glanced back toward the farm buzzing with judgmental relatives. No, now wasn't the right time or this, the right place. That moment was coming soon enough. "I get tired of their constant preaching and always trying to convert me. It turns me off."

"What about Marcus? There's more to it than you not taking on his beliefs, and I know it's more than being competitive."

"Because there is more. The argument goes way back."

"Janet, right? I could tell, when you showed me their picture, there was jealousy between you."

Jealousy? The word rumbled through his thoughts. "Maybe at first. That was a long time ago. I broke up with her and didn't realize what I'd given up until Marc started dating her. I'm afraid I was never too kind to him about it, either. I didn't like to lose, still don't, especially to my brother. I'd say the feelings are more from a lost competition than jealousy. We've both let it fester over the years."

"Why don't you come clean with him? Apologize? Something? Can you imagine how tough this has got to be on Janet?"

His gaze wandered to the water, fixing on the low, rolling waves. "I suppose it is. I haven't been around to notice."

"Take my word for it, whether she shows it or not, it must bother her being the root cause of her husband and brother-in-law not getting along."

"There's more to it than that." *A whole lot more.* "But, I suppose it wouldn't hurt to make amends where Janet's concerned."

"It would make things better."

He nodded, although he didn't necessarily agree. Only a miracle would mend things between him and his brother.

"You like to hold things in, don't you?" Sheila's manicured toes dug a hole in the sand.

"You're trying to figure me all out in one day, aren't you?"

She drew her knees close to her chest, wrapped her arms

around them and turned her head, her eyes meeting his. "You're an enigma to me. The puzzle pieces of your life don't fit. You're an extraordinarily bright man over-employed as a janitor and, I'm not putting janitors down, but you don't fit the part. You've got expensive taste that doesn't fit with a janitor's salary and, judging by the rest of your family, I don't see an inherited wealth."

"I've invested well." Which was true, but only a portion of the truth.

"Hm, hmmm." Lifting a hand to his cheek, she spoke softly. "You've been nothing but a gentleman to me. I wish you'd be a less of a gentleman."

His hand covered hers. "Believe me, there are times when I'd rather not be a gentleman either." He kissed her, thinking back to the cornfield, thinking of places he couldn't go, he so wanted to.

"And that's a problem?" Her forehead rested against his as she probed his eyes.

You have no idea. He stood and searched the beach for stones.

"See what I mean? I think your family's religion has affected you more than you believe. And they regard you as a black sheep? Personally, I don't think they know you very well."

"Unfortunately, they know me all too well," he mumbled and realized he only added pieces to her puzzle. Wanting to change the subject, he scanned the sand. Weeds mottled the beach and rose up through the water. When he was a teenager, the lake was used daily and weeds were never allowed to take root. Maybe if he hadn't turned from God, the weeds wouldn't be clogging his heart.

He rolled his head in an attempt to clear away the unsolicited sermon.

Feeling Sheila's hand on his back helped.

He pointed toward the middle of the lake. "We used to have a raft anchored out there. Marc and I built it out of two-by-fours from an old corncrib. We attached the metal slide from an old swing set. Rusty barrels helped it float. The raft was nothing to look at, but we didn't care. We didn't need the fancy rafts and slides and trampolines kids now demand."

There was a time when he didn't think he'd ever miss the

simplicity of farm life, but right now, he wanted desperately to go back to those days and start all over again.

"So what happened, Richard?" Her hand traveled from his back and down his arm until she held his hand. "What did you do after college? Before Wharton?" Her voice was soft and infused with concern, not the curiosity that was usually there.

He clenched his jaw. *I can't tell you.*

Her finger traced the scar peeking out from his shirt sleeve. "What caused this?"

Tension strained his muscles. "We've been over this before." Well, not really. She asked the question before. He always avoided answering, just as he would do now.

"I care for you. Let me help you."

Her free hand reached for his, but he refused it and released the one he held. His gaze landed on a flat stone. He squatted to pick it up along with a few others. He flung one outward toward the water ... one ... two leaps, and then it disappeared. He threw out another. This time four skips.

"Richard ..." Sheila's voice blended with his self-induced fog.

He couldn't tell her. Not yet.

"You know, you were right." Anger stole the affection from her voice. "I should've stayed home."

He didn't watch her leave. This was exactly what he knew would happen today. There was nothing he could have done to prevent it, short of explaining his history, but that would have been worse. He reached up and clutched the front of his shirt, grasping the chain beneath it. Yes, explaining would be far worse.

He hunted for more stones and skipped them across the water. How had things changed so drastically? A mere twenty minutes ago, his heart skipped as if experiencing a high school crush. Those feelings sank along with the stones. He couldn't wait until the meal was over, so he could go home and not face the pressures his family, and now Sheila, placed on him.

CHAPTER *eleven*

Richard eyed the stone making its sixth leap when Debbie's voice sounded behind him.

"What's your record?"

"I'm not sure. Ten, twelve." He braced himself for an impromptu therapy session as she stopped at his side. His sister had been wise to go into counseling. She always got more out of his jumbled thoughts and emotions than anyone else had. She knew more about that wretched night than anyone. Still, even she didn't know everything, and he swore she never would.

"Ha! Mine's fifteen." Bending over, she selected a rock. "Found the perfect stone and happened to throw it at just the right angle." She side-armed her stone toward the water. "It seemed to keep going and going and—"

"And then it sunk." Her stone disappeared. The analogy to his life was almost frightening. "Just like me. Fifteen perfect years. Thought it would go on forever. Then, without warning, I find myself sinking to the bottom."

"You're a good swimmer, Ricky."

Yeah, right. "I'm good at treading water." He waited for her to end with some corny statement about God being a life preserver. Gratefully, she was smarter than that.

"Come, sit." Her hand brushed his arm as she turned away.

He followed his sister and sat next to her on a bench. Like Sheila, Debbie allowed him a temporary retreat, but it wasn't nearly long enough. He was tired of his psyche being poked and prodded which was exactly what his sister came to do, although Debbie was so smooth at it, he rarely realized what she was doing until midway through the conversation.

"Is Sheila the one you stood me up for?"

Recalling the theater date, his mouth tipped up. He'd initial-ly promised to take Debbie. "Yeah. But, I made it up to you, remember? I'm sure you didn't mind going to the show with Jerry, plus dinner, plus hotel. I seem to remember Jerry thanking me profusely for the evening out."

"But, you wouldn't watch the girls. That would've made the night complete."

"Overnight, by myself?" He shook his head. "No way. I'll give you a couple hours any time, but I'm not ready to deal with the bedtime ordeal. Besides, Mom thrives on watching her grand-daughters."

"Chicken."

"Guilty as charged."

"To be honest, I was just happy you were dating again. I would've given you the ticket. And to see that you're still with her, she must be special."

His lips curved up even more. Far more reaction than he wanted to show. "I guess. Maybe." He shrugged. Debbie didn't need to think he and Sheila would last.

"So what did you two argue about?" Whoosh. The coun-selor deftly swooped in beginning her session.

He set his jaw in answer.

Her hand rested on his forearm. "Come on, Richard, you know you can talk to me."

She called me Richard … Shaking his head, he stared out over the water. May as well get it over with. "What do you want to know?" He leaned back, crossed his arms, and stretched his legs out in front of him.

"I'm concerned for you. We all are. Apparently, so is Sheila."

Same old song. "Well, Sheila can't figure out what all your concerns are about. She sees who I am now. I don't party. I don't drink anymore. I don't even …" He sighed, letting Debbie fill in the blank. "That part's really driving her crazy. Me too, to be honest. I've changed so much already. Why can't the family accept it?"

"Because you're not dealing with that night very well. We

can all see it—feel it when we're around you. You're on edge all the time, running away from it."

"And just how do I *deal* with it, when it doesn't let me rest? When I relive it every day?"

"You've been forgiven. Have you forgiven yourself?"

"Forgiveness." He laughed without humor. How often would he hear that word this visit? "Could you forgive yourself under the same circumstances? It was *my* fault."

"But, they said—"

"I don't care what they said. It was entirely preventable. I'm guilty, okay? And you all wonder why I'm not handling it well. Would you be able to?"

"I don't know."

"Because it never would have happened to you."

"Maybe. I just know that when I face the tough times, it's my faith that gets me through, knowing God won't ever desert me, even when I mess up. He helped us when we found out about Lilly. When Jerry and I had problems. He's our constant."

"You know I can't—"

She rested her hand on his arm, silently telling him to listen. "We've all noticed the changes you've made and are ecstatic about it, but those changes are all on the surface. You're still running away from God. I wish you'd stop running and seek him again."

He raised his arm, shook off her hand, and pointed upward. "Oh, I know exactly where he is. He's sitting on his throne allowing losers like me to ruin lives."

"That's what you think?"

"It's what I know." Bending down, he picked up a cat that had followed Debbie to the beach. He raised it to his shoulder hoping its purr would calm him. "Do you know I prayed that night? I hadn't prayed in years."

She remained silent, staring out at the lake.

"I begged him to take me, but he didn't listen."

Debbie closed her eyes and sighed. After a moment, she opened them and turned toward him. "He listened. He just has other plans for you."

"Oh, I know." Giving his best imitation of a TV evangelist, he spouted a verse forever imprinted on his mind. "'For I know the plans for you,' declares the Lord, 'plans to prosper you and not to harm you, plans to give you a hope and a future.' My hope and future are pretty bleak."

"You may think so, and I can sure understand why you would feel that way, but I see hope in that you remember his promise."

His eyes narrowed and bore into hers. "I remember everything, Debbie." He wasn't just speaking Bible verses.

"Do you still believe?"

The ache in his sister's voice was clear as he stroked the cat's fur, deepening its purr. Faith was important to her. It had been that way for him once, too, and he did remember everything. He'd been raised on Biblical principles, memorizing verses and applying them to his life. All too often Bible verses still floated through his head. The lessons his parents taught frequently confronted him.

He gazed at the blue sky mixed with stretched cotton clouds. When had it changed? When did he turn away? Did he still believe? "That God exists? I guess so. That he's a personal God who wants a relationship with us? I don't know. It's been a long time since I've made the effort. It was easy not to try in New York. But, then I come here and see the kids, I see the beauty in creation. It makes me wonder what I've given up."

"You should come home more often."

"And face Dad and Marcus? Not happening."

"They're hard on you because they love you."

"I'd like to be loved a little less. For once I'd like to come up here and enjoy the family without feeling I have something to prove."

"Do you want me to talk to them? Ask them to lay off a bit?"

"Wouldn't help. The easiest thing to do is stay away."

"Or run away," Debbie mumbled.

Richard glanced her way. Did he hear her correctly? She'd always been his biggest supporter. Had he lost her now too? What did he have to do to regain their trust? Hadn't he changed enough? Sacrificed enough for them?

A tear rolled down her cheek. "God can help you through this, Ricky."

He hated seeing the dampness in her eyes, but he couldn't

do what she wanted. How could he return to God now? There could never be forgiveness for what he'd done.

"If you don't give this up to him, we're all afraid you're going to self-combust, and I won't have my big brother anymore."

"What? You too?" That's what they all worried about? If anything, this past year taught him how precious life was … even his own pathetic life. "That's not a problem. I just look at life differently now. Stop worrying about me. I'll be fine. Sheila brings out the best in me too, usually … So, what do you think of her?" He needed to direct the discussion away from himself.

"Sheila?"

"Yes."

Debbie shrugged. "It's too early to tell. I haven't had a chance to talk with her. Does it matter?"

He gazed at the water. "I didn't think it did, but now that we're here, I'm finding I want everyone to approve of her."

"The girls adore her. She seems to have a natural gift with children. Does she work with kids?"

"No, not at all. Doesn't have any family to speak of, either. I was shocked at how well your girls took to her and vice versa. Who knows, maybe she'll be a good mom someday."

"You're not thinking about marriage?"

"Marriage?" Until now, the thought hadn't crossed his mind. He still debated whether he should even be dating Sheila, much less considering marriage. "No way. There are a lot of things we have to deal with before marriage is even an issue."

"So, you haven't told her about New York yet?"

"No. Thought about it right before Sheila stormed off, but this isn't the time or place. She knows I'm hiding something, and I know it's bugging her." But then, no one in his family knew the whole story from that dreadful night, and they never would. If they found out, he'd break their hearts more than he'd already done. "I do plan on telling her. Soon. Then I'll be alone again."

"Don't be so sure." She touched his arm. "Maybe you need to give her a little more credit. After all, she's seeing the best of you now. If she's a decent person, she'll understand."

"Guess I'll know soon enough."

"Make it soon, okay? She deserves the truth."

"I know." But, the truth was awfully frightening to face, and he wasn't ready yet. He placed the cat on the ground and stood. "I think I better head back up. I've got some crow to eat if I want a peaceful ride home."

She stretched an arm around his back, hugging him. "You know we love you, Ricky."

He forced a smile for her benefit. "Yeah, I know."

As they walked briskly back to the house, Richard's thoughts raced. What did it matter what the family thought of Sheila? That, in itself, said he cared too much. He never allowed himself to get close. Life was easier that way, less complicated, and the last thing he needed was more complications. But, the fact was, he did care for Sheila, and he needed to make it up to her.

Back at the house he spotted her throwing a football around with his nephews, with Prince chasing after the ball. Richard caught himself smiling. The competitive boys had discovered a tough challenger, and Prince a new friend. He sat on the ground and silently watched. Sheila either didn't realize he sat there or intentionally ignored him. A fitting payback.

"Food's on!" his dad yelled behind him.

About time. Richard jumped up, intercepted a ball thrown to Sheila, and ran toward the picnic tables. Prince raced at his heels. Something slapped the back of his legs, and his knees buckled beneath him, pressing his face into the grass.

Kaitlynn squealed. "Auntie Sheila tackled Uncle Ricky!"

What? He spun around and felt his eyes grow wide. The little stinker was right.

Sheila grinned with her arms still wrapped around his calves. "That'll teach you to ignore me." She let go and extended a hand as she stood.

He accepted it, stood, and pulled her close, whispering, "You're showing me up in front of my family. I'll never live this down."

"You deserve it," she said smugly.

Not caring about the eyes trained on them, he kept her close. "I do deserve it, and I'm sorry. But, there are things I can't talk about, not today."

A smirk formed on her face. "So someday you'll confess

that you're a secret agent?"

He grinned, rubbing his chin, liking the image it conjured up. "Something like that."

"Fine. I forgive you." Her mouth straightened. "Just remember, I don't like being ignored."

"I'll remember." He sealed his promise with a quick kiss, but her hand pressed into his back, keeping them close.

"Making up is fun," she whispered in his ear.

Tell me about it. Feeling his body's temperature rise, he pulled from her grip.

Yes, he'd tell her. Someday. "Let's go join the family before they have more to gossip about."

CHAPTER *twelve*

Sheila watched with raised eyebrows as Richard and Marcus walked together up the hill, steering away from the lake. They seemed to be getting along. She glanced at Debbie who sat next to her on the sand. Debbie's gaze was on the brothers, too, and her wide-eyed stare told Sheila this was not a common occurrence.

But, for the moment they didn't matter. She had Debbie to herself—she and the five kids playing in the water—and it was time to get some answers. "Tell me about your brother." The direct approach usually worked best.

Debbie diverted her eyes from the hill and smiled. "Awe, the ever elusive Ricky Brooks." Debbie's smile faded as she turned back to the lake and counted, on her fingers, the number of heads in the water. "He never used to be that way, you know. There was actually a time when I'd have to remind him we didn't need to know everything. He knew that, of course. He just wanted to …" Debbie forced out a breath as she turned, letting her gaze climb the hill again. The brothers had disappeared.

"So what happened? Why did he change?"

With cloudy eyes, Debbie looked at Sheila. "I'm sorry, but if he hasn't told you, it's not my place to say anything. I'm sure it's frustrating, but he does have his reasons, whether I agree with them or not."

"I know he came from New York." Maybe this one thread of evidence would open the door for more information.

"Yeah, he did." Debbie turned back to the lake and counted the kids again.

Sheila counted them too. Even with her frustration, she couldn't help but smile as she watched them play. The boys swam in deeper water, racing and wrestling. Kaitlynn and Jaclyn sat on the beach building sand castles, decorating them with evergreen sticks and multi-colored stones. Lilly played by herself, sitting half in the water, half out, fingers digging in the sand. The little girl's eyes suddenly lit up, and then she stood and ran toward Debbie, fisting her hand.

Lilly's almond eyes were the same intense blue as her uncle's. But unlike Richard's, hers glowed with a happy twinkle. Saying nothing, Lilly unfisted her hand, displaying a small black stone with pinpoints of white sparkles. A common, everyday rock.

"It's beautiful, sweetheart." Debbie stroked it as if it were a costly gem.

Lilly's smile broadened on her round face.

"Lilly, may I see your treasure, please?"

She lifted her hand close to Sheila's eyes.

Smiling, Sheila touched the rock. "It's the most precious jewel I've ever seen."

Lilly brought her hand closer keeping her palm flat.

Debbie touched Sheila's arm. "She wants you to have it."

"Really? For me?" Sheila splayed a hand over her heart, and her throat knotted up.

Grinning, Lilly nodded.

Firmly convinced it was a precious gem, Sheila accepted it. "Thank you, sweetie. I'll keep it forever."

Lilly's pudgy arms curved around Sheila's neck and squeezed.

"Oh, Lilly," Debbie said. "Please don't get Auntie Sheila wet."

"I don't mind." Sheila returned Lilly's hug. The soggy embrace felt more precious than the gem.

Just as quickly, Lilly loosed her grip and returned to her digging.

"You've made a friend for life." Debbie touched Sheila's arm.

With her thumb, Sheila rolled the stone in her hand. "I think I could bring her home with me. Any of them, as a matter of fact."

"I'd be careful about saying that out loud. We might take you up on it. But, you'll have to wait in line. Ricky gets first dibs."

"He lives for those kids, doesn't he?" Sheila nodded toward the water.

"He really does. Even on his worst days, they can get him to smile."

"He's had a lot of those 'worst days,' hasn't he?"

Debbie nodded, and her smile faded.

"What happened to him, Debbie?"

Sighing, she looked down at her hands.

"You're not going to say anything, are you?"

Debbie shook her head. "I've noticed one thing today: you make him smile too." She smiled at Sheila. "The family's thrilled. Ricky's had his share of girlfriends, but he looks at you differently. We all see it. You're not just someone he brought out here to show off. He cares about you, and he wants to tell you what happened. When he's ready, he will."

"Maybe I can't wait until he's ready."

"That's understandable. My guess is he's almost trying to drive you away. If you leave him, he won't have to face his problems, and he can wallow in his pity again."

Sheila pinched her eyes shut. All she'd wanted from Richard was a nice, uncomplicated relationship: go on a few dates, have some fun together, and move on to the next person. She hadn't expected to care for him, but now that she did, she wasn't ready to give up yet. "I'll give him some time. Not much, mind you, but I think he's worth it."

"I'm so glad to hear that." Debbie wrapped her arms around Sheila. Another loving hug from someone who didn't even know her. Debbie backed away, looking sheepish. "I'm sorry. I love Ricky. He's always been my best friend, and it kills me to see him so sad. I want him to be happy again. I'd love things to work out for you both."

Work out for us? Was this family thinking her relationship with Richard was heading toward something permanent? Commitments were too painful. Gazing at the water, she recounted heads. "I guess we'll see what time brings."

Sheila already knew what time would bring: when they got too close, it would be time to move on. Let her be the one doing the abandoning.

RICHARD DEBATED HIS WORDS AS HE WALKED with his brother through the former cow pasture. It had been years since cows left their mark on the gentle hills now colored in varying shades of green. It had been years since Richard left the resentful mark on the relationship with his brother, only that had never been restored. Was it even possible to revive the relationship? Sheila was right. He had to give it a try.

Breathing in deeply, he dug his hands into his front pockets before letting the words spill out. "I need to apologize." *Hmmm, that wasn't even difficult.* "I've dragged this feud on long enough, and I'm sorry."

Marcus stopped. He said nothing as his left foot kicked at a two-foot-high thistle.

Richard took that as a cue to continue. "To be honest, I'm really happy for you and Janet. The two of you are good together. You've been good parents and have great kids. I've been wrong to carry this grudge."

Marcus stared at the ground. His foot worked at the thistle, tearing at its roots. Richard's contrition had muzzled his brother. that was a miracle in itself.

"So anyway, I'm tired of the fighting and, since everyone's so bent on talking about forgiveness today, I was wondering if you could forgive me?"

Marcus' foot stilled. The thistle lay mushed beneath his foot.

The apology clearly caught his brother off-guard. Richard rarely admitted he was wrong about anything, especially to Marcus. It even felt good to say those words. Maybe this admission would improve his relationship with his family. He was tired of the fighting. It had grown old long ago, but he'd been too stubborn to admit to it.

Marcus raised his head toward the distant farmhouse. "I should have dropped it long ago. I'm sorry to have kept this going. Forgiven?"

Richard nodded. They exchanged a brotherly hug, the first one offered out of kindness in years. It felt good.

Maybe restoration was possible after all.

CHAPTER *thirteen*

Sheila rested her head against the car seat, closed her eyes and patted her pocket. The gem was still there. "Your nieces are adorable." Talking about Richard's nieces would certainly revive that smile she'd seen so much of today. She opened her eyes and looked his way. Yes, she was right. His focus remained on the road, as he drove toward home, but his smile was clear. "I've never been around children. I'm surprised at how much fun I had with them. And they even like me." She dug in her pocket and pulled out the stone. The sunset provided just enough light to make the rock sparkle. "Lilly gave me a gift."

Richard stole a quick glance and his smile grew, but it faded just as quickly and his jaw tightened. "I can't believe I ..."

"What?"

He shook his head. "Nothing."

The set of his jaw said it wasn't nothing. She rested her hand on his arm. "Talk to me."

A pick-up whooshed past as he sighed. "Debbie was a few months pregnant when she learned Lilly had Down syndrome." His grip tightened on the steering wheel, and his words were barely audible. "I had the gall to ask if she was going to keep Lilly."

The gall? Sheila's stomach roiled as she stared down at Lilly's stone. "I don't see what's wrong with that. It can't be easy raising a special-needs child. Abortion would be a prudent thought."

"Prudent?" Anger tinged his voice. "Suggesting Debbie kill Lilly was—"

"Whoa." Her hand squeezed around the stone, and her stomach turned even more. "That's a bit strong, isn't it?"

The car accelerated. "Just being honest."

She clenched her fingernails into trembling palms and willed away tears. "So, you'd call rape or incest victims, murderers?"

"Now who's—" He slammed on his brakes as a sharp curve approached.

Sheila grasped the sides of her seat as he maneuvered the S curve.

He rolled his shoulders. "Listen, I don't have all the answers." His voice had lost its edge. "I just know it's a life, a human life, and in spite of the circumstances, life should have a chance."

"How noble of you." Good thing he couldn't see her roll her eyes. Typical answer of the pro-life crowd. So willing to inflict the sentence of parenthood on innocent victims. Forcing babies to grow up unwanted. Unloved.

Abandoned.

She wiped a tear and hugged herself, trying to calm the shivers. Those people had no clue. No clue at all. "So you don't think a woman has a right to make her own health care choices?"

"Health care?" A sneer filled his tone. "Talk about selfish. It's all about the mother. Not the child—"

"It's not a child—"

"And what about the father?" His voice became a near whisper, and the car slowed.

The father? Right. Like they cared. "It's her body. Her choice." She clutched her stomach, hoping to hold down the bile threatening to claw up her throat . How could Richard have such an old-fashioned attitude? He'd never come across that way before. She stared out her window at the shadowed scenery. It was a good thing they were having this discussion now, so she could see the man for who he really was.

"Well, maybe if women would make the right choice in the beginning …"

RICHARD QUICKLY BIT HIS TONGUE. WHAT A HYPOcrite. When had he ever made the right choice in the beginning? For over twenty years "no" wasn't in his vocabulary, and he counted himself fortunate for not having to face the issue sooner. But, in the end, it was his beginning choice that set up his fall.

"I realize you are this paragon of virtue—"

"Virtuous? Me?" He laughed at the absurdity and pressed harder on the gas pedal.

"Yes, Mr. Boy Scout, the real world isn't like you."

If she only knew. He gritted his teeth. "I'm no Boy—"

"Men don't have to deal with the fallout of an unwanted pregnancy. Women can't walk away from the pregnancy or throw money at it and say she's supporting the child."

"That's not always—"

"She has to sacrifice everything: her career, her life, her integrity. He gets to go on with life as if nothing ever happened."

You are so wrong. His knuckles whitened on the steering wheel as he allowed her the victory in this battle. He'd heard all the arguments before, all ignoring the truth. Men did have to deal with it. While it took two to create life, only one was given a choice in ending it. The father's opinion was unwanted, so they dealt with the loss—their hurt—in silence. Alone.

And with Sheila stewing silently next to him, memories of that fateful night swarmed through his thoughts, forcing him to relive the agony once again.

Drunken laughter. Head-pounding music. Too many people.

Escaping the party's chaos, Richard gripped his Manhattan and withdrew to the expansive cedar deck on his boss's home. Blissful silence greeted him; he still preferred solitude over loud parties. The parties were just a necessary part of his job. He stopped at the railing overlooking the landscaped grounds of the country estate. It reminded him of home.

Home ... It had been a long time since he'd visited. A long time since he'd seen his nephews and nieces. Jaclyn just turned two the last time he flew out. His gut ached with missing them. Yes, he'd let the kids down, but he couldn't face his dad or Marcus. They didn't approve of his chosen lifestyle and were never shy about expressing it.

Home was rarely peaceful, but right now, this place was. Basking in the quiet, moonless night, he slowly sipped his drink, numbing himself, blocking out the voice of God who refused to let him be.

"There you are, Richard." A woman spoke softly behind him.

He set his drink on the railing then turned and watched Marissa approach. She looked good tonight— better than good in her low-cut, figure-hugging dress. This night was going to end well.

He didn't love her, and she certainly didn't love him. Did he even know what love was? She stood quietly next to him. He rested his arm around her waist, but she didn't flirt. Something serious was obviously on her mind.

"Richard, I'm pregnant."

A smile tugged on his lips. She probably expected shock, anger even, but he loved kids, especially his nieces and nephews and always felt he was missing out. She couldn't have delivered better news. He squeezed her into a hug she didn't return then leaned back and explored her stoic face. Naturally, she wouldn't be happy about this, but time would take care of that. He'd see to it. "When are you due?"

She pulled from his grip. "It doesn't matter. I'm not going through with it."

Paralyzing panic spread through him. His arms collapsed at his side, and he felt the blood ebb from his face. "You can't do that, Marissa. It's a baby."

"You're kidding, right? I thought you'd hand me some cash and tell me to take care of it."

"No. Never. I wouldn't do that to you." Or my baby. "So, if I want it, you'll keep it, right?"

"Absolutely not. I'm scheduled to go in this week. I thought you should know."

No. She couldn't. He swallowed the golf ball-sized knot clogging his throat. "There are other options, Marissa." He tried to process the alternatives, but the alcohol slowed his thinking. "We can get married ..."

She laughed. "Married? To you? Please. We both know you're not the marrying type. It would last until you saw the next set of legs walk past." Her eyes narrowed and darkened. "You know that's not what either of us wanted from this relationship."

Of course, she was right. Their "relationship" was built solely on physical attraction. He didn't even really like her. She was too needy, too demanding, but she knew how to meet his physical needs, and that was what had been important. That was where he had to make his appeal now. He folded his arms around her, found her eyes and spoke softly, hoping to see his way to her heart. "Fine, forget marriage, but have the baby. You know I can support you. You'd both be well taken care of."

She laughed dryly. "No. I don't want to be 'taken care of,' and I especially don't want a child interfering with my career."

Richard released her. His voice pitched higher. "Then I'll raise it!" It was a sacrifice he'd gladly make.

"No! I'm not going to ruin my life so you can suddenly become noble."

He pushed away from the railing, needing to get away from her, wanting to shake her to her senses. How could she do that to his child? Breathing slow and deep, he paced, searching his thoughts for a solution. Nothing. He had no choice. For the first time he could ever remember, he was powerless. "Please, Marissa, don't do this." His voice quivered. "There's got to be some way ..."

He stopped pacing as she approached.

Tears pooled in her eyes. "You don't understand." Uncertainty shivered in her voice. "How would I explain this to anyone? To my mom? I'd be such an embarrassment to her. And at work? This is not a mistake a career woman makes. I can't bear the thought of everyone whispering and talking behind my back. It's easy for you to say you want it. Guys don't have to bear the shame. If I end it now, no one has to know, and I can go on with my life as planned."

That was what she was worried about? How she'd look to everyone? The selfish little ... He pressed his arms to his side. "Ending the pregnancy won't make your problems go away, Marissa." His tone was low but intense. "It may create a whole set of new ones. If it's your reputation you're worried about, I'll stand with you. You won't go this alone."

"The decision is mine and mine alone to make." Marissa wiped her eyes. "And my mind's made up. Nothing you can say will change it."

A murmuring crowd had gathered inside the patio doors. Let them watch. What did he care? He narrowed his eyes as her obvious motive dawned on him. "How much do you want?"

"You think I want money? That's your answer to everything, isn't it? Well, I don't want your money, and I don't want this baby. You have no say in the matter." She turned toward the house.

He grabbed her arm, spinning her around. His grip was firm, but she stood straight, with confident shoulders and jutted chin.

A slight smile curved at her lips as her eyes narrowed, obviously enjoying his desperation. Her choice, this act of power, unexpectedly dropped him to his knees. No one else ever achieved such a feat, and it clearly affirmed her decision. Glaring in his eyes, she spoke with cold conviction, loud enough for the spectators to hear. "Let go of me and don't ever touch me again."

He loosened his grip, and she sashayed away, his brokenness adding a swagger to her hips. With her newly unveiled power, she divided the onlookers like Moses parting the Red Sea.

Richard turned his back to his colleagues and fisted his hands. Never had he felt so weak, so unable to control a situation. The other employees must be relishing this moment.

He strode to the railing, picked up his drink and stared at it. The glass was over half-full but no longer enticing. How many had he drunk? Three? No, this was his fourth in four hours. Probably not enough to make him legally drunk, although he felt a slight buzz. Certainly he was okay to drive, wasn't he? He had to get in his car and go somewhere. But where? Did that even matter? Anywhere would be better than here.

Not giving the crowd the satisfaction of witnessing a glass-throwing outburst, he placed it on the railing. His heart thumping, he pressed his way through the masses crowding around him, whispering, gossiping, suffocating him.

He got in his car, and no one tried to stop him.

A flash of light and a honking horn jarred his thoughts back to the present. An oncoming vehicle whizzed past and Richard broke out in a sweat.

It almost happened again.

His heart sprinting, he wiped perspiration from his forehead. Calm down. He glanced at Sheila. Her eyes were closed and her arms hugged her body. Everyone was all right.

What would Debbie do? That's right. Inhale ... One ... Two ... Three ... Four. Exhale. Five ... Six ... Seven ... Eight.

Repeating the process, he kept one hand secure on the steering wheel, and reached inside his shirt collar, clutching the chain.

The innocent would never forget; he shouldn't either.

AS THE LINE OF PINE TREES SIGNALED HIS HOME was near, the reality of the day hit him. He certainly hadn't planned on getting involved in the emotional dispute with Sheila, nor was he prepared for living through the argument with Marissa again. It was in the past, and that's where he needed to leave it.

If only it would stay there.

He stole a glance at Sheila who'd been silent since their quarrel. Her head was angled toward the passenger window. Either she was resting or purposely ignoring him, as he'd ignored her.

Pain stung his heart. That alone told him his feelings for Sheila delved deeper than he'd been willing to admit.

Marissa was wrong. He was the marrying type. He just hadn't met the right person, at least not until now. He never felt for anyone what he did for Sheila, but if things didn't change, she'd most likely move on.

He didn't want her to.

Yes, she deserved to know about his past, and he'd tell her. Soon. But, the confession needed to be carefully prepared and scripted. A process he hadn't yet begun.

It was nearly eleven when he pulled in his driveway. Even with the gravel popping beneath his wheels, she didn't stir. He pressed the remote, the garage door opened, and he drove inside a well-lit garage.

Sheila's eyes fluttered open as he pulled the key from the ignition. "We're home." He squeezed her hand gently.

She blinked several times, then slowly lifted her eyes to his. "Are you mad?"

"No." He sighed, shaking his head, momentarily closing his eyes. *Leave it in the past.* "Why don't we agree to disagree? I won't change your opinion any more than you'll change mine."

"Agreed." Sheila yawned. "All that fresh air today has totally wiped me out."

"Not to mention the turkey."

"That too, so I better get going. I'll sleep well tonight." Sheila helped herself out of his car. The horn chirped and the lights flashed on her sedan as she walked toward it. She opened the door and stood behind it as he approached.

He positioned himself outside the car door, leaning into it. It was a safe closeness. He reached up, wiped the hair from her face and twirled it between his fingers. "Thank you for today."

"For what?"

"For finding joy in my family, even if I couldn't. I promise to try harder next time." His voice remained a near whisper as he tried to read her face. Would she want there to be a next time?

"I'd like that." She smiled.

Warmth spread through his body—it wasn't over.

She yawned again. "I really have to get going."

"You sure you're okay to drive? Let me grab a cold pop for you."

"No, I'm fine."

"Call me when you get home." He ran his hand through her hair, down the back of her head, and gently pulled her in. No resistance. He kissed her; his lips lingered softly on hers, calming her tremble. She did care for him. Perhaps there would be a future with her, if he didn't blow it along the way.

Saying nothing, she sat, and he closed the door behind her. She shot him a quizzical glance then started the car.

He inhaled, filling his lungs with the air's summer freshness as she backed out of the driveway. Yes, he would tell her.

Soon.

SHEILA PULLED THE BLANKET UP TO HER CHIN and closed her eyes, remembering the day: the walk through the cornfield, catch with the boys and the monster-dog, Lilly's wet hug. She reached over to her bed stand, picked up the stone Lilly gave her and sighed. Why didn't she know, before, how precious children were?

Now, she would never forget.

Warmth coated her body as she relived Richard's goodnight kiss. She licked her lips sealing in its memory. It had been so loving and so tender, one that spoke of how much he cared for her even with their disagreement. The physical attraction was still there, but what she felt for him grasped beyond. For the first time in her life, she truly cared for someone and wanted to make the relationship work.

Picturing Richard's tilting smile and gentle laugh coaxed in her slumber. Sleep took over; his face and smile faded. Moving shadows filled his place. Veiled beings swayed in the background, moaning *Amazing Grace*. A man's muffled voice said it wouldn't hurt; everything would be all right. She shivered and a tear dropped off the side of her face. A whirring buzzed in her ears. Was it a fan? A dentist's drill? Cramping pain seized her stomach. Hadn't he told her it wouldn't hurt?

Sheila opened her mouth to scream, but nothing came out.

Trembling, she awoke, the nightmare fresh in her mind with a sense of déjà vu. How could something so insidious be familiar?

She drew her knees to her chest. Closing her eyes again tonight would not be an option. She slipped out of bed and shuffled to the kitchen. Black coffee would keep the ghosts away. Tonight, that was more important than sleep.

CHAPTER *fourteen*

White Plains, New York

Justin should have been nineteen today.

Meghan stared at the calendar on the kitchen wall and wiped her eyes. The day was unmarked, as if her brother never existed.

How could they do that to him, the good child, the one everyone always said was chosen especially by God?

But, if God had such wonderful plans for Justin, why would He take him so soon? How could Justin possibly do God's work if he was dead? Didn't this prove Justin had been wrong? God had been number one in Justin's life, but God let her brother down.

Just as she'd done.

She shivered. Would she ever be able to forget her part in Justin's death? If not for her, he'd still be alive. No one else knew, especially not her parents. Why did God punish Justin for her mistake?

Meghan wiped her forearm across her face. No crying allowed. Kneeling down, she opened the lower cupboard door and pulled out a cake pan. She placed the pan on the cupboard and turned on the oven to 350 degrees. How appropriate. That's exactly how hot she felt toward her mother and her mom's unwavering faith. How could her mom let God off the hook so easily?

Her dad, she could understand. How often had her father stared up at the ceiling and asked, "Why Justin?" always to be answered with silence.

Meghan shook her head, attempting to jolt the depressing thoughts. Concentrate on the cake. Inhaling a deep breath, she searched the cupboard and refrigerator for all the ingredients. As she combined them, unwanted thoughts of God flitted through her mind again, expanding her stomach with an empty ache. Where was He?

With a sniffle, Meghan plopped down on a kitchen chair. Their family should have been celebrating together. Instead, her parents were off remembering or honoring Justin, each in their own way, leaving her alone.

Her dad had gone to the spot where Justin died. A wooden cross, etched with loving words of remembrance, still stood there in commemoration. Meghan had gone a few times, but it didn't give her any peace as cars flew thoughtlessly past the spot. Did drivers even take a moment to think, "What happened at that cross?" Did they care that Justin breathed his last breath there?

Her mom always said she hated that spot, the cross a daily reminder of Justin's death. She wanted to remember how he lived: playing piano, running track, volunteering at the local food shelf. Today, her mom worked at the food shelf, claiming she couldn't think of a better way to honor her son, especially on his birthday.

His unmarked birthday.

Meghan wouldn't leave the day blank. Justin deserved better.

She dried her eyes. No more feeling sorry for herself. She poured the cake mix into the pan and eased it into the oven. Thirty minutes later, she slid the pan out and breathed in its dark chocolate scent. Justin had loved that smell. Did chocolate exist in Heaven? What about lasagna? Was Justin up there right now celebrating his special day with Jesus? If not, he could look down and celebrate with her.

She prepared the lasagna, Justin's favorite of course, and then rested on the living room couch. Her parents should be home soon.

With tears ever-present, Meghan covered herself with a fleece blanket and adjusted her head on the sofa's arm, Maybe, just maybe, this last year had been a nightmare. Maybe Justin would come singing through the front door as he always had. If he did, she was going to be ready for him, with nineteen candles topping a cake slathered with thick fudge frosting. She even bought and wrapped a gift. A book of piano music. She never listened to him play before—not voluntarily, anyway. What she'd give to listen to him now.

She blinked, forcing her eyes open, listening, waiting. Certainly he'd come through that door any second now.

But, of course, he never did. Her dad slouched in the door and spent the evening in isolation in front of the television, clicking robotically through its channels.

Her mother slipped through the front door and went immediately to bed, complaining of a migraine.

The lasagna sat uneaten. The candles were never lit—were never blown out. The gift remained wrapped.

Justin was forgotten.

It was all her fault.

CHAPTER *fifteen*

Sheila turned off her car's ignition and stared at Richard's house. He was obviously home. The garage door was raised showcasing the Audi and Silverado. Both vehicles appeared to be recently cleaned, but had she ever really seen them dirty? Hardly. Even the garage was uncluttered. Tools hung from pegboards. Oil and paint cans were arranged according to type and size. What must he think of her disorderly desk?

For that matter, what would he think about her showing up at his door unannounced? Would he say yes to her invitation? If only she could tell him how she needed him to hold her at night. To protect her from the nightmares that inhabited her sleep.

Ignoring the butterfly war in her stomach, she stepped out of her car into July's heat and strode to his front door. In the three plus months they dated, she'd been at his home once and hadn't seen past the living room. Today, that would change.

Peering through the door's window, she rang the doorbell. Its bell chimed through the living room's open windows. No movement inside. She counted to ten then turned the doorknob. Unlocked. She pushed the door open a crack. "Richard?" Silence answered.

Her heart beat accelerated as she stepped into his living room. The once dingy walls were now painted an earthy tan playing off the color of the fireplace stone. But, still no artwork. A trip to the art gallery would remedy that. Hardwood floors replaced the carpeting, adding rustic warmth. She thumbed through the magazines and newspapers on the end table. Updated and arranged with precision. Of course.

Obviously, she wasn't going to discover who he was in this room.

She walked through the living room and entered a small open kitchen. Cupboard doors lay stacked on a counter. The cabinet facing appeared freshly sanded. An open window above the sink offered a view of a rectangular deck and wooded backyard. No sign of him there, either. She cupped her hands around her mouth and yelled through the window. "Richard." Birds tweeted, but otherwise, no response.

She glanced at her watch. Plenty of time before she had to leave. She walked down a short hallway, passing a bath and a small bedroom, and entered what had to be his master bedroom. A queen bed, covered with a navy comforter, was centered against the wall opposite the door and oak side tables stood on both sides of the bed. Lamps with bronze bases and rectangular shades sat on each table, and a Vince Flynn novel rested beneath a lamp. Typical.

Oh, but Richard was far from typical.

Stuffing down her frustration, she strode to the headboard-matching dresser angled in a corner. His billfold lay on top. She picked it up and breathed in the scent of real leather. She began to open it then stopped. How would she feel if Richard snooped through her purse? Some things needed to stay private.

Peeking in his closets wouldn't invade his privacy, would it? She pulled open the bi-fold doors opposite the bed. Her eyes widened, and her jaw dropped. At last, something out of the ordinary. She fingered ten crisply pressed, evenly spaced suits: Hugo Boss, Polo Ralph Lauren, the Italian suit he wore the night of their theater date, and more. Her fingers stopped at the Armani, caressing it. An image of Richard wearing it flashed through her head. How sweet she would look hanging on his arm.

She spun the carousel of silk ties. Conservative red to stained glass window flamboyant. And the quantity of dress shoes would even make Imelda Marcos jealous.

Why would Richard—a farm boy turned lowly janitor—own such a wardrobe?

Images flew through her head. He hadn't denied her secret agent remark. Was he CIA? James Bond? No, that was absurd. Wasn't it?

Who are you, Richard?

She closed the closet doors and turned to the wall to the left of the bed where a collage of four pictures hung. The large, center picture was a family portrait, the caption beneath read "Marlene and Bernie—40 years!" Jaclyn was the only one absent although, if Janet's very pregnant belly were any indication, Jaclyn would make her appearance soon.

The other three pictures were the real treasure. One was taken from behind of Richard and his two nephews sitting on a dock, swinging their legs above clear blue water below a cloudless sky. The three sat fishing poles in hand, all with the same posture, each holding their poles at the same angle, as if planned.

Another picture was taken at Easter. Judging by the looks of his nieces, it was probably taken this year. Richard knelt on one knee in the grass in one of those expensive suits punctuated with a colorful tie. Only for his girls would he risk a grass stain. Jaclyn sat on his knee, Kaitlynn and Lilly leaned into his sides. The three girls wore flowery dresses and lacy tights, black patent leather dress shoes and bonnets. Each held their Easter basket filled with rainbow tinted plastic eggs he most likely helped them discover. Richard's smile was genuine, and, for that brief moment, sadness escaped his eyes.

She drew her finger down the fourth photo, clearly a snapshot of his heart. Wearing the hospital's requisite blue gown and cap, he held newborn Lilly close to his face. Love beamed from his toothy smile.

All glimpses of Richard unguarded, with genuine joy glowing from his face. What she'd give to have him look at her like that.

With a sigh, she left the room and angled to the right entering the other bedroom. All it held was a full-size bed and a single nightstand. A framed Twins Homer Hanky hung on the otherwise bare walls. This closet concealed no surprises, just pillows and blankets and winter clothing. With the exception of the expensive suits, it was as if he'd erased his past.

So where was he? The basement? No. He'd have heard her rummaging above him. But, it was one final place to search.

A motor rumbled from the backyard as she headed for the basement. She hurried to the kitchen window and watched Richard emerge from the woods on a four-wheeler, pulling what was left of a felled tree devoid of branches.

A grin grew on her face. His well-worn T-shirt no longer had sleeves and the August heat and humidity stained it with dark blotches. He parked the ATV and jumped off showing jeans frayed at the bottom and worn thin at the knees with paint splatters coating them.

Even his hair escaped the comb today or rebelled against it. The man was absolutely gorgeous. Armani had nothing on this look. She remained at the window, resting her elbows on the sink rim and her chin on folded hands, memorizing every inch of the new Richard.

He grabbed a chainsaw and divided the trunk into neat, round logs. Once completed, he placed a log upright on a stump sitting just inside the trees. With the precision of someone who'd done this many times before, he swung an ax down, his muscles glistening with sweat, splitting the log in two. The two halves looked equal. Always, a perfectionist.

Well, it was time to make her presence known. She grabbed two water bottles from the fridge then rushed outside and reclined on a padded patio chair.

He took several more swings, then glanced up at the house.

She grinned and waved. There was that smile from the pictures. The smile usually reserved for his nieces. The unguarded smile, which for a solitary moment, held only joy. And this time the joy was for her.

How could he say no to her invitation?

He glanced down at his clothes and ran his hand through his hair, then over his unshaven face. Unguarded joy fled his eyes.

Still, his crooked smile remained as he laid the ax on the ground and sauntered toward her, removing his gloves and stuffing them into his back pockets. "How long have you been sitting here?" He climbed onto the deck and sat in the lounge chair next to her.

She handed him a bottled water, her gaze scanning his body. "Not nearly long enough."

His eyes met hers. Uncertainty rested there. "You have me at quite the disadvantage, you know."

"I'd hoped to catch you at a disadvantage and, I must say,

this is more than I hoped for." The pressed clothes, the neat hair, the precise look was clearly all part of his persona. For once, he was deprived of his costume and didn't know how to play the part without it. With him stripped of the façade, he almost seemed vulnerable.

He looked away and unscrewed his bottle cap. "I thought you had meetings in Duluth this weekend."

"I'm on my way. Just took a slight detour, hoping to see you. You're not too far off I-35." She shot him a flirting smile. "I'm glad I stopped."

"Me too." He smiled back.

Precisely the reaction she hoped for.

Leaning back in his chair, he sipped his water. "So, what did you learn?" Without turning his head, his eyes shifted toward her.

"Pardon me?" She reclined in her chair, mimicking his posture.

He sipped more water, but his grooved cheeks gave away his smile. "My house is wide open. Knowing you, I'm sure you took advantage of it, didn't you?" He sat up, swung his legs off the side of the chair, and looked directly at her.

With a blush warming her cheeks, she kept herself angled away but turned her head in his direction. Time to play coy. "Advantage of what?"

"What did you find?" His lips tilted up to the right, and his eyes sparkled.

Simply breathtaking. She opened her mouth then clamped it closed. So, he knew what she did and wasn't angry. That, in itself, was a small victory. Keep the game going, and she might win the battle too. "I like the changes you made: the floors, the paint job, but you're sadly in need of some artwork."

He chuckled. "I agree. It hasn't been my top priority."

"Perhaps I could help you out."

"Be my guest. I trust your judgment."

A hummingbird flitted around a feeder attached to the siding. "I confirmed you're obsessively neat. I'll bet your mom loved you."

"She did. Now Marcus and Debbie, they got tired of hearing Mom say, 'You should be more like Ricky.'"

"The Homer Hanky in your spare bedroom—is that an original?"

"From 1987. The ones given out before the first play-off game. Marcus and I managed to call a temporary truce for those games. I probably keep the Hanky more in remembrance of the truce than the actual World Series. It was a special time. I'm glad you encouraged me to make amends with him. It's nice to have a brother again."

And it was nice to see Richard smile when he talked about Marcus. Her next topic would broaden his smile. "The pictures in your room are telling. You've got a soft spot for girls."

"Guilty." Richard lifted her hand, his thumb lightly caressing her fingers. It didn't matter that his hand was darkened and gritty from logging.

Feeling her cheeks heat, she purposely changed the subject. "I didn't have a chance to look in your basement. I'm assuming that's where you keep all your skeletons."

He laughed. "Of course. Skeletons and workout equipment plus some spiders to keep me company."

"So I'm glad I skipped it."

"Probably." His eyes narrowed. "You're avoiding my question."

She eyed his face. Was he ready to explain his past? Regardless, she could no longer put off the tough questions. "You've got exceptional taste in clothing. You clearly like to look good. Of course, I already knew that, didn't I?"

His smile turned up more. "I guess you did."

She placed her legs over the side of her chair with her knees barely grazing his. It didn't matter that she was dressed for a meeting. Being on the verge of a breakthrough, maintaining an immaculate wardrobe was insignificant. Her heart pumped faster. "What I don't know is why you have them."

He shrugged, and his eyes clouded. "Like you said, I like to look good."

"For where? For what?"

He dropped her hand, reclined in his chair and stared straight ahead. "Church. Theater. Concerts."

His open door was slamming shut, so she jammed her foot

back in. "You're full of it, you know. A farm boy turned janitor does not have a closet full of suits costing over a thousand each."

He bolted upright and leaned toward her, his cheeks taut, and intensity sparking in his eyes. His fisted hand jabbed at his chest. "This is me. Okay? The person you see at work. Here. On the farm. This is who *I am*. You don't want to know who I was. That person no longer exists. If you can't accept me for who I am now, if a custodian isn't good enough for Miss High and Mighty Executive, then maybe it's time to call it quits."

Her fingernails dug into her palms. Oh, how this man could infuriate her. His quick-change, flip-flop moods were the one thing holding her back from seriously considering a long-term relationship, but she wasn't about to give him up because of them either.

"Oh, you'd like that, wouldn't you?" She sat up straighter in her chair. "Then you could sit here and feel sorry for yourself for whatever it is you won't tell me. Well, I'm sorry. I've invested too much of myself in you to let that happen."

"You think I haven't?"

You're on a roll. Don't stop now. "You're wrong about your job."

"Oh, really." He squished the half-full water bottle between his palms. "Can you honestly tell me that you aren't bothered by dating a janitor?"

"Sure, it mattered at first, but that was ages ago. I don't care what you do if it's what you want, if it makes you happy, but I know it doesn't. Frankly, the only one who isn't satisfied is you."

Richard's eyes lost their intensity and the distant look returned as he slumped in his chair. She'd clearly hit on something. Waiting for his response, she clamped her mouth shut. Please, please respond.

He sucked the last drop of water from his bottle and toyed with it, speaking in a barely audible tone. "You're right. It's not what I'm meant to do, but I can't ever go back. I'm where I need to be, where I deserve to be." A chuckle filtered through his nose. "I don't even deserve you." He sat up and faced her again, his eyes pleading.

She wanted to turn away from those hurting eyes, but her body remained frozen.

"I'm sorry." He reached over and caressed her cheek. "I don't want to break things off, and I do understand your frustration. I need more time. Do you understand?"

No. She closed her eyes and swallowed. *Time. More time.* Yes, she'd give him more time, but how much more, she wasn't sure.

But then, maybe time wasn't what he needed. She'd stopped by today with an invitation. Why should that change? Maybe if he'd come with her to neutral ground: get away from work, his home, his family. Maybe a change of venue would relax him and allow the truth to come out as it almost had moments ago.

Taking his hand again, she nodded toward the back yard. "Why don't you take a break from this? Come up to Duluth with me and relax. I've got an early dinner meeting tonight and nothing afterward. I hear Canal Park is lovely at night. Tomorrow, I have a breakfast meeting, but I'm free afterwards. A drive up the north shore would be romantic, don't you think?"

Silence greeted her invitation.

RICHARD RECLINED IN HIS CHAIR AND SIGHED. Oh, how he wanted to confess what he'd done; how he needed to tear the weight of his past off his shoulders. Was he ready? Would the majesty of Lake Superior's northern Minnesota shoreline somehow soften what he had to tell her?

He rubbed his whiskered chin. Nothing was more calming than the drive up old Highway 61 along the north shore. But, to go up with Sheila? Now? It would lead to one thing. That, in itself, was enticing.

But, no, now wasn't the right time. He just wasn't ready.

"I can't." He placed his empty water bottle on the wire mesh table in between their chairs. "As you saw by my kitchen, I've got projects to finish, and I hate leaving things undone. Maybe the end of September, first part of October, when the leaves are peaking. We can go up then." By then, she'd know what he'd done and, if she hadn't tossed him aside, he could think commitment.

Hah! Who was he kidding? That big "C" word had filtered through his thoughts since they returned from the farm, the big "C" word he hated the thought of until he met Sheila.

"I'll hold you to it."

"I expect you to." And he wanted her to. The north shore at peak season? Gooseberry Falls. Split Rock Lighthouse. There could be nothing more romantic. But first, he had to climb over his mountain of guilt to get there. Could he do it and come down unscathed? Sure, Sheila might tell him she accepted him for who he was now, but putting those feelings into action would be a whole different story once she knew the truth.

She leaned over and kissed him, then stood. "Since I can't convince you to come with me now, I better get going. It's going to be a very lonely drive."

He followed her through the house and out to her sedan. Once again, he strategically placed the car's door between them. It was safer that way. Leaning over, his lips met hers. If not for the barrier between them, he might not let her leave. And that wouldn't be right. She needed the truth first. He'd already begun to plan how he'd tell her. Now he needed the courage to follow through.

"Stop in on your way home." His gaze captured hers. "I'll be here." They kissed again before she drove off.

SHEILA HUGGED HERSELF AS SHE GLANCED OUT her Duluth hotel window at the moonlight glistening off Lake Superior. What she'd give to have Richard's arms around her instead.

He was weakening. She'd felt it in his kiss today. Maybe soon. If only he understood how much she needed him.

She pulled the blinds shut then snuggled beneath her bed's covers, pretending it was Richard's arms enveloping, protecting her.

Maybe that would stave off her reoccurring nightmare.

Her body trembled at the thought of the dreams that filled nearly every night with the shadow man's wickedly calm voice.

She pried her eyelids open, but they fluttered and fell shut. *Think Richard. He's holding me. Keeping me safe.*

Yes. Happy. Safe.

The shadow man rose from the floor and tore Richard's arms

from her. His ghostly tentacles gripped her, and he laughed, deep and guttural. Evil. *Richard, where did you go? I need you.* A spectral ensemble misted through the walls, shouting out *Amazing Grace*, drowning out her calls.

With a scream, Sheila shot up on her mattress, perspiration saturating her silky chemise.

Who were those people? What did they want with her?

Shaking, she slipped out of bed. With wobbly knees, she walked to the bathroom and took her migraine-preventing prescription. It had been years since the headaches had tormented her. Now, they were just another byproduct of her nightmares. With a glass of water in hand, she walked to the desk and turned on her laptop. No way could she face those phantoms again tonight. Not alone.

And if Richard refused her again, she'd find someone who wouldn't.

Her stomach soured at the thought.

CHAPTER *sixteen*

Late August's humidity dripped down Meghan's cheeks as she stood in the University parking lot and waved at her parents' Buick LeSabre. It drove away carting a small trailer. Madison, Wisconsin was a long way from her home in White Plains, New York. A thousand or so miles. Hopefully, that would be distance enough.

Her parents had stayed in town for a few days, met her roommates and toured the college. Meghan assured them she'd be fine, study hard, use good judgment, and be responsible. They said they trusted her. The worry in their eyes said otherwise. They pointed out the Christian groups on campus and hinted it would be good to get involved with one or more knowing of the temptations even Christian students face in college. Yes, it would be a good idea, but she never said she'd join. Those groups were the very ones she wanted to stay far away from.

And, if her roommates' FaceBook pages were at all indicative of their personalities, Emily and Kalyn wouldn't be attending any on-campus ministry meetings. But, a frat party? That was a different story. Did she want that too? Justin wouldn't have. But then, she'd never been like Justin.

She didn't want to be like Justin.

Meghan waved one last time as the Buick rounded the corner and disappeared. She stood still, waiting for a rush of sadness or loneliness or fear, but a smile formed instead.

Freedom! Finally.

She ran up two flights to her dorm room. Her roommates would celebrate with her.

Kalyn—tall and model skinny with hair too blonde to be

natural—was packing her clothes into school-provided drawers. She peered up from her suitcase toward Meghan, then over Meghan's shoulder. "Your folks gone?"

Meghan nodded, and her smile broadened like it used to, before Justin died. "I'm finally on my own. Free."

Petite Emily looked up from where she had splayed herself across the bottom bunk. The girl didn't look a day older than fifteen. "You too?" She sat up, her ponytail swinging, and clutched a stuffed elephant in her arms.

"Me too!" Meghan flopped on her bed hard enough to bounce—she'd never do that back home—and lay on the bare mattress. With her hands supporting her head, she stared at the ceiling, soaking up some of this freedom. Later today, she'd cover the mattress with her new comforter set. But not yet. Nope. Only when she was good and ready.

"I swear this was the longest summer of my life." She eyed a spot of paint peeling from the ceiling. "I had to do everything with Mom and Dad. It's like they were trying to fit a lifetime of experiences into one short summer."

"You poor things." Kalyn snapped her suitcase shut and climbed up on her top bunk. "I had an open relationship with my dad and step. They wanted me to experience life, especially while I'm young. Got the hotel room for me and my prom date. Of course, we snuck in the champagne."

"No way!" Emily pouted. "I still had to follow curfew on prom night. The guy never asked me out again. And if I came home with even a hint of beer on my breath, I'd have been grounded for life." She giggled. "Didn't stop me though."

Meghan swallowed hard as she sat up and reclined against the wall, a single pillow propped behind her back. Just the thought of being with some guy was nauseating. Maybe if she hadn't …

Nope, that was a thousand miles behind her. Boy, she had a lot more learning to do than academics. Sounded like Emily and Kalyn would be good teachers and doors would open to a life she never dreamed of.

Kalyn plopped on Meghan's bed and crossed her legs. "My brother tells me there's a huge party off campus tonight."

Meghan's stomach seized. Did those doors have to open so

soon?

"Normally freshmen aren't invited, but Doran, my brother, can get us all in. It'd be a great way to get school started off right. What d'ya guys say?" Kalyn looked at Emily first.

"Absolutely!" Excitement, not fear, glittered in Emily's eyes. "Will there be beer?"

Kalyn laughed as if mocking the question with an obvious answer. "Kegs full."

Emily squeezed her stuffed friend. "And guys?" She looked way too young to be worrying about guys.

"Lotsa guys. Older. With experience."

Meghan folded her hands between her thighs, and her stomach flip-flopped again. Was this really how she wanted to begin her college experience? She'd never been drunk. Didn't even like alcohol. People said it was an acquired taste.

Maybe she could go tonight and not drink.

Biting her lip, she glanced at Kalyn.

"You're coming, aren't you?"

Would she make any friends if she didn't?

"C'mon Meghan." Emily flounced between Meghan and Kalyn. "It'll be wicked fun. Just think, seniors will be there."

Did she want to meet the kind of guy who would be at a keg party? They certainly wouldn't be the kind she'd want to take home to Mom and Dad.

Or maybe they would be experiencing their first steps of independence like she was. That didn't make them bad. In fact, it would make them normal. She was the one who wasn't normal.

If she didn't go tonight, if she didn't drink along with the rest, she'd be labeled with the same party pooper reputation she earned back at home.

Forging a smile, she nodded to Kalyn. "I wouldn't miss it."

She inched forward and slid off the end of the bed. It was time to make the bed after all. Keep herself busy so she wouldn't think about tonight.

The afternoon passed quickly as the three explored the campus, meeting new people, making new friends from around the country, even the world. But that didn't stop the flutters in Meghan's stomach. How could she get out of going to the party and still be friends with Kalyn and Emily?

At close to six that night, with no good excuses, she found herself following Kalyn and Emily into the party house. Her eyes began to water and her nose stung. The combination of alcohol, cigarettes, and other scents she didn't recognize—probably didn't want to recognize—added to the nausea already brewing in her stomach. Music thumped through her body and tingled her ears. An unseen hand pressed her forward, her foot landing in something soft and mushy. *Don't even look.*

That same hand glided to her shoulder with a hairy arm scruffing her neck. "Hey, babe. You new?"

At least that's what she thought he said. Shivering, she shrugged away from the arm, refusing to look at his face, and searched for the safety of her roommates. Kalyn held up a glass brimming with an amber liquid, and waved her over. Meghan breathed in and squeezed between perspiring bodies. If only she had the courage to leave.

She reached Kalyn and someone placed a filled plastic cup in her hand. Looking over, all she saw was emerald eyes.

The student winked and held out his hand. "Welcome … Meghan? Is that it?"

Her cheeks heated as she nodded and accepted his hand.

He held on to hers. "I'm Doran. Kalyn's brother. Glad you could make it."

"Me too," she said softly. Oh, man, what was wrong with her? She was proving freshmen were idiots.

He pointed to her glass and smiled, wiping an errant curl of blond hair from his face. "Have a drink. It'll help." The smile added sheen to his eyes. He winked again and released her hand. "I'll see you around."

All she could do was nod as she watched him snake between guests to greet newcomers.

"Don't even consider it." Kalyn broke Meghan's stare.

"Huh?" Meghan squinted at Kalyn.

"My brother. He's wanted by every girl on campus. Probably gone out with half of 'em. You don't stand a chance."

"But, I—"

"I saw that look." Kalyn pointed to the beer in Meghan's

hand. "Take a drink. By the end of the night it won't matter what they look like."

Meghan stared at her glass and breathed in deeply. What would her parents say if they knew she was here? What would Justin think?

Nope. Their opinions no longer mattered. It was time she grew up. She raised her glass to Kalyn's. Maybe this would help her finally forget. "To growing up."

Kalyn smiled. "To independence."

Meghan brought the drink to her lips and swallowed freedom's bitterness.

CHAPTER *seventeen*

Sheila stared at the spreadsheet on her computer monitor while massaging her temples, hoping to ward off an impending migraine. It had been years since she allowed one to steal her day, and she wasn't about to let that happen now. Still, the numbers she'd tried analyzing over the last hour meant nothing. What was wrong with her, anyway?

She pushed away from the desk, rolling her chair backward. Standing, she gazed out her office window. Glass skyscrapers reflecting muddy clouds filled her view, adding to her melancholy. Fatigue weighed on her eyelids. Maybe a nap would help.

She buzzed her secretary and asked not to be disturbed before curling up on her brown leather loveseat. Her eyelids closed, but instant panic forced them open. Heart racing, she sat up, clenched her hands, and tried to slow her breathing. Nightmares dwelt in closed eyes, not just the night.

And last night's dream lasted longer than usual. Another form hid in the shadows and his phantom-like presence felt more menacing than the first figure. As in so many previous nights, fear awoke her. Would she ever be able to sleep again? Even worse, how could she prevent the visions from invading her day?

Regardless, it was time to get back to work. She stood, straightened her skirt and walked to her desk. She sat and again attempted to focus the numbers dancing on her screen. With a sigh, she leaned back and stared at the ceiling. Perhaps what she needed was a diversion, something to take her mind off her job and her nightmares.

For the first time today she smiled. Yes, she knew of the ideal distraction.

"YOU MAY GO IN." SHEILA'S ASSISTANT LOOKED AT
Richard and laid her phone down. He curved his hand around her
doorknob, but didn't turn it. They'd always been discreet about
their relationship, and he didn't want that to change. The call to
maintenance claimed her cooling system wasn't working. That in
itself wasn't out of the ordinary. The system installed building-
wide this past spring had too many bugs in it, and he'd spent
much of the summer exterminating them. Still, his gut said this
wasn't the typical call.

He took in a breath and pushed open her office door. Sheila
sat at her desk rifling through papers. Her hair was pulled up off
her neck, and her silk blouse was unbuttoned a few too many
buttons for his comfort. She peered up, smiling seductively. But
then, she always smiled like that for him.

"It's good to see you." She rocked back in her chair, fanning
herself with a file folder.

He raised his eyebrows and looked away, not daring to tell
her how good she looked. "I understand your air's not working."
The room did feel muggy, so maybe he was letting his imagination get in the way. Sheila tended to do that to him anyway, but
not usually at work. Well, he was here to do a job, not flirt.

As he crossed the room to check the controls, the office
door clicked shut behind him. He glanced down at the temperature sensor and frowned. "It's turned off, Sheila." His voice was
intentionally harsh.

Arms circled his waist, and her chin rested on his shoulder.
"Goodness, you are right. Here, let me turn it on." Lips like silk
caressed his neck. The woman clearly knew how to ignite his
senses. In times past, he might have let her follow through. Not
anymore.

He squirmed from her grasp, raised his hands and backed
away. "Whoa. May I remind you we're at work?"

"If this were a soap opera, you know what we'd be doing?"
She approached him again, her knee-length, linen skirt clinging
to her curves. The three-inch stiletto heels nearly put her eyes
level with his. Almost every inch of him wanted to reach out, kiss
her, and give in to her. It was the *almost* part holding him back,

the inner voice that had become so familiar again, and learned to listen to over the past few months.

"Enough, Sheila." His voice cracked. *God, why can't I give in? Just once?* Why was he asking for God's permission?

"Killjoy." Pouting, she strutted away.

A relieved breath flew from his lungs.

She reclined in her chair, crossing her legs on top of the desk. Clearly, her game wasn't over yet. "I didn't sleep well last night ... I haven't been sleeping well, period."

"Why? What's wrong?"

She grimaced and shook her head. "Just work. You know how it is."

Only too well.

"Now today, I've dealt with nothing but problems, and my concentration is non-existent.. I needed a diversion, something to brighten this afternoon, and you came to mind."

He crossed his arms and allowed a smile. "So, I'm simply a diversion to you?"

"A very good diversion, mind you."

He chuckled, looking for an excuse to leave. "I can feel it's already cooling off in here." Personally, he wouldn't cool off until he was far from her office.

"No thanks to you." Sheila stuck out her lower lip.

"You know, I actually have work to do." And he better leave right now and get it done.

"Yeah, me too. That's the whole problem." She pulled her legs from the desk, sat upright, and buttoned her blouse.

Thank you, God!

"Give me a call after work and ... and thank you."

"For?"

"For being professional. I'm very sorry. I think I need some time off."

Him too, apparently.

Maybe they could spend the time together. He smiled, thinking of the ideal plan. "Well." He stepped toward her desk, maintaining a safe distance. Yet, even from several feet away, her seductive perfume called out. That's what he deserved for giving her Dior's Midnight Poison. "How about a game of hooky tomorrow? I haven't missed a day since starting. I know you're exhausted. You're working too hard. A day off would do us both some good."

Her mouth scrunched, she reviewed the paperwork piled neatly on the corner of her desk. "I can't …"

She peered, up and he winked. His boyish grin would convince her. It always did.

"And do what?"

"How about a day at Valleyfair?"

"Valleyfair?" Her shoulders drooped, and she frowned at her paperwork.

"You know, roller coasters, merry-go-round, cotton candy."

She shook her head. "You can't be serious."

"What? Don't you like rides?"

"To be honest, I've never done fairs. Never went as a child. Been too busy as an adult. I thought we were passed that stage by now."

"Oh, no way. There's nothing like an amusement park to bring back your childhood and forget about your responsibilities for the day. To be honest, I haven't been there in years. I think it would be just the thing we both need. What do you say?"

She sat silent, glancing from paper pile to keyboard to monitor and back to him. Finally, she smiled. "Okay, but if I don't have any fun, you will owe me." She threw him a beguiling glance.

He ignored it. "You will have fun. I guarantee it. I'll pick you up tomorrow around nine. Wear something cool and comfortable. Shoes for walking. Something you don't mind getting wet."

Her eyes widened.

He grinned. "I'll take care of lunch."

"I'm so excited." Sarcasm laced her voice.

She would have fun; he'd make sure of it. Feeling like an excited ten-year-old, he strolled out her door, humming to himself, anticipating the coming day.

CHAPTER *eighteen*

Sheila tucked her hair into a ponytail as Richard practically dragged her through the amusement park entrance along with throngs of other visitors. As much as Sheila had dreaded the day, seeing this exuberant side of Richard was making it very worth her while.

They skirted the Snoopy fountain centered in the park's entrance, and a young woman with a camera strapped around her neck, stepped in front of them. "Take your picture?"

"No, thank—"

"We'd love it." Richard removed his sunglasses and pulled Sheila in tight.

Maybe it wasn't such a bad idea.

Sheila combed her fingers through her bangs and made sure no stray hairs escaped her ponytail.

The photographer snapped one picture then stepped forward for a close-up.

"See, that was painless, wasn't it?" He grinned as the young woman handed him a card indicating their picture number.

How could Sheila not smile back? She poked his chest. "Just keep it that way."

"Not a problem." Grasping her hand, he led her between early-twenties replica buildings advertising dentist-disdained treats: fudge, rainbow suckers, and of course, cotton candy. She felt her teeth rot just smelling the sugary confection scent.

Once they passed the buildings, he veered slightly to the right aiming for the carousel. "How's this for starters?"

She studied the rows of prancing horses circling slowly beneath a canopy. Looked tame enough. "Okay, why not?"

Which was exactly what she said when he pointed out the antique cars. He even let her drive the puttering vehicle around the track. Okay, not too bad so far. Maybe today wasn't going to be terrible after all.

Grasping her hand again, he pulled her along the asphalt path, and pointed. A wicked grin filled his face.

"Uh-uh." Just watching the ride in front of them made her dizzy with its octopus-like arms circling, rising and falling around its mechanical body. Spinning cars, filled with screaming children, clung to the end of the arms. "No way, in this lifetime, are you going to get me on that."

"Aw, come on, please?"

No. Do not look at him. His adorable grin and those mischievous eyes would not persuade her.

With his finger, he lifted her chin, then kissed her. "I'll promise you more if you ride with me."

"Oh yeah?" Rats. Now she looked him in the eyes. Why didn't he put his sunglasses back on? The man was too clever. Well, she could easily match his wit. Bracing her hands on her hips, she purposely stared in those eyes. "Just how much more?"

His eyebrows waggled. "I guess you'll have to wait and see, won't you."

Grabbing his hand, she dragged him toward the queue. She was no better than those permissive parents who'd be paying the giant dental bill. Her chiropractor would love this. "You realize you will owe me big time for this, don't you?"

He laughed. "I look forward to it."

Biting into her lower lip, she considered where this day might actually lead. Definitely, something to look forward to.

SHEILA'S HEAD SNUGGLED AGAINST HIS SHOULDER, the sickly green fading from her face as the train carried them to the front of the park. Richard swept hair from her face. Okay, maybe the Monster was not a wise choice for an amusement park newbie, but they both had enjoyed the benefits of the ride's centrifugal motion. Once she got a little something in her stomach, she'd be ready to go again. This time no spinning rides.

He kissed her forehead, and her dimples smiled their approval. The two of them certainly didn't need outside forces pressing them together. In Sheila, he finally found the missing part of his life, the puzzle piece that made him feel whole. Maybe it was time he showed her his whole picture. The thought upset his stomach more than the whirling ride.

If he showed her, would she leave him? If she left him now, loneliness would infuse his days. He squeezed her shoulders and kissed her again.

Regardless of the unknown answers, it would be unfair to put it off any longer. All the more reason to make this day as memorable as possible.

SHEILA FELT LIKE SHE WAS IN A SCENE FROM some Cary Grant / Doris Day movie as Richard covered the picnic table with a grape-leaf tablecloth and matching napkins, followed by fine china and crystal goblets. From his cooler he brought out finger sandwiches, berries, watermelon, and sparkling grape juice.

"I see your mother's influence." Sheila sat on the cushion he placed on the worn bench.

He grinned, obviously appreciating the comparison with his mother.

She picked up a triangular sandwich layered with ham, cheese, and mayonnaise. "Is this normal fare for amusement park picnics?"

"No, only for you." He sat across from her and filled his plate. "I wanted to set this trip apart from the rest, but I think we've already achieved that."

No doubt about that. Who knew childish amusement could be so much fun? That it would draw her even closer to him?

A comfortable silence settled between them as they ate, and she studied the man of contradictions seated across from her. The wealthy and brilliant janitor. An Armani-wearing farm boy. The adult who'd gifted her with a child-like day, the very kind of day she'd missed out on growing up. A Boy Scout who called himself a rebel. The serious man whose rare smiles and laughter had broken the vault guarding her heart. A strong man whose arms embraced her with protective tenderness. A gentleman whose kisses could melt Antarctica …

Whew. She fanned a hand in front of her face. If someone had told her six months ago she'd be dating a janitor and going to amusement parks, she'd have laughed straight out. Even funnier, five months of dating and they never even …

Her fanning hand picked up speed. Tonight, that would change. He wouldn't be able to say no.

"What are you thinking?"

Heart quickening, her eyes rose to meet his. "About tonight."

"Tonight?"

She nodded. "I'd like you to come home with me."

His lips curled up into a sexy smile.

Yes! He's finally going to say "yes!"

But, his smile sagged.

"Please?" How could he expect her to hold out any longer? He looked down.

"Well?" She rounded the table, sidled next to him, and kissed him. A kiss he wouldn't soon forget.

"I can't. Not yet." His voice squeaked out, betraying feelings he couldn't hide.

Sheila pushed away. Oooh, this man could be so infuriating. "I don't get you." Her voice rose several notches. "I know you want to. What's holding you back?"

He fingered a napkin, his eyes hooded. "Before I came to Wharton I dated … a lot … and usually those dates ended back at my place."

You've got to be kidding. So, he wasn't a Boy Scout after all. But then, she'd always known that, hadn't she? No one without experience kissed like he did.

"Frankly, it was a lifestyle that left me empty." He peered up, his jaw working from side to side. "That behavior's largely to blame for the rift with my family. It's not something I'm proud of. I made a vow when I moved here, I wouldn't sleep with someone again until there was a commitment between us."

Commitment? Whew. Thank goodness. For a second Richard sounded too much like Joe. "You scared me for a moment. I thought you were going to say marriage. I once dated—"

"Actually, that would be the ideal."

Sheila flinched. She couldn't possibly hold out until marriage.

"Reality says I don't have the strength to wait."

Okay, that she could handle. "What exactly do you mean by commitment?"

He rubbed his chin. "I guess, engagement, a firm promise of a lifetime spent together." His eyes narrowed. "You're not ready, are you?"

"I don't know." Could she ever commit to a lifetime spent with one man? "The whole idea of marriage scares me, but what I'm finding even more frightening is thinking of the future without you in it."

He looked outward toward the Minnesota River and said nothing.

"You don't feel the same way?"

"I care for you, Sheila."

Nausea coated her gut. Care? *He* cares *for me?* She was way beyond *caring*.

"I can't think commitment yet. There's too much in the way."

"Too much what?"

"You don't really know me." He grasped at his chain.

She squinted. What significance did that chain hold? "Then tell me." Did she really want to know?

Maybe not. Then she'd have to share her secrets. If he knew what she hid from him, they wouldn't be discussing a future. Did a commitment mean their pasts had to be unearthed? Nothing good could come from that, could it?

He was right. Commitment's trap was ensnaring as a spider web. How could she get him to think past that antiquated, moralistic conviction and bring their relationship into the current century?

She slipped her hand through the crook in his arm. "So, does that mean there's hope for us?"

His eyes gazed into hers.

Yes, she could spend a lifetime looking in those eyes.

He cuffed his hand over her cheek, his thumb caressing her

skin. "I'm not going to leave you."

"Then I have something to look forward to." She turned her head and kissed his hand.

His mouth curled to one side as he leaned forward to kiss her. "A lot more than that."

She took his hand and stood. "I suggest we go enjoy the rest of our day."

"Good idea." He nodded to the rollercoaster careening out over the parking lot. "Do you like heights?"

The ride would certainly fit her emotions. May as well give it a try.

THE WATER-DRENCHED MAN HOLDING SHEILA'S hand was completely certifiable. So, what did that make her? Sure, she survived the roller coaster with its two-hundred-foot, sixty-degree drop. She even enjoyed the tower that launched them nearly three-hundred feet into the air before bouncing back to the ground. It was the Viking ship, which literally hung them upside down over one-hundred feet in the air for what seemed an eternity, that sent her over the edge. Richard's ears probably still echoed with her flowery exclamations.

Never again.

So, getting soaked on a water ride? Piece of cake. It was fitting he got drenched, while she remained fairly dry.

Wringing the front of his shirt, he led her to a bench by the ride's exit. He removed his tennis shoes and dumped a waterfall onto the asphalt pavement. Waterlogged socks clung to his feet. He peeled them off and wrung them out. It didn't help, poor guy.

She almost felt sorry for him. Almost. He'd just have to squish around for the remainder of the afternoon. At least she had the wisdom to wear sandals.

"You do deserve this, you know?" She giggled.

Shaking his head, he stood and tugged off his clinging wet shirt.

A whistle blew through her lips. The man didn't have a six-pack, which was perfectly fine with her, but he was lean, his muscles defined from hard work, not repetitive machines. A chain linked down his chest, with a solitary key pulling it into a V.

She reached out to touch the key, but he slapped his hand over it.

"What is that for?" She grasped his hand and pulled.

Clutching the chain, a quiet curse flew from his mouth. "Just a key." He turned around and drew on his drenched shirt.

One more intriguing puzzle piece to her mystery man. "The key to your heart?"

His shoulders heaved before he turned back, still smiling, but his eyes had lost some of their spark. "Precisely."

She pressed her hand into his sodden shirt, and traced the key's outline with her thumb. "Let me guess, someday you'll tell me, right?"

"Someday soon."

Oh, really?

He clasped her hand. "Yeah. Soon." Hand in hand they continued through the park.

Truthfully, the individual pieces detailing his life didn't matter anymore. All of those pieces, good and bad, composed this boyish man who walked beside her now. There was nothing about him she'd change.

THE AFTERNOON GREW INTO EVENING, painting the sky in swirling red, orange, and purple pigments. For Richard, it seemed to be the perfect end to what had been a nearly flawless day.

"Now for the *pièce de résistance*." After indulging in the requisite fair food of cotton candy and corn dogs, there was one final attraction. For him, it would be the ideal way to end this part of his day. He grasped Sheila's hand, pulling her toward the front of the park to his favorite ride. Colorful lights lit up the rectangular building. Sparks flew from the ceiling as the ride slowed to a stop.

"Bumper cars?"

"Of course. This is where the true Minnesotan comes out."

"Really?" She wrinkled her nose.

Man, she was gorgeous. "You take a group of us passive aggressive Minnesotans and give us permission to show aggression. I swear Debbie and Marcus have given me whiplash."

"And that makes me want to go on this ride?"

"Absolutely." He tugged on her hand, forcing her to follow him into the building. The line was short, and they were able to select their cars immediately. He chose a blue one and nodded to the green car next to his. "Just give it a try. You won't regret it."

"Whatever you say, but I have no clue how to drive one of these things." Sheila sat and buckled her shoulder harness.

"All you do is press the pedal. When the ride turns on, you go. If you get stuck, keep turning your wheel. You'll figure it out."

"Oh, I know I will, and you'll pay for it too."

Exactly what I'm hoping for. Electricity zapped from the ceiling, propelling his car forward. As anticipated, Sheila briefly struggled to get her car moving, and he took full advantage of it too, ramming her on all sides. But, shortly, she had it figured out, and it was payback time.

For all he cared they could have been the only two in the building. Other cars crashing into them were like pesky bugs trying to interrupt the fun. Despite warning signs placed on all the walls, and an announcement by the ride operator to *Avoid Head on Collisions*, they squared up for a collision, and he floored his accelerator, as if he could go faster than one speed.

Determination tensed Sheila's face, magnifying her dimples, as they drove toward each other. Absolutely beautiful. The cars stopped inches from a crash. A sexy pout covered her face.

He jumped up and helped Sheila out of her car, and the ride operator enunciated, "Please wait until all cars have completely stopped before exiting your vehicle."

"Oops. I believe it's time to go." Richard took her hand and led her toward the park entrance. They strolled past the game area and the circling Scrambler Sheila refused to ride. That was all right. She'd done far more today than he anticipated. They walked in between the old-time buildings leading to the entrance fountain.

"Want to check out our pictures?" He pointed to the photo booth near the park's exit.

"Absolutely. I don't have one of you."

"They could be lousy. I don't photograph well."

"Yeah, right."

He handed the clerk his ticket.

She brought two pictures up on a monitor hung on the back wall. Both had excellent clarity, especially the one with the close-up.

"Rabbit ears? You gave me rabbit ears!" She hip-checked him, setting him off balance, but he didn't fall. "I can't believe you would be so infantile. No. No, I take that back. After today, I should have expected it."

"I'll take one of each." He grinned at the worker.

The park employee printed out the pictures and inserted them into white cardboard frames.

Sheila snatched the close-up. "This one's mine. No one else is going to see that I'm dating an oversized child."

Frankly, it didn't matter which picture he took as long as he had some tangible reminder of Sheila. If their relationship unraveled, he'd always have the picture to look back on and remember the day.

He led her from the park and through the darkened and empty picnic area, fighting against the urge to kiss her. Losing the battle, he stopped and pulled her close, her body melding perfectly with his. He tipped her chin up, silencing her voice but not her heart as it quickened against his chest.

This day had been so perfect. She was so perfect. He'd never known anyone like Sheila who made the word *commitment* sound like a good thing not a life-sentence. "Sheila, I …" He stopped his sentence short of saying, "I love you." Those words had passed his lips before, but never in truth, never with Sheila.

Reaching behind her head, he released her ponytail. Her hair fell softly, framing her face. He ran his fingers through her hair, cupped her face in his hands and kissed her. A simple, *thanks for the fun day* kiss. The kiss deepened, months of stifled passion and longing spilled out. Knowing they were in a public place was the only thing keeping his hands firmly on her back.

"Are you sure you won't come home with me?" she whispered as his lips brushed over her cheek.

He raised his head, pulling it back just enough to read her expression. Hope. Pleading. What he'd give to say yes. But, he couldn't, not until she knew the truth.

It was time.

Tonight would be the night.

The words were already scripted in his head, now he just had to set them free. "Let's stop at Marcello's—"

"Marcello's?"

"You know, real food, no artificial sweeteners."

She held her face within centimeters of his, her lips lifting in an inviting tease. "And then?"

His lips skirted hers, tempting him to skip Marcello's altogether. "And then I think I'd love to stay the night."

He prayed it would get that far.

CHAPTER *nineteen*

Richard sat across from Sheila in a private booth near the back of Marcello's. A single candle lit the table illuminating Sheila's face, accenting her dimples. His Sicilian scampi sat cold and untouched. He eyed it for several minutes, moving it around with his fork, then set his fork on the table. Hoping to hide in the shadows, he leaned back in the booth, not wanting his face to betray his feelings as the words formed on his lips.

"Sheila, it's time I told you the truth. I should have told you long ago but, to be honest, I never believed we'd last."

Worry lines creased her forehead, and she cuffed both hands around her daiquiri. "Richard, whatever it is, it doesn't matter." Her hand reached for his. He ignored her hand, and she slowly pulled it away. "I know who you are now. Isn't that enough?"

"No, it's not," he said softly. How he wished it were. "You'd find out sooner or later anyway. I'd rather you hear it from me. Like I told you before, this job isn't what I'm born to do. It isn't where my passion lies, and it isn't what I did before I returned to Minnesota."

Sheila chewed on her lower lip.

"I used to work for ACM Technologies in New York City. Vice President of Operations. Even had a window framing the city."

Her eyes widened. "I don't understand."

Neither did he. How could he have been so stupid? "I worked with failing branches and subsidiaries of our company to make them profitable again, and even did some consulting on the side. You said I can fix anything? Well, that includes businesses. I understand the marketplace. I've got great instincts and can find a solution for most problems. If the company accepts the solutions I offer, they're soon

141

back in the black. I was good. Very good. I was highly respected—in and outside of ACM—and, I believed, an invaluable asset to the company."

Gripping his knees, he watched Sheila's impassive face as she raised her drink to her lips. *Say something. Please.*

Her silence spurred him on. "Of course, with the job came all the perks of a high level position, and I took advantage of them all: money, nice cars, expensive apartment, parties ... women ..." He cringed. How had he allowed himself get so out of control? It was all so contrary to how he'd been raised.

"I was arrogant and self-serving and used people to get what I wanted. My position reinforced the attitude. Too many times I had to advise scaling back or even eliminating a branch altogether. So there I was, making an obscene amount of money, advocating hard-working, budget-straining people lose their jobs."

"But isn't that just business? The ultimate goal is profit."

"I know, but you can't forget you're dealing with people's lives. Looking back, I believe I made the right financial assessments, but each time my calluses grew a little bit tougher and eventually I forgot I was dealing with real people. Then ..."

He swallowed a deep breath, closed his eyes, and clenched his fists beneath the table, trying to prevent the tears from coming, trying to get rid of the mass swelling in his throat. He lifted the napkin to his eyes, wiping them as they reopened.

"I left a company party knowing I had a lot to drink. You know how it is; you think you're invincible, you're not really impaired. The sad thing is, I don't think anyone even tried to stop me. I'd made so many enemies in the company, I believe there were people who wished something bad would happen."

"Slow down a bit." Gripping her glass, Sheila leaned forward. "That's not you. Maybe I've only known you a few months, but the last word I'd use to describe you is arrogant."

"Well, a person changes when ..." He calmed the tremor in his voice before dragging the chain from beneath his shirt, drawing the key along with it.

Clutching the key, he swallowed hard and stuffed away his emotions. It was the only way to get through it again. "It was a dark night. My mind was reeling, thinking about a nasty encounter I had at the party." Sheila didn't need to know the details of that encounter. She would stand with Marissa. "It was the reason I left, and my mind wasn't on driving."

The memories drew him back in time, forcing him to relive the horrors of that night.

Richard sank into his 1997 Mercedes' leather seat and held his head. His hair was damp. Seventy cool degrees, yet he was perspiring. Now he knew he was in trouble. Where was his dispassionate demeanor, the one that allowed him to make complex judgments without breaking a sweat? All it took was one single phrase— "I'm not going to have this baby"—to melt his icy certitude and remind him, he was a fallible human being.

Fallible.

Broken.

Broken things could be fixed.

There had to be a way to fix the situation. There was a solution to everything. For now his solution was to drive, to get far away. He inserted the key into the ignition, simultaneously stepped on the clutch and the brake, and turned the key. The engine's quiet purr was soothing.

He glanced at the clock. Why weren't his eyes focusing? He lifted his hands. They were steady. He talked aloud— no slurring, no difficulty speaking. He didn't have that much to drink, did he? Not even four drinks over four hours. It had to be his turbulent emotions.

Slowly releasing the clutch, he accelerated away. The car headed straight on the road: no swerving, no weaving, but doubt still niggled at his conscience. If he didn't have to get away so badly, he wouldn't drive, but staying was not an option. There would be no speeding or showing off tonight. If he had too much to drink, he certainly didn't need to make himself obvious.

He stepped on the clutch and shifted into fifth gear. The fluid transition was calming. But, where was he going? Not back to that apartment in Brooklyn Heights. Having lived there ten years, one would think it would be a home.

Instead, it was his showplace. It impressed the women, if not himself. It had never been home, and he'd find no solace there.

Could he go home? Home … He laughed dryly at his word choice. Ironically, in his fifteen years in the city, he never referred to New York as home. Home should be more than where you sleep and eat. It should be where you find love and comfort. Isn't that what he was supposed to have here?

Maybe, but the home he thought of was over a thousand miles away. A home with Johnnycake, hugs, fresh air, star-filled skies, his mom … his dad, Marcus, preaching, jealousy, resentment. How could he go there, especially now? But, the ache to see his mother, to talk to Debbie, maybe they could help him through this. And the kids … More than ever he needed to see them. He wouldn't take them for granted anymore.

Maybe a surprise visit wouldn't give Marcus time to prepare a mental list of all the things he'd done wrong. Maybe they would be happy to see him. Mom, Debbie, the kids, even Dad? Yes. Marcus? Never. But, he could always leave when it got bad. Maybe if they promised to lay off him, he'd stay longer.

But then, maybe they were right. Hadn't tonight already proven that? His choices, ones he'd been taught to flee, now wickedly mocked him, and Marcus would join in the mocking. Or would he? Maybe he'd provoked his brother to that. Nothing was clear.

Too much thinking. Just make a decision and go. Go home. Go home. Good idea. The airport wasn't too far away, either. Ten minutes tops. He should make it there without incident and surprise his family tomorrow afternoon.

He pulled his Blackberry from his belt and scrolled until he found his flight application. LaGuardia had a flight leaving in two hours. Perfect.

He secured his reservation in first class.

Home. He grinned. He was going home.

Whistling, he returned his phone to his belt, and looked back at the road.

The red traffic light sped past him, and a car pulled out in front. Richard slammed his brakes and tires screeched. Metal crunched metal. Glass shattered. Airbag exploded like a shot gun and pummeled his face, his body. Smoke and dust drenched the air. Airbag deflated.

Absolute silence …

Richard pried his eyes open and blinked, wiping airbag dust from his face. He breathed in the grimy air and coughed.

But, he was still breathing, thank God. His arms, hands, legs, and body ached, but they all moved. "Thank you, Lord." The words poured from him without thought. But, what had he hit? He forced himself to look ahead. It was too dark to make out fully through the airbag's residue and his spider-webbed windshield.

With a bleeding hand, he pushed down on the door handle. Stuck. He rammed his already aching shoulder into the door and winced as broken glass sliced along his upper arm. A curse crossed his lips when he looked down. Red already bled through his new Brooks Brothers shirt-sleeve. The shirt was ruined.

Shaking the pain away, he stepped onto the asphalt, grabbed his cell phone, and dialed 911. The road signs blurred as he gave his location, affirming his unstable condition. Then he trained his eyes on what was in front of him. Breath deserted him as he staggered to the crumpled vehicle, dropping his phone on the ground, leaving the operator suspended. "Oh, God, no! Please, God, they have to be all right. They have to be alive!"

Did God listen to prayers of those who turned their backs? Of course he did. That's what he learned growing up, wasn't it? Miracles happened all the time. Jesus raised Lazarus from the dead. Surely, this wouldn't be any more difficult.

Richard reached through the shattered window and cuffed his hand around what was left of the driver's bloody wrist. Nothing. He pressed shaky fingers to the driver's neck. Clammy stillness. Richard's stomach churned, and bile burned up into his throat erupting onto the pavement, leaving its impression on his Gucci loafers and Prada trousers. It kept surging until dry heaves overtook his body.

He stumbled back to his car, trembling.

Why didn't he just stay at the estate? He could have lived with humiliation, but this? Never. He sank against his car, plugged his head between his knees, and wept. "God? Why?"

Sirens cried in the distance.

Heart pounding, Richard blinked the restaurant and Sheila back into focus. Outside the restaurant, sirens faded away.

He lifted his gaze to Sheila, but she'd tucked herself against the back of the booth, shadows obscuring her face.

"Is there more?" Her voice trembled out of the darkness.

"That's the worst of it, but yeah, there's more." He stuffed the key from his Mercedes back into his shirt. "When I heard the sirens, I shut down. I realized my drinking had contributed to the accident. I had killed someone ..." Just saying those words made him sick again. How was he any better than Marissa? "I could hear my parents' voices in my head, warning me to slow my life down. Marcus always told me I'd live to regret my behavior one day. He was right. I lived, and I knew I deserved whatever was about to come my way."

Deathly silence echoed across the table. Oh, Sheila must hate him. It didn't matter now if he told the rest. It couldn't possibly worsen her opinion of him. Still, it was best to release the truth now. No more holding back.

"I don't remember everything that happened. I guess I've tried to block it out. I remember answering the cop's questions, the stitches, the time in jail." Jail. The ultimate equalizer. No, to be truthful, it equalized nothing. Rather, roles were inverted propelling him from the top to the very bottom of the food chain.

He subconsciously massaged his wrists, the bite of the handcuffs was ever-present. Leaning forward, he retrieved his wallet from his back pocket and flipped it open. His driver's license once peeked through the plastic window. The license was still there, but his Nick Nolte-like mug shot, flaunting his pasty face, wild hair and bloodshot eyes, concealed the license. It always would.

He handed the wallet to Sheila.

She accepted it as if being handed a dirty diaper, then covered her mouth. "This is you?" Gravel grated in her voice.

"Hard to believe, huh?"

Handing the wallet back, her head bobbed one slow nod, then she grabbed her napkin and dipped her hands into her lap.

To wipe away the filth she just held, he was certain. How often had he done the same thing with his own hands?

"My attorney called Mom and Dad. I couldn't. I'm sure they were proud of their successful son. It wasn't until the next morning when I found out who I'd ..." The words refused to come out. "It was just a boy celebrating his high school graduation. He was sober."

"Oh, Richard." Sheila shoved her drink to the middle of the table.

Just as he figured, he'd broken her ideal perception of him. The Boy Scout had become a criminal.

Those broken pieces would soon be shattered, scattered and beyond repair—just like his life. "Of all people, it was Marcus who flew out to help me through the mess. I wasn't thrilled to see him, but what bothered me the most was the look in his face. Disappointment. My little brother was disappointed in me. I couldn't even imagine the disappointment of my parents.

"Marcus didn't condemn or make a scene. He was even kind. I wanted him to be angry. I expected torrents of judgment. Disappointment was much more difficult to live with, so I goaded him to get the reaction I wanted. Debbie insisted I get some counseling. I did, only to appease her, but never took it seriously."

Richard kneaded the back of his neck, listening to Sheila's screaming silence. "My employer couldn't take the bad reputation I brought to their company and let me know it. I resigned before they could fire me."

"Is there anything else I can get you?" The waiter seemed to materialize out of nothing.

How about a clean start? Richard shook his head. "Just the

bill."

The waiter laid the leather bound bill holder on the table. Richard stuck his card inside frowning at the costly tab for untouched food.

He looked back at Sheila. The damage was done. May as well get it over with. "I faced the judge a couple months later. The charge was just Careless Driving because my blood alcohol level registered at only .068. Talk about pure luck. If I'd finished my drink that night, just another half a glass, I'd most likely be serving time with a felony vehicular manslaughter charge.

"I pled guilty. I was guilty, and I knew it could have been a lot worse. I've got a mark on my police record, but it's not what I deserve. A stinkin' half a glass of booze kept me out of prison." A low huff escaped his throat as he shook his head, still struck by the absurdity of his sentence.

"In my mind it was a technicality that got me off. I'm guilty of murder. *I* drove the car after I'd been drinking. *I* was on the phone when my eyes should have been on the road." He swallowed hard. "That young man should be alive, going to college. He's not because I killed him. I. Killed. Him." And right now he wanted to die. It had been months since he'd relived that night and had forgotten about its jarring impact on his psyche.

He waited for some response from Sheila, something that would tell him what she was thinking. Piercing quiet announced her thoughts so he continued.

"Sentencing was months later. I had to pay a fine and put in a lot of hours doing community service, mostly speaking to driver's ed classes or student assemblies about safe driving. I don't know if anything I said registered to them. When the kids looked at me they saw someone who got off with a misdemeanor and minor injuries. They didn't consider there was an innocent person in the other car."

"All set?" There was the stealth waiter again.

All set. Game, set, match. Loser.

Richard pushed the bill toward the waiter and watched him scurry away. What Richard would give to hurry from his confession, but Sheila needed the whole truth. Her stillness already shocked the air with tension. It couldn't hardly get any worse.

"At the sentencing Marcus finally showed what I'd been expecting from him. He wanted to see me punished, especially after how I had treated him and the boy's family. I think he believed I'd somehow bought my way out of a harsher conviction. I swear I didn't. Even I don't believe I got what I deserved. Apparently, that's not how I came across, though. Marcus told me he couldn't believe I could be so heartless, and I needed to show some concern or care for the boy's family.

"But, I was terrified. I knew if I didn't remain calm and keep my feelings in check, I would fall apart. I was sorry. I still am. I always will be. I couldn't express it. Everyone believed I was this horrible, heartless monster. I don't know. Maybe they were right. I never did apologize." Maybe he was cruel and heartless. If not now, he must have been at that time.

He wiped his eyes. What he did know, what never made sense to him, was the family's response. Their kindness only magnified his guilt. "The boy's parent's reaction wasn't what I expected at all. Here I am, facing a minor charge for killing their son. They should hate me. But, they … they forgave me. I couldn't even forgive myself. I still can't, and I need to live with that realization for the rest of my life.

"And the ultimate kicker? They refused to file a civil lawsuit, offering me mercy." He laughed ironically and tugged on his chain. "They had no clue that mercy was the worst punishment possible."

He rubbed his thumb over the weathered links. Mercy's chain had merged permanently with the shackles he'd forged in his adult life, link by selfish link, just like *A Christmas Carol's* Jacob Marley. "I took a chunk of my savings and put it in a trust fund for the boy's sister. It could never be enough to cover what I took from them, but what else could I do? What do you do when you commit an unforgivable sin?"

He didn't expect her to answer. No one had a real answer. His family repeatedly talked of forgiveness, but that term no longer made sense to him.

"I sold my home and my Mercedes once it was fixed. I rented a small U-Haul, emptied my closets and bookshelves and left everything else behind. I realized I needed my family. I know

I haven't spoken to them much but, they're a security net for me, in spite of our differences. They stood by me even though I didn't deserve it."

All he heard was the steady cadence of Sheila's breathing. Deep and purposeful. He reached for his water glass. Why hadn't he ordered something stronger for the night? Something to help him through? Just one wouldn't have hurt. He downed the water, put the empty glass on the table, and stared down at its emptiness ... at his hands clasped around it.

"I contacted Ethan. Told him I wanted a menial job, one that would simply keep me busy. I wanted to stay low-key. It's what I earned." He paused, searching for Sheila's face in the shadows. Bottled emotions began bubbling out. "You came along and complicated matters."

Her continued silence was unbearable. "Sheila, please say something." He rounded the table to sit beside her. He needed to see her face—needed to know what she was thinking.

With his fingers, he tipped her chin up, but her eyes flitted away.

"Take me home, Richard."

He pressed his lips to hers anyway. "I'll stay tonight," he promised thickly, hoping to guide her emotions.

"Call me a cab, Richard." She wiped her lips. "I need time to think."

That's okay. She just wants to think.

The waiter returned and set the bill on the table. Perfect timing. "Would you please call us a cab?"

"Right away, sir."

Richard pulled his VISA from the bill holder and signed the invoice as Sheila stood and hurried toward the entrance.

He rushed after her, stepping outside into air that had cooled dramatically. She stood next to the curb, hugging herself with goose bump sprinkled arms.

"You're cold." He stretched his arm around her shoulders.

"Brilliant deduction." She shook him off and moved away.

Sighing, he leaned against the side of the brick building giving her some space.

Minutes later, a yellow cab pulled to the curb. Richard

opened the door and paid the driver.

Sheila sat without looking at him, without talking. The car motored away, Sheila's eyes fixed straight ahead.

It's over.

His breath slowly released as he shuffled to his car and got in. He drove off, trying desperately to erase Sheila from his mind. Baseball. That'll help. He tuned in the game. An image of Sheila in her Twins jersey filled his thoughts.

At a red light, he punched the radio's scan button. The scanner stopped with Jimmy Buffet's *Margaritaville* depressing the air. Boy, could he relate. Waiting for the light to change, he glanced at neon sign flashing "liquor" on one corner of the intersection.

The light turned green. Taking the *go* signal as a *yes*, he tripped his blinker and took a hard right. Margaritas weren't his style, but a chilled twelve pack? Nothing would taste better.

Once at home he collapsed on the couch, turned on the baseball game and, for the first time in over a year, popped open a can.

LONGING FOR THE PEACE OF FORGETFUL SLEEP, Sheila stared out the cab window, but was oblivious to the night-life partying in the streets of downtown Minneapolis. She'd read Richard's story on the internet months ago, but hadn't believed the *Richard Brooks* described in the articles could possibly be the man she knew. There were no accompanying pictures on the sites she perused, and the descriptions of his prominent career at ACM and arrogant personality bore no resemblance to *her* Richard.

Her eyes stung, and she blinked away tears. *Her Richard.* Could he really be hers if she didn't know who he really was? She'd quickly discounted that internet story along with all the others she found of men bearing the same name. Who knew it was such a popular name? No, if she were truthful to herself, she hadn't wanted it to be *her* Richard and therefore denied the obvious evidence.

Did it matter what or who he'd been? She rubbed goose pimpled arms hoping to generate some heat as she played Richard's confession in her head. His former career path sounded exhilarating. She could definitely see him succeed, and she could easily envision herself being together with him. If only she'd known him before. What a duo they would have made. A slight smile pulled on her lips.

But, did she want to know him?

The cab thumped down a pothole-pocked street. Jostled from her reverie, she gazed out at blurred streetlights. Richard's story had distorted all the noble images she once had of hm. He'd taken the life of someone—a child. The act was unintentional, still her gut seethed. Maybe she saw too much of herself in his actions. It could have happened to her just as easily. How often had she driven under the same circumstances? Too often to count. Would she have handled the situation any differently? Probably not, but it hadn't happened to her, and what he had done did matter.

She'd thought it wouldn't. Before tonight, she thought she could deal with whatever he hid from her. Maybe tomorrow she could handle it, but not now. She pulled a tissue from her purse and wiped at burning eyes. It was imperative to get away from Richard, and her tangled emotions, and look at the situation objectively.

The cab swerved around a whiskered man pushing a wobbling grocery cart, probably filled with his lifelong possessions. A person needing a stranger to reach out.

How could she comfort a stranger if she couldn't comfort the man she'd grown to care for, maybe even love. She sniffled and pulled another tissue from her purse. Part of her had wanted to reach out and console, to return his tender kiss and tell him "yes." But, wouldn't a real man have stayed and faced the problem? Not run and hid a thousand miles away. Wasn't it running that caused his accident in the first place? Would he run from her now too? Abandon her like her Joe? Like her parents?

A knife-twisting pain sprouted behind her eyes as the cab turned onto Fourth Avenue. She dug into her purse for aspirin. Perhaps she should make that move first. Was she strong enough to withstand the ache of let him go? Was she willing to lose someone again whom she started to love? Did she really love him?

Before tonight? Probably. But now?

She swallowed three aspirin. That should postpone the headache for now anyway. If she and Richard stayed together, was she avoiding the inevitable? Eventually. she'd have to reveal what happened between her and Joe. Richard would hate her for that. Yes, maybe it would be best if they broke up. Next time she'd be more careful in choosing a relationship. Someone she could no way fall in love with. Someone that wouldn't make her heart ache.

The cab pulled to the curb in front of her condominium. Thanking the driver, she stepped out. Robotically, she climbed the steps to her door, slid the key into the lock, and entered her empty home. Empty by choice. He would have come home with her tonight. Had she been wrong to tell him no? Maybe she should call him. Forgive him. He would come. Wasn't he worth it?

Tonight there was no suitable answer. Just go to bed. Sleep. Tomorrow she'd likely see him again.

She slipped beneath her satin sheets and closed her eyes, hoping for restful, forgetful sleep.

A cacophonous choir floated in the shadows and a phantom loomed over her. Laughing maniacally, he touched her and pain racked through her body.

She opened her eyes wide and sat up, shivering. Sleep no longer offered solace—it had become her enemy.

CHAPTER *twenty*

The doorbell echoed through his ears like a gong and propelled Richard off the couch onto his hardwood floor with a thud. Empty cans clattered around him. A sharp pain knifed his back. He leaned over, grasped the offending beer can, and hurled it across the room. It rattled off his stone fireplace and pinged onto the floor adding reverberation to the drumbeat in his head.

Sitting up, he attempted to focus. A rolling headache forced his eyes closed as he tucked his head between his knees.

The doorbell sounded again—its vibration pulsed in his brain. "Sheila?" He shook his head. No, it wouldn't be her. This was much worse.

He forced his wobbly legs to stand, and he eyed the five empty beer cans lying crushed on the floor. "Five? Just five and I feel like this?" Before the bell would sound again, he yelled in the door's direction, "I'm coming." His head hammered. "Be right there." With his foot, he swept the empty cans under the couch. He ran his fingers through his hair and tucked his shirt back into his shorts.

Gluing on a smile, he opened the door. "Hey, Marcus, Nate, Josh. Come on in." He waved them into the room, taking full notice of the contempt in his brother's face. Quick, think up an excuse. "I had a late night last night and am not quite ready. Have a seat, guys. Make yourselves at home." Oh, brilliant.

"Sweet, Uncle Ricky's got a massive TV." Joshua plopped on the couch. "Can we watch something? Have any video games, Uncle Ricky?"

He didn't answer, but hurried to his bedroom, pretending he didn't hear his nephews' questions or his brother directing the boys to

155

wait on the couch.

"Watch some TV," Marcus said. "I need to talk to your uncle."

Terrific. Here it comes. Richard rested his back against the dresser, burying his fingers in his front pockets.

Marcus entered without knocking.

Maybe that's a good thing. Richard lifted his head just enough to view his brother.

Marcus held up an empty beer can. "Found this on your end table."

Okay, make that six.

"I'm assuming this isn't the only one."

Richard glowered back with his head drumming and his eyes straining to focus. So, he'd royally messed up again, but he wasn't about to admit it to his brother. "What's it to you?" He growled. "I had a lousy day yesterday and had my first beer since coming back to Minnesota, so lay off me."

Marcus stared at him, then sighed. "Where's your aspirin?"

Richard told Marcus, watched him leave, and then collapsed on his bed. What had he done? This wasn't how he dealt with problems. Not anymore. His brain bruised with each thought. *Shower. Go shower.*

He walked to his bathroom, his body shaking, and sagged against the wall. Bloodshot eyes stared back from the mirror opposite him. Last night he'd conveniently forgotten about the after affects of alcohol. The memories returned in pummeling waves.

Marcus stepped into the room and frowned in the mirror. "Here, this should take the edge off a bit." He set the medicine and water on the counter. "I'll tell the boys you can't make it."

"Don't. Wait." Richard stood, fighting to maintain his balance. The last thing he wanted was to let his nephews down. They had looked forward to this day, a guy's day out at a baseball game with no mothers, wives, or girlfriends to remind them of their manners. He wasn't about to blow this day for them. He'd have to suffer through what was to come. "Give me a minute to get ready." He steadied himself at the sink. "Just tell the boys I ate some bad meat or something."

Marcus' reflection scowled back.

WITH ONLY FIFTEEN MINUTES LEFT UNTIL FIRST pitch, Richard sat in the unforgiving stadium seat and crammed his legs in the narrow space. When they designed stadiums, they must have imagined all sports fans were five foot six and smaller. Good thing his seat was on the end of the row so he could stretch ... and probably escape.

Nearly every seat was occupied with screaming fans eager to watch their team clinch the division title. He massaged his temples as the din in the building escalated and reverberated. How could he have been so stupid last night?

With his head throbbing, he glanced two sections over where Sheila held her season passes. Oh, she was there all right. His pain increased as the client draped an arm around her shoulders and planted a kiss on her cheek, before she leaned into his shoulder.

How dare she?

Richard fisted his hands, and his breathing quickened. Just give him one moment with that slime—

"Uncle Ricky." Nathan tugged on Richard's arm. "That lady down there looks like your Sheila."

"It is." Richard growled and crossed his arms, wanting to pull his gaze from her, needing to give his nephews the attention they deserved, failing on both counts.

"Is she the problem?" Marcus nodded toward Sheila.

"Gee, how'd you figure that out? She knows I'm here. She's playing me, trying to make me jealous, and, to be honest, she's succeeding."

"Just try to ignore her. Don't give her the benefit of a glance. You're here with me and the boys."

"Yeah ... right." He gulped some water and stared down at his scorecard that wouldn't come into focus. The sellout crowd roared at the introduction of the lineup and grew louder when the defense ran onto the field, jack hammering his head.

It was too much.

"Guys, I need to get a drink."

Marcus glared at Richard.

"Not that kind of drink." Although, it did sound like a good idea. Maybe ...

"But, the first pitch is coming up." Nathan pointed to the starting pitcher stretching on the mound.

I couldn't care less right now.

Marcus patted his son's knee and whispered in his ear.

Nathan nodded.

"I'll be back," Richard mumbled and climbed the concrete steps, two at a time, to the concourse. It teemed with an ageless range of people and obnoxious vendors. The stench of hot dogs, popcorn, and jalapenos assaulted his senses, urging on the drumbeat in his head. There had to be some quiet place somewhere.

He wove among the thinning crowd. Deafening cheers erupted as Richard spotted an empty table off in a corner. *Perfect.* He strode toward the table, then stopped by a refreshment stand. *Beer $6.00.* His stomach roiled. Okay, not now. Save it for tonight. He ordered a large Sprite, and claimed the table, slumping in his chair, with his scorecard laid out in front of him.

With a sigh he glanced outward to see if the field was visible from here, and he cursed. What was she doing out here? He pulled the bill of his cap below his eyes and held the scorecard in front of his face, trying unsuccessfully to ease the tremors in his hands.

A shadow crept over him.

"You can't hide that easily, Ricky," Sheila said with an obvious smile in her voice. After her little display of playing him for a fool, how dare she think of smiling?

"That term is reserved for use by my family." He talked into his scorecard, keeping his voice low.

"Fine." She dragged a chair next to his and took his hand.

Her hand felt good in his—too good.

He pulled his away. Sure, last night's binge embarrassed him, and he wanted to hide it from her, but really, he was the only one harmed by it. Her flirting was a deliberate stab at him. The searing pain in his chest told him she succeeded.

"I saw you leave, so I came out to see how you're doing. Maybe talk."

Great, now she wants to talk. He shifted his jaw. Why

couldn't she talk last night?

"You look awful."

He laughed and glanced up. She looked perfect. Naturally. "Thanks so much, and, may I say, you look outstanding." Sarcasm dripped from his voice. *Cool it, Richard. Just shut your mouth.* Hangovers always made him say the stupidest things. "You know, I'm really not feeling well and would prefer to be left alone." There. Nothing inflammatory. No harm done. "I'll call you tomorrow."

"If that's what you want." Her fingers caressed his arm. Why did it have to feel so good?

"It's what I want." Or maybe he should wait for her to call him. She's the one who walked out on him last night. She was the one playing games with his emotions. "You know, I'm gonna return to my seat. My nephews have looked forward to this game, and I plan on enjoying it with them." Every nerve-splicing second of it. He stood and took a step. His foot caught on a chair leg, and thrust him downward. His cap flew off, and he stretched his arms out just in time to keep his face from kissing the concrete.

"Are you all right?" Sheila took his arm.

He lifted his gaze to hers and allowed her to help him stand. The shadows below her eyes suggested she hadn't slept well either. *Good. She deserves it. Whoa, careful, Richard.*

Sheila dropped back on her chair, her eyes narrowing.

Here it comes.

"You've been drinking!"

He was right. "Yeah, so what? People drink." *Brilliant come back, genius.*

"But, you don't. I always assumed that—"

"I'm an alcoholic?" He'd heard the accusation before, courtesy of Marcus of course, and had even undergone an evaluation following the accident. At least it got Marcus off his back. "No. I gave up booze after the crash. Realized what a demon it was, but last night I discovered it's not so bad after all."

"I did this to you." Guilt softened her tone and eyes.

"No, I did it to myself, but after your display down at the field, I'm thinking I've got at least six more cold ones back home." *Don't be an idiot.*

"You saw that?"

"Oh, come on, you knew I was watching." *Stop, right now. Don't say another word.*

Her lips pursed.

Gotcha. "I realized something today, watching you. Marcus accused *me* of having you as a trophy. He's got it all wrong." He pointed a finger at her heart. "I was *your* trophy, hopefully another conquest to place up on the shelf next to Joe ballplayer and who knows who else you've used along the way. I'd really been blinded by you, but, today, you opened my eyes."

Sheila sat mute as he strode toward his seat.

You blew it, man. You blew it big time. Turn back. Apologize. Do something. But, his feet stubbornly moved forward.

"Go ahead. Run away again. Just know that if you keep going, we're through."

He spun around and glared at her standing with arms crossed and jaw set. "That's what you want, isn't it?"

"Want?" She chuckled and pulled her hair back behind her neck. "What I want, what I *need* is someone stable. Someone who doesn't change moods with the wind. Someone who's honest."

His anger drained away as her piercing, but truthful words lanced his heart.

Stable.

Honest.

He'd been none of that.

She deserved better, but then he'd always known that, hadn't he? Maybe he should be fair and let her go.

Clenching and unclenching his fists, he walked back to her, searching his numbed brain for a solution. What was the right thing to do? He stuffed his hands in his back pockets and nodded toward the table. "Can we talk?"

"I don't know. Can trophies talk?"

Ouch. "I didn't mean that. I'm just not …" He sighed. "I'm not myself." Again, he nodded at the table.

She shook her head. "You see there's the problem. I don't know who your real self is. Are you the fun loving guy I saw yesterday, or are you someone who drinks to face your problems? Are you a janitor or a smooth talking, finely dressed business player?"

"I'd like the opportunity to show you." He took her hands, pulled her close and let her find his eyes, no longer caring that they were streaked with red. "Now that you know the truth about me, I have nothing else to hide." He leaned in and kissed her but she didn't return it.

"Please. Don't." A thud of finality pounded in her tone as she pulled away.

He dropped her hands and stepped back, nausea coating his throat. "This is it, isn't it?"

Her eyes closed and her head tilted downward. "I don't want to hurt you."

"I think it's a bit late for either of us to say that, don't you think?" A dry chortle escaped his throat. "But, hey, you're probably right. Until I get my head screwed on straight, I'm not being fair to you. You deserve more."

"Richard?" She peered up, tears collecting in her eyes. "Will you be okay?"

No. But the six pack back home would make it better. "I've got family support, remember?"

"They love you." Tears charted a path down Sheila's cheeks.

"I know." He kissed her tears. "I love you too." He didn't look for her reaction; he just turned away and strode back to his seat.

Her silence followed him.

CHAPTER *twenty one*

"What are you doing here, Janet?" Richard slammed the door of Marcus' Suburban and frowned at his sister-in-law sitting on the steps of his house. The last thing Richard wanted was more company. He wanted to be alone and couldn't wait for Marcus to pack up the boys and leave.

Janet glanced up at Marcus.

"I asked her to come." Marcus closed his door. "I'm staying the night with you."

Richard's neck slumped into his shoulders. *There goes the six-pack.* His lips pinched together. Of course, Marcus must have instinctively known that. Richard lifted his hands and rolled his eyes in Marcus' direction. "If that's what you think you need to do. Just don't count on me listening to any sermons."

Was there no kindness in him today? Janet and the boys certainly didn't merit the impact of his sullen attitude. He sighed and waved to his nephews. "Nate, Josh. Let's give your parents some space. I've got Schwan's bars in the freezer. Meet me in the back yard."

He hustled to his refrigerator. Six cans remained, just as he thought. *Later.* He closed the fridge and opened the freezer. The mere thought of eating ice cream curdled his stomach. He grabbed two ice cream bars and carried them to his deck where his nephews waited.

"Can we explore the woods?" Nathan pulled his ice cream bar out of the paper wrapping.

Yes. Please do. "Go ahead." Ice cream in hand, they ran off, and he dropped his bone-weary body into the outdoor lounge chair. Its cushion did little to comfort the ache permeating his bones, but at least there was silence. *Heavenly silence.* He shut his eyes. Within minutes, he was asleep.

"Time to go, guys." Marcus' voice woke him. "Your mom wants to get home before it's too dark." Richard raised an eyelid just enough to see his backyard through his eyelashes. The house now cast a long shadow across the yard indicating he'd probably slept for nearly an hour. He shut the eyelid and pretended to sleep. He'd make it up to the boys another time.

Unfortunately, he couldn't shut out the sounds as well as his sight. "Dad, why is Uncle Ricky so sad all the time?" The pain in Joshua's voice was palpable. "Doesn't he know Jesus can help him?"

"He used to, Josh," Marcus said in a near whisper. "Just keep praying for him, okay?"

How could a child be so smart—so observant?

Of course, Richard had been much like Joshua once upon an eternity. *God, don't let Joshua follow my footsteps.* He pinched the bridge of his nose. Why wouldn't God leave him alone? Richard wasn't ready to give in to God yet.

Instead, he gave in to sleep.

SLEEP ELUDED SHEILA. HOW COULD SHE POSSIBLY sleep after what she'd done? She fluffed her pillows and grabbed the book off her nightstand. A thriller void of romance. Exactly what she needed.

She opened to the bookmark and read the first paragraph. Then she read it again. And again. And she still didn't know what it said. Rather, Richard's sad eyes and his whispered "I love you" played over and over in her mind like a broken movie reel.

But she couldn't take her words back. Not when his confession niggled at her conscience. Seeing him yesterday, broken and hurting, stabbed at her conscience even more. He was right. He had been her trophy. At first. But then he'd grown into so much more, more than she deserved. If she didn't cast him off now, he'd do it to her later when he knew her whole story, and she couldn't take that, not again.

Sure, he hurt now, but he'd close this chapter of his life and move on just as she'd always done when abandoned. It built strength and character, even if the initial pain seemed unbearable. He'd survive and be better for it.

She slapped her book closed and tossed it on her bed stand. It skidded off and clattered to the floor, the bookmark fluttering aside losing her place.

How fitting.

A tear drifted over her cheek, and she wiped it away. So, tonight she was floundering a bit, but she was an overcomer. She'd built a successful life entirely on her own. Without parents. Without Richard. Tomorrow she'd turn the page and begin the next chapter in her life.

Another tear drifted down. Never before had turning the page proven so difficult.

RICHARD BLINKED AND SQUINTED AT THE dawning son. A blanket covered him, but the morning dew still chilled his bones. At least his head was back to normal. His frustrations and anger from the day before seemed like a dream. His biting conversation with Sheila surged in his thoughts. It wasn't a dream. No. It was a nightmare.

They were over, just as he'd anticipated. If he'd only kept his mouth shut, maybe they could have worked through it.

If only.

If only.

Too many "if onlys" littered his past.

It was time to let it go, move on, this time make the right decisions, the ones he'd been raised to make. But, could he go on without Sheila? Perhaps not, but she'd be fine without him.

He could do it without God. He'd always known the difference between right and wrong but didn't fear the consequences of making the wrong choices. He learned that lesson. Now to move forward in honesty—and perhaps some kindness toward his brother.

He showered then returned to the living room where Marcus was just waking up. "Sleep well? That couch isn't the most comfortable thing, you know." Marcus had obviously chosen the less comfortable bed in order to safeguard the fridge. Last night there had been no guarantees it wouldn't be an issue. This morning Richard was thankful it hadn't been. "You could have used the guest room." At least he could pretend he didn't perceive Marcus' motives.

"I'll remember for next time." With a yawn, Marcus sat up and stretched out his back. "Hhow are you feeling this morning?"

Richard plunked himself into the recliner. "Physically, better. I'm reminded why I gave up drinking in the first place. It solves absolutely nothing."

"At least you realize that."

"It's not how I prefer to learn." But, this lesson had cost him everything important to him—once again. "Why don't we grab a bite to eat before we get into things? That is why you stayed last night, right? To lecture?" The question was even asked with a crooked smile. In truth, he was grateful for Marcus' company this morning.

"Would I do that?" Marcus caught on and returned the grin.

"Every chance you get."

"I'll shower first."

RICHARD SET A PLATE OF TOASTER WAFFLES ON his deck table along with a carafe of warm maple syrup. "Sorry, they're not homemade."

Marcus speared two waffles. "Just makes me appreciate Janet more." He spread butter liberally over the waffles and drowned them in syrup. "If you have to live in the city, it doesn't get better than this." He chased the bite with orange juice.

Richard followed his brother's gaze and smiled. A doe and her fawn grazed among the trees oblivious to their human observers seated on the deck. "Yeah, it's a little slice of the farm. I should finish remodeling the house this winter, so next summer I can concentrate on outdoors. I plan on putting in a pond and adding some koi. Probably plant some vegetables. Won't Mom be proud of me when I bring home fresh veggies?"

"You'd leave the rest of the family in a state of shock."

"At least that would be a good shock. It'd be nice to do that for once."

"Don't sell yourself short."

"You tell me to be truthful; well that's what I'm doing. I figure if I keep myself busy around here I won't have time to let women get in the way. I won't have to worry about hiding my past." He poured some juice and drank it, his rejuvenated taste buds appreciating the tangy citrus.

"So what happened, Ricky?" Marcus placed his juice on the table. "What happened Friday that caused this?"

Richard stared down at the glass wrapped in his fingers. "I told her. Everything." In between sips of juice, he reviewed the day, told Marcus about the entire day's events. Why? He wasn't sure. Perhaps because Marcus was trying so hard to help, to listen and not put him down. Besides, Richard needed a confidant. More so, he needed a friend.

"Where does it leave the two of you, now? Or don't you know?"

"It's over." Richard closed his eyes. The ache in his stomach would probably never leave. "Sheila searched me out yesterday. I tried to avoid her. I know how dreadful I am when I'm hung over. I said some things …" Things he could never take back, things that had cost him way too much. "Besides, I'm sure 'killer' isn't on her list of desired husbandly traits."

Marcus had no clever comeback. Maybe his family could offer forgiveness, but no intelligent woman would look twice at him knowing what he'd done. But, keeping the secret wasn't any better. Maybe he was meant to be alone. The thought terrified him. "So, what do I do now? I know I've had my share of girl-friends, but they've never stayed. I guess I've never found anyone I really wanted to stay with—not until now. I care for Sheila more than anyone else I've known."

"That's saying a lot." Marcus knew all too well his history with women. Richard made sure Marcus knew of each and every relationship.

"I realize it's too late for me and Sheila—"

"Are you sure?"

"I destroyed her trust." He crossed his arms. "Even I know you can't build a relationship without trust. If *I* can't get past what I've done, how can I expect others to?

167

"First, you have to start caring for yourself."

"Right." His tone was deliberately cynical. "And maybe forgive myself?"

"I'd say first you need to turn it over to God. Ask for his forgiveness. You know he died for you, that you're supposed to cast all your burdens on him. You don't have to carry this around anymore."

"I know the rhetoric, Marcus."

"You're not saying no. That's progress."

"Perhaps."

"What are you going to do now?" Marcus pulled the sports section from the paper. "I don't expect you'll want to stay on at Wharton."

"You're right." Richard finished his juice. "I've been researching starting my own business. There's a definite market in the Twin Cities metro area for my expertise, especially in this economy. I've already got good leads on clients. There's even an office available downtown with an awesome view. I haven't made a commitment to it yet, though. I miss my old job, but that lifestyle cost far too much."

He drew out the paper's business section. He shouldn't have done that either. "Look here, Marcus." Richard pointed out a short article buried near the back page. "ACM Technologies Suffers Sixth Straight Quarterly Loss." His lips turned up in a sardonic grin. "Do ya think they miss me now?" He laughed through his nose. "I know exactly what they're doing wrong. If only—"

"You wouldn't consider going back there, would you?"

"Like I said, I miss the job. For the most part, they were a good company to work for. If they came and groveled a bit …" Another thought entered his mind. "Maybe that's what I need to do. If I went back to them and groveled, maybe I could work out of the Chicago office."

"You've got to be kidding. That's the last place you should go." Marcus shook his head before stuffing a waffle in his mouth. "Listen, I have a better option." He waved his fork through the air, talking with his mouth full. "Take some time off and come back home. You know Mom would love to have someone at home to take care of. To be honest, I could use another hand this fall too." Marcus suspended his fork in the air.

Richard reclined in his chair. Really, it wasn't a half bad idea. He wanted to get away from here—being alone right now could be dangerous—and the farm was as good an escape as any. Better than any. Warm breakfasts. Wrestling matches with Prince. Nieces and nephews to dote on. Acceptance. He wouldn't have to hide who he was with them. They already knew all the ugly truths— almost all, anyway—and they still loved him. That reality was finally sinking in.

Besides, it had been a long time since he'd helped Marcus. He loved building: the feel of a hammer in his hand, power tools, and the satisfaction of seeing the finished product. It would give him time to think about what he wanted to do. The physical work of construction would get him away from Wharton. It would take his mind off Sheila and everything that reminded him of her.

"Well?" Marcus set his fork on the table.

Richard sat up. "Did Mom send you here to bring me home?"

Marcus chuckled. "No, but I bet she'll make me one or two of her pecan pies as a thank you if you come home."

"I'll be sure to help her."

"No way. I prefer my pies without the tang of arsenic."

Another smile for his brother. It had to be a record. "I'll talk with Ethan tomorrow morning and hand in my resignation. So, I get to start all over, once again."

"You'll have our support, you know."

"Yeah. Believe it or not, I'm finally beginning to appreciate it."

SHEILA PICKED UP THE FRAMED PORTRAIT FROM the corner of Ethan's desk. "Your family looks happy." She didn't smile. Experience had proven to her that families smiling for a camera did not always equate to happiness. Too many families concealed their discontent behind a grin.

Still, Ethan smiled at her. "We are." His smile appeared to be genuine. "Now."

Ahh, yes. His qualifier proved her point. "You weren't always." She replaced the photo and wrapped her arms around her midriff trying to still her shivers. His office was cold. This whole old building was cold. Richard wouldn't have allowed it.

"Not so long as my job was more important than them. The move to Minnesota was what kept my marriage together. As a matter of fact, it was Richard who encouraged the move."

Her body stiffened. Staring at Ethan, she said nothing.

He nodded. "He told me you know everything."

No, that wasn't true. She didn't know everything. Not the most important thing. "Where is he, Ethan?"

He raised a single eyebrow and cocked his head to the side. "You don't know?"

She shook her head slowly then stared out his office window at the brown-brick building across the street. Rectangular holes that once framed glass were empty. The structure was vacant. Abandoned. "He's gone," she whispered. Disappeared. His phone was disconnected. E-mails bounced back. A stranger answered his door. It had barely been two weeks since their fight, since he said he loved her, since she watched him leave. She turned back to Ethan, refusing to cry. "Where is he, Ethan?"

He sat up in his chair, crossing his hands on his desk, and shook his head. "I can't help you, Sheila."

"Come on, Ethan. As a friend."

"As a friend, I need to respect Richard's wishes. As a professional, you know I can't say anything."

Yes, she knew, but she'd hoped. Perhaps if she told Ethan that Richard said he loved her, that she'd been foolish, that she needed Richard to help her through her dreams. Why had she kept them a secret?

Ethan reclined in his chair, his hands resting in his lap. "Give him time. He'll call." He sounded so confident.

She wished she shared his certainty. "If he calls you, will you tell him …" Tell him she loves him? No. That needed to be done in person.

"Tell him what, Sheila?"

She stood and walked to the door. Her hand clasped the knob before she looked back. "Tell him, what he did doesn't matter."

CHAPTER *twenty two*

Meghan shuffled over the uneven sidewalk, following Kalyn and Emily to September's last weekend party. After several weeks of partying, she still wasn't comfortable with it, even though, for the first time in her life, she was popular. For a college Freshman, wasn't that the important thing? Wasn't that what college was all about? Right, tell her that tomorrow when she was sprawled out on her bed all day. But, how else was she supposed to meet anyone?

She kicked at a stone lying on the concrete. It skittered onto the road. She could listen to her parents. When they called earlier in the evening, they asked if she'd joined any of the groups they recommended. Sure, and be the pious hypocrite who prayed for show, then partied for fun. Several would be at the bash tonight. No, she wouldn't attend meetings with a bunch of frauds. She'd told her parents she didn't have the time.

Besides, parties were where you meet people. She'd even been asked out a couple of times—by guys she'd never be alone with again. She shivered just thinking about those dates who grew tentacles once they got her alone. Did they all have to be like that guy back home? Surely not all men were like him. Hopefully, not Doran, Kalyn's brother. A smile hinted on her lips as she recalled her real reason for coming tonight.

The party music echoed down the street before the house came into view. A familiar knot tied her stomach. Images of Justin appeared in her head, and the knot in her stomach twisted. He'd be disappointed. That bugged her. Why did disappointing her brother even matter? It hadn't when he was alive, why should it now? A few beers always took care of that. Alcohol had a wonderful way of erasing all bad memories.

Drunken laughter seeped through the house's windows as the three girls climbed the concrete steps to the house. Kalyn and Emily charged in ahead of her, always eager to lose themselves. Was life so bad that they all needed to anesthetize themselves?

Maybe sometimes, but tonight might be different. Meghan pulled open the screen door and pushed through the crowd, searching. Kalyn had hinted that her brother Doran expressed interest in Meghan, a measly little freshman. It didn't make sense. Still ...

Someone handed her a drink. Meghan stared at it. Nope. Tonight she was staying sober. If Doran talked to her, she wanted to remember it. With the beer clutched in her hand, she walked around the room, visiting, watching, waiting, and sneaking peeks at Doran to see if he glanced her way. Not even a peep from him.

But, he sure was sweet to look at with those twinkling emerald eyes. Every girl on campus crushed on him. Who was she fooling to think Doran would notice her?

Nearly an hour later, she stared down at the full cup, now warm in her hand. Doran had no clue she even existed. Kalyn was obviously wrong, or maybe she'd outright lied. Like that would be a big surprise. Not. Her roommate hadn't proven herself to be the most trustworthy person. Hadn't she told Meghan not to bother with Doran earlier, and now Kalyn was saying the opposite? How gullible could Meghan be?

She took one more glance around, searching, and spotted him escorting a girl into one of the bedrooms.

That's it. No crying now. She slammed her cup on a table. The beer sloshed on the already gunky table and the matted-down carpet. Like anyone here would care. Meghan strode to the door. Oh the things she was going to say to that lying roommate of hers.

She twisted the doorknob, and a voice sounded behind her. "Leaving so soon?"

It couldn't be, Meghan swallowed and pivoted around. "Doran ..." *Hurry, make up an excuse.* "I guess I'm not into the scene tonight. I don't want a headache tomorrow." She squeezed her eyes shut. *Ooh, he's gonna think I'm a party pooper.*

"Hey, that's cool."

Her eyes popped open. *That's cool?*

Placing his hand on her back, he gave her a gentle shove. "Come on outside where it's quiet. We can talk for a bit."

Her body trembled. Why didn't she have something to drink, something to calm her jitters?

He motioned for her to take a seat on the steps.

She sat, crossing her ankles on a lower step, and folded her arms in her lap.

He sat to her right, his thigh lightly grazing hers. "In case you haven't noticed, I don't drink much either."

No, she hadn't noticed. "So it's cool if I don't?"

"Very cool." Doran picked up her left hand that crossed over the right.

Her pulse galloping, she trained her eyes on his hand holding hers. With his index finger, he lifted her chin. She looked down, but felt his eyes on her.

"I've been watching you for a long time, Meghan."

She pulled away. Yeah, her and every other female. "What about that girl you brought into the bedroom?"

He laughed. "She was about to pass out. I just got her out of the way. I like to keep an eye on everyone, make sure people are safe. Especially you. How do you think you got home that first night?"

"That was you?" Why couldn't she remember?

He shrugged and leaned close like he wanted to kiss her.

She turned her head. "Please, don't." Where did that come from? How stupid could she be?

He backed away.

Her head stayed down. She'd blown it big time now.

"No wonder I like you." He patted her leg.

He likes me? Her heart accelerated.

"You gotta lotta guts for a freshman. Most don't know the word 'no.' I respect that in you."

"Thanks." She stared at her feet.

He lightly touched her arm. "What would you say to coming with me to a movie tomorrow night?"

Her heart pattered again. What did he see in her? "Sure," she said so soft she wondered if he heard.

"Listen, if you wanna head back to your dorm, I'll walk with ya. I'll ask a buddy to keep an eye on things here for a few minutes. I'd prefer you don't walk back by yourself."

Each nerve in her body pulsed. "I'd like that." She tried to speak a little louder, sound more confident.

"Great. I'll be right back." He bolted into the house and returned seconds later with a red University of Wisconsin letter jacket. "It's a little chilly out here. Thought you'd need something to keep you warm."

"Thanks." She slipped the coat on. Why couldn't she think of anything else to say?

"Could I take your hand?"

She looked up at him. He was still smiling. Oh, and he had a great smile. Her legs shook as she stood and accepted his hand. Boy, did it feel good.

CHAPTER *twenty three*

"Janet wants to set you up."

Richard's shot circled the hoop then rimmed out. He frowned at Marcus' statement and the missed basket. He never used to miss such an easy shot.

"H." Marcus' voice echoed in the small church gym that retained the gamy aroma from an afternoon of hoops.

Two games of one-on-one had established Marcus' superiority. But, this was H.O.R.S.E. Richard never lost. He'd just spotted Marcus one letter. It would be "lights out" from here on in.

"I don't need help getting dates." The truth was, he had no desire to date. For the first time in his memory, he'd lost his attraction for women. There was only one he wanted, and she no longer wanted him.

Marcus set up for his next shot and let it go. The ball swished through. "That's why you're still single."

"You've always told me I date too much." Richard's follow-up shot hit the board then flew off to the side. Man, what was wrong with him today?

"O," Marcus said.

Richard chased after the ball, removing his sweat soaked T-shirt along the way. It had been a long time since he'd worked up this good a sweat. Marcus' blind date idea made it worse.

Marcus drove in for a lay-up and banked it in. "Well, now, we think you need some help. You haven't chosen wisely in the past."

Richard's lay-up whooshed through. *Finally*. "And you think you could do better?"

"Janet thinks so." Marcus' shot from the free-throw line hit the rim and bounced back.

So, his brother was human after all.

"What's it been? A month?" Marcus asked.

"And a half." Richard knew the exact number of days that had passed since he saw Sheila but wasn't about to admit it. He dribbled to the three-point line and arched a shot. It glided in. *Two in a row.* "Nothin' but net." Maybe he was finally getting his rhythm back. "So it's not some ploy to make me forget Sheila?"

"Would it help?" Marcus netted the three pointer.

"Probably not." Richard tried for the dunk, missed and crashed to the ground, scraping his hands and knees. He held his breath and clenched his fists as he worked through the burn.

"You're not young anymore." Marcus offered a hand. "You used to kill me with that move."

"I need a little practice." He stretched out his limbs making sure he still had movement and no broken bones. Tomorrow would be the true test.

"And a hoop that's ten inches lower." Marcus eased in a free throw.

"You wound me." Richard's shot hit the rim and bounced over the backboard.

"R."

Richard gave chase again and considered Marcus' offer. It had been six weeks. And three days. He glanced at the clock. Plus one hour and twenty-five minutes. Maybe it was time to move on. "What do you know about her?" Richard dribbled back onto the court.

"Her name's Karen. She's a long-time friend of Janet's."

"Go to our school?"

"Nope. Private school in town." Marcus made a shot from the top of the key.

"Don't you miss anymore? I used to be able to beat you in seven shots." Richard threw one up that completely missed the backboard. "And I can't hit the broad side of a barn."

"S. I've got the boys to challenge me." Marcus cleared a perfect hook shot.

I need to get in some practice. Sheila would have been a good opponent.

It all came back to her, didn't it? It was definitely time to move on. "What else do you know?" Richard rolled his hook in.

"She's a CPA, a widow." Marcus pointed to two brown metal folding chairs set at the side of the court. "Water break time."

Richard jogged over retrieving his water bottle. Could he date someone besides Sheila? His gut ached just thinking about it. "Is she pretty?" Richard sat on the floor, stretching out his legs and arms, preparing for a come-from-behind victory.

"That's subjective." Marcus smiled. He sat in a chair and guzzled a drink.

"Oh, real promising."

"Look, she's a nice woman and, yeah, I think she's pretty, but she's no New York babe."

Not such a bad thing. "I don't know." It didn't feel right. "Just talking about it makes me think I'm cheating on Sheila."

"She broke it off. You're free." Marcus shook his head. "Sheesh, I didn't think I'd ever see the day when you had it this bad for someone."

"Me neither." Richard laughed dryly. "It sort of ruins my rep, doesn't it?"

"That's good."

How true. They finished their water and jogged back onto the court. "So, what does she know of me?" He had no desire to open himself up to more hurt. Explaining the past did precisely that.

"Probably everything. Like I said, she's a good friend of Janet's."

Good, there would be nothing to hide. "When and where?"

"Saturday night. Bowling."

"I haven't bowled in years. Do you think my ball's still at the house?"

"Saw it the other day."

"I don't know."

"We'll play for it." Marcus dribbled to the top of the key, set himself, then arched a perfect shot into the basket. "Okay, this one's for all the marbles. You miss it, you spell H-O-R-S-E, you go on the date."

"I sink it, I'm off." Richard stood where his brother had

been, bounced the ball twice and eyed the basket, giving a careful aim. No way would he miss this.

"She's got an eight-year-old son."

The ball dribbled off the end of Richard's fingers. "Convenient omission." Frowning, he ran after the ball.

"Slight oversight." Marcus stood beneath the net with his arms crossed.

"That doesn't count." Richard dribbled back into place.

"You bet it does."

He attempted the basket again. This time the ball swished through. "Two out of three?"

"Sorry Ricky." Marcus draped a clammy arm around Richard's shoulder. Richard held his breath. They were both in desperate need of a shower. "Think of it this way. Your loss is still a win. You'll like Karen."

"COME ON, SPIN IN, THERE YOU GO. THERE YOU go!" Richard pumped his fist as his bowling ball struck the one pin, just off center, and the remaining nine pins lay back like precisely spaced dominoes, adding to the clamor of pins falling and bowlers cheering throughout the alley.

Even after all these years, he hadn't lost his touch. The last time he'd picked up a bowling ball was during his college days when bowling was synonymous with beer and cigars. Smoking was no longer allowed indoors, but its ghostly tentacles had permanently stained this ancient alley's walls, ceiling, and even the air. And beer? It still flowed, but no longer appealed. Perhaps he should give Sheila a call and thank her for soiling his craving for a Heineken.

Perhaps he was nuts to even think it.

He wiped his hands on a towel and glanced at his watch. Stomach bubbling, he looked to the door. They'd be here soon. How in the world did he let Marcus talk him into a blind date? No way was he ready to start dating again, not when Sheila still dominated his thoughts.

Would he ever be ready? He slumped in a seat, wiped a towel across his face, and closed his eyes. How long did it take to get over someone?

Well, they would bowl tonight. He'd pretend to smile and have fun. He'd thank Karen for the evening then tell her he wasn't up to dating. It had nothing to do with her. That would be the truth, no matter how the evening turned out.

A burst of cold air warned him that the outside door opened. He peered up as a petite blonde-haired woman entered, followed by Janet and Marcus. His lips curved into a true smile. Marcus was right. She wasn't New York pretty—glamorous, like he was used to. Like Sheila. Rather, she was what he'd call country or "girl next door" pretty, cute even with straight hair cut short and tucked neatly behind her ears. Her jeans, tan blouse, and denim jacket were typical dress for this small town. *Sheila wouldn't have been caught dead in that.* He shook his head. Forget her!

He hurried to greet them and offered his hand. "Hi, I'm Richard. You must be Karen."

"Nice to meet you." Her gaze briefly acknowledged him before darting away. She tugged her hand away too.

Oh boy. This was going to be a fun evening. "Let me help you with your ball. Our lane's right over here."

"Thank you." A smile flickered on her face before she peered down and walked ahead with Janet.

Marcus grabbed Richard's arm, stopping him. He stood mute until the ladies reached the lane. "She's shy." He kept his tone low.

"No kidding!" Richard whispered and shook off his brother.

"She'd be good for you. Make you think of someone other than yourself for once, rather than build up your ego."

"My ego's suffered enough lately."

"She's fragile. Needs someone to treat her gently, someone who could be a good father to her son."

Oh, now it all made sense. "Is that what this is all about? You want some kid to have a father?"

Marcus shrugged. "I guess that's partly true. I know how much you like kids and frankly, your time is running out."

"That's not the reason to date someone. Kids are the one thing I feel I've missed out on. I was hoping with Sheila—"

"With Sheila you'd be single and miserable for the rest of

your life. Now Karen's another story."

"You've got the wrong person. She's not my type."

"She's the type you need, and you'd be good for Ryan."

"I'd just hurt her and the boy."

"At least give it a try."

Oh, he'd be his charming self for the night, but that was it. He shot Marcus a warning glance. "You owe me."

Marcus grinned. "By the end of the evening, you'll be thanking me."

Yeah, and Antarctica's a great place for a honeymoon too.

Just a couple hours, and it'll be over.

Gripping Karen's bag, he and Marcus joined the women. He sat next to her as Janet typed their names into the computer. Time to turn on his Brooks charm.

He touched Karen's arm and smiled. "Thanks for coming tonight."

Biting into her lip, she glanced up. "I'm glad it worked out for you."

"Yeah, me too." He resisted the urge to roll his eyes. "Marcus tells me you're a CPA. Do you work for a firm?"

"Self-employed." She angled her head toward the alley as Janet threw a gutter ball. "I've always been able to be home for Ryan."

"Ryan. He's your son?"

She looked back at him with a sincere smile. Not a bad smile, either. Definitely no ulterior motives behind it. "Yeah, he's my son."

"Tell me about him."

She reached into her purse and pulled out a school picture. "He loves reading and music. He's good at school too, most any subject. Sports haven't been his thing, but then he never had his dad to play with him. He died when Ryan was two."

"I'm sorry." What else could he say to that?

"Thanks." She put the picture away and turned toward the alley just as Marcus threw a pin-exploding strike.

She stood quickly and retrieved her ball as if she couldn't get away from him fast enough.

He rested his forehead on his fingers. *Thank you, Marcus.*

This was going to be one long evening.

But once it was over, he could get back to the farm, sleep, dodge church in the morning and drive in to Minneapolis tomorrow. He'd thank his neighbor's college-aged son for house-sitting and let the boy know he'd be moving back soon. He'd check on his new office, find a hotel room for the night, and make business contacts on Monday.

Just the thought of returning to the business world excited him. At least he had something to look forward to.

But until then, he wasn't about to give up on his date. Karen deserved that courtesy, even if Marcus didn't.

Crossing his arms, he leaned back in his chair and watched her lay the ball on the lane as gently as he'd cradle a baby. Her ball floated lazily down the lane then touched the one pin just off center, and all pins slowly laid down.

He grinned at her when she walked back to the seat. "Quite the style."

She peered down, but still showed a glimmer of a smile.

There was something appealing about her unassuming shyness. Sure beat the games Sheila played.

So why did he miss Sheila so badly?

He picked up his ball, strode to the lane, and fired it, releasing his frustrations. Two lousy pins fell. Wonderful. He rotated his shoulders and waited for the ball to return.

It was time the phantom of Sheila stopped interfering in his life.

Inhaling a cleansing breath, he grasped his ball. *Focus.* He eyed the pins, took three steps and released. The ball hugged the gutter then curved back in and knocked the remaining pins down. "Yes!" He pumped his fist.

"Your style's not too bad either." Karen glanced up, wearing a cautious smile as he sat across from her.

"Now, don't go stroking his ego like that." Marcus leaned back in his chair, wincing at Janet's failed attempt to stay out of the gutter.

"She can stroke it all she wants."

Karen's smile grew into an adorable grin. "Marcus tells me you're starting a business."

And this was a conversation he'd love to have. "He's right. I'm opening an office in Minneapolis. Marc begged me to stay with him, but the pay is lousy."

"My good workers get paid very well."

Karen gave Marcus a shove. "Go throw your ball."

"Getting pushy now, eh?" Grinning, Marcus stood.

Okay, the lady's got chutzpa. Anyone who can push Marcus around can't be all too bad. Maybe tonight wasn't going to be so bad after all. Maybe this was the perfect remedy for forgetting Sheila.

SWEAT GREASED RICHARD'S HANDS, LIKE A KID on his first high school date, as he drove Karen home. No, he wouldn't kiss her. That, in itself, was a change. Did he want to ask her out again? She was undeniably different from other women he'd dated. Whether that was good or bad, he was unsure yet. Perhaps he should try again, without the hawking eyes of his brother. Would it hurt to ask?

He pulled his truck up to the curb by her house, but his thoughts still waffled. Karen stepped out of the pickup before he had a chance to stop her. Keeping his arms at his sides, he hurried around the truck to accompany her to the entryway. He held the screen door as she unlocked the other.

She took a step inside before looking back, and smiled without peering down, a sign that her shyness was fading.

That convinced him. "Would you care to try it again? This time without the chaperones?"

She laughed. A glorious, uncalculating laugh. "Sure. What do you have in mind?"

He shrugged. "I guess I haven't thought that far. But, Saturdays work best for me."

"Oh." Her smile faded. "I've got plans for next Saturday."

"Oh, okay." Surprisingly, it wasn't. "Maybe another time."

"You could come along."

"I could?"

"It's a hayride. A church-sponsored singles event complete with roasted hot dogs and s'mores, if you go for that kind of thing."

"I'd enjoy it. I'll see you on Saturday." Bowling and a hayride. What his former girlfriends would think of his dating habits now. Truly, it didn't matter. He actually looked forward to the next Saturday night.

CHAPTER *twenty four*

Sheila closed her condo door and wilted against it. Another dating failure. The second this month—the third since Richard, to be exact. It wasn't that they were bad men: a gourmet chef, an art museum curator, and the last, a sportswear salesman—a competitor whom she'd known for years and finally said "yes" to. They were all interesting, but their personalities didn't click with hers, giving her no reason to pursue a relationship.

Perhaps it was too soon. Or, perhaps dating had become more than a game. Perhaps dating now served a higher purpose, the pursuit of a committed relationship rather than meaningless evenings out. Escaping the stresses of work by going out with an endless stream of men no longer constituted time well spent. Rather, it had become a worthless, waste of time.

She straightened and walked to her dining room table. The rose was wilting in the vase. Tomorrow she'd buy another Saturday rose.

Richard was at fault for this ritual.

Following their breakup the shriveling blossom on her table reminded her too much of him so she removed the flower and vase completely. But then, her table appeared sad and empty. She substituted flowers of varying types and shades, but none seemed to fit her home as precisely as the orange rose. It was amazing how well Richard knew her right from the beginning.

Finally, she gave up on trying to improve on the perfection of the original and returned to it. It had been a few months since she'd seen Richard. With a few dates in between, she was certain the simple centerpiece would no longer be a reminder of what she gave up. She stared at the lifeless flower and fingered away a tear. No, she didn't miss him.

She yawned and covered her mouth. Time for bed, but if she went to bed now, she'd first see Richard and his tilting smile, and she'd smile back. Her eyes would close. Richard would disappear, and the shadowy monsters would take his place.

No, she couldn't sleep now. Maybe if she stayed up long enough, wore herself out enough, she'd be too tired to dream or remember them come morning.

She glanced around her living room. There had to be something to take her mind off her fatigue and failures. Definitely not TV, and the classical novel she was attempting to read would put her to sleep much too quickly.

Her gaze landed on the artwork resting against the wall next to her loveseat. It had been a gift to Richard, a piece of contemporary art he frowned at. He claimed he didn't *get* the four brown lines heading in a straight line toward the end of the print or the single line that started out straight and brown, like the rest, then gradually shifted to a shade of blue before the line meandered over the canvas. It would have matched his living room perfectly, would have given it a more eclectic feel.

It reminded her of him.

He'd told her he was grateful for the thought, but wanted to keep his home rustic, peaceful. At the time she said she understood, so they chose a print by a local artist instead: one with a log cabin tucked in the woods, with deer drinking from a narrow creek snaking between the trees. That was the serenity he strived for.

Well, he could just have his pastoral picture.

She kept the modern painting for herself, but never put it up. Now was as good a time as any. It should go right above her fireplace. All she needed to do was find picture hangers and her hammer. They should be in the drawer in her kitchen—the drawer she was afraid to open because it was the resting place for all her seldom-used and frequently forgotten miscellaneous items. It would be difficult to close once open.

She pulled on the drawer's handle. It glided out smoother than anticipated. How could she have forgotten? Richard had arranged it shortly before their breakup. First, he'd laid dark blue contact paper. Then he'd tied up loose cords, sorted nails and screws into small containers, and used a grated silverware divider to separate the hammer, wrench, and screwdrivers. He had done the same with her entire home, with her blessing of course.

He'd been so good at sorting through her chaos. *Boy, could I use him now.* The thought escaped her heart before she had time to close it.

Scrunching her lips together, she took a breath in through her nose. *Stop thinking of him and hang the picture.* She released her breath. The container labeled picture hangers was right in front, the hammer next to it. She lifted the hammer, revealing something white beneath the divider.

No. Leave it alone. But, she couldn't resist. She raised the divider and retrieved the white envelope. *Breathe.* She lifted the flap and looked in. The card was still there of course. Why did she expect otherwise? She slipped the card out and opened it.

She smiled.

Then tears trickled down her cheeks, stealing her smile.

Of all the dates she had, of all the sophisticated men she'd gone out with, only Richard would do bunny ears.

BEFORE RICHARD HAD MARCUS' OFFICE DOOR closed, his brother smirked with his characteristic eloquence. "Dumped you, huh?"

Richard shot his brother an angry stare then eyed the ceiling before taking the chair on the other side of Marcus' desk. "You know?"

"I am married to Karen's best friend."

"Three dumps, three strikes in a row, now. Marissa. Sheila. Karen." He swung his arms as if swinging an imaginary baseball bat. "Does that mean I should leave the batter's box? Give up dating altogether?"

"Could you?"

"I doubt it, but I'd sure like to." He hadn't felt serious about Karen but enjoyed their few dates. She'd taken his mind off Sheila, so that was more than anyone or anything else did.

Marcus rolled his chair backward and rested his head in his

hands. "So what happened? What did you do?"

"I did nothing!" Richard combed his fingers through his hair. "Maybe I should have. Is it okay to kiss someone after four dates?" He wanted to after the third, but when he escorted her to her door it didn't feel right. That had never stopped him before. "I don't know what's proper anymore. I thought I was being respectful."

"I doubt that was the problem."

"Then what was? I don't know what I did wrong. She said she didn't see a future for us, and if I became serious it would be harder to break it off. She'd rather do it now. I hadn't even thought that far out yet. I was enjoying being with someone. Someone different. Someone straightforward, who doesn't play games to get noticed, someone who knows about me, so I don't have to convince them I'm not who my past says I am."

"You don't see it, do you?" Marcus rolled forward, folded his hands on his desk and smiled.

"What?"

"She was tired of being compared with Sheila."

"Sheila? What does she have to do with Karen? I never brought her up."

"Oh, maybe not her name, but look at what you told me. All the things you like about Karen are the things that drove you nuts about Sheila. Sorry, Ricky." Marcus leaned back in his chair and shrugged keeping the cocky smile on his face. "I hate to say this, but you're still not over Sheila."

Richard moaned. Marcus was right. Again. "So tell me, how do I make that happen?"

"Come back to church. Give her up to God."

Same old pat answer. Should have expected it from Marcus. Well, he wouldn't do it. Without saying another word, he stood and stomped from his brother's office, slamming the door behind him.

MEGHAN HUGGED TEXTBOOKS AGAINST HER winter coat and opened her dorm room door. All she needed was her Norton Anthology, and then she could hurry to Doran's house. It was hard to believe studying could be so much fun.

Kalyn looked up as she entered. The girl's puckered mouth and narrowed eyes warned Meghan to be quiet. Her roommate could be such a head case at times. Kalyn and Doran were so different.

Meghan crossed the room and pulled her book off the shelf.

"You're seeing my brother again tonight?" Kalyn's glare flung darts toward Meghan.

But Meghan smiled anyway. "Yes, I am." Doran's sister would not spoil this evening.

"I wish I never introduced the two of you." Kalyn crossed her arms and fell back onto their dorm couch. "I can't believe how boring both of you have become. Doran hasn't hosted a party in weeks cuz he's too busy seeing you. Everyone's bugging me about it too. They all wonder what's happened to him."

"Just tell 'em the truth. He needs to study to get good grades. He's going to grad school. That's all we're doing tonight, by the way." Why did she justify Doran's actions? He didn't have to answer to his little sister.

Kalyn sat up and smiled. Not a happy smile, rather a sarcastic one. "You're studying. At his place. Alone. His roommates will be at the party."

Wrongo. Her relationship with Doran wasn't at all like that.

"I can't believe how naive you are. Let me give you a little heads up on what my brother will be studying."

Just leave the room. Ignore her. Meghan stuffed the book into her backpack and crossed the room to the door.

"My first guess is that he'd really like to study anatomy—hands on, if you get my drift. I guess I won't expect you home tonight."

Meghan grasped the doorknob and squeezed. "You don't know your brother very well." She flung the door open.

"Right." Kalyn giggled.

Meghan stomped out and slammed the door behind her, but Kalyn's laughter filtered through. Meghan clenched her teeth, holding in a scream. Thank goodness, it was a ten-block walk to Doran's house. The crisp November air should help her cool off.

Holding tight to the metal railing, she descended the dorm's icy steps. When she reached the bottom, she zipped her coat and pulled gloves from her pockets. Her toes were already chilled, but she wasn't about to go back and get her boots.

Kalyn had no clue what she was talking about. Doran had always respected her. She wasn't ready for a physical relationship, and Doran never forced the issue. That was one of the many things she liked about him.

Her pace slowed as she turned onto the sidewalk, and her throat tightened. His reputation did concern her though, and always lurked in the back of her mind, courtesy of Kalyn, no doubt. What if Doran hadn't changed? What if she was only seeing what she wanted in him? What if he got bored with her?

She kicked at a flattened beer can. It skidded a few feet ahead. Maybe she was worrying too much. She kicked the same can. It flew a few yards this time. She wasn't afraid to say "no." At least she'd learned that much growing up, and it saved her more than once. She quickened her pace and smiled. Doran liked the fact that she wasn't easy.

Minutes later, she stood at his door and rang his doorbell. The door opened before she removed her finger.

"Meggie." His eyes twinkled as he bent to kiss her, warming her all the way to her frozen toes. Kissing was okay. Better than okay, really. Perhaps there was something to be said for dating an experienced guy. "Come on in." He held her gloved hand and pulled her through the door. "The guys are gone—probably for the night." He shut the door and took both her hands, removed her gloves, and leaned in for another kiss.

Hearing Kalyn's words echo in her head, Meghan turned away.

He dropped her hands. "Something wrong?" Concern sounded in his voice, not anger thank goodness.

"Uh, not really. I'm just eager to get studying." Forcing a smile, she removed her jacket and shoes. "I don't want to get distracted, you know?"

His smile was genuine and, boy, was it gorgeous. "You're probably right." He threw her jacket on the back of his couch. "Come in the kitchen." He waved for her to follow him. "I've got my books set up there. I can make some hot chocolate to warm you up, or a cappuccino, if you'd like."

She relaxed. Doran wouldn't have set up the study area in the kitchen if he had other motives. "Hot chocolate would be great." She followed him to the kitchen and dropped her backpack on a chair. His books and notes occupied much of the space. "What are you studying?" She picked up a thick book covered with a paper grocery bag and paged through it.

"Mostly poli-sci and anatomy ..."

Meghan didn't hear what came next. Kalyn's silly insinuations just wouldn't go away. She dropped his book and placed her anthology on the table before slumping in an empty chair.

He set an insulated red Wisconsin Badgers mug in front of her and handed her a spoon. "What's up, Meggie? You seem far off tonight."

She stirred in the marshmallows until they blended with the chocolate. "Oh, just thinking about something." She lifted the spoon and tasted. Its warmth traveled down her throat.

Doran took the seat opposite her and placed a similar mug by his books. "Talk about it so you can get to work."

Arghh. If she told him, he'd think she was a whiner.

He picked up a pen and reclined in his chair, clicking the end of the pen. "Come on, what's up, Meggie?"

She glanced down at her closed book. "I had a fight with Kalyn tonight."

Doran laughed. "Let me guess. She's upset with me. She thinks I've become boring."

Shrugging, Meghan kept her head down. "That's part of it."

"Oh? And the rest?"

Biting into her lower lip, she peered up. "She thinks I'm going to stay the night."

Doran's eyes narrowed. "I wouldn't mind, you know."

She looked back down. Oh, yeah, she knew. "I can't. I'm not ready." Please, oh, please, don't let this chase him away.

"Then we wait till you're ready. I've never forced myself on anyone."

How many *anyone's* were out there? "You won't breakup with me cuz I'm not ready?"

"That's what your problem is?"

Nodding, she bit into her lip again.

His chair scraped against the linoleum floor. He circled the table and squatted to her eye level. "Meggie, I like that you stand up for yourself, that you don't have to follow the crowd. You're more mature than most girls your age. So study. Don't worry about me. I'll walk you home at a decent hour."

"Thanks." Moments like this always seemed to leave her with the one-word answers, but he didn't seem to mind.

Before he stood, he stole a quick kiss. "Now that's it for the night. Study." He pointed to her book, then returned to his chair.

Boy, was she lucky. She peeked through her lashes as Doran dragged a highlighter across a sentence. Maybe she'd be ready sooner than she thought.

She opened her calculus book and set her calculator on the table.

Two hours later, her eyelids begged to close.

"Meggie."

"Huh?" Her shoulder shook.

"It's time to go. You keep falling asleep."

"Oh." Sitting up, she yawned and stretched as he gathered her books, stuffed them in her backpack and slung it over his shoulder.

Half-awake, she leaned on Doran during the walk back to her dorm. By the time they got there, the cold air had awakened her, but she didn't let him know. His arm around her back, supporting her, felt too good to disturb. The walk back to her dorm passed much too quickly.

They stopped outside her building, but he kept his arm tight as he leaned in for a kiss, then he rested his forehead against hers. "We'll do something fun Friday night, okay? No books."

Friday? Drats! She forgot to tell him. "I'm leaving right after my last class on Friday."

"Really?" His shoulders slumped. "Where to?"

His disappointment lit a smile inside her. "Home. Mom and Dad are going on a vacation, and they'll be gone over Thanksgiving. I'm flying home for an early celebration."

"Bummer."

"Yeah, I know, but I'll be back Monday afternoon. I'll only

miss a few classes."

"Then I'll see you Monday night."

"Monday night." Her eyes locked with his. The emerald seemed to sparkle even more tonight. Was this what love felt like? Would it really be so bad taking that next step with him? Her stomach gurgled as she considered it. Good thing Doran was willing to wait. "Kalyn is wrong about you, you know."

Bringing a hand to her cheek, he whispered, "Kalyn doesn't know me very well." He kissed her again. "That's so you don't forget me."

Like that could happen. She bit her lip and grinned. "Hardly."

"Good night, Meggie."

"Night, Doran." She glided into the dorm.

CHAPTER *twenty five*

Richard stood by his pickup in his parent's driveway with the frigid November air swirling freely around him. The entire family had come to see him off, to hug their good-byes, to show their support for him and his business that would officially open in the morning.

It had been too long since he'd been on his own. Nearly three months. Three months of working for Marcus, home cooking, pleas for his salvation, quiet walks under the stars—lonely walks he wanted to share with Sheila.

Three months, and she still occupied his thoughts.

His business should take care of that. There wouldn't be time to think of her. He'd be too busy marketing and drawing up proposals and supplying his services. He should be able to lose himself in his work and hopefully find success along the way. And success would come with sheer honesty.

There would be no more deceptions, half truths, or stretching the truth. If some inquired about his absence from the work force, they would know the truth as well, even if it cost him clients. There would be no more secrets and no more burdens to carry around. His services would be supplied with integrity, something this family surrounding him could be proud of.

He hugged his nieces first, and his sister, and promised to stop by often. The nephews couldn't wait to visit him. Probably during Christmas vacation. He looked forward to that time nearly as much as Nathan and Joshua, if not more. He accepted his dad's hand and was pulled into a bear hug that didn't want to release. His mother kissed his cheek, before hugging him. Then, she handed him a wrapped gift the size of a large shirt box.

He eyed the box in his arms with suspicion. It was heavy. Too heavy to be cookies which would have made a wonderful going-away present. He turned it over to rip the paper and felt his mother's hand on his.

"Not now." Her eyes misted. "Wait until you get home. We love you so much, Ricky."

"Love you too, Mom, Dad, everyone." He looked down so they wouldn't see how this farewell was affecting him. Bittersweet. His family had been convinced his stay at the farm meant a return to his faith was imminent. Disappointment misted their eyes, and lingered in their hugs. Again, he had let them down.

Their chorus of well wishes and promised visits tugged at his heart.

And pricked his conscience.

He couldn't do what they wanted. Perhaps it was the last bit of pride he held onto, the last piece of himself he dragged from New York, the last flicker of familiarity with his former way of life. Everything else—every little bit of him—had been destroyed, stolen, sold, donated, or left behind, and he refused to give up that piece of himself. With each embrace, the force of the chain and the key pressed into his heart. How could he return to a God who punished the innocent and let the guilty go free?

He opened his truck door and tossed his mother's package onto the passenger seat. Taking a breath, he turned around and smiled, grasping onto the door. "I'm just a couple hours away. Call me anytime, or come visit even. You know you're all welcome." Anytime.

Man, was he going to miss them, but it was time for him to grow up, to stop running, to face life head on.

He sat in his pickup and drove off, venting a heavy sigh as his truck rumbled down the gravel driveway aiming for home.

Home ...

Hopefully his house would soon earn the title. It would have been easier if Sheila were alongside him making it a home, but that obviously wasn't going to happen. He'd make the best of it on his own. A dog would be nice. One just like Prince. But, his business required too much time. Even a dog deserved more attention than he had to give.

He steered his pickup onto the county road, stealing one more glance at the farm. It felt good to leave. It was time. He'd been away from the business world far too long and couldn't wait to dive in again. Four clients were already lined up, and he was writing proposals for several more. Creating *Integrity Business Solutions* was truly looking like the right decision.

That was a much easier decision than the one to be made about the box riding in his passenger seat. He glanced over at the package. For some reason, its unknown contents disturbed him. Knowing his mom, it was bound to be something presenting a spiritual challenge, a challenge he didn't want to face tonight. When he would be ready, remained to be seen.

RICHARD SANK INTO HIS OFFICE CHAIR ABSORB-ing the scene around him: the scent of the new black leather chair, the rustic beauty of two wildlife prints framed in cherry wood, the softening texture of green foliage sprawling over his credenza and poised in the corners. His mother's touch was effective. Impressions were vitally important in his business, and he needed to begin with the greatest possible impact. The picture window view overlooking downtown Minneapolis made the deepest impression. It wasn't New York City. No. It was better. It was home. This was where he belonged.

It felt so good to be in an office again, to be wearing a suit again. This was the world that motivated him—one where he'd flourish. Now that he had his priorities straight, he wouldn't leave. It was probably the first right decision he made in years, and he took it in like a kid in a candy shop: playing with his electric pencil sharpener, whirling around in his chair, setting up his computer wallpaper with pictures of his family. For months this was the moment—the freedom—he'd waited for, longed for and at last, it was here.

The intercom beeped, interrupting his musings. "Yes, Emma." His newly hired assistant, Emma Hatch, inspired complete confidence. Ethan recommended her as someone who thrives in a small office setting. Already, Emma proved Ethan correct.

"Mr. Hamilton is here for his appointment."

"Thank you. Send him in."

It was time to go to work, and he was thrilled. But, his heart still felt an emptiness. Was it for Sheila or was it for something much deeper?

No time to think on it now as Mr. Hamilton walked through the door.

"ARE YOU SURE YOU'RE OKAY?"

Sheila heard the concern in Ethan Johnson's voice, even over the phone. She smiled for the first time in weeks as she leaned against her kitchen cupboard, momentarily taking her mind off the prescription bottle waiting on the counter behind her. It wasn't atypical for Ethan to stretch the boundaries of his job. His friendly counsel had proven invaluable on more than one occasion.

"I'll be fine." There was little truth in her reply, but it would make Ethan feel better. "Again, I feel I need to apologize for bringing the boss down on you."

"Hey, don't worry about it. Griggs was going to find out anyway. Now I don't have to anticipate it anymore. Our jobs are intact. That's all that matters."

"I guess you're right." She turned around and picked up her prescription bottle. Yes, Ethan's employment was secure. Her career was another story. It had been months since she performed her duties to the high standards she spent years honing and perfecting, standards Wharton expected from her, and rightly so.

Today, Wharton's CEO, Spencer Griggs, had given her a stern reprimand, letting her know he was fully aware of her recent ineffectiveness. He'd been blunt, telling her she looked awful, and needed sleep. He demanded she take the remainder of the week off, return next Tuesday and Wednesday for the board meetings, and then not until after Thanksgiving. He told her to take a vacation. She almost laughed in his face. What possible benefit could she gain from vacationing alone?

"... and don't be afraid to contact the counselor, either, Sheila." Ethan's voice jerked her back to the present, and she juggled the phone receiver between her hands. Her attention span, like everything else in her life, was failing. "Their lines are answered twenty-four-seven."

Facts she knew all too well. It hadn't helped. "I'll remember." She covered her yawning mouth.

"Good. Now get some rest. We'll see you next week."

"Thanks, Ethan." She hit the end button, disconnecting her link with the human race. That was good. No more smiling to make a sale, to prove to others she was happy, to convince herself she could go on.

Go on to what? What would she do until next week? Maybe her work performance had been subpar lately, but taking the time off would only make it worse. It would make her worse. She rolled the prescription bottle in her hand. Hopefully, this was the panacea she sought.

She pushed down the lid unscrewing it from the bottle and dumped one blue convex tablet onto her hand, laughing ironically at its size. Control of her life rested in this miniscule object. She hadn't relinquished control since she left home some eighteen years ago. Now her happiness, or to be honest, her sanity, rested in the pill's effectiveness. It was supposed to provide the sleep she'd been deprived of, deep enough sleep to bury her nightmares into her subconscious.

She placed the bottle on the cupboard and opened her fridge. Yuzu Perrier would wash it down. After that, she'd find comfort in her bed. She swallowed the medicine and half the container of designer water, then picked up the medicine bottle to twist the cap back on.

A thought flitted past. *How many would it take for her to never wake up?*

She stared at the bottle, tipped it over, and counted them out stopping at ten. Ten? Would that do it? No, better make it fifteen. *Eleven, twelve …*

Oh my God, what am I doing? She dumped the pills from her hand into the sink then threw the bottle onto the cupboard scattering the remaining tablets. Goosebumps broke out on her body. How could she even contemplate such an action? She hurried upstairs to her bedroom, and slammed the door to her room and the drug's lure. When she awoke tomorrow, she hoped—she prayed, the temptation would be gone.

CHAPTER *twenty six*

Richard's garage door lowered in cranky descent shutting out winter's howl. It was good to be off the roads before they got too icy. The first snowstorm of the season was always a treacherous one for Minnesota drivers who tended to forget, over the summer, how to maneuver on snow frosted roads. Home was the safest place. Besides, he'd accomplished what he wanted today.

He set his briefcase beside the end table before settling into the recliner. His eyes closed and a contented smile rose. One week complete. One exhilarating week, ending with a victorious Saturday morning meeting. He hadn't lost his touch. Not that he worried about it, but over nine months had passed since he ran from Manhattan.

No more running for him.

He opened his eyes and frowned. If he was done running, then why did the gift from his mom remain wrapped? It lurked by the fireplace hearth, right where he'd placed it Sunday night, proffering a challenge. Who was he to back away? "Okay, Mom, I'll do it." Wherever she was, he imagined her smiling.

First, though, the mood needed to be established. He changed into worn Levi's and a sweatshirt. A lit fireplace chased off November's chill, scenting the room with woodsy pine. He selected a light-rock station and set the volume just loud enough to understand the lyrics, providing a tranquil background. All he lacked now was wine and a woman. He chuckled. *Oh, yeah. Real funny.* That was the last thing he needed.

He nuked a container of his mom's beef stroganoff. With the leftovers his mom sent from home, he'd be eating well for the next month. Another crafty ploy by his mother. She knew he'd return for more. He devoured the beef, soaking up every drop of gravy with a slice of bread.

Finally, it was time.

He carried his mom's package to the couch, removed the paper, and folded it to be reused. He tugged on the cover and stopped, his heart pulsing an erratic beat. Did he really want to know what she sent? It was probably something deep, something to influence his beliefs. He was doing just fine without those beliefs. His new business was proof of that.

Still, there would be no more evading.

He raised the cover and blew the breath from his lungs. The Bible he'd used during his teen years lay on top. He picked up the book with the cracking black cover and swallowed hard as he zipped it open. The dog-eared pages and texts, highlighted in a rainbow of hues, emphasized what this book once meant to him. When he flew to New York, he intentionally left it behind.

He placed the Bible on the coffee table then took out the remaining item. A scrapbook. A classic *Mom* gift. Moisture clouded his eyes as he spread the book open next to his Bible. Blinking away the tears, he leaned toward it resting his elbows on his knees.

The first pages held coloring sheets from Sunday school. One featured a picture, crayoned in blue, bypassing the lines. He laughed. Apparently, he'd never liked staying within the borders. Beneath his artistry it read, *Be patient, God isn't finished with me yet!* Next to the picture his mom had calligraphied a verse from Philippians. "He who began a good work in you will carry it on to completion until the day of Christ Jesus."

He who began a good work in me must be extremely disappointed.

A cartoon frog and the letters F.R.O.G. filled the next page. Fully Rely on God was typed below it. Right. It had been years since he relied on anyone but himself …

And look where it got him. Shaking his head, he flipped the page.

More pictures. More Bible verses and entreaties from his parents. All showing what God had once meant to him.

All highlighting what he'd thrown away.

He leaned back into his couch, tenting his hands in front

of his face. "What happened?" he mumbled. When did he stop calling on God and seeking him? When did he stop praying?

When had the world taken him captive?

That's exactly what had happened, wasn't it? He fingered the chain anchored around his neck. Could God really set him free?

The doorbell rang as if in answer. Richard glanced out his picture window that featured churning snow creating whiteout conditions. The storm's breath whistled through cracks Richard didn't realize the house had. Who in their right mind would be out in this weather?

He hurried to the door and opened it, holding tight to the knob to prevent the door from slamming against the wall, and felt his mouth drop open.

This was how God answered prayer?

"I'm really sorry to bother you," said a young man disguised as a snowman. He held up a baby carrier shrouded with blankets of fleece and snow. "I really thought I could beat the storm."

"No bother." Richard waved the man in, then forced the door closed. "I think it blew in earlier than the forecasters said it would."

"Tell me about it." The man set the baby carrier on the floor and pulled off the blankets revealing a sleeping infant's face. "My wife's not gonna be happy." He stood, frowning, and removed his gloves and jacket. "She's missing this little guy."

Richard accepted the man's coat and offered his hand. "Name's Richard Brooks."

"Max Belden."

Richard draped the coat over his arm. "You were heading home?"

"To Des Moines. They said south of the cities isn't supposed to get hit. Thought if I could just get there ... Man, Gina's not gonna be happy."

"I'm sure she'll be happy you two are safe." Richard glanced at the baby, amazingly content, fully trusting his father. *Maybe my child would have been like that.*

"I suppose so." Max scratched his neck. "I do appreciate you taking us in. I mean, it was scary out there, you know. I was just praying and praying that God would keep my car on the road

205

and not get stuck and then I saw your driveway. I'm afraid I'm blocking it, though. My little Honda's not too good at plowing through drifts."

Richard looked away from the napping baby and smiled at his guest. "We'll take care of it in the morning. Snow's supposed to let up this evening."

"I don't want to impose. I mean, I could leave once the snow stops."

"You're not imposing. Besides, the roads won't be cleared till tomorrow." Richard motioned to the couch. "Please, sit."

"Be glad to. I guess I'm pretty stressed." Max toted the carrier.

"I'm more than glad to help you and your ..." Richard glanced at the baby. "Your son?"

"Yep. Little Logan. Ten months yesterday."

My child would have been about ten months.

"You got any kids?"

I should have. He shook his head. "Lifelong bachelor."

"I once thought that was the way to go, but then I met Gina and now, well, I wouldn't give up this life for anything."

A life he could have had with Sheila.

Why was God shoving this in his face?

"Make yourself comfortable. I've got a phone in the kitchen—"

Max reached into his pocket and pulled out his cell. "Yeah, better give Gina a call."

"I'll hang your coat and prepare the guest room."

"Oh, I should go to the car first." Max stood. "Logan's formula's in there and his travel crib and diaper bag—"

"Just sit. I can get it for you. I don't think you want to leave your baby with a stranger."

"Uh, yeah, I guess you're right." Max sat and tossed his keys to Richard. "I do appreciate this, you know."

"Glad I could help." He was more than glad to leave the house now filled with reminders of how he'd messed up. God had some sense of humor, answering both his and the kid's prayer by plunking him on Richard's doorstep, showing Richard what he could have had if he'd only behaved.

CHAPTER *twenty seven*

Okay, God, I get the picture." Richard yelled into the storm as he trudged through the snow carting mounds of paraphernalia required to care for a baby for one night. Once in the house, he delivered it to his guest room.

He returned to the living room and found Max cuddling Logan while staring at the scrapbook.

"This you?" Max pointed to a picture taken outside a church of a dozen high school kids surrounded by several boxes of school supplies.

Richard sat next to Max and nodded. "The tall string bean. For a tenth-grade project, I organized the drive to collect donations for a mission trip to Guatemala. We helped build a school." There was a time when he put others first. Clenching his jaw, he flipped the page.

He wished he hadn't. His eleventh-grade prom picture glared back, mocking him. The string bean had filled out, and he knew it. Cockiness burned in his eyes and showed in the upturn of his mouth. He and Janet looked like an odd couple with him rising a foot above her, but her spunk more than made up for what she lacked in stature.

"She's really cute." Logan let out a tiny squawk and Max circled his hand over the baby's back.

Richard massaged his neck. "Yeah, she was." He'd loved her dancing green eyes and curly locks.

Even in the picture, mischief sparkled in those eyes. That was the last time they smiled together—as a couple anyway. He'd pressed her that night, wanting to go way beyond kissing. And she'd responded with a slap to his face.

One he deserved.

The five-mile midnight walk home should have taught him a lesson, but it made him more determined. When he broke up with her, he called her a prude.

The baby let out a piercing cry. "Guess someone's hungry. The diaper bag is where?"

Richard pointed toward the hallway. "First door on the left."

"Thanks." With Logan fussing on his shoulder, Max hurried to the bedroom and returned carrying a diaper bag. He pulled out a bottle and a can of premade formula.

"Can I help with that?"

"Sure. That'd be great. Gina's good at this three-handed thing, but me? I don't think I'll ever get the hang of it."

Richard wished Marissa had given him opportunity to try.

Logan's cry grew shrill as Richard carried the formula and bottle to the kitchen where he filled the bottle. He stored the remainder of the formula in the fridge and brought the bottle to Max. Seconds later Logan's cry quieted.

Richard rejoined Max on the couch and watched the child suckle from the bottle. What a life babies had—to be completely reliant on another person for their daily needs.

Which was what God wanted from him.

How could a grown man surrender to that?

"Mind if I keep looking?" Max nodded toward the scrapbook.

Richard stared at the picture of him and Janet. At that point in his life, he'd begun his surrender to the world.

Was that any different from surrendering to God?

Max pointed to the picture. "You keep in touch?"

Richard laughed as he stood and walked to the bookshelf. He picked up Marcus' family portrait and carried it to Max. "She married my brother."

"Oooh, sorry." He scrunched his nose. "Awkward, huh?"

If Max only knew. "She got the right brother." Richard hadn't seen tears when they broke up, but apparently, Marcus had. His brother had the sense to see brokenness and picked up the pieces. Richard's jealousy destroyed a once-close relationship. How could he have been so stupid?

"What about this girl?"

Richard's senior prom portrait faced the junior photo. By then, his surrender had been complete. He squinted, trying to recall the brunette's name. Kerry? No ... Kim? Uh-uh. Not that either. Bile stirred in his stomach. "It didn't go beyond the prom." Although, he was certain he slept with her on prom night. One of many to which he'd surrendered his body and ultimately his soul.

"You don't mind me looking at this, do you?" Max stuck his finger beneath the page but didn't turn it. "My wife's big into scrapbooking. I think I like looking at her albums as much as she likes making them."

"No. I don't mind." Nothing in here could embarrass him. Just glowing highlights of his faith-filled youth. Richard mentally rolled his eyes.

Max turned the page. It was blank.

More empty pages followed. Nothing of his life after high school. None of his grandiose achievements since then were worthy of a scrapbook. But then, success, money, and possessions don't display well in a memory album.

He graduated from college, ran to New York, and never looked back. Perhaps to run away from the fact that his brother had married his girl, the one he threw away, the only one he ever cared about.

Until Sheila.

Enough memories for now. Richard lifted the back to close the book and noticed a letter stuck inside the rear cover. Shaking his head, he read the note. A Bible verse—no surprise there—written by his father. "Return to the Lord your God for he is gracious and compassionate, slow to anger and abounding in love."

Richard closed the album, chuckling. His father never gave up, did he?

Did he really want his father to give up? Did he want his mom and dad to keep their faith silent? The bile in his stomach roiled.

Never.

"Your family Christian?" Max dug in his diaper bag and pulled out a cloth diaper. He flung it over his shoulder then propped Logan against it and tapped the baby's back.

"Very."

"Cool. Me too."

Logan released a juicy burp. If only life's problems were solved that easily.

Maybe if he stopped trying to do it all on his own ... Richard looked away to dab his eyes. "Just remember to cling to that faith." Wise words from a stupid man.

"I plan on it."

The churning in his stomach threatened to claw up his throat. It was time for a change of topic. Something safe. "I'm sorry, I've been a poor host." Being busy always kept God at bay. It had worked for years. He slapped his thighs and stood. "You must be freezing. Could I offer you a hot chocolate? I don't drink coffee, but I always keep some instant decaf." He aimed toward the kitchen.

"Hot chocolate would be awesome."

"How about a sandwich?"

"I ate just a bit ago, but thanks anyway."

Richard twisted the knob on his range lighting the gas burner beneath the teakettle, then removed a jar of homemade hot chocolate mix—courtesy of his mom, of course—from the cupboard. Still, the busyness didn't prevent his mind from ruminating.

During this past year, he blamed Marissa and that devastating night for everything. Losing his baby. Justin's death. Quitting his job. Even the break up with Sheila. But if he were honest with himself, that night was a summation of his grown up years. He'd brought it all on himself.

Richard stole a glance into the living room, at the memory book shouting at him, and wiped his eyes. Yes, he'd changed now and was better off for it. So, why didn't he feel better? Why wouldn't God's voice remain silent?

The whistle sang on his teakettle.

God sure had a strange way of communicating.

Maybe it was time to consider listening.

Tonight, he'd sleep on it.

"IT'S MOVING, DOCTOR. WHAT DO I DO?"

Through a foggy haze, Sheila detected the anxious face of a woman wearing a bright pink smock. The nurse's eyes centered on a man dressed in a white coat, a stethoscope draped around his neck. Another doctor, an older man, stood in the background laughing; an unending, insidiously evil laugh biting into her bones. The younger doctor's eyes reflected the nurse's anxiety as they stared down at the object in her hands: a bloody mass of tissue.

But, the mass moved.

The nurse wiped it, toweling blood away.

Chilling laughter persisted.

The fog cleared, and it became apparent what the nurse held. A baby. Too little to survive, but a child, none-the-less, with two legs and two arms.

A girl.

The infant's head was oversized, but her face already showed personality and recognizable features, even with sealed eyelids. Her skin was pale—translucent, like cellophane. A pearl-tinted skeleton and a brown liver were easily seen through it. The miniature child even had little fingers and toes no bigger than a Barbie doll's. She didn't appear to be fully human, but she moved, breathed, and probably felt pain.

"Let it die!" The scream tore from Sheila's throat.

The infant stilled.

Sheila awoke trembling, her breathing shallow, fast and fragmented. Those faces living in her dreams had names. They were real. It didn't make sense. They had told her she'd be all right. They promised her there would be no side effects, no pain. She believed them.

They had lied to her.

Why had she flushed away those pills?

Maybe after Wednesday, following the board meeting. Maybe then, she'd have the courage to permanently terminate her pain.

"LITTLE ONES TO HIM BELONG—" THE YOUNG father's melodic voice greeted Richard as he stepped from his bedroom Sunday morning. "They are weak, but he is strong."

Richard peeked into his living room where Max sat rocking Logan, the wide-eyed infant sucking in nourishment from a bottle.

"Yes, Jesus loves me. Yes, Jesus loves me. Yes, Jesus loves me. The Bible tells me so."

Richard leaned against the wall, hiding from Max, and gazed at the ceiling. Would he ever have a child he could sing to? Would he ever see that clear innocence, experience unflinching trust? He wanted to be more than Uncle Ricky. His arms ached to have someone hug him and call him Daddy. At his age, the door to fatherhood was rapidly closing, leaving precious little time to find someone to be his wife and mother to his children.

It could've been Sheila.

He clenched his fists, banishing her name.

Max's voice was pure, truthful. Max believed the sermon he was singing to his child. He believed Jesus loved him simply because the Bible told him so. The same Bible that said God loved the *world*, not just the churchgoers, not just the ones who awoke with praise on their lips. He loved the sinners too.

Richard leaned against the wall. Isn't that what he learned in Sunday school? What his parents' lives demonstrated? That God loved everyone so much he sent Jesus, his only son, to shoulder the burden of everyone's sins. Richard knew how heavy they felt to himself. How much more would they weigh on Jesus?

"Jesus loves me, this I know—" Max repeated.

How could you possibly love me, Jesus? Richard dragged his arm across his eyes. *Get a grip, Brooks.* He clenched his teeth and stepped into his living room wearing a glued-on smile.

The smile the young father returned was genuine. "Hey, good morning. Hope I didn't wake you. Logan's got a big set of pipes."

"I didn't hear a thing." Not until a few minutes ago, anyway. The song still reverberated in his head. He looked out the window, away from the beaming father. Sparkling sunlight filtered through his drapes. "Looks like I'll be able to plow you out no problem." The sooner, the better. "I'll throw together some breakfast, then head out."

"You really don't have to do breakfast for me." Max raised

Logan to his shoulder and patted his back. "I can grab something on the way home."

"No trouble. Breakfast consists of Wheaties and orange juice. Wish I could do more, but you wouldn't want to eat what I make."

Max laughed. "I'd tell you the same thing."

Richard walked to the kitchen and set breakfast out.

Max followed, placing Logan's car seat on the table. He pulled his wallet from his back pocket before sitting and pulled out two twenties. "I want to thank you again for taking us in. It meant everything to me, and to Gina, knowing Logan was safe."

Richard frowned and waved his hand. "Put that away. I'm just glad I could help."

Max shrugged and returned the money to his wallet. "I wish I could do something for you. I have this bad habit of needing to be rescued."

"Oh, really." *Don't ask. Just feed him, clean the drive, and let him leave.*

"Yeah. Maybe I could tell you Logan's story."

Let me guess, God. This has something to do with you. God's fingerprints were smeared all over this weekend. "I'd love to hear Logan's story." *Just be polite, listen, and then erase God's voice by clearing the snow.*

Max grinned and rocked the carrier. "When Gina and I got engaged, we planned our whole futures out. You know, we'd get married in a year, get our careers going, have kids five years later."

"Didn't work out that way?"

Max humphed. "Gina told me she was pregnant two weeks into the engagement."

"Ouch."

"Tell me about it. I didn't take it too well. I didn't like *her* messing with *my* plans so I headed to the nearest bar, got drunk, and cheated on her."

Whoa. "You really don't have to tell me—"

"I know. It's not something I usually talk about." Max looked down on Logan. "But, I think I'm supposed to."

Thanks, God. "I guess I'll listen."

"I appreciate it. That was just the beginning of my stupidity. The woman was a friend of Gina's, so I knew she'd find out eventually, then she wouldn't want to have anything to do with me. I broke the engagement before she had a chance to dump me. She left me messages all the time saying she forgave me. I never returned them. I was going to live my life as I planned it."

Max wiped his eyes and lifted Logan from the car seat and cuddled him. "I wasn't there when my son was born. I missed a miracle because I wouldn't receive forgiveness."

Richard shifted in his seat. A lump congealed in his throat. "You still got together."

"Because Gina never gave up on me. A week after she had Logan, she showed up at my apartment. With him." He kissed the baby's forehead and moisture dropped from his cheek. "She said Logan needed a father, and she'd like that father to be me. I abandoned her, but she never stopped loving me. She pursued me. Does that make any sense?"

No sense at all. Richard reached behind him for the tissue box. He handed one to Max, hoping Max wouldn't see that Richard used one too.

"I didn't know how she could love me after what I did to her, but she did, and I finally accepted it. Wisest decision I ever made. We had a small ceremony right away. Parents, siblings, best friends, but I guess it isn't the ceremony that counts, is it?"

No. It's the life lived once the commitment is made. Sorrow stewed in Richard's throat. "I need to be excused." He hustled to the bathroom and gently closed the door. *Okay, God, you've got my attention.* He crumpled to the floor and laid his forehead on his knees letting the jeans absorb his grief.

Minutes later, Max's voice filtered under the bathroom door. "—Bible tells me so. Little ones to him belong—"

You are that little one. A voice whispered in Richard's head. He looked upward, opening his eyes wide. *Me?* His heart burned, craving to believe.

"Yes, Jesus loves me. Yes, Jesus loves me—"

Yes, you!

Me ... I'm sorry, God. I'm so sorry. Will you let me come home?

Warmth hugged his body. He was too weak to resist it as he'd done in the past. So long ago as a child, he'd known with every fiber of his being that Jesus loved him, that Jesus was Lord of his life. Somewhere along the way to human success—human captivity—he'd forgotten. Now, thanks to an unborn child, and this precious infant God delivered to his doorstep, he desired to be a child of God once again.

His joy came out in tears. The infant he'd never see and never hold had served a divine purpose. A little over a year ago, his and Marissa's unseen child pointed Richard toward home, back home to his loving Father. Richard had felt—he had heard—God's call that night. At last, he was paying attention.

Not caring about his tear-stained face, Richard rejoined Max in the living room, blending his out-of-tune voice with the father's. "Yes, Jesus loves me. The Bible tells me so."

Max looked up, raising his brows. "You okay?"

Richard grinned and blotted his tears. "There's a Bible verse that says 'A little child shall lead them.' I want you to know how true that is."

"Really?" Max boosted Logan to his shoulder and stroked his back.

Richard nodded. "Since we can't make it to church, how about having our own little service here?"

"I'd love it."

Logan rewarded the father with a healthy burp.

Both men laughed.

Richard sat next to Max and held out his arms. "Mind if I hold him?"

Max passed Logan over.

Richard snuggled the child against his new heart, taking in the clean fragrance of baby powder. He picked up his Bible from the coffee table. It was time to put it back in use. He opened it, paging to Psalm fifty-one. Those words, first prayed by King David three-thousand-years ago, now pierced his heart and became his fervent prayer. "Create in me a clean heart, O God and renew a right spirit within me. Cast me not away from your presence and take not your holy spirit from me. Restore unto me the joy of your salvation and uphold me with your free spirit."

For the first time in nearly twenty years, Richard was free.

CHAPTER *twenty eight*

Richard pulled the cord on his drapes, encouraging the sun's light to bathe his home, and watched Max steer onto the newly plowed road. The snow bordering it still glistened. Few things were as breath-taking as fresh snow greeting a winter-blue sky, as if the earth was receiving a second chance at purity.

As God gifted to him.

He was done walking around in darkness and shadows. He was done living by the world's standards, which had proven to be no life at all. He wanted more out of life than to simply exist. Thanks to the two snow angels God placed on his doorstep this weekend, he would.

This was the news his family had longed to hear for over twenty years, but he couldn't wait for a face-to-face to tell them. He relaxed in his recliner and dialed the farm. Four rings later, the answering machine picked up. He left a simple message, "Mom, Dad, I returned." They would understand.

He hit the end button, and Marissa's name floated through his thoughts. Turbulent emotions swelled in his gut. For well over a year, he'd hated and resented her, faulting her for his life's upheaval. He'd been unforgiving, though others had forgiven him.

It was time to release that burden. He set the phone on an end table, ambled to his bedroom, knelt beside his bed, and forgave her.

His child wouldn't be forgotten. That was impossible. But, hate would no longer command his life.

His next action was much more difficult, but it was necessary and long overdue.

217

WITH HIS PULSE POUNDING, RICHARD STEERED
the rented Equinox onto Western Drive. He hadn't touched New
York soil since he fled the state an eternity ago. At the time, he
swore he'd never return, but circumstances had changed. Everything had changed.

Just four houses down on the right. His breath quickened
as he passed each house, drawing closer to the man he'd upset
on the phone earlier in the day, to the family he'd ripped apart
without even a token apology.

Still, they were willing to open their home to him on short
notice. That alone showed the high character of this family. Now
it was time for his character to grow. His first painful spurt was
about to occur.

White knuckled, he drove up the blacktop driveway iced
with freezing precipitation. He stepped onto the slick drive and
took baby steps across the sidewalk and up the stairs. He raised
his hand to the doorbell and stopped. He could still turn and
run and again avoid doing what was right. The door swung open
before he had a chance. A tall, burly man filled the entrance. The
father's cheerless eyes hadn't changed.

"Mr. Keene? I'm Richard Brooks." Richard removed his
glove and offered his hand. It was ignored.

"I haven't forgotten you, Brooks." The father remained in
the doorway.

"Vernon," a voice beyond Mr. Keene said, "let the poor man
in. He's come a long way, and we owe it to him to speak his mind.
When he's finished, you may speak yours." Mary Keene appeared
at the door. She didn't smile, and her eyes were red and rimmed
in shadows, but Richard didn't see the same bitterness implanted
in her husband's eyes. "Please come in, Mr. Brooks." Her voice
was even welcoming.

Vernon stepped aside.

Richard removed his shoes while Mary hung his jacket.
She led him into a combination living/dining room still decorated with the muted peaches and greens popular in the 1980's.
Pumpkin-scented candles glowed on the dining room table. She
gestured toward the couch. "You may sit here. May I offer you a

drink?"

He sat, bracing his hands on his knees. "Water would be fine. Thank you, Mrs. Keene."

Vernon settled into a chair directly across from Richard and stared at him as if trying to bore into his mind. On the wall behind Vernon hung senior portraits of their deceased son and the recent one of their daughter. The daughter smiled in the picture, but her eyes didn't reflect happiness. Yes, he'd been placed on this couch specifically.

"That was my son." Vernon nodded upward toward the picture. "He was a good kid. Had a bright future ahead of him."

Richard swallowed hard, his cheeks tightening, but he said nothing.

Mary returned with the water. "Vernon, Mr. Brooks is well aware of our loss. Let's please listen to what he's come to say."

She offered the drink to Richard then sat in a chair adjacent to Vernon's. Her eyes were kind and encouraging, but she didn't smile either.

The least painful thing would be to keep his head down, avoid eye contact. What he had to say would be easier if he couldn't see their expressions, but this was not about doing the easy thing. He sipped his ice water then placed the glass on a coaster on an end table next to the couch.

He dug his fingers into his knees. "I know I should have said this when the accident occurred, and I apologize for not speaking sooner." He looked at Mary. Her eyes closed. He shifted his gaze to Vernon who glared. Richard sighed and swallowed. "I am sincerely sorry for your loss."

Vernon didn't flinch.

Richard didn't expect otherwise. "I have nieces and nephews, and if something happened to them ..." He'd be devastated. "The loss of a child would be unbearable." *Even an unborn child.*

"Thank you, Mr. Brooks." Mary's mouth lifted slightly, although tears misted her eyes.

He looked down to regain his composure, sniffling lightly. His throat felt as if a tennis ball was lodged in it. That couldn't stop him. Too much was left unsaid. He peered up as Vernon swiped at his eyes. Mary didn't seem to care about the tears tracing the outline of her cheeks. Richard's stomach turned. Once again, he was causing distress in this family.

He gulped his drink, loosening the tennis ball. "I also apologize for my abhorrent behavior following the accident. I realize I came off cold and insensitive. For that, I'm very sorry. You would have been right to hate me."

Mary rotated her eyes toward her husband. The hard lines in his face were softening. Her gaze shifted back to Richard. "You were always forgiven."

Unearned forgiveness. Richard smiled half-heartedly. Still, they deserved an acknowledgement of the grace they extended. "Yes, I remember you saying that, and for your forgiveness I am forever grateful. It was the initial motivation for the changes I've made in my life. But it wasn't until recently I remembered what forgiveness is all about. That's why I'm here."

He closed his eyes, sucked in a breath, and puffed it out. He drained his water, leaving the glass one-third full with ice. "Prior to the accident I was a person who had achieved a phenomenal success in business. I thought only of myself and made sure everyone else knew how important I was. In the process, I ended up hurting a lot of people and didn't think anything bad could happen to me." Tears fell unrestrained.

Mary stood, retrieved Richard's glass, and excused herself. She returned with more water and a tissue box and handed both to him.

Nodding his thanks, he placed the items on the end table. He yanked out a tissue and swabbed below his eyes. "I had become a horrible person. My family didn't even recognize me anymore. This past year I've taken a journey—one that's led me back to my roots—back to the faith of my childhood. This morning I finally decided to come home to Christ."

Vernon's eyes closed, and his body relaxed.

"I would give anything to have that night back. Anything. I know what I've cost you. I wish I could have taken his place, but …" *God, it should have been me.* He wiped his tears again, and chugged water down his raw throat. "Unfortunately it took the accident for me to realize my life isn't about me, it's about living for God."

"Praise God." Mary closed her eyes and folded her hands, bringing them to her bowed head. After a silent moment she looked up. A full-faced smile appeared. "I've prayed for this from the beginning."

"You've been praying for me?" His shoulders slumped. How could a parent possibly pray for their son's killer?

She nodded. "I knew God could change your heart."

"I've been blessed with a lot of people praying for me. My whole family's been praying, for forever, that I return to God."

Vernon stood and approached. A slight smile now curved at the father's lips as he extended his hand. "Welcome home."

Richard rose and clasped Vernon's hand, using all the control he could assemble to keep from sobbing. He didn't deserve their mercy.

"Let's offer up this moment in praise." Mary gripped Richard's and Vernon's hands. "Dear Lord, you have said you would work all things together for good, for those who love you. We thank you and praise you for bringing this moment of healing into all of our lives. We praise you for freeing us from the bondage of sin through your holy and precious Son." Together they said, "Amen."

The outside door flew open and a young woman walked in. The girl with sad eyes displayed in the graduation picture. "Whose car's …" The girl's cheerful face contorted with contempt as her gaze turned his way.

"What's he doing here?" She pointed at Richard while glaring at her parents. Her breathing became forced. "He should be in jail, not here receiving your blessing."

Richard swallowed and looked at the carpet. She was right.

"Meghan." Mary spoke with a gentle firmness. "He's come to apologize. He's turned his life over to Jesus. He's part of God's family now."

"That's a family I don't want to have any part of." Meghan flung the words, then ran down the hall. Mary followed close behind.

Richard secured his hands in his back pockets. He deserved what the girl threw at him.

The speechless father glanced between Richard and the

hallway.

Richard took the cue, hoping to spare Vernon further discomfort. "I want to thank you again for opening your door to me. I offer my sincere apologies for your loss. I'll see myself out. Go. Take care of your daughter."

He left the home, his heart lightened by the forgiveness offered, yet torn by the grief he inflicted on the girl. If the same had happened to Marcus or Debbie, he'd have found it nearly impossible to forgive.

To be honest, he didn't want her to forgive him. He didn't deserve it.

MEGHAN FLUNG HERSELF ON HER BED AND tried to hold back the tears. Tears were cleansing. She didn't want to be cleansed. She wanted to be angry, to taste the hate. Justin's death was that man's fault, not hers. *He* drove the car. *He* ran the red light. So what if Justin was on that road because of her. It still shouldn't have happened.

Her mom hurried into the room probably hoping to offer comfort, but Meghan wanted no part in it.

"What's *he* doing here, Mom? What were you doing with *him*?"

"He came to apologize. He's sorry for what happened." Her mom sat on the bed and reached out.

Meghan shrugged her off, then grabbed a pillow and clinched it to her chest, erecting a barrier between herself and her mom. "It's a little late for that, don't you think? Do those apologies bring Justin back?"

"No, sweetheart, I know nothing can ever bring Justin back."

"Well that guy killed Justin, just as if he'd taken a gun and shot him down. And he didn't even care."

"I felt that way too, Meghan." Her dad filled the doorframe. "For a long time, but it's not good to hold onto hate. It'll tear you apart. That's what it's been doing to me."

Meghan looked beyond her dad. "Is he gone?"

He nodded.

"Good. I never want to see him again. And if you two ever

have anything else to do with him again, you'll lose me too."

The silence from her parents confirmed they knew she meant it.

RICHARD SLUMPED INTO THE SEAT OF HIS rented SUV and closed his eyes. The tensions flaming in the house were incited by him. Not only had he robbed the family of a son and brother, he was responsible for pitting daughter against parent, and against God.

He folded his hands and silently prayed, calming his churning emotions before driving off. Overwrought passions had convinced him to run that awful night. Controlling them now took priority over driving.

Only then did he glance at the clock. In one hour, he needed to be at the airport. There was plenty of time, although he didn't look forward to doing what God required of him.

He shifted the car into reverse and backed out of the driveway. The intersection was only five minutes away. The boy had only been five minutes from his home. A split-second turned those five minutes into eternity.

Richard spotted the intersection from far off. There were no trees, no buildings, no obstructions whatsoever. He hoped there would be something he could fault for blocking his view, although he knew this is what he'd find.

The blame—the guilt—landed entirely on him.

Several hundred feet before the crossroad, he steered onto the gravel roadside. He wiped tears from his eyes and eased on his gloves before stepping out of the car. Tears flowed and iced on his face, threatening to freeze his eyes shut. His leather jacket offered little aid in his attempts to dry them. Still his feet carried him forward.

A wooden cross, painted white and blending with the snow, pointed upward in tribute. Bouquets of silk flowers surrounded it. Messages and signatures decorated the cross. He knelt in the snow reading, clutching both arms at his stomach, yearning to relieve the mounting ache. This young man had truly been loved and was now greatly missed.

Brenda S. Anderson

He, Richard Brooks, former youth leader, former Manhattan executive, was personally responsible for this grievous waste.

No, he couldn't repair anyone's grief, but there was one small thing he could do. "Justin." Richard spoke quietly with his voice shivering more from remorse than the cold. "I promise you your death will not be in vain. I promise I will never run from God again, and I pray God will use your story—my story—to lead others to him."

He reached behind his neck and raised the chain over his head. He freed the key and chain onto his open hand and stared at it.

No. He couldn't do it. Not yet. There was a family, a girl, back at that house suffering because of him. Who was he to be released of this yoke when they never would be?

He returned the chain and key to their rightful home. Noosed around his neck.

"Oh, God, please forgive me." Richard doubled over and wept.

Somehow, mercy's shackle weighed heavier than before.

CHAPTER *twenty nine*

Richard rubbed his eyes then reviewed the pink message slips spread out on his office desk. His body was no longer accustomed to red-eye flights and early mornings. He arrived at work at nine this morning, nearly two hours later than normal, but still felt drained. Maybe he was just getting old, but he felt like he'd aged a lifetime in these past twenty-four hours. Life had been easier without faith, but "easy" certainly didn't equate with "good."

He picked up the message on the left. In one week, Emma had already figured out how he liked things organized. He jotted a mental note to give Ethan a call thanking him for the recommendation. But, business needed to come first.

He sat back in his chair assessing the first memo. Mr. Hamilton liked the proposal and wanted to sign a contract. That was good news and a perfect way to begin the new week, really his new life. He returned Mr. Hamilton's call and set up an appointment for early afternoon.

The next three messages forced a chuckle. Everyone from his family had called inquiring about the cryptic message recorded on his parent's answering machine. They left the same messages on his home voicemail. He'd return their calls tonight, make them wait just a little longer.

It was the last memo that deflated his smile. What could Spencer Griggs, Wharton Sport's CEO, possibly want with him? And how was Sheila involved?

MEGHAN OPENED HER DORM DOOR, PEEKED IN, and sighed. Kalyn and Emily were gone, thank goodness. She couldn't face them yet, didn't want them around when she called Doran. They would figure out she was up to something.

She called Doran, and the phone rang once before he answered. "Hey, Meggie."

She fought against tears upon hearing his voice. "I'm home."

"Boy, it's good to hear from you. I've missed you, ya know."

He'd missed *her*. Meghan Keene, freshman. "You have no clue how much I've missed you." She had to be the luckiest girl on campus. Maybe what she had to do wouldn't be so difficult. "Can I come over?"

"Sure. I'm already done with homework."

"I'm on my way."

Apprehension stirred her gut as she dressed for the walk. She was about to do something drastic, make a sacrifice, battle her inner fear. Was revenge reason enough? She zipped her jacket and pulled on her gloves. Yes, it was. Doran's sexy smile appeared in her thoughts. Really, it wasn't a sacrifice at all.

RICHARD HUNG UP THE PHONE AND SHOOK HIS head, chuckling. Wharton Sports wanted his help. How ironic. He told them "yes," even though part of him warned it was unwise. But, this was business and having Wharton on his resume' would help open doors to success.

Sheila had given the recommendation. Spencer Griggs, the company CEO, admitted as much after complimenting Richard on his prior work with ACM Technologies. How Sheila had discovered him was a mystery, but truthfully it wasn't a surprise.

He pulled his calendar up on the computer. Only two days to prepare a proposal. Two days to figure out what he wanted to say to Sheila. Act professional and treat her in the same manner he'd treat all clients; with practiced detachment. He'd done that often enough in New York with clients. Even so, it wouldn't be easy.

Why, when his life finally headed on the right path, when

he believed he could move on without her, why did she have to intrude again?

He rolled his chair to the credenza and opened the middle drawer which housed room enough only for a few extra pens and pencils. Its purpose was more aesthetic than functional, but he invented a use. No sense in wasting anything. He removed a white envelope from beneath the pens. It should have been discarded months ago. He'd even pitched it in the trash several times, but lacked the courage to leave it there.

He slid the card from the envelope and opened it, revealing their Valleyfair portrait. With his index finger, he traced the outline of Sheila's face, drawing out his smile. What he'd give to caress the silkiness of her skin, and taste the tenderness of her lips again. They'd been so happy that day. Funny how things changed, literally overnight. Too bad his affections hadn't changed along with those circumstances.

How would he react when he saw her? Had she moved on? Was this another one of those games she excelled at? Did she have a new boyfriend? Would it matter if she did? No doubt, it would. What if she wanted to get back together? Would he want that? Emotionally? In a heartbeat. Logically or spiritually, it would be unwise.

He slipped the photograph back into the envelope and secreted it once again in the tiny drawer. Partnering with Wharton was a practical business decision. Whatever happened with Sheila, well, he'd leave that up to God.

MEGHAN WALKED QUICKLY TO DORAN'S, trudging through heavy snow that had fallen during the day. She was eager to see him, to tell him what she'd kept bottled up for what seemed forever. Hopefully he was alone. She climbed the steps to the house and the door opened as her foot touched the last step.

"Hey Meggie, it's good to see you again."

"You too." She kicked the snow from her boots then stepped into the house.

He took her coat and hung it on a hook next to the entry.

"You sounded worried."

"Can't a girl miss her boyfriend?" She removed her boots and positioned them on a carpet square beneath her coat just like she would do every other visit.

Only this wasn't every other visit.

He clutched her hand. "Yeah, but there's more to it, isn't there?"

Butterflies awoke in her stomach. Did he know her plans?

Doran led her to a green and formerly-white floral couch that belonged in the town dump. For all she knew, that's where it came from.

"Am I so transparent?" She shifted her weight on the sofa searching for a spot where the springs wouldn't poke her bottom.

"Sometimes." Doran sat next to her. "But, today you've got a little edge. I rather like it." He leaned in to kiss her and Meghan grabbed on. His response was precisely what she sought. Their kiss deepened and his hands began examining places they'd never explored, making her feel things she never felt before.

So this is how it feels when it's right.

He pulled away. "Whew, girl." His face crimson, he stood and paced.

How sweet that he was respecting her.

"You really missed me, didn't you?" Crossing his arms, he looked down at her.

"Oh, yeah." She patted the space he vacated.

"Uh-uh. Something's up. This isn't like you."

Her lips formed a straight line as she crossed her arms beneath her chest.

"What's wrong, Meggie?"

At least he cared enough to ask. How many other guys would? "My parents." She picked at imaginary lint on her lap. "They betrayed me."

He sighed before sitting, his arm circling her shoulders. "I don't understand."

"They hurt me." Willing away unwanted tears, she stared at the freckles on her clasped arms. "It's a long story. There are things I haven't told you."

He crooked a finger under her chin lifting it up. "Then tell me. You know I'll listen."

Yes, she did know. How did she ever get so lucky?

His arm left her shoulders. "Let me grab us some drinks first." He stood and looked back at her. "What can I get you?"

That was easy. "A beer." She smiled. That alone would upset her parents.

Doran eyed her then shrugged. "If it's what you want."

"Absolutely."

He returned with a can for each of them and popped the tab before handing it over.

She gulped a long swig, hoping it would loosen her up. Again, he sat next to her, bracing his arm around her, snuggling in close. The faint scent of his Axe cologne implored her to come nearer. She would. Soon.

He kissed her forehead. "Talk to me, Meggie."

Needing strength to get through the conversation, she guzzled more beer, then placed her half-empty can on the dark-finished coffee table, another treasure from a dumpster dive. No need for a coaster. Actually, the lack of coasters had etched a distinctive image. Her drink would add one more dimension. Doran cuddled his beer next to hers. Side by side, their new design would be created.

She wiped her mouth, and toweled her hand on her jeans. "It began over a year ago, the night my brother graduated from high school." She wouldn't tell him the story actually began the night before. That was her secret.

"Hold on a second." Doran scratched his forehead. "You have a brother?"

"*Had* a brother." She wiped a stray tear. "Justin." She said his name softly. "He was a year older than me and he'd just graduated. After the ceremony, he drove around to different grad parties." She blotted another wayward tear. "You had to know Justin. He wasn't one to stay out late. He wasn't a rule-breaker at all, so when it was after midnight, and he wasn't home yet, Mom and Dad got real worried. They started calling around to see if anyone had seen him. A lot of parties were still going on, but everyone said Justin had left long ago."

Only she knew where Justin had been heading.

"Then the police arrived. They wanted to talk to Mom and Dad alone, so they took them outside. But, I watched. I saw it in their faces. I knew what had happened when Dad had to hold Mom up."

Doran squeezed her shoulders and stroked her arm. "What happened?"

"It was a drunk." *It was* his *fault, not mine.* "Drove right through a red light. Justin didn't have a chance. They said he died instantly."

"Oh, Meggie, I'm so sorry." Doran's fingers walked through her hair as he kissed her cheek.

"And the drunk, he barely had a scratch." She clenched her fists, concentrating on breathing. "The thing is, the guy didn't care about Justin or us. He never talked to Mom and Dad. Never apologized. Never looked sorry. Even got off on a technicality 'cause he wasn't legally drunk. You know what Mom did? She went and forgave him, right there in the courtroom. How could she do that?"

Doran drew her closer, stilling her shuddering body. "I don't understand what that has to do with now? What happened this weekend?"

She shrugged out of his arms and reached for her beer. "This guy—the drunk—was at my folks last night. I saw him, in my house, praying with Mom and Dad." The tears wanted to come so badly. Her throat ached and her insides throbbed from stuffing them inside. "How could they do this to Justin?"

Doran kneaded her shoulders. "What did they have to say about it?"

She positioned her beer can back on the table taking care to put it in precisely the same location. "Get this, they said 'we've forgiven him, and he's part of God's family now.'" Sarcasm tinged her voice.

"They're pretty religious, huh?"

She nodded. "To the extreme. I used to buy into some of it. Was raised that way. Justin always believed, but I don't, not anymore. How can I? If God can forgive him for murdering my brother, I don't want any part of Him or religion. There's no way I want that man forgiven."

She saw Doran glance at her beer. Before she could stop him, he grabbed both cans.

"So, you're getting back at a drunk by drinking?" He carried the cans into the kitchen and set them on the table.

"I hadn't thought of it that way." Her shoulders slumped.

He leaned against the narrow wall separating the kitchen from the living room and crossed his arms. "He wins if you do that. Don't give him any power over you."

"Right." Meghan sagged into the couch, pouting and rocking. It hurt so badly. She missed Justin so much. He should be alive.

For Justin, she needed to get back at the man. For Justin, she needed to teach her parents a lesson.

For Justin.

For justice.

Was she ready?

Doran was. He'd been ready a long time. Still, first-time jitters restrained her. That, and memories of the night before Justin died. Well, that was in the past. She was a new person, infinitely more mature, and wouldn't hold back any longer. When she told her parents, they would regret what they had done.

She peered up at Doran still leaning against the wall. "Will you hold me?" *Please don't notice how nervous I am.*

Doran sat next to her and enveloped her in his arms.

She snuggled in, nuzzling her face into his chest, breathing in the blend of aftershave and alcohol. An intoxicating combination. She looked up and kissed him deeply, tasting his hungry reply.

His hands began to roam. This time he didn't pull back. There was no stopping now, for either of them.

She'd seized her revenge.

CHAPTER *thirty*

Today she was going to see Richard. With a smile, Sheila lifted her gaze to the mirror hung in her walk-in closet, and watched her jaw fall, dragging her smile down with it. The full-length mirror reflected a stranger. Shadows had settled beneath her eyes, eyes devoid of luster. Richard once told her they shone like warm maple syrup. The syrup had grown cold. Even her hair lacked its usual sheen.

More appalling was the fit of her clothes. She specifically chose the burgundy pencil skirt that ended just above her knees, and the cream cashmere sweater with the scoop neck, scooped just enough to draw attention, yet remain professional. It always drew Richard's attention. The outfit once hugged the curves she was proud of, but now it hung loosely. It would not do for today.

Did she own anything that would suffice? She scoured her closet for an outfit less fitting. Perhaps in the anorexic world of models, she'd look fine, but being stick-thin was never something she aspired to be. Besides, Richard had appreciated her figure.

Nothing. This outfit would have to do. It still looked good, but it had lost the *wow* factor she wanted to pull off; the one where his eyes would widen and his mouth would silently form the exclamation.

She plodded to her bathroom and applied another layer of concealer below her eyes before dragging a brush through her hair. The alien staring back from the mirror wouldn't leave. Once upon a time, the mirror had been her friend. Even that had turned against her.

Would Richard have the same reaction? Would he be angry? Would he ignore her? He was awfully good at ignoring her, and that would be worse. He was her final hope.

She turned away from the stranger, hoping never to see her again.

RICHARD ARRIVED AT THE CONFERENCE ROOM several minutes early allowing him time to set up before board members arrived. The room wasn't what he'd grown accustomed to in New York City. There were no cherry wood tables or cushioned ergonomic leather chairs with high backs and arm rests. Rather, this table was overlaid with wood veneers. The leather chairs were probably purchased from the local discount store. The windows in Manhattan framed panoramic views of the city's soaring skyline and the Hudson River. These windows overlooked Minneapolis' warehouse district.

Truthfully, it didn't matter. Expensive seating and magnificent views were as much veneer as was on this table and were used to camouflage ACM Technologies' humanity, its imperfections, of which there were many. Too bad he hadn't comprehended that fact years earlier.

This room was functional. It bore no pretense. Just the way he liked it. Wharton Sports was a sensible company, managed by a group more attentive to quality than image. The company just needed a little fine-tuning to attain the excellence to which it aspired. He'd be proud to work with them, knowing he could aid them in achieving their goal. Likewise, they would be helping him realize his. If he got this contract and performed the job flawlessly, which he would, other companies would take notice.

Those thoughts energized him for the meeting, sustained by his renewed faith. He wouldn't be going this alone anymore. He glanced at his watch. Five minutes till show time. He sat in one of those low-cost chairs and prayed, something he'd never done before, asking God to be with him, laying out concerns about seeing Sheila again.

Sheila. It always came back to her, didn't it? No, he hadn't gotten over her and didn't want to make any more poor choices where she was concerned.

That was in God's hands now. Richard double-checked his notes and tested the projection system. Everything was ready.

Within minutes, the door opened. Spencer Griggs entered, introduced himself, and then lauded Richard for his accomplishments at ACM, mercifully ignoring the scandal overshadowing those accomplishments. Richard humbly accepted the praise as more board members arrived.

Each time the door opened, he peered up, and then looked down, disappointed. Eight times that happened before Sheila finally stepped in. He held his breath and smiled as he caught her eye, hoping no one could hear his heart hammering.

She mimicked his greeting.

But, his smile hid concern. To most people she probably looked put-together and professional, but fatigue slowed her walk, and gauntness hollowed her cheeks. The confidence in her eyes was waning. Confidence had never been an issue. Yes, he needed to speak with her following the meeting. He wouldn't be able to treat her strictly as a client.

The group settled into their chairs. Murmured conversation hummed until Mr. Griggs called the meeting to order. The CEO then made introductions. At Sheila, he modified his briefing. "I believe you've already met Sheila Peterson."

"Yes, I know Ms. Peterson quite well." Richard smiled at her, trying to calm the butterflies in his stomach. *Did she blush?* He couldn't tell as her makeup had been applied heavily. Another oddity.

Regardless, those thoughts were irrelevant. His concern needed to be directed at his presentation. "Could I have someone dim the lights, please?"

"One moment." Sheila raised her chin. "Before you begin, Mr. Brooks, we would like you to address a concern of ours."

He glanced in her direction, raising his eyebrows.

Her gaze focused beyond him. "We are aware that for several months recently, you were employed by Wharton Sports in the capacity of maintenance engineer. Could you please elaborate on why you would give up a Vice Presidency at ACM Technologies for such a position?"

Sheila's question didn't surprise him, but the fact that she'd asked it, not another board member. Perhaps she wanted to demonstrate she wasn't partisan, but more likely, it was her way of getting back at him for going away, for running away.

I won't let her get to me.

Besides, he deserved the question, had expected it and prepared a diplomatic answer. "Yes, Ms. Peterson." This time he didn't smile when he briefly caught her eyes.

Her gaze darted away.

"I anticipated your question and hope you will all find satisfaction in my response." He cleared his throat. As he spoke, he made eye contact with each board member. "While I was in the employ of ACM Technologies, I made several ill-advised personal decisions, one which led to the death of a young man in an alcohol related accident." He swallowed a breath and waited, allowing the information to sink in.

Some members showed surprise, others nodded—perhaps they were aware of his history—but most maintained a poker face. No one spoke.

"Following the accident I took a yearlong sabbatical to examine my prior behaviors and to make the necessary changes in my lifestyle." He looked directly at Sheila. "I have since made amends with the family of the young man."

Her brows lifted, as expected.

"I believe that my management skills have been enhanced through this period of reflection and self-examination, and I believe I may now offer a stronger and more honest service, hence the name of the business, *Integrity Business Solutions*."

Again, he intentionally made eye contact with each member, sensing approval of his explanation. Only then did he move forward with his PowerPoint presentation, enthusiastically highlighting what steps he'd take to enrich their business. When finished, he excused himself to the reception area just outside the room allowing them privacy to review his plan.

Not more than ten minutes later, as he worked through another proposal, he felt someone sit in the chair next to him. He looked up into Sheila's eyes, and quickly glanced away. Redness had replaced the spark that once lived there.

"Hi, Sheila." More words wouldn't come. How did one begin a conversation with a former girlfriend if he couldn't tell her how fine she looked? That had always been the groundbreaker. To offer any compliment would be a lie, so he said nothing personal. "How did things go in there?" He nodded toward the boardroom, bracing his hands on his laptop, fighting his natural impulse to take her hand.

"They loved you, Richard." Her tone was soft. "When you finished, you had the look of a ballplayer who just hit a walk-off home run."

He grinned. "I felt like it." She still knew how to read him. What was he supposed to make of that?

Her fingers grazed his arm, resting there.

His body stiffened. He'd forgotten how her touch made him feel.

"I wish I could have known this side of you before." Sorrow pervaded her hushed voice.

"You should have." It was difficult to resist the urge to hold her, to learn how he could help. "I was wrong to be dishonest with you, and I'm very sorry."

She removed her hand and folded it with the other. Her face became impassive. "We can discuss that later. Right now, they'd like to see you again."

"Right." Sighing, he stood and followed Sheila back into the boardroom.

He accepted the chair Sheila wheeled out for him and switched into business mode.

"Mr. Brooks." Mr. Griggs folded his hands on the table. "We are all impressed with your proposal and believe it is one that would greatly benefit Wharton Sports. Would you be willing to join us for lunch to discuss terms of a contract?"

Yes! Inside, he was doing handstands and somersaults, but he maintained his cool demeanor. "Lunch would be perfect."

Following that, he'd deal with Sheila.

LUNCH WAS PERFECT, ONCE HE GOT PAST THE fact that they were meeting at Marcello's, the place he'd laid his life out before Sheila, and she'd decided he wasn't worth the risk. Richard shouldn't have been surprised. It was most likely another one of Sheila's games to make him uncomfortable. Well, he wasn't playing.

He gave no hint of being unsettled by the meeting's location, rather he applauded the group for choosing the fine establishment. They, in turn, complimented him on his plan to turn Wharton around, offering a contract that would place *Integrity Business Solutions* well on its way to solvency.

This merger was precisely the springboard required to catapult his newborn company from obscurity. He assured the board they would be pleased with his work. They would be. It wasn't an arrogant thought; years of experience taught him he rarely disappointed his clientele. This would be no exception.

Following the meal, the board members individually excused themselves, each, once again, acknowledging their confidence in his abilities, until he and Sheila remained alone, seated across from each other.

Sheila leaned forward. "Can you stay?"

"I planned on it." He sat back in his chair, maintaining a distance between them. As she glanced across the circular table, he felt a touch of déjà vu. Perhaps the locale was appropriate after all. Perhaps they could turn this setting, where their romance had fractured, into a place of reconciliation.

It wasn't even romance he desired. Although friendship was exactly what Sheila needed, the idea of friendship didn't sit well, either.

"I've missed you, Richard." Sheila reached out, placed her hand on his and sought his gaze. "I didn't realize till you were gone what an integral part of my life you'd become. I felt so alone when you left."

He stared down at their hands. Amazing how a simple touch electrified his whole body. From the beginning, their relationship had bordered on intimacy. The night of his confession, he'd been more than willing to leap over that boundary. Now, with whatever was going on with her, those boundaries had to be reestablished. The lines needed to be pushed way back as he could easily cross over again. How he'd dated Sheila for so long, without giving in, was a mystery to him. God must have been with him all along, providing that strength.

Still, in order to reestablish those boundaries, or even to

reconcile, truth needed to come out, no matter how much it hurt. He turned his hand over, grasping hers. "I wouldn't have left if you hadn't wanted me to."

Sheila tugged her hand away and sat upright. "If you had told me the truth from the beginning, I wouldn't have had a reason to break up with you."

"Because we never would have been together in the first place. If you couldn't take what I'd done, after knowing me for so long, how do you think you'd have reacted if I told you right away? There wouldn't have been an *us* to break up."

She looked down.

He did too, wishing he could retract the biting words. Pointing fingers would only rebuild the barriers. "I'm sorry." He peered up. "I didn't come here to fight. I've missed you too." There, he said it. The truth. "You're right. I misled you. At first I didn't think it would matter because I've never handled relationships well. With all the obstacles we already faced, I didn't expect we'd date for long. Once we became close, I was too afraid to tell the truth. I didn't want to lose you, and I knew the truth would break us up."

She wiped her cheeks with her fingers.

He'd give anything to reach over and do that for her, but didn't dare. Such an action would be too intimate and wasn't the message he wanted to deliver. "None of that makes what I did right. I should have been honest from the beginning, and I'm very sorry I wasn't. You deserved better. I hope you can forgive me." He scanned her face, hoping.

She raised a napkin and dried tears. "Me? Forgive you?" A single chuckle escaped her throat. "Since Ethan told me about your business—"

"Ethan?" His friend had a big mouth.

Sheila even smiled. "Yes, blame Ethan. I needed a new assistant. He said the best one had recently been hired by a friend starting a new business. When I mentioned your name, he didn't deny it."

"Remind me to thank him."

"I will." She smiled, and her dimples emerged.

Oh, how he missed her smile.

"He even got in trouble because of you. Griggs came down on him for hiring you in maintenance."

Richard frowned. Ethan was another casualty of his dishonesty.

She waved her hand. "Oh, don't worry. Ethan's job is secure. Griggs just had to blow some steam. Now, he's ecstatic to have access to your expertise. He's glad you're back." Her dimples deepened. "So am I."

"Me too." Maybe not for the same reasons, though. They left too much unsaid. There was so much more he needed to tell her now.

Her dimples hid as she steered the conversation back to where it had veered off. "I've anticipated this meeting hoping you could forgive me. I behaved poorly those last days we were together and have regretted it, more than you can know. I understand why you didn't tell me the truth, and I do forgive you. I hope you can do the same for me." She leaned forward, extending her hand.

"I already have." The manicured hand waiting for his was far too tempting, so he clutched his hands over his thighs. "I don't think either one of us behaved very well. You may regret the breakup, but I don't. It forced me to examine my life, and I wasn't too happy with what I found. I believe our breakup was the best thing for me—for us."

Disappointment flickered in her eyes. "You're probably right. I'm glad to see you've returned to the business world. Obviously, it's where you belong." She added with a flirting smile, "I could get used to seeing you in the office setting. I like you in a suit."

He tugged on his tie. "Beats the janitor uniform, doesn't it?"

"Definitely." She grinned.

"Beats cafeteria lunches too."

For just a second, the old glint shone in her eyes as she laughed. "Give me a place like this any day."

He laughed along. "So am I to assume you chose this venue for our meeting?"

"If I did?" Her laughter ceased.

"I'd say it's appropriate."

"Well, I didn't recommend it."

He smiled. "I'm glad to hear it." It hadn't been a deliberate plan to hurt him.

"I do agree it's appropriate, though." She leaned forward. "I made a mistake leaving you that night. Maybe this is fate's way of telling us we belong together."

Fate? Hardly. A fresh start was what he longed for, but those feelings couldn't be expressed aloud. He'd changed too much in the past months—in the past days alone. A mere week ago, he'd have leapt at the opportunity to get back together. But, now? It would be wrong to pursue a relationship if she didn't share his re-found faith. "I don't know, Sheila."

Her eyes worried. "Is there someone else?"

Karen flitted through his thoughts. She'd been right to end things so quickly. "No. No one else. It's just that I've changed since I saw you last. I'm not the same person anymore."

"It shows. I can tell it's a positive change."

"It is. You've changed too."

She squeezed her eyes shut, and her lashes glowed with wetness.

What happened to you, Sheila? He couldn't wait any longer to find out, to comfort her, so he circled the table, touched his chair to hers and placed an arm around her shoulders. A hushed gasp escaped his mouth. Bone protruded from shoulders that were once round and muscular. He removed his arm, cupped her chin and pried her face toward him. "Sheila, what's wrong?"

Tears hugged her cheeks. "Can we go somewhere private? There are things I need to tell you."

What things? What could possibly have happened to destroy her like this? He wavered before making the offer. "Come back to my office. We'll have privacy." Not too much, though, so long as Emma was around. He wanted Emma there. "Ride with me." Sheila was in no condition to drive.

But was he in any condition to listen to what she had to say without stepping across his newly defined boundaries?

CHAPTER *thirty one*

"Emma, could you hold all my calls, please?"

"Certainly, sir."

Richard grasped Sheila's arm, led her into his office, and closed the door. Whatever she was going through required his undivided attention. Hopefully, he could help her through this, but he feared it went way beyond what he could deal with.

Sheila slid her pumps off and stretched her legs out on his leather loveseat, crossing goose-pimpled arms over her chest. His thermostat's digital numbers read seventy-six degrees. How could she possibly be cold?

"Could I get you a coffee? Hot chocolate maybe?"

"No, thank you." Even her voice shivered. If she fell asleep on the loveseat later, he'd sneak over to Macy's and purchase a blanket. He removed his suit coat and handed it to her. For now, it would have to suffice.

He sat hard into his desk chair as she blanketed her legs with his jacket. The tie had to go. He yanked it off, unbuttoned his top two buttons, then rolled his chair to the loveseat. Her hand lay limp in her lap, crying to be warmed. Ignoring the boundaries he drew earlier, he cradled her frigid hand between his. "Tell me what's going on."

Her eyes lifted. "I'm not sleeping at night." Tears floated over her cheeks. "I'm too frightened."

"Frightened?" He clenched a fist in his lap. "Has someone threatened you?" If so, he'd—

"No, no, nothing like that." Her cheeks flexed. "I've been having nightmares or flashbacks." She looked toward the ceiling and closed her eyes. After inhaling a deep breath, she brought her head down dragging her shoulders along with it. "I'm not even sure any more. But, when I sleep, I see … I feel these *things* happening to me."

"Flashbacks?" He squinted. "I don't understand?"

"I'm dreaming about things I did, or allowed to happen. Things I didn't know were bad. I'm not so sure anymore."

"What things?" He scratched his head. This wasn't making sense. She never mentioned any event in her life that would trigger nightmares.

She kept her head down, her voice toneless. "When I was sixteen I had a steady boyfriend. A missionary's kid. My parents even liked him. He was a senior, and I was a sophomore, so I thought I was pretty special. One evening, he stopped taking 'no' for an answer. Back then, they said I asked for it. Today they call it date rape."

Oh, God, no. No wonder she despised religion. He squeezed her hand, hoping to offer assurance. "I'm so sorry."

"I'm over it." An expressionless voice responded. "I've dealt with it enough. I didn't think I needed to dredge up those memories again."

"It wasn't your fault."

"I know, but what happened next was. You see, I became pregnant."

Pregnant? Richard dropped her hand. He rested his elbows on his thighs, and his forehead on folded hands. She didn't, Lord, she couldn't have …

"I was probably about fourteen weeks along when I told my parents. I was naive and didn't understand, or maybe I didn't want to believe why I missed those months. I was afraid of my parents' reaction, and Mother didn't disappoint. When I told her I was pregnant, she couldn't wait to get me in the car and drive me to a clinic."

Richard swallowed the melon-sized knot in his throat.

"Naturally, Mother didn't believe my righteous boyfriend had done anything wrong. She was certain it was all my fault, that I led him on. Then she gave me this lecture on different methods of birth control. Even got me a prescription for the pill. I told her I'd be sure to put it to the test and, believe me, I did."

How could a mother treat her child like that? Thank God

he had parents who loved him through his problems and didn't heap more on top.

"I hated that she didn't trust me, but I should have expected it. The reaction was normal for her. I knew then there was no way I'd bring a baby into our house. We actually agreed that having an abortion was the only thing to do, and it's a decision I've never regretted."

Not regret that she killed an innocent baby? He fisted both hands and squeezed. *Breathe, Richard, breathe.*

Sheila raised her arm, slid off her sterling silver bracelet, and held it up. "A peacemaking gift from Mother, assuaging her own guilt. My only memento from her."

Richard gazed at the bracelet that had always circled Sheila's wrist. What he'd give to grab it and throw it away. Sheila didn't need that kind of reminder.

"Frankly, I don't know why she felt guilty." Sheila slipped the bracelet back over her hand. "It was the right thing to do. I never even gave it a thought until I started having the nightmares."

Thoughts of Marissa and her "choice" tumbled through his head. He'd forgiven her, hadn't he? But, this was different. Sheila's choice wasn't born out of selfishness, not like Marissa's.

So why did he ache to punch the wall?

The last thing Sheila needed was his self-righteous judgment. With his fingers, he squeezed his knees hoping Sheila wouldn't see his tension. "Tell me about the nightmares."

Red swollen eyes peered up, standing out against a pale face. "I'm reliving the abortion, Richard. Every night." Her words were slow and deliberate. "Every single night I relive it. In the dream I'm in the operating room. In the background I hear the accusations of anti-choice zealots as the doctor is doing the procedure."

He winced at her word choice. Would she place him in the same category? *No judgment, Richard. She was sixteen.*

"I hear every sound, can almost taste the smell, remember every sight, feel all the pain ..." Her arms barricaded her stomach.

No wonder she couldn't sleep. "What can I do?"

Sheila's gaze found her lap again. "Listen," she whimpered.

"There's more?" His eyes narrowed, and his body stiffened. What else had she gone through?

She nodded, keeping her head low. "You've wondered what happened between me and Joe."

"Do I need to know?" He massaged tightening shoulders. Did he want to know?

"I think you do. I didn't love him, but I loved the idea of dating a ballplayer and the perks that came with it. I loved being seen with Joe."

"You've always loved attention." He forced her chin up and smiled, hoping to lighten the heavy moment, but she pulled away.

A sigh slid from his throat. "Go on."

"He was so much like you. Grew up in a religious family. Why is it I keep dating these religious kooks?" She shook her head.

Oh, boy. What would she think when she found out about him?

"Joe had these outdated ideas about sex belonging only in marriage. That certainly wasn't the lesson my mother taught, and I looked at him as a challenge. I made it my goal to change his mind. He never did, but I caught him at a weak moment, and he …" Sheila raised a hand to her face, wiping her cheeks. "He cried, Richard. I made him cry."

The details of her relationship with Joe didn't surprise him. They sounded way too familiar. Richard had been heading down the same road Joe took, but at that time, he'd have deliberately chosen the easy path, had even anticipated it. He wouldn't have realized, until too late, he'd taken the wrong road again.

Could he take up with Sheila again and not give in to temptation? Would she even want to get back together now that he'd become one of those kooks she despised? He studied her lying on the couch. In spite of everything, he was very much attracted to her. He still cared for her—more than cared.

Three months had passed since he confessed his love for her. Three months of absence hadn't changed those feelings. Wasn't she worth another try? He could deal with what she told him. It was obviously wearing on her, and she needed someone to listen to her, support her, encourage her. She didn't need romance. No, she needed a friend. He could fill that need, couldn't he?

Again, he took her hand. "You have to remember, you didn't

force anything on him. It was his choice, even if the decision was made in a weak moment."

"I know. That's what I told myself. Later, he said so too. He didn't blame me, but he started to keep an obvious distance from me. But, that isn't why we broke up."

Tingles electrified Richard's spine. Maybe he should stop her. Tell her it didn't matter. But, it would matter. Somehow, he knew that. "What happened, Sheila?" He asked the question even though he didn't want to hear the answer.

"I was pregnant."

Oh, God. He was right. Richard pinched his eyes shut as if that would close off his ears. He didn't want to hear her flimsy excuses.

"Marriage wasn't an option, and with my career, I was in no position to raise a child. Obviously, Joe couldn't either. The game takes him away for so much of the year. He couldn't be a good father, so I took care of it, without telling him."

No! She couldn't possibly ... Richard's eyes remained sealed as memories forged through again. He tried to swallow, but the clot in his throat wouldn't let him. Anger tensed his body. Who was he mad at? Sheila? Her mom? Marissa? All of them?

He stood and paced, coursing his fingers through his hair, trying to purge his emotions.

Sheila was quiet. He felt her eyes seeking to penetrate the wall he built up. *Don't look at her.* He couldn't show her what he was feeling. No. *Keep quiet. Listen. Pray.*

"The first abortion never bothered me, but for some reason this time I felt—I feel guilty."

You should feel guilty. He studied a picture on his credenza, the one taken this past Easter of his parents surrounded by all their grandchildren. There should have been one more child in that portrait.

"It's never far from my mind."

There's a reason for that.

"I hadn't planned on telling him, but then Joe proposed. We never discussed marriage. It was a subject I intentionally avoided. I had no desire to get married. But, he brought out the diamond and told me he wanted to make us legitimate.

"I started crying. I felt awful for lying to him. He was obviously puzzled by my reaction. That's when I told him about the abortion. He started shaking and said, 'You killed our baby.' I tried to explain, but he wouldn't listen.'"

Out of the corner of his eye, Richard watched her toy with her ring finger. *I know exactly how Joe felt.* He grabbed a bottle of water from his fridge and resumed pacing.

"Then I saw you." Her voice lifted slightly.

He leaned against the credenza, drinking his water, wishing for something stronger.

"When I saw you at Wharton, I knew you were perfect. I wanted to make him jealous. I was mad at him for walking out on me when what I did was the best for both of us."

Right. Don't give the father a choice. His fists ached to smack something. When he got home, he'd hit the weight machines. Go for a run. Scream. Pray?

"I figured you'd be honored to go out with me, you know, being a janitor."

He rolled his eyes.

"It wasn't quite as easy as I thought." Sheila glanced up.

He looked away. She wouldn't want to see what his face would tell her. He hadn't felt this angry in a long time. Not since Marissa.

And see where that got him. He might have to sleep here tonight. Driving wasn't an option.

"In my nightmares, there's always this second doctor."

God, can't you make her stop? Please?

"He's laughing at me. To him I was just another number. He performed some rote procedure, then left. It was painful, humiliating. Now I'm seeing that doctor again, nearly every night."

Richard paced to his picture window. The sun was setting, but city lights illuminated a downtown bustling with cars. The scene normally refreshed him. He'd hoped the tranquil view would wash away his anger. But, it didn't.

How someone could deliberately do that to their own child, a defenseless baby, was beyond his scope of understanding. To him, her excuse was simply that: an excuse. This last abortion was a selfish solution to a problem created by her own behavior.

Behavior that had continued with him.

Perhaps that's what really upset him. If he and Sheila hadn't broken up, would they now be facing the same issue? Could he have survived the loss of another child? If she despised children so much, there could never be a future for them, and he may as well tell her tonight. Someone else would have to help her through this.

Her hand rested on his shoulder. "Tell me what you're thinking."

He kept his gaze outward. "It could have been us."

"I don't understand. We never—"

"No, but I wanted to. If we hadn't broken up that weekend, I was anticipating ... I was longing to deepen our relationship. It was only a matter of days." He turned to her, crossing his arms at his chest. "What if you'd gotten pregnant again? You know I never would have approved—"

"There's a difference now."

"Really?" As if it mattered.

"I still believe a woman has a right to make her own choices, but my feelings have changed." Sheila forced his arms down until she held his hands. "You've helped me see how much I love children."

He pulled away and dropped into his chair "Perhaps you started having the dreams because you saw how wonderful children are."

Sheila sat and drew her knees up against her chest, covering up with his jacket again. She wrapped her arms around her legs before resting her chin on her knees. "I didn't know I loved children. I never wanted children before. That day at your farm made me wonder what I'd given up. Maybe that's why I attacked you on the way home from the farm. Maybe I needed to convince myself I had done the right thing. Now that thought's always on my mind. I'm not certain, anymore, if I did the right thing." Tears dripped again.

Because you didn't do the right thing! So what if you love children now? It's too late, isn't it?

He refused to look at her, remembering the butterflies he'd felt a few hours earlier. Why, when he was so angry, did his attraction for her pull so strong?

It was necessary to remain aloof, keep his distance. Reclining in his chair, he crossed his arms again, watching Sheila rock on the love seat. "What do you want from me?"

"Will you? Can you hold me? Can you tell me the nightmares are going to stop, the pain will go away?"

Hold her? He'd probably squeeze the life from her. "Sheila, I can't fix this. You need to find a therapist, someone who's dealt with these issues before."

"I have seen someone. When I told her about the dreams, she told me I'm letting society influence me. I don't know, is that it? Am I feeling guilty because some right-wing nuts are telling me to?" She stilled, and her face deadpanned. Lifeless eyes stared into his. "Richard, I can't live with these dreams."

He kneaded his neck. There was no way he could deal with that. *Okay, God, I could use some help here.*

No answer came. No words of comfort.

For a brief moment following his accident, he'd wanted to die, but he hadn't sunk this low and couldn't imagine the desperation she must be feeling.

Debbie could help. If he could get Sheila to rest, then he'd call his sister. If he could get Sheila in to see a counselor, then he could forget about her and move on with his new life.

At least that's what he'd like to do. He breathed in through his nose and blew the air out his mouth.

Forgive. The word passed through his head.

Forgive? No way! Not this, God. There is no possible way I can forgive this.

You've been forgiven.

Sure, he'd been forgiven. But, this was way too hard. *We're talking infants here, God.* He could forgive anything but this.

Forgive! The command nudged stronger this time.

He looked up at his ceiling. *Jesus, do I have to?*

Forgive.

Fine. He sat next to Sheila and held her, just as she requested, stepping way beyond the boundaries he set only a few hours earlier. God had called him here for this, not to be judge and juror, but to be a friend.

"I can't help you. You need to change counselors, maybe take a break from work. From what I saw today, you don't want to be there."

"That's not a problem. I've been ordered not to return to work. Not until after Thanksgiving."

"Oh." He rubbed his forehead. That meant she'd be alone for the next week and a half. Wouldn't that be dangerous for her in this state of mind? But, staying with him wasn't any better. Getting involved with her again would distract him from his faith, and he couldn't afford to let that happen. *God, what do I do?*

"Can you …?" Her hollow eyes pleaded. "Will you be here for me?"

No way could she be left alone. "I'll be here." He remained next to her, silently praying, trusting God to show the way.

THE CLOCK READ 6:11. RICHARD PUSHED AWAY from Emma's desk and stole a quick glance at his office door. Good, it was closed, and Sheila slept soundly behind it, warmed with a blanket he slipped away to purchase.

That comfort would be brief. Debbie would know how to make it permanent.

If he called now, she'd probably be in the middle of supper, but he needed to speak to her before Sheila awoke. He rested an elbow on Emma's desk and punched in the number.

The phone rang once. "Hello."

"Hi, Debbie."

"Ricky! It's so good to hear from you!" Excitement oozed from her voice. That would change quickly enough.

He combed his fingers through his hair. "Yeah, we'll see."

"What's wrong?"

"I need your help." He eyed the closed door again. His family wouldn't be happy with this revelation. "It's about Sheila."

CHAPTER thirty two

The knock on Richard's front door interrupted his breakfast, but it didn't come any too soon. So what if his *Wheaties* became soggy. They tasted bland anyway. He backed away from the table, hurried to the door, and was greeted with his sister's warm smile. He smiled back. "Thank you so much for coming.

"Anything for you." Debbie set her overnight bag on the floor, removed her boots and hung her jacket on the coat tree before grasping him in a hug. "And guess what? I even called Mom and asked for help. Aren't you proud of me?" A few years ago, his self-sufficient sister wouldn't have dreamed of asking for help. That pride had cleaved a rift in her marriage.

"You bet I am." He'd played an instrumental role in mending that fracture. Now if she could help with Sheila. "You didn't tell Mom about—"

Debbie laid a hand on his arm. "No. I just told her you needed me. That's it. She was thrilled to come watch the girls. Even said she'd stay the night, give Jerry a break."

"You plan on sleeping here?"

"If you want."

"I'd love it." He gestured to the couch. "Can I get you something to eat? Drink, maybe?"

"No. I'm fine."

He glanced at the kitchen, then sat next to Debbie. His cereal was unimportant. "She's sleeping again. Slept all night curled up on the loveseat in my office. If I weren't meeting some prospective clients today, I wouldn't have come home, but I had to shower and change. No way was I going to leave her alone at her place."

"Which is why I'm h—"

"Why are you here, Debbie?"

Richard and his sister looked up at Sheila standing, hands braced on hips, in the short hallway leading to the bedrooms.

"I'm—"

"She's here because I asked her to come."

Sheila's scowl warned him this wasn't going to be good, but the fire lighting her eyes was a positive sign, considering the lifelessness he'd seen there yesterday. "You didn't tell her—"

"Yes, I did."

"How dare you! I told you that in confidence!"

He leapt up from the couch. "So I can stand by and watch you disintegrate?"

Her eyebrows tented, and her lips pinched.

He stepped toward her, holding his hands away from his body. "Listen," he said softly. "I can't help you, not the help you need."

"I do not need a shrink." Her fists clenched on her hips, but the flames in her eyes had cooled.

"I'm not here as a shrink."

Richard felt Debbie at his side.

"I'm here as a friend."

Richard prayed that would be enough.

FRIEND IS SUCH A SUBJECTIVE WORD. SHEILA peered through the front door's window, watching Richard steer his pickup onto the county road. If Richard ever uttered the line about being *a friend*, she'd have to laugh in his face. They'd zoomed right past that stage in their relationship. If she hadn't sent him away …

The thought was too depressing.

She stepped away from the window and scanned his living room. Little had changed in three-plus months. The serene forest print enlivened the wall behind the couch. Admittedly, it did fit the style of his home better than the linear work she'd given him.

Did she fit into his life anymore?

The fact that she was here, at his house, and not in her condo medicating herself meant he still cared, but the physical distance he spaced between them told her he didn't want to care. If the word *friend* exited his mouth, and it might, it wouldn't be honest.

There had to be a way to narrow the gap.

"I take it he's gone." Debbie walked from the hallway leading to the bedrooms. Richard insisted Debbie sleep in his room. He'd take the basement couch.

"Yes," Sheila whispered. What she wouldn't give to exchange rooms with Debbie, to sleep in his bed. Being surrounded with his masculine scent was an intimacy she longed for, even if he didn't share the bed with her.

"Good." Debbie grinned and strolled to the bookshelves bordering the stone fireplace. She pulled out a book then squeezed it in two books away.

Sheila dropped onto the couch and closed her eyes. Debbie's use of the word *friend* carried an entirely different meaning. Richard had versed Sheila on Debbie's knack for sneaking in counseling sessions before the counselee was aware of what was happening. She wouldn't allow Debbie to get that close.

"I know what you're doing." Sheila kept her eyes shut.

"You do?"

"I don't need a babysitter."

"Babysitter?" Debbie laughed. "You think that's why I'm here?"

She's a great actor too. "I *know* that's why."

Sheila's body lifted as Debbie sat next to her. "You are very mistaken. I'm a mom twenty-four-seven-three-sixty-plus days per year. You think I would spend my day off babysitting? Not hardly. Frankly, this is an answer to prayer. The girls have really been getting on my nerves lately, and my temper's been short. And poor Jerry gets the brunt of it. If I had to stay home one more day, I might have gone crazy."

Sheila laughed sarcastically and opened her eyes. "You expect me to believe you?"

"Ah, so you've been listening to my brother." Debbie shook her head. "He's got me enthroned right next to St. Peter. He should know better. As a matter of fact, he's the one who probably saved my marriage the one time I wigged out."

Sheila didn't want to listen, but the notion of mild-mannered Debbie *wigging out* made her curious. "I'd like to hear about it."

"Naturally." Debbie rolled her eyes. "I guess I'd rather you hear it from me than Ricky or Marcus, though. It's an epic saga to them now." She drew her legs onto the couch and crossed them beneath her. "When we found out Lilly had Down syndrome, Jerry began pulling away."

"I thought Richard said you wouldn't talk to *him*?"

"Oh, yes. That's another piece of the story. Ricky said something I didn't like so I shut him out. I just couldn't handle one more issue at that time so Ricky was collateral damage. You see, Jerry was married before, and he had a son ... Christopher ... Christopher had Down syndrome, but Jerry didn't care. He loved his son. Problem was, Christopher had a bad heart, and surgery didn't save him."

She reached over and grasped Debbie's hand. "I'm sorry. Richard never told me."

Debbie shrugged. "I guess it's one of those things we don't talk about anymore. That's actually part of the problem. When we found out Lilly had DS, Jerry was afraid it would happen again. He couldn't let himself get close to someone else who would leave. Like his father left him as a child."

What kind of monster abandons their child?

"When Lilly was born, Jerry wouldn't hold her. Wouldn't have anything to do with her and, since she was a fussy baby, and I held her a lot, he stayed away from me too. Now, you would think a Marriage and Family Therapist would know she needed to talk things out with her husband, but I was so busy trying to be a good mom and patching things up with Ricky and planning our parent's fortieth wedding anniversary, I didn't make marriage a priority. I kept telling myself that we'd talk after the anniversary party."

Debbie fingered her eyes dry. "Shoot. I never get emotional."

A smile tugged on Sheila's lips. "Richard said he calls you Spock."

"Oh, that turkey!" She giggled.

Sheila squeezed Debbie's hand. "Did it improve after the

party?"

"I left Jerry."

Sheila gasped. "What?"

"It was just for one night, but I needed a break, so I forced Jerry into caring for Lilly. The problem was, while I was gone I went on a little spending spree, then drank too much, and one thing led to another. The worst part was waking up in my hotel room with another man."

"No." The word blew over Sheila's lips. "Does Jerry know?"

Debbie smiled. "He sure does. Turns out, the *other man* was Ricky. He took care of me that night, paid all my bills, and even sprung for an extra night for me and Jerry. Accepting help from him was one of the hardest things I've ever done. But not accepting or asking for help was what got me into trouble in the first place. I got smart and gave in. Jerry and I finally talked. When we got home, this counselor became the counseled, and we slowly glued our family back together."

"Oh." So, that's where the story was heading. To advocate counseling. She tugged her hand away and crossed her arms.

"The point is." Debbie touched Sheila's hand. "We all mess up. We all need a friend who'll listen when we do mess up. Ricky was my friend then and probably saved my marriage. I'd like to return the favor."

Sheila bit into her cheeks and looked up at the ceiling.

"Which means." Debbie stood and moved to the end table where she swapped the top and bottom magazines. "I do *not* plan on babysitting. Actually, I could really use your help in picking out a dress for Jerry's Christmas—" She cleared her throat. "Er, 'holiday' party at his school. Public school. Can't say *Christmas*." Debbie rolled her eyes.

Shopping. The idea compelled a smile.

"And then I would really, really like to see a movie that has no singing mermaids or talking sponges."

"Chick-flick?" When was the last time she had watched a movie with a girlfriend?

"Doesn't have to be. I like crashes and superheroes too." She motioned toward the kitchen. "We can pig out on buttered popcorn and chocolate."

Sheila appraised her bony arms. Maybe buttered popcorn and chocolate wasn't such a bad idea. She followed Debbie and stopped in the doorway, squinting as Debbie switched the salt and pepper shakers around on the table. "What are you doing?"

Debbie grinned. "Tormenting Ricky."

"Excuse me?"

"I'm sure you've noticed my brother's a little anal."

Sheila huffed. "Just a little."

"Marcus and I used to do this to his bedroom. Instead of messing things up, we just swapped things around. Drove Ricky crazy. When he gets home, you'll see."

Sheila glanced down the hallway. "Any room fair game?"

"Any room at all. But, if you really want to drive him nuts, change all his radio stations to country, and don't forget the one in his car."

"Now that's just plain mean." And ingenious.

"That's the fun of having brothers." Debbie opened a cupboard door and moved a coffee cup from the bottom shelf to the top.

Sheila walked to the bookshelf and squatted next to his tuner. Turning it on softly, she found a station broadcasting old-fashioned country twang, then quickly shut it off. It grated like fingernails on a chalkboard. Richard would agree.

The bedroom radio would be her next victim. Before heading down the short hall, she peeked in on Debbie. "When we're done, you want me to help you pick out a dress?"

"Oh, please. I have absolutely no fashion sense. Don't ask me why Ricky got it. It's so not fair." Debbie opened the silverware drawer and swapped the knives and spoons. "I'd really like something that would dazzle Jerry. Something to show him I do have a feminine side, you know. Something sexy, romantic."

Romance. Now that she could do with excellence. Excitement bubbled inside her as she assessed Debbie's appearance. Faded jeans. Worn sweatshirt. Jewelry limited to gold stud earrings and wedding ring. Mousy brown hair pulled into a tight ponytail. No makeup. A clean canvas begging for Sheila's artistic touch. She hadn't felt this energized in weeks. "How about starting out at my salon? Get our hair and makeup done. Manicure. Pedicure. The works." A day of pampering would do wonders for both of them. Then Richard wouldn't be able to ignore her.

Debbie rested a hip against the countertop. "Oh, that sounds heavenly, but I'm afraid my budget is limited to the dress."

"Let it be my treat."

"Oh I can't—" Debbie bit into her lower lip before smiling that familiar Brooks smile. "Okay, this is where I hear Ricky telling me to stuff my pride and graciously accept help."

"Your brother's a smart man. You should listen to him."

A grin stretched over Debbie's face, and she stood straight. "I'm ready to go."

"So am I." The grin was contagious. "Sounds like something friends do together."

"Exactly."

RICHARD HUMMED AS HE STEPPED INTO THE small mudroom attached to his garage. In spite of the insanity of the past two days, the meetings had gone well, producing two new clients. His alliance with Wharton was already bearing fruit. He'd prayed, throughout the day, that Debbie's afternoon with Sheila was equally fruitful.

Since it was past ten, the women had plenty of time alone and should be preparing for bed. He'd greet them with the obligatory "How was your day?" then escape to the basement and collapse on his sofa bed. Solving the latest Patrick Bowers mystery would occupy his mind, leaving no room for thoughts of Sheila sleeping a floor above him. Tomorrow morning would be early enough to fret about what she was going to do for the coming week. Rather, he'd kneel on it tonight and let God do the worrying.

Giggles drifted toward him as he draped his winter coat over a hook on the wall, proving he had no cause for worry. Talk about a heavenly tune! The scent of homemade popcorn mingled with the laughter as he noiselessly made his way out of the mudroom into the kitchen.

And stopped.

Something wasn't right. He studied the kitchen. The countertops were clean, the sink empty, the stove ... The stove! The grates all covered the wrong burners. Salt and pepper shakers were switched. Salt belonged on the left. Debbie knew that too. This was the penance he paid for asking for help. He strode toward the living room.

"Deborah Brooks!"

Laughter answered.

He crossed his arms over his chest and stopped in the doorway separating the kitchen from the living room. The television emitted the only light, yet he felt the same disquiet he experienced in the kitchen.

"It's Verhoeven, dear," Debbie said. "Has been for several years, in fact."

"Ha ha." He scanned the living room. "You sabotaged my home." His magazines, books, kids' toys. Even the cushions on his couch.

"Just need to remind you a little disarray is good for you."

His attention turned to Sheila. "I'm assuming you helped." The smile she returned convinced him disorder wasn't such a bad thing. Even in the dim light, she looked a hundred percent better than she had twenty-four hours prior.

"It's only fair that I chip in." Sheila patted an open space on the couch then put a finger to her lips. "You need to be quiet. I've never seen this movie before."

He eyed the spot thinking how much he'd love to cuddle next to her and watch a movie like old times. But, cuddling led to other things he didn't want to battle. He wasn't certain he'd win.

It would be so easy to forget these last months had happened. But, those months couldn't be disregarded. He couldn't abandon his faith again. Instead, he slid into the recliner trying to ignore the tell-tale droop of Sheila's shoulders and her down turned eyes.

He closed his eyes and bowed his head. Obviously, one day with his sister wasn't going to be enough. This whole stupid situation was too complicated. Sure, he could spend time with Sheila this weekend, check up on her next week, maybe bring her to the farm for the Thanksgiving celebration, but then she'd get the wrong idea from his attention. Yet, leaving her alone wasn't an option either. *God, this is your issue. I can't handle it.* His knees were going to receive a workout tonight.

Debbie paused the movie. "We'll be leaving tomorrow morning."

"Huh?" He peered up, praying he heard correctly. "You said *we*?"

"We." Debbie nodded. "Since Sheila's got till after Thanksgiving off, I invited her to my house. It'll be wonderful to have an extra set of hands for the week."

"And I might learn to babysit." Sheila's slight smile didn't draw out her dimples, but it was sincere.

Personally, he felt like doing handstands. *Thank you, God!*

"I'll drive in to Sheila's place first so she can pack."

"After Thanksgiving, you can bring me home?" Uncertainty rang in Sheila's voice.

He walked to the couch and sat next to Sheila, avoiding touching. "You're sure about his?" He wanted to read the truth in her eyes.

They brightened in affirmation. "Debbie convinced me it's okay to accept help, especially from a friend."

And now, he had nearly a week to prepare his heart to face Sheila again, thanks to a beautiful little sister.

THE CAMPUS MEDIA CENTER WAS NEARLY EMPTY as Thanksgiving break called the majority of students home. The students who remained on campus all seemed to be partying in Meghan's dorm. That building was never quiet. One would think she'd be used to the sound barrage by now, but studying was still easier in the library's isolation.

She wound her way through the maze of tables and chairs until she reached the back. There would be fewer disturbances here. She dropped her books on the table and draped her jacket over a chair.

Although it would be odd not being home on Thanksgiving day, what she had to look forward to far outweighed any homesickness. Doran promised to treat her to The Admiralty, a fine dining establishment located on Lake Mendota's shore, a place boasting romantic sunset views. If she hadn't spent the morning shopping for the perfect dress, she wouldn't be here now, but once Doran saw her, he'd definitely agree with her priorities.

Studying with Doran was no longer an option. They'd tried the last couple of nights, and always ended up, well, distracted. Not that she minded, terribly, but there would be time for that later. She giggled aloud just thinking of him. Exacting her revenge was so much fun, she almost regretted waiting so long.

But more fun would have to wait. That pesky English Lit paper was due right after break. If she could finish it today, the rest of the week would be open. She rummaged through her notebooks and cursed. It must be back in her room. How absent-minded could she get? Now she had to trudge back into Wisconsin's outdoor icebox and run all the way across campus. That stupid paper would never get done.

If she didn't complete it tonight, Doran would be disappointed, but even he prioritized studying. He'd understand. She put on her coat and gloves. Her books would wait here.

When she stepped out of the building, she heard his familiar laugh. It was far off, but no one laughed like Doran. Maybe he was coming to distract her again. Smiling, she tracked the sound around the side of the building. A heavily jacketed couple stood making out in the cold. The guy's face wasn't visible, but the girl was easy to identify. Meghan's pixyish roommate had hooked another sucker.

Only Emily could get away with wearing the powder-puff pink jacket with white fur circling all its openings, the kind Meghan envisioned on preteens. But, who was that with her? It couldn't be Doran. The guy's stocking cap matched Doran's, but not the red and white letter jacket. Doran's jacket was an older style. So was his roommates'.

The laugh came again. Boy, it sounded like him. She had to be imagining things. She just had to be.

Daring one last glance, she watched the couple scurry hand-in-hand past the library, heading off-campus. In the direction of Doran's house. But more than half the campus lived that way. How could she suspect it was him, even for a second? Doran had no reason to cheat on her. Not anymore. Especially with Emily. She was so not his type.

Still, it wouldn't hurt to finish her paper and surprise him tonight, make sure he'd never want anyone else.

CHAPTER *thirty three*

Richard kicked off the snow clumped to his boots before knocking on Debbie's door. Anything to avoid seeing Sheila again. The first arrows fired at his reborn faith couldn't be sharper, striking his armor at its weakest. Women. But, he was older now, wiser, and he knew how piercing those arrows were when he left God behind. That could not happen again. With a prayer on his lips, he fisted his hand against the door then let himself in.

There was no mudroom or porch to ease his entrance so he steeled his legs for the first wave of attack. Good thing he did as little arms circled each leg as soon as he stepped onto the carpet square. If this were the worst thrown at him, then life wouldn't need any armor.

He squatted and lifted his nieces up in his arms taking swift notice of their normally straight hair, curled in a fashion that would make Shirley Temple envious, and their cherubic faces layered with child-applied makeup. Had to be Sheila's doing. Debbie's idea of mother-daughter bonding involved hammers and screwdrivers, not curling irons and makeup brushes.

He grinned and kissed Kaitlynn and Lilly on their cheeks, coating his lips. Heavy doses of a citrus perfume assaulted his nose and throat. He glanced away to cough and held his breath as he spoke. "Am I the lucky prince who comes to rescue the pretty princesses?"

"I don't know, are you?"

His breath escaped with the sound of her voice. He glanced to his right. There sat Sheila, next to a table smothered in child cosmetics. But the table wasn't the only thing. Apparently, his nieces had used Sheila's face as their practice palette. Green eye shadow was caked on from her eyelashes to her brows. Bright blush circles on her cheeks reminded him of Raggedy Ann, and Sheila's already full lips were painted in the form of a football. Her hair hadn't eluded the girl's hands either, as ponytails and braids projected out around her head.

She never looked more beautiful. *God, why are you doing this to me?*

Sheila held out her hands displaying fingernails buffed in a rainbow of colors. "Like the new me?"

You have no idea. His mouth betrayed him by tilting into a smile. He released his grip on his nieces, letting them slide down his legs. "Go stand by Aunt Sheila. I need to see my princesses altogether." And record a permanent memory of it.

As Lilly and Kaitlynn eagerly climbed onto Sheila's lap, all three wearing the comfortable smiles of familiarity, he unclipped his phone from his belt.

"Oh no you don't."

The life he heard in Sheila's voice was precious. Last Wednesday, he wondered if she'd ever sound that way again. He raised his phone and aimed. "You think I'd copy this to Ethan?" Who would immediately post it on Wharton's blog.

"You wouldn't!"

He snapped the photo. "Of course I would."

"And then you will die!"

Death by Sheila ... Could definitely think of worse ways to go. He studied the photo, and clipped the phone back on his belt. Only then did he realize what had just happened. Twenty-five seconds into seeing her, and he'd already dropped his guard. The sooner he told her about his renewed faith, the better. She wouldn't be so quick to flirt with someone she despised.

He pulled a chair out from the table and sat down to remove his boots, needing to do something to distract him from Sheila. "Where's Debbie?" He could really use her right now.

On cue, the basement door opened and Debbie stepped up. "Ricky!" A smile brightened her eyes.

"Hey there." He stood and squeezed her with a hug. "It's good to see you."

"You too," she said before socking his arm.

"Hey, what did I do?"

Debbie flitted past him and pointed at her daughters. "It's a mutiny. Five and a half days here, and my tractor-riding tomboys suddenly want to be Southern belles. Just tell me, what am I supposed to do when Sheila leaves?"

Sheila laughed, and what a beautiful laugh it was.

He put his hand over his mouth covering a smirk. "You could join them."

"And you could buy your wardrobe at Wal-Mart."

"You know how to hit a guy where it hurts."

"And, by the way." Debbie pointed to her jeans. "There happens to be nothing wrong with shopping at Wal-Mart."

"While you two hash this out—" Sheila set the girls on the floor and stood. "—I promised to give the princesses a bubble bath."

"Yippee." Kaitlynn galloped toward the bathroom.

Lilly skipped after her.

Sheila brushed past Richard, whispering on her way. "I might just join them."

Whoa. And a cold shower called to him. *Okay, God, she's firing those arrows. I can't stop them on my own.* He rotated his shoulders and strode to the refrigerator. "Got a Pepsi?" Not waiting for an answer, he flung the freezer door open, letting the cold blast him.

Debbie cleared her throat. "Uh, generally speaking, I keep Pepsi in the fridge."

"Ha, ha." He closed the freezer and found a twenty-four ounce pop in the fridge. He downed a third of the bottle before looking at his sister. The smirk in her eyes said she understood. "Jerry home?" Some guy time would be excellent medicine.

"Not yet." She waved to the table and shook her head. "Would you look at this mess? My girls are traitors."

Grinning, Richard shoved everything to one side and sat.

"Jerry's at school yet." Debbie sat at the table's head. "Had some things to finish up before vacation so he doesn't have to go back in till Monday."

Hearing the water turn on in the bathroom, Richard shook his head hoping to erase unwanted images.

Debbie's hand rested on his arm. "We've had some very good days."

"Oh?"

"I honestly didn't think Sheila'd last one day, much less five."

"You and me both." He poured another third of pop down his throat.

"We're so different, but we've really clicked."

"You're not as different as you think."

"Maybe you're right." Debbie shrugged. "All I know is, she actually listens to me."

She always listened to me too.

"We all know why I invited her, but I think God meant this for my good too. I've got lots of friends, but when it comes right down to it, I'm always the listener. No one, other than family, let's me get past the role of counselor. I think we've stayed up every night talking and giggling." Debbie turned away and brushed her eyes.

She's crying … If Spock was crying, there was a reason behind it. "Are things okay with you and Jerry?"

"What?" Genuine surprise lit her face, then brightened into a smile. "Oh my gosh, no. I mean, yes, things are fine with me and Jerry. Better than fine, actually." She blushed and crossed her hands on her stomach. "It's just that I've prayed forever for a special girlfriend, someone who really understands me, and he's finally answered. So, if the girls suddenly go all girlie on me, I won't mind because I just have to call Sheila and ask 'What do I do now?'"

Richard briefly eyed his sister's stomach then glanced up. "You're not …?"

She grinned, nodding.

He stood to hug her, his smile rivaled hers. Nothing could make him happier than becoming an uncle again. Well, nothing except becoming a daddy, and only God knew if that would ever happen. He should have been a daddy, nearly ten months already. He shook off the depressing thought and sat down. This was a celebration, not a funeral.

"I need details."

"He's three months—"

"He?"

"Yep. Healthy little boy—"

"Healthy?" That word sounded glorious after what she'd gone through with Lily.

"Thankfully." She fingered a bottle of finger nail polish. "Does that sound selfish of me?"

"Selfish? To be thankful for a healthy child?"

"I feel by saying that, I diminish Lilly." She returned the polish to the table. "I would never wish for her to be different, because then she wouldn't be Lilly, and she's an amazing child. But, I also know the road ahead is difficult. For me and Jerry, not so much for Lilly."

He reached across the table and took her hand. "Hey, you don't have to explain it to me. I understand that you all have challenges ahead of you. But, you've also got family to help you through."

"We really are blessed, aren't we?"

He nodded. "When are you due?"

"The end of May."

"Same time as Kaitlynn?"

Her head rocked from side to side. "Could be, but that would make him two weeks early, although Lilly was early."

"And you're doing fine?"

"If you discount crying over every little thing, I'm doing wonderful."

"I figured so much. When you cry, I either need to congratulate Jerry or strangle him."

"I'll tell him you said that."

Richard finished his drink. "Does the family know?"

"It's Kaitlynn's job to tell them tomorrow, but I'm glad you know. The godfather should be the first."

"Godfather? Really?" He was finally going to be a godfather!

"We can't think of a better prayer warrior for our son."

"I promise, I won't let you down." Splashes and giggles drifted from the bathroom. He'd love to join in the fun. "I just hope I can let Sheila down without hurting her too much."

"Who says you have to. She's a keeper, Rick."

He swallowed. "Right. There's just this little thing about being unequally yoked in my way."

"Yeah, I know, and she does have issues with religion, Christianity in particular, and not without viable reasons."

"So you know about when she was sixt—"

"And probably a lot more than you."

"More?"

"I said, we've been talking. That one event colored so much of her life. How she views religion, sex, men in general."

"So what do I do?"

"Be a friend."

"Come on." He shook his head. "You know as well as I that friendship isn't a possibility. You heard her remark on the way to the bathroom. You saw how it affected me, and she's constantly pushing."

"Because to her, sex is power. It's control. It has nothing to do with love. That's what she learned from the rape."

What he'd give to have a moment alone with that guy. Sure, like that would solve anyone's problems. To be honest, sex had never been about love for him either.

He put his hand on his chest, imprinting the key on his palm. "I'm not strong, Debbie. There's one place friendship would lead to, and that's between the sheets. You know it too."

"That's where you're wrong. It didn't happen before you turned to God—"

"What?" He released the key.

"As I said, we've done a lot of talking."

"Wonderful. My baby sister's talking about my non-existent sex life."

"I remember someone bragging about his active—"

"Yeah, yeah, yeah." He pressed his back into the chair and crossed his arms.

"The point is." Debbie rested her hand on his forearm. "The point is, even without God, you waited."

"Oh, he was there, reminding all along."

"Exactly. And that's when you were trying to tune him out. Just think of what you can do when you actually listen."

His sister was more confident than he was. Personally, at this juncture in his life, he'd rather not risk the temptation. It had been a very long time … and Sheila was no ordinary temptation.

More giggles erupted from down the hall. A vision of Sheila

splashing with their own children, flashed through his head. Well, that was a fairy tale, and he didn't believe in Cinderella stories. This prince must abandon his beautiful princess even if it was the most difficult thing he'd ever done.

"We'll see how things go tonight." When reality would take place. The evening was already planned and prepared. He needed to tell Sheila about his renewed faith before Thanksgiving, before the family dropped the news on her. Knowing how Sheila felt about religion, he probably didn't need to worry about being friends. In that respect, it would all work out for the best.

So why did the thought of never seeing Sheila again make him heartsick? And why did God's armor feel so heavy?

SHEILA HUGGED HERSELF AS SHE TRUDGED behind Richard along the moonlit path toward a windbreak of trees. All day, she'd looked forward to this evening out alone with Richard. But, wading through foot deep snow in a forest somewhere in central Minnesota wasn't what she anticipated. Wearing a down jacket and Thinsulate gloves to deflect against twenty-degree air certainly wasn't conducive to cuddling and handholding.

She should have expected it, really, since he hardly grazed her arm since the day of her breakdown. This was private all right, but not the least bit romantic. Still, she'd hoped. Could still hope. Who was she to give up so easily?

Warding off her disappointment, she followed in his footpath, her gaze taking in the scenery about them. The sky was cloudless, and the moon full. The heaven's lights multiplied here in the country. She'd never seen so many stars. If it weren't so cold, it truly would be a romantic setting.

Up ahead, Richard inhaled a deep breath. "Don't you love the smell?"

So the man speaks. She breathed in, but said nothing. They passed between rows of pine trees flocked with the wet snow. Out here, snow stayed white, unlike city snow that seemed to take only minutes to turn various shades of brown, gray, and black. Yes, winter in the country was an entirely fresh experience.

Conversation would intrude on the grandeur.

Moments later the trees parted unveiling a baseball field-size clearing. Low-backed benches sat around a fire pit dug in the clearing's center. Branches were already arranged in teepee form. No surprise, the evening had been preplanned.

She settled on a bench while he added newspaper. Soon a warming fire blushed from the wood. Maybe romance wasn't out of the question.

He removed a blanket from a sports bag he'd carried along, and draped it over her shoulders. Then he pulled out a Thermos and filled two insulated cups with steamy hot chocolate before dropping a handful of mini marshmallows in each. Next, he took out Graham crackers, Hershey bars, and large marshmallows and set them on a tray he balanced on a stump. He'd thought of everything.

"Ever have a real s'more before?" He sat next to her, whittling the end of a tree branch with his jackknife.

"No." She tugged the blanket tight around her. "Another childhood event I missed out on."

"We're going to try and make up for some of those missed experiences." He skewered two marshmallows on the end of his stick.

"You already have."

He handed over the branch.

She accepted, purposely covering his hand with hers, her hand lingering a moment longer than necessary.

Clearing his throat, he yanked his hand away. "There's an art to making one correctly. Hold the marshmallows over the red embers—not the flame."

She extended her arm, aiming for the embers.

Stretching his legs out in front, he leaned back, resting his head in gloved hands. "Brown the outsides lightly." From the corner of her eye, she glanced at him. This man looked unbelievably content, replacing the serious man she'd fallen in love with. "Keep rotating the stick. The insides will begin to melt."

Sort of like her heart. This process was slow, but that was okay. Funny how her attitude had changed in a few short minutes. She could stay out here forever.

After a minute or so, Sheila pulled the branch away from the embers to check the marshmallows. A bark brown coated most of the outside. She showed Richard.

"Perfect."

His praise spurred her smile as she squeezed the marshmallows from the stick onto a cracker already covered with chocolate.

He completed the sandwich with another cracker. "It's yours. Give it a try."

One bite sent her to heaven. Beat Fig Newtons any day. Food, in general, tasted better this past week, but this treat surpassed everything.

"You should see the northern lights from here." Richard held the thin branch over the fire again. "Marc, Debs, and I would bring our sleeping bags out here, lie under the sky, and fall asleep watching them." His voice was low and reflective. "They're spectacular. Scientists may give some drab explanation, but God has a way of making natural scientific occurrences appear dazzling."

God? She choked on a bite and stared at him.

His chin was tilted up, eyes probing the universe. "There's something I need to tell you."

No. The chocolate suddenly tasted like tar and congealed in her throat.

He poked at the fire with a separate stick, rotating the wood to generate more heat. "Before we broke up, you'd become my life. Thinking of you always made my day better and being with you, well, it was a high I'd never experienced before. I believed I finally found what would clean out that rotten ache in my gut."

It was the same for me. She nibbled on the tasteless cracker while staring at the seething fire.

"When we broke up, I think I finally realized I needed something more. I needed someone who would never let me down. No matter how much people love you, they will always hurt you."

"I never meant to hurt you."

"I know. Just like I didn't want to hurt you, but we're human. It's going to happen." He poked the stick into the fire again. Embers crackled and flew into the air flitting about like orange lightening bugs.

"Over the years I convinced myself my reasons for avoiding

home centered around Dad and Marcus but, to be honest, that was an excuse. I think it's because I knew what would happen. I knew if I came home, I would hear God calling. God's voice has such clarity here."

Sheila followed his gaze to the pine trees circling the clearing. Their spired tops formed mountain-peaked shadows against the evening's indigo backdrop. Yes, it was inspiring, breathtaking even, but how did that clarify God?

"It wasn't so clear when I left." He jerked back his stick; the marshmallow flamed at the end. "That's what happens when you get too close to the fire," he muttered as a gooey substance fell into the blaze.

He dropped the branch to the ground and reclined. "Back, then, I felt the world revolved around me—an attitude I carried until the accident."

Sheila trapped her hands beneath her armpits. When she didn't force the world into orbit around her, it was too easy to get caught up in its spin, leaving her life a dizzy mess. Like she'd allowed the dreams to take charge. Not anymore. Since staying at Debbie's, Sheila had relearned to control her nights, and with ample sleep, once again she ruled her days. God had nothing to do with it. She found herself rolling her eyes as Richard's admission continued.

"Sadly, it was easy to turn my back on God. I attended a secular university and bought into their humanistic philosophy. From there I went straight to New York and ACM. I was successful from the start, and all reminders of my past were gone." He looked up at the sky. "In Manhattan, I didn't even have these bright stars to remind me."

Sheila inched away. Romance was no longer a desire. How could he surrender? It was fine for his family; she could tolerate their beliefs, but she wasn't in love with them.

"I didn't need God anymore, but he never left me alone. I just did whatever I could to drown him out. To be honest, I never stopped believing, but by ignoring him, I didn't need to live by his morality code." The fire crackled, and a log shifted igniting flames. "Deep down I knew what I was doing was wrong, but let's face it, if there's no God to answer to, then there's no moral standard to live up to either. As long as I pretended God didn't exist, I could live life how I wanted. I could throw off the guilt from my behavior. It was all about me."

Her stomach flamed like burning wood. Even in the chill of the night, her body perspired with anger. He made self concern sounds so evil. Where would she be now if she hadn't taken care of herself? No one else ever lifted a pinky to help her.

"I'm sorry, but I don't understand what was so wrong with your life." She flung her s'more into the fire. "You had one bad night. Made some worse decisions. But, it was one night out of a thousand."

"It was one night built on the shoulders of those other thousand. That one night ..." His voice tremored. "My choices ... people's lives ..." He sniffled and raised a hand to his eyes. "None of it would have happened if I'd ..." A sob broke from his throat and his hands stretched over his face.

She wanted to comfort, but couldn't. Not now. Again, he was throwing too much at her. Too much to process at one time.

The fire hissed and a log rolled off the top, splitting the logs into two burning piles.

He'd become her enemy.

"Mother went to church." The confession tumbled past her lips.

His hands slid from his face. "Your mom?"

"Oh no, not Mom, Mother." She laughed and looked upward. Clouds were creeping in, slowly dimming the night's brilliance. "Mother went to church. The one all the power brokers attended. She'd drag me along and make me fold my hands while she pretended to pray to this God of love. Then she'd haul me home only to make sure she didn't have to look at me for the rest of the day. Neither she nor Father played with me or read to me like Debbie and Jerry do with their kids. To them, I was this terrible inconvenience they couldn't wait to get rid of.

"Mother taught me what God's love is all about." Sarcasm blazed through her words. "The missionary's son only confirmed it."

"I didn't know." His hand rested on her arm, the touch she'd longed for earlier. Why did it have to feel so good?

She whisked her arm away and Richard sighed. "They called me shortly after I left for college. Told me they sold the house. Said they'd send their forwarding address, and left my things at the neighbor's. I never went back. All they left behind was bad memories. Never did get their new address, either. I would have loved to send a good riddance card."

"I can't imagine how much that had to hurt you."

"At first, yes, but they actually did me a favor. I was totally, completely done with them and never looked back. Never tried to find them, and they've never contacted me. It's not like I'm difficult to locate."

She swallowed, dousing the anger burning up her throat. "I took control of my own life and my own body." So why was it shaking from the inside out? She clenched her fists and inhaled a deep breath. "I swore I would never do to another human being what they did to me. I would never bring an unwanted life into the world."

Richard's arms surrounded her.

She wanted to melt into them, let him still the chills, but couldn't. He was now her adversary. She tried to pull away, but he held fast.

"Sheila," he whispered close to her ear. "I'm so sorry for what you've gone through."

"Are you?" She pushed him away. "If there's one thing I learned about churchgoers, it's that they show their pleasant face in public, then their ugly true self comes out at home. After they've used you up, they abandon you, forcing you to scrape together the pieces they tore apart."

His hands moved up her back and cupped her face forcing her to look at him. "We're not all like that."

She laughed and glared into his eyes. "You've already abandoned me once. Can you honestly say it won't happen again?" *Please promise me you won't leave, you won't hurt me. Show me you're different.*

His hands slipped away, and he looked down, his shoulders heaving with breath. "I can't," he whispered. "I can't stay with you if you don't share my faith. It wouldn't be fair to you."

Just as I thought. She gritted her teeth, fighting against tears.

Joe once said the very same thing. She'd been willing to overlook his religion, yet he said it wasn't enough. Of course, everything changed when …

She restrained the smile tugging at her lips. Everything changed that one night.

Richard would be no different. Especially now. And, if things went as planned, no God could force Richard to abandon her.

She put her arm around his back drawing his body to hers right where it belonged. "It's okay."

His head lifted. "Do you want to go home?"

Eventually, absolutely. "We can wait till after Thanksgiving. Tomorrow night's soon enough."

She could hardly wait for tomorrow night. After that, she knew Richard well enough to know abandonment would no longer be an issue.

CHAPTER *thirty four*

Richard trailed Sheila up the steps to her condo, lugging suitcases. Less than one week away required three bulky bags. How was that even possible?

Sheila stopped at her door and rummaged through a purse large enough to hold his bowling ball. It was probably just as heavy.

Waiting, he shifted his weight. Knowing her penchant for clutter, it could take hours to locate her keys. God was teaching him patience.

"Yes!" The metal jangle announced her victory. She slid the key into the lock and pushed the door open. "Is there anything I can offer you before you go?"

He patted his overfull stomach. "You think I can eat?" Not tonight, anyway. A good workout tomorrow should even things out a bit.

"I don't think I've ever eaten so much in my life!"

"Welcome to a Brooks Thanksgiving." He followed her into the home examining her jacketed frame. Beneath that thick winter coat was a body still pleading for nourishment. So, seeing her eat with abandon today told him she'd accepted his faith turnaround. That was the first step in commencing this "friendship." He just needed to keep his ears tuned to God's voice, and friendship was a definite possibility. God would handle whatever came next.

"Is Christmas the same way?" She removed her coat and slung it over the back of the couch.

"Pretty much." He hefted the luggage. "Where do you want this?"

"Oh, sorry." Deep dimples proved her genuine smile.

Okay, maybe "friendship" wasn't going to be that easy, but it was necessary.

"If you wouldn't mind bringing them up to my room, I'd be grateful."

"Not a problem." As long as it was in and out, so he could go home and call Debbie to tell her which model tractor he bought Kaitlynn for Christmas. Without releasing the bags, he slid off his boots and headed for the stairs, hearing Sheila pad behind him across the hardwood floor. He carted her luggage up the steps, past a bath and second bedroom, into a suite scented with Dior's Midnight Poison. A gift from him months ago when he anticipated a sexual relationship. Its venom still knew how to infect the body.

It didn't help that her queen-sized bed was intentionally positioned opposite a bowed window framing the river. What a sunrise she must awake to! A sunrise he once longed to share with her.

Ah, who was he kidding? That longing never left.

He clutched the suitcase handles, tensing his muscles. "Where do you want these?" It was time for him to leave.

"You can put them in the closet. I'll deal with them tomorrow."

"Fine." He hurried to the closet, listening to her footsteps fade away. *Good.* Kiss her on the cheek. Tell her goodbye. Drive home and take a cold shower.

He deposited the luggage on the floor and stepped out.

"Would you mind waiting a second?" Her voice came from the master bath.

"Only one second." He scratched his head. "I really need to get going." Drumming his fingers on his thighs, he walked to the window and watched the river's flow resisting the freeze. The struggle would soon be lost to a persistent winter that wouldn't be denied.

"Nice view, huh?"

He cleared his throat. "Um, very nice." When he turned around, he saw her seated on the edge of her bed, one leg crossed over the other. *Nice view, indeed.* A silk robe covered her decently, thank goodness, but even so … "Listen, I really do have to go." His thoughts at the moment had nothing to do with friendship.

"I know." She patted the space beside her. "I just want to talk for a second. Tell you thank you."

That should be harmless enough. Listen, then leave. He sat on the bed, measuring at least twelve inches between them, and crossed his arms over his chest.

She folded her hands in her lap. "I wanted to say thank you, again, for all you've done. For Debbie, Thanksgiving. Everything. Even for being honest with me last night. I know that wasn't easy."

His arms relaxed at his sides, hands on his legs. "I hope you remember you can always come to me or Debbie."

"I'm realizing that. It was so nice to be invited on their shopping day tomorrow, to be included as one of the girls. But, it was time to come home. I didn't want to wear out my welcome."

"Or could it be you didn't like the idea of battling crowds at six in the morning just to save a few dollars?"

"So true. I'd gladly spend extra to avoid the hassle." She lifted her chin but couldn't disguise its tremble. "This whole week I've been treated as one of the family. I just wish …" She raised a hand to her mouth.

That things could be different between them? "Yeah, me too." How was it he could complete her sentences when he barely knew her? At times like this, their connection truly scared him.

Her hand settled on his thigh as the gap between them shrunk to six inches. "When Kaitlynn told your family her brother's nest was in her mommy's tummy, I don't think I've ever laughed so hard."

He shifted a few inches away. "Everyone got a kick out of that one."

Her fingers walked over his thigh. "Do you know what I would have given to hear that reaction?" She wiped her eyes.

Without thinking, he circled his arms around her, pulling her close. Dior's Midnight Poison filled his being. Good thing he never removed his winter jacket. "Someday," he whispered into her ear.

"You really think so?" She nuzzled her face next to his.

Danger, Will Robinson. It's time to leave.

Her lips skimmed his cheek, tickling his whiskers.

"Hmm, hmmm." He returned the kiss. First her cheek, then her neck, her skin silky against his lips. His response was so natural, it couldn't be wrong, could it?

Definitely, time to go.

"One second." She breathed the words.

He sat back, paralyzed, permitting her to unzip his coat while he eyed her robe. Loosely knotted. One little pull should do it. Sure, it had been a long time and that scared him slightly, but it would all come back. He helped her slide his arms from the coat sleeves before aiming for her full lips, capturing them with a venomous fever that hadn't burned for forever. *Just this one time. That's all I want God. Just this once.* Words he probably prayed over twenty years ago when he committed his first mistake. He didn't wait for an answer this time, either.

As her slender fingers undid his shirt buttons, he reached in his back pocket for his wallet then pulled back. "Um, I don't have anything." *That's God telling you "no."* He'd tossed it into the fire last week, symbolically proving he was a new person.

"Do we really need anything?" With a sultry smile, she unfastened the final button. Her brown eyes connected with his as she splayed her hands over his T-shirt.

He swallowed hard. *This is God telling you "stop."*

"I mean, would you be upset if …?" A hand curved over her stomach.

If she became pregnant? The smile lifting his face couldn't be suppressed. God blesses mistakes sometimes too, doesn't he? At least, he forgives them. Richard had learned that much this past year.

Her fingers glided down his chest, stopping on the key. "Do you need this?" Her eyes lifted to meet his.

He gulped. That chain had shackled him since the courts granted his freedom.

Without waiting for an answer, she pulled the chain over his head, then clutched the key in her hand. "You said it was the key to your heart."

He nodded. *And my soul.* At this moment, a worthy sacrifice to be united with the woman he loved. He and Sheila and …? What a glorious thought. It had to be God ordained, didn't it? A quick trip to Las Vegas tomorrow could make it legal.

He tugged the belt on her robe. It slipped away, just as he anticipated. He hadn't lost his touch. His hands slowly slid the robe from her shoulders. The robe cascaded downward, exposing a revealing orange chemise. Fascinating.

If he were going to fall, becoming a Daddy would be one heckuva way to go.

Tomorrow, when he watched the sunrise paint the river, then he'd ask for forgiveness.

CHAPTER *thirty five*

Y ou're sure I can spend the night?" Meghan wrapped her arms at her waist as Doran hung her coat. His roommates were gone, just like he promised. Would be until Monday. Her plans were just for the night, but who knew what tomorrow would bring?

"Would you rather spend tonight with my sister and your other roommate, uh, what's her name?" Doran walked toward her, his eyes probing her body.

"Emily." When the sales associate first showed her the black evening dress, Meghan had cringed. Its V neck cut a little low for her comfort, but she did like the way the material flared out from an empire waist, stopping just above her knees in front and draping slightly longer in back. When she tried it on, she decided showing off a little cleavage wasn't so bad. Considering the way Doran eyed her all evening, she definitely made the right decision. His eyes didn't think of wandering.

He cuffed his hands over her shoulders. "Oh, yeah, her." Whispering, he pulled Meghan in tight, then leaned down for a kiss.

Meghan squeezed her hands up to his chest and pushed out. "Uh-uh. Not yet." If she were going to spend her first full night, she'd make it one they would both remember.

"Not yet, huh?" He crossed his arms. "I'm intrigued."

"You should be." Her fingers lightly grazed his arm as she flitted past him to retrieve her overnight bag. Yesterday, she thought she spent too much money buying the dress, scented candles, Cartier perfume, and the most important purchase, a satin chemise. It would be well worth it. Besides, she'd barely touched her college trust fund. Might as well do something fun with it too.

She picked up her bag and peered over her shoulder as she entered Doran's room.

His eyes narrowed to slits. "Don't take too long."

"I'll take as long as I need." She blew an air kiss before closing the door. It was so fun being special. To be Doran's one and only. She faced the mirror on his door and reached behind to unzip her dress. If she'd been thinking, Doran could have done that part, then he'd really be sweating.

She slipped the dress off her shoulders, and a flash of red caught her eye. She studied the image in the mirror. Her heart rate sped up as she slowly turned around. No, it couldn't be his. It had to be one of his housemates'. It just had to be.

She pulled the dress back over her shoulders, rezipped it, and inhaled a deep breath before pulling the bedroom door open. "Doran?" She cleared her throat. "Could you come here a second?"

The blaze in his eyes, as he sauntered toward the room, warned her what he was expecting.

Please let me be wrong. He entered and Meghan pulled the jacket from the bedpost. "Is this yours?"

"Uh, yeah." His brows knitted together as he closed the door. "Just got it a few days ago. Why?"

She thumbed a tear from below her eye. No tears allowed. That meek little freshman was gone for good. "Were you at the library yesterday?"

He dug his hands into his front pockets, eyes avoiding hers. "For a bit."

Meghan bit into her cheeks. No, she would not cry. "Making out with, uh, *what's her name?*"

Doran's cheeks flamed. He brushed his hands through his hair. "It's not what you think."

"Really?" She slung the jacket at him. "Enlighten me."

"I, uh." He leaned against the door and stuffed his fingers back into his pockets. "It was a one-time thing. She, uh ... I, uh ..." His shoulders heaving, he looked down at the floor. "I'm sorry, Meggie." He looked back up, bringing damp eyes to hers.

Her arms stiffened at her sides. She refused to look away. "And just how many other *one-time things* have you had since we've

…" Since I surrendered myself to you.

His gaze found the floor again.

"You jerk!" She hurled a few four-letter epithets in his direction. The shock in his face told her she'd struck him square on.

Guys. They were all jerks. She should have learned that lesson her junior year of high school. Justin's death obviously wasn't a big enough lesson.

Her hands fisted into tight balls. "You need to move."

"Meggie, please …"

"Now!"

Doran shuffled away from the door. "I am sorry."

"Right." Meghan yanked the door open, letting it crash against the wall.

The sound of glass shattering behind her accompanied obscenities as she slipped on her boots, coat, and gloves.

Not caring about the late hour or the evening's darkness, she stepped from the house, slamming the door behind her. Only then did she let herself cry.

"IT'S YOUR PHONE." SHEILA STROKED THE SCAR on Richard's solid bicep.

"Let it ring." His mouth captured hers again and the generic ringtone faded in the background.

The evening may have begun as a seductive game, challenging herself to win the greatest prize of all. Of course, she had unfair advantages, but games were won by utilizing all assets to strike at weaknesses. Something she'd done with glee. The victory of a lifetime relationship was within her grasp.

But, the game had changed. Rather it had become not a game at all, but an outpouring and sharing of love. His passionate kisses and exploring caresses told her she was to be cherished, not used. Perhaps her triumph was in discovering that true love was freeing, love delighted in putting others first. It wasn't all about her.

Stopping for breath, she rested her forehead against his and smiled. "The call could have been important." The man was so fun to tease.

"More important than you?" His finger traced the drooping neckline of her chemise.

"Could have been your family."

He groaned and flopped back on the pillow. "Thank you for that picture."

She lay still, waiting, knowing he was powerless to resist her. "Could have been Debbie."

Richard rose to his side and pulled her close. No barrier existed between them anymore. "I'm just going to have to keep you quiet."

She closed her eyes anticipating the rush from feeling his lips on hers, but heard him moan a low oath instead. "What?" Her eyes opened as he pushed her aside flinging the covers away.

"Debbie." He growled the name and sat up, slinging his legs off the side of the bed. "I was supposed to call her."

Oh, no. How could they have forgotten? He should have been home long ago. They would worry.

Not quite true, Debbie wouldn't worry. She'd know the truth.

Kneading the back of his neck with one hand, he punched a number into his phone.

Sheila pulled her knees to her chest, restraining sobs. The night had been so perfect.

"Debbie. Hey, I'm sorry I missed your call." His shoulders hunched, elbows rested on his knees. "No. Not yet." He smoothed his unruly hair with a hand. "Sheila's." His voice was barely audible, but his sniffle was obvious. "No. Nothing's all right."

Nothing? How could love be wrong?

"One second." He pulled the phone from his ear and held it to his chest as his torso turned. He glanced her way, his blue eyes glazed. "I'm so sorry, Sheila. Can you forgive me?"

Forgive him for what? Loving her? Her mouth opened, then clamped shut. There was nothing to forgive.

He raised his arm to his face, wiping his eyes. "I thought so. Here." He tossed the phone on the bed. "You talk. I need to go."

Sheila numbly picked up the phone and stared at it.

"God," he mumbled as he dressed. "Can you forgive me?

One more time?" Without glancing her way, he grabbed his chain from the bedside table, hurried from the room and clomped down the stairs.

"Ricky? Sheila? Somebody there?"

Sheila put the phone to her ear. "Hi, Debbie." Her voice came out in a whimper.

"Sheila, what's wrong? Is Ricky okay?"

The outside door slammed sending a tremor through her body. "No, he's not, and it's my fault." This was what she reaped for playing games with his emotions. Why couldn't she have left him alone? Let things happen naturally? She sniffled, but let tears wash her face. "I think he may be gone for good."

Gone forever. Just like Joe. Just like her parents.

"Talk to me, Sheila. Do you want me to drive down? Jerry can watch the girls."

"Not tonight, please. How about I meet you tomorrow? When you're done shopping?" Not even shopping would be therapeutic tomorrow, but a heart-to-heart with a friend? Debbie would understand, then convince Richard. She had to. Sheila didn't even want to think of living a life without him or his family.

"I'll hold you to it. I'll give you a call when we're done tomorrow. You know we love you."

We, as in Debbie's family. All but Richard. He probably hated her.

"I'll be waiting." Hoping. Maybe even praying.

CHAPTER *thirty six*

Two minutes. Sheila lowered her arm and stared out at the amusement park occupying the mall's center. It was fitting for Richard to choose the Mall of America. Meeting at the third level food court two weeks before Christmas insured a large crowd. He wouldn't have to worry about her playing any games.

Swigging her cappuccino, she surveyed the food court. Fast food reigned up here, surrounded by giant LEGO creations hung from the ceiling, and joyous screams from rollercoaster riders. Some shopper's paradise. Give her downtown Minneapolis any day. She eyed her watch again. *Come on Richard, it's time.*

On cue, she heard his laugh. Her traitorous heart dancing, she followed his voice, spotting him several tables away. Even her mouth disobeyed as it lifted into a smile, seeing his eyes light up.

With arms wide open, he approached.

She stood, and his open arms circled another woman. The hug was brief, thank goodness. The woman, who wore little or no makeup, stood at least a foot shorter than Richard. A denim jacket, with patchwork Santa's circling the hem, clashed with her faded jeans. Must be a friend. She was not at all Richard's type. So why did Sheila's stomach lurch watching them talk and laugh together?

Richard glanced at his watch, laughed again, and kissed the woman on the cheek. On the cheek, thank goodness, like he'd give his sister. Had to be a friend.

The woman walked away, and he scooted around tables surrounded with harried women, whining children, and handled shopping bags. He drew close and his arms opened up again. This time, Sheila waited until he reached the table before standing and receiving his quick hug. Almost as short as the one he offered the stranger. Then he kissed her.

On the cheek.

Two weeks following their intimacy, and he gives her a peck on the cheek. How dare he?

Smile, Sheila. Don't let him know it hurts. She sat, and he pushed in her chair. Ever the gentleman, but he'd do that for any woman now, wouldn't he? "I see you met a *friend.*"

He sat in the chair opposite her and glanced out at the food court. Guilt splayed across his face. "Oh, yeah. A friend of Janet's."

That she could handle.

"Actually, no."

No?

"I mean, yes, she's a friend of Janet's, but she and I dated some."

Richard dated Miss Down-Home Country Girl? Had to be ages ago. "Back in high school?"

His lip twitched. "Uh, no. After you and I broke up."

The nausea in her stomach rolled up to her throat. "You told me there was no one."

"And I told you the truth. She's ... just a friend."

Sheila laughed. "Like me."

A sigh blew from his mouth. "Not at all like you."

"So you'd like to date her again?"

His hands clenched on the table. "I didn't ask to meet you here so we could argue."

So, he didn't deny it. How could he move on so quickly? "Then, please tell me." She sat up straight, nice and professional. "Why did you need to see me?"

He smiled, and his midnight eyes sparked with a new brightness.

How dare he bribe her with his smile?

"First, I want to tell you how great you look."

Don't drop those defenses. "Thank you." Keep it steady.

"Debbie says you've been seeing a new counselor. She says it's really helping. I guess I'd have to agree."

Sheila folded her hands on top of the table. "Why don't you

just get to the point of why you wanted to get together? Why you've waited two weeks to call."

His Adam's apple bounced. "I need to apologize."

"Apologize?"

"For Thanksgiving. You know, at your place. Nothing was supposed to happen."

She laughed. "Nothing was supposed to happen. Oh, how nice. I always thought when two people loved each other—"

"They respect each other. What I did, was not showing you the respect you deserve. I was thinking of one thing. Myself. Not you. Not love. Especially, not God."

"That's the ultimate issue, isn't it?"

He nodded. "For once, I want to do what's right."

"I guess the question of love being right or wrong is one we'll never agree on."

"Remember, it wasn't too long ago, I would have agreed with you."

"Where does that leave us? And don't even think of saying you don't love me." She'd probably slap him if he did.

A smile edged up on his mouth. "Not a chance, but as far as you and I being an 'us,' it can't happen. I've told you that. I can't let anything come between me and God again."

"But, you'll let your God stand between us?"

"Yes." He peered down. "I'm sorry."

"Tell me why. I know plenty of other couples, happy couples, with interfaith relationships."

"True. But, what happens when you get tired of me attending a Bible study every week and church every Sunday?"

"It wouldn't hurt to miss now and then, would it?"

"For me it would. It keeps me honest, accountable, even recharges me. I can't let it go by the wayside again. But, the big issue is children. If we had children, and you know I want children, how would we raise them? Would you allow me to teach them that Jesus is real?"

Would she? "I don't know."

"Exactly. I need to pass my faith on to my kids. It's too important, too real to me. I can't live my life apart from God anymore, and I need a spouse who will encourage my beliefs, not scoff at them. I know life will never be perfect, but at least now I can rely on God's strength to get me through."

She gazed out at the amusement park, at the rollercoaster circling inside, thinking back to the steel coaster at Valleyfair. To say she'd been afraid of riding the speeding demon, flying over the tracks seemingly out-of-control, was an understatement. But, Richard had grasped her hand as the chain dragged the car, clanking, toward the top of the two-hundred foot hill. With the car peaking at the top of the hill, he kept his hand tight around hers, transferring his strength to her before the ride accelerated on its descent. His hand secured hers the entire time, around the unexpected twists and curves, and even when the train pitched down into darkness. When it had finally pulled to a stop, his hand remained, steady and strong.

His fingers grazed her arm. "Are you okay?"

She turned back to him and nodded. How nice it would be to believe God would be her strength. "I think I understand. But, I can't believe in Him just because you want me to. I can't unlearn what Mother taught, I can't undo what the missionary's ..." Her eyes clamped shut and she focused on breathing.

"I know. That's what makes this so dratted hard. I know you don't like the word friend. Personally, I hate it, but I promised you I wouldn't abandon you, and I intend on keeping that promise."

Her jaw clenched. How could *friend* be such an ugly word?

He glanced at his watch.

"Need to be somewhere?"

"Uh, well, I promised Karen—"

"Karen?"

"Yeah, um, the woman I ..." He nodded toward the food court.

"Ah, yes. Karen." The name grated over her tongue. "A Christian woman, no doubt."

"Yes, but—"

"You promised her something?"

He slumped in his chair. "She's got a son. Nine years old. Needs some advice on what to get him for Christmas."

What a neat little package for Richard. A ready-made family. "You mustn't be late."

"Sheila, we don't have a set time. I need to be with you."

She glanced at her watch. "Oh my, it is getting rather late, isn't it?"

"Come on, Sheila. I'm trying here."

And I'm dying. She raised her hands as if to surrender. "Fine. I'll behave."

"This isn't easy for me, either. My feelings for you are just as strong as ever, but I've made too many mistakes following feelings instead of leading them."

"I'm a mistake, now." *Tears, go away.*

He closed his eyes and shook his head. "I'm sorry. I'm handling this badly. Yes, I care for you."

"Care?"

"Love! Okay? Is that what you want to hear? I love you, all right? You're the most incredible woman I've ever met. I love your smile, how you listen to me, how when I was just a nobody you saw something special in me. I know in my heart there will never be anyone else. Not Karen. Not anybody."

But, it's not enough. She wiped her eyes with a napkin. "I can never be friends with you."

He nodded. "I understand. But, Debbie—"

"I can easily visit Debbie without you."

"Okay. Good." He checked his watch again then kept his gaze toward the ground and sighed. "I suppose …"

"Go ahead. Make some little boy happy." *While I go home and cry.*

He stood, keeping his arms at his side. "Um, Debbie mentioned she invited you for Christmas. I know you're hesitant because of me. I don't want to stand in the way of your friendship. You've been good for her."

She sat up straight again. "I appreciate the offer." As if she'd ever spend another holiday around Richard, continuously reminding her of what she'd never have. "But, I've got plans. I'm going to Jamaica with …" Her gaze rolled up to meet his, and her lips lifted in a devious grin. "With a friend."

"Oh, I see …" His Adam's apple moved again. "Good for you."

Yeah, good for me. If only it were with you.

"Hope you have a good time. Oh, and I got you a little something." He dug into his jacket pocket and removed a two-inch square box wrapped in satiny green paper. "Just a little something to remember me by. I planned on giving it to you at Christmas, but since you'll be … since you won't be with us, you can have it now."

He crammed his fingers into his jeans pockets.

She tore the paper, and raised the velvety box cover. Her tears couldn't be restrained as she stared at the expensive brooch.

A single orange rose.

CHAPTER *thirty seven*

"Your turn, Uncle Ricky."

Richard leaned over and raspberried Kaitlynn's cheek before placing a bite-size peanut butter cup on his birthday cake. For years he'd wanted the train cake for his birthday, just not enough to bring him home from New York two weeks after Christmas.

Then just one year ago today, with one timely letter, God's mercy had brought him home; at that time Richard hadn't imagined a worse punishment.

He swirled his hand through Kaitlynn's hair. Now, he couldn't be more grateful for the amazing blessing.

Even if Sheila wasn't with him.

He popped an M&M into his mouth to help him swallow the hurt of missing Sheila.

"I saw that, Uncle Ricky. Now I get one too."

With a nod, he raised a finger to his lips. "Just don't tell your mommy, okay?"

"I don't tattle."

"Atta girl." He picked up a bite-sized Reese's peanut butter cup and handed it to Kaitlynn. "Can you put on the final piece for me?"

"Of course." She unwrapped the candy and placed it at the end of a perfect row of other mini-Reese's. She was his niece, for sure.

"All done, Katydid." He blew another raspberry on her cheek then studied his cake, memorizing it. With four small loaf cakes topped with M&M's, licorice, and crumbled Oreos, all his favorites, he'd have to take a small slice of each. If his nephews didn't beat him to it, that is. He'd have to share the engine and the caboose as well. That was okay. Better than okay, really. Sure beat spending his birthday with some woman he hardly knew, which had happened too often in the past. Today, he couldn't wait to share it with his family.

Giggling, Kaitlynn wiped her cheek. "Did I do good?"

"Absolutely the best ever."

She placed a hand on her hip. "I know."

"Don't you love my humble daughter?" Debbie and Marcus walked into Richard's kitchen. "I really shouldn't let her spend time with you. Between you and Sheila I don't …"

Debbie's words fogged in his head. He knew the two women talked and frequently got together. It was nice for Debbie to have this new best friend. Why did it have to be Sheila?

"Hey, earth to Rick." Marcus' voice dispersed the fog.

Richard looked up as a paper airplane nosedived into his chest.

"Whew, for a second, I thought we lost you there." Marcus popped a handful of M&M's into his mouth. "Kaitlynn, see what happens when you get old?"

"Is he old as you?"

Richard didn't even try to stop his laugh. "Katydid, I have trained you well."

"Ha, ha, ha." Marcus dipped back into the candy. "I might have to take back my present."

"Go right ahead. You'll be needing that cane sooner than I will."

"Will your hair fall out like Daddy's did when he got old?"

Richard ruffled Kaitlynn's hair. "I'm sure your daddy would love to hear that."

She picked up four candles from the table. "This isn't enough."

"Not hardly." Marcus took a candle from Kaitlynn and stuck it on one of the cars. "Each candle means ten years. Do you know how many that is?"

Kaitlynn stared at her fingers, touching each one with deep concentration, before her head bobbed up. "About a hundred?"

"Bingo," Marcus said. "And see all that white in his hair? It's a sure sign he's a hundred."

The doorbell rang, thankfully interrupting the humiliation.

"I thought you were on my side, kiddo." Richard passed his

hand over Kaitlynn's head as he hurried to the front door. He just might kiss whoever was there.

Kaitlynn's feet pattered behind him. Smiling, he pulled open the door.

The smile instantly flattened as his eyes connected with the uninvited visitor. Debbie was in big trouble.

"Auntie Sheila!" Kaitlynn bumped past him and raised her arms.

"Hi, sweetie." Sheila scooped Kaitlynn into her arms, grasping her in a tight hug, burying her face in the girl's hair. "I've missed you." Sheila peered up at Richard.

No way would he acknowledge he missed her too. He nodded to the living room and said with a straight face, "Come on in." A little warning would have been nice. His sister was dead meat.

"Sheila!" His treasonous sister greeted Sheila with a hug. "I'm so glad you could make it."

"That makes two of you anyway." Frowning, he stomped to the kitchen and looked out the patio door at his family playing in the snow. It was time he joined them. Help them build a snow fort. Launch a few hundred snowballs.

"Got a problem?" Marcus stood next to him.

"Check out my living room." He pulled out a chair and reached for his Sorel boots.

Marcus sat alongside. "Our little sis ambushed you, huh?"

"You could say that." He tugged on a boot.

"Maybe it's time for you to show Sheila what it means to be a friend."

"Huh?"

"Listen, I know what she means to you, and I know you've used that awful word 'friend.' Sort of sticks in your gut like peanut butter, doesn't it?"

No kidding. "Your point is?"

"My point is, by coming here, she's reaching out. It's up to you to decide what to do next."

Richard stared down at his snow boots. Some friend he turned out to be. Some Christian witness. He couldn't even manage a smile for Sheila.

Marcus stood and patted Richard on the shoulder. "I think I'll go help Janet take on the boys."

"I'll be out shortly." After he took care of important business. Sheila had been right to scoff at the word friend. He pulled the boots from his feet, and forced his facial muscles upward. *That's it. You can do it.* He stepped toward the living room, stopping in the doorway when he heard Debbie.

"Are you feeling better now?"

Sheila was sick again? He glanced at her face. Fatigue rimmed her red-streaked eyes, but her cheeks had regained their previous fullness, and her figure? Whew. Nothing wrong there. Clearly, hunger was no longer an issue.

The women sat side by side on the couch with Kaitlynn cuddled in Sheila's lap.

"I'm feeling a little better, but the nausea ..."

Nausea? No. Couldn't be that, could it? Could be a million other explanations. Clenching his fists, he kept the smile on his face and stepped toward the couch. "Am I interrupting?"

A shy smile lit Sheila's eyes. "No. Please join us."

He sat on the edge of his recliner, resting elbows on his knees. "Sheila, I'm sorry. That was rude of me. I really am glad to see you again." At least that wasn't a lie. He looked from Sheila to Debbie. "As a matter of fact, if you two want time to talk once family leaves, you're welcome to stay here. I'll drive Debbie home."

Debbie glanced at Sheila who nodded, then turned to Richard. "Thank you. We'd love it."

He wished he could say the same.

MEGHAN SAT UP IN BED AND RUBBED HER EYES before focusing on the clock. Noon? This sleeping-in had to stop. Come Monday morning at seven-thirty she'd be in her calculus class taught by a professor who barely spoke English. Who in their right mind thought it was a good idea to schedule calculus at seven-thirty? And what good would calculus ever do her, anyway?

Maybe nothing, but getting good grades was her only motivation to keep moving. It didn't help that apparently Emily and

Doran were the hottest couple on campus. According to Kalyn and Emily, anyway. Good for them. Personally, she didn't need a jerk for a boyfriend.

She dragged herself from bed and shuffled to the sink. After turning on the cold water, she splashed it on her face. It didn't ease the fatigue that consumed her days. Gallons of coffee hadn't helped. Food didn't wake her either. Food had become an unwelcome ally or perhaps a consoling enemy as it satisfied her emotional cravings while finding home at her midsection. She lifted her sleep shirt and glanced at her stomach. The dreaded freshman fifteen had finally attacked. That had to be the cause. It just had to be. Later today, she'd have proof.

She released her shirt's hem watching it fall neatly back into place. If only she could go back in time, see Doran for the cad he was, then she wouldn't have to prove anything.

Like she'd made good choices in the past. Justin had paid for those choices. Richard Brooks should have paid too.

Well, that was out of her control. She studied her image in the mirror. Dark eyes, pale cheeks, frizzy hair. Was this the image she wanted to show Doran? That he had the power to reduce her to this? That she was the mousy creature he met at the beginning of the school year? No way. She grabbed her towel and toiletry bag off a shelf and strode to the shower room.

Good. It was empty. Most students were probably sleeping off last night's hangover. If that's how they chose to waste their college freedom, it was their problem. The party scene was for losers like Doran and Kalyn and Emily who chose to live their lives out of control. She wouldn't live that way anymore.

After stepping behind the shower's privacy curtain, she shed her pajamas. This new quarter would begin with a clean slate, with her living her new life as a studious undergrad. She'd eat healthy, get lots of sleep, and definitely avoid the guys.

The water ran warm over her body, cleansing and reviving her. It was time to take control of her life, stop worrying about what might be.

She peered down at her stomach and nausea swept over her, just like it had for the past week. Reality said she had good reason to worry.

CHAPTER *thirty eight*

Richard stuffed the final piece of the caboose cake into his mouth and leaned back into his chair. He loved his family, but he sure appreciated the quiet when they left. The two women conversing in his guest room wouldn't make too much noise either. He had to admit, Debbie and Sheila were good for each other. Now, if he could just avoid them for the next hour or so until Sheila left.

Reading in his bedroom should do the trick. One particular book, as a matter of fact. The only one that could give him the strength to make it through the day.

He finished his cake, washed it down with a swig of milk and headed for his bedroom. The guest room door was open a crack, allowing their conversation to drift through. He knew he shouldn't eavesdrop, but their words caught his attention and wouldn't let go.

"It's more than just nausea," Sheila said. "I feel dizzy. Strong scents really irritate me. I'm tired all the time, even though I'm getting sleep finally. But, it's never enough."

Richard dragged his arm across his forehead and hurried to his bedroom. Those symptoms could only mean one thing. The Psalms would do the trick. They always provided comfort under stress. He reclined on his bed taking his teen Bible with him. It was hard to believe he'd been so wise at one time. Now, the wise young man he'd once been, taught the older man who should have been wise.

As he reread Psalm 51, a knock sounded on his door. He placed the open book in his lap and ingested a deep breath. "Come in." Holding his breath, he watched the door open, then he gladly puffed it out. *Debbie.*

"Hey there." Her smile was contagious. "How's it going?"

"Not bad." He scooted to the side of his bed and patted it. "Just enjoying the quiet."

"Tell me about it." She plopped next to him, relaxed against the headboard, and closed her eyes. "My favorite time of day is when Kaitlynn leaves for school and Lilly's still sleeping. I think silence has to be my favorite sound of all."

"You'll be adding another voice to that soon."

"Crazy, huh?" She grinned.

"Nah, you're a terrific mom."

"And you're too nice. Must be old age."

He flung a pillow at her. "Happy now?"

"Much better."

"So did you just come in to shoot the breeze or do you have something else on your mind?"

"You know me too well."

"Could come from knowing you your whole life."

"Okay, here's the deal." She faced him. "Sheila's asked to have a moment with you. There's something she needs to tell you."

He leaned back and stared at the ceiling. *More proof.* "Okay. Fine." Better to get the news out right away. Nothing could be gained by avoiding it. "Why don't you tell her I'll meet her in the kitchen? You can watch a movie in here."

"Can I watch your *Jonny Quest* DVD's?"

He laughed. "Is that why you gave them to me? So you could watch them yourself?"

"With you, of course."

"Naturally. I'll join you later, after Sheila leaves."

Debbie laid a hand on his arm. "I do appreciate you letting me stay the night. Good thing Marcus brought the Suburban so he could bring Jerry and the girls home."

His hand covered hers. "You know I don't mind, especially with Sheila here. There's no way I could have this talk with her if you weren't here to chaperone."

"I swear, the two of you drive me nuts."

"Yeah, me too."

She squeezed her arm. "What she has to say isn't going to be easy for her, but I know you'll support her."

"Of course." He smiled. It was time he did the right thing.

PURSE IN HAND, SHEILA HURRIED FROM THE bedroom to the bathroom. Looking in the mirror, she fingered the rose brooch pinned next to her heart. This coming encounter demanded perfection. She opened her Coach handbag and stared at the chaos inside then snapped it shut.

It was time to stop hiding behind her mask of perfection and show him who she really was: a vulnerable young woman seeking approval, asking for love, willing to settle for friendly support.

What a better place to ask for it than in the heart of a family home: the kitchen. She walked into his kitchen and ran her hands across the smooth granite countertop, stopping at the cake. Normally, she wasn't keen on chocolate, but at the moment a bite-sized piece of cake was just what she craved to calm her nerves. A life lesson learned from Debbie.

Only one piece. Getting hooked on chocolate would be too easy. After downing the bite, she took two bottled waters from the fridge then sat at the table to wait. If she were a praying person like Debbie, and now Richard, this would be a perfect time to ask for help. It would be nice to rely on someone other than herself.

He walked into the kitchen as she unscrewed the bottle's cap.

She had to look away.

Why did his blue eyes have to look so understanding? His smile so friendly?

"Debbie said you wanted to talk." He pulled out a chair and sat across from her.

Even his voice was calming. She peered up and forced a smile. "I'd like that." First, she needed to soak her dry throat. She swallowed a third of the bottle before setting it down. "It's my turn to apologize." Her eyes connected with his. "Last Thanksgiving, it was …" She closed her eyes and blotted them with her fingers. "It was my fault. I planned it all to entrap you."

He smiled.

How dare he do that?

"I know. In hindsight, it was pretty obvious. I just didn't want to see it at the time. I appreciate the apology, and I do forgive you. Hopefully you can forgive me."

"Forgive you? For what?"

"For not being strong enough. For proving to you Christian's are the hypocrites you say we are."

"I never thought that about you."

"Well, you should have. I sure did. You know, maybe that's why I turned off God in the first place. No matter how hard I tried, I couldn't be perfect."

"And for a perfectionist, it's got to be difficult to accept."

"Exactly. So, instead of trying to be perfect according to God's rules, I found perfection in humanity's moral ambiguity. I'm finally learning I don't have to be perfect. I won't be perfect. Thanksgiving proved that out. But, if I can take responsibility for my actions, repent and accept God's forgiveness, I can finally grow."

"I hope what I have to tell you won't stunt that growth."

He sat up, shoulders straight, chin forward, and folded his hands on the table. "I can handle it."

Squeezing her hands in her lap, she wet her lips and swallowed hard. "When I went to college in Madison, I was pretty outspoken."

"Just in college?"

She bit her lip. "I mean about abortion."

"Oh." His straight shoulders drooped, and fear filled his eyes.

She didn't want to hurt him again, but it was important to be honest. "I've been asked to speak at the rally on January twenty-second."

Confusion replaced his fear, and he fisted his hands. "The anniversary of Roe v. Wade."

She nodded. "Exactly. I spoke for them my senior year. They want to bring me back."

"And you'd speak for them yet? After what you've gone through?" His fists tightened, and he leaned into the chair's back.

Just the reaction she expected. *Take a deep breath. Breathe out. Good girl.* "Absolutely. that's why it is so important I speak out. So women and girls can understand what abortion is about, how it affects us. I was never told. If I had been, I could have planned for it. I would have been prepared. Now I know what to expect."

"Haven't you learned anything?" He pushed away from the table and began pacing the kitchen.

"I need to understand."

"Understand what?" He shook his head and anger darkened his eyes. "I sure don't understand you."

"Please sit."

He leaned against the breakfast bar and crossed his arms.

She hated upsetting him like this, especially on his birthday. For a second she considered dropping the subject altogether, but that would solve nothing. Her views would be more convincing if she thoroughly comprehended his position. Few people demonstrated the passion Richard held. If she could capture a fraction of why he was so zealous about abortion, her message would have the power to affect women's choices. Maybe her own future choices.

It was worth the argument.

She steepled her hands below her chin. "Please?"

His eyes glaring, he flipped the chair around and straddled the back, resting his arms on top. "What's so hard to understand?"

"Why you're so opposed to abortion."

Was that a tear?

"Okay, I'll tell you. Four years ago, Debbie called me, crying. Told me her baby had Down syndrome. You know what I said?" He leaned toward her. "I said she could always have more children. Then I played the God card and said God would understand if she didn't keep it. He wouldn't want someone to have to face the struggles this child would bring."

Didn't they have this discussion months ago? "That's a logical recommendation." Sheila loved Lilly, but the child would require a lifetime of special care. Maybe Debbie and Jerry could handle it, but how many other people would?

"Logical? To end a baby's life because it isn't perfect?"

Sheila's chin dropped to her chest, and she gazed at her stomach. Yes, sometimes it did make sense, but she'd never be able to convince him, not until she understood where he was coming from. "I'd like to hear more."

He twisted the top off the water bottle and chugged it down then slammed the bottle on the table. "I thought Debbie'd never talk to me again. She said Marcus had been right about me all along. I was a self-centered egomaniac who didn't care about anyone but myself. They were both right. Debbie'd always been there for me and then, the first time she comes to me for help, I tell her to kill her baby. She didn't talk to me for months. It gave me time to think about what I told her. I realized I blew it again. I knew I had to make it up to her somehow.

He reached into his back pocket, pulled out his wallet and flipped it open. An accordioned picture holder sat in the middle next to his mug shot in the driver's license slot. He stretched the plastic framing open and pointed to a newborn's photo. "That's Lilly. The opportunity to reconcile came when she was born. I swore to Debbie I'd be there for Lilly's birth, no matter what, and I was. Got a reprimand from my boss, but I got my sister back, and I got to hold the most beautiful baby. I fell in love with Lilly from the start and really knew what a jerk I'd been."

Sheila took the wallet and stared at the picture of Lilly then glanced at all the other photos of loved and wanted children. Not all babies were wanted like these were. Some were better off never having lived.

"When I realized how beautiful, no, how absolutely perfect Lilly was, I took a hard look at my stance. I'd been ready to write her off because she wasn't going to be the perfect human being Debbie and Jerry prayed for. Turns out she was exactly who they prayed for, and we've all been blessed by her."

Sheila handed back the photographs but said nothing, letting him vent.

"It made me wonder if I was wrong about other things too. After all, I was raised in a pro-life family. I left that belief behind with all my other beliefs. When Lilly was born, I think that's when I started wondering what my life was about. How had I become someone with such a cavalier attitude toward life?"

"There's more to your decision than that, isn't there?"

He nodded, grimacing. "I started doing some research. For me, it came down to a basic question. When does life begin?

There's no comfortable answer. If you can't give me a solid answer of when human life begins, how can you decide when it's okay to take that life? It's why I have to go back to conception. For me, it's the only concrete answer."

"Your decision was that simple?" There was nothing simple about choosing abortion.

"Simple? Hardly. I had to convince my head what my heart already knew."

"How?"

"How ..." He rubbed a hand over his chin, the glare from his eyes began fading. "I'll be right back."

As he left the room, she stared out the patio door at the once-virgin snow, now trampled and dirty from well-intentioned play. How often did her good-intentions wind up crushed and stained? Even Thanksgiving evening was lived with good intentions. That was why today she had to listen and understand, so she could convince him she was making the right choice.

She jumped when a soft thump hit the table in front of her. His laptop. Oh, the man was cunning, using knowledge to persuade her.

He logged on to his WI-FI provider.

"Now what?"

"Google something simple like fetal development."

She typed in the words. The search engine displayed over ten million hits.

"Ignore the ones that seem overtly pro-life or pro-choice if you don't want to be influenced by their spin." He moved away but didn't sit. "Medical websites tend to be good. If your question is, 'when is a baby a baby,' those sites should be able to help you."

"Is that it?"

"Hardly." He crossed his arms. "As someone who's always considered herself pro-choice, you claim the constitutional right to privacy, right?"

"Absolutely. That's the very foundation of Roe v. Wade."

"So, tell me, where is privacy found in the Constitution?"

"I believe the Fourteenth Amendment is the main basis, but the First, Fourth, and Ninth Amendments are referred to as well." Certainly, she'd done her homework. She'd have been a poor champion of women's rights if she hadn't.

"Have you ever read the Fourteenth Amendment?"

"Of course I have." Although she couldn't recall verbatim what it said. Okay, she'd look that up. Memorize it this time. "What else should I consider?"

"You asked me what I did. I looked at the facts. I know you will too."

I already have. She'd give it one more go, for his sake.

"I'll leave you alone."

Sheila glanced up as he strode away from the table.

He reached the living room, and turned back, his mouth set in a dour line. "Don't forget to consider the father's point-of-view."

The father? Frowning, she looked back at the monitor. Like the father would care.

Joe did. An ultrasound photo of an eight-week-old fetus showing arms, legs and even a little nose filled the screen. *Exactly how old Joe's baby was.*

Her hands rested over her stomach. How could she convince Richard, when she struggled to convince herself it was the right thing to do?

CHAPTER *thirty nine*

Richard debated hitting the weights in the basement as he stomped away from the table. It was a good thing Debbie was here or he'd seriously consider the six-pack stored in his basement fridge. Right, and keep that wicked cycle going. But, there was nothing wrong with exercise.

He clutched the basement doorknob, and he felt a hand on his shoulder. Why wouldn't she leave him alone?

"Give me some time." His words came out in a snarl.

"Time for what?" Debbie said.

Sighing, he spun around. "Sorry. I'm just …" He stole a glance at Sheila who seemed to be engrossed in her research. *Please, God, let her see your light.*

"I understand." Debbie tugged his arm. "I need some company, if you don't mind."

"Good idea." Better to give in right away than argue. That would be pointless. He followed her to his room, shut the door and sat on the end of his bed facing a flat screen television. The cartoon was paused. He scanned his bedside table for the clicker.

Debbie sat next to him. "I hid it."

"You did what?"

"I knew you'd want to lose yourself in TV, so I hid the remote. Now, you've got to talk."

"Is this a method you learned at school?"

"The school of life, yeah."

He stared at the motionless characters. "What do you want to talk about?"

"About those snow angels who appeared on your doorstep right before Thanksgiving, Max and little Logan."

"So we're heading straight into the counseling session, huh? No easing into it?"

"Would you prefer I talk about *Jonny Quest* for a bit? I can if you want."

"Nah, give me the straight talk. Let's get it over with."

"I figured you'd want it that way."

"Naturally." He cupped his hands over his knees. "Lay it on me."

Debbie put an arm over his shoulders. "Whenever you mention your snow angels, you talk about how much you recognized yourself in the father. He met you on common ground. You understood each other and that helped you see the good God could do in your life, even with the choices you made in the past."

"True. He helped show me God never stops pursuing me, no matter what wrong I've done."

"Exactly." She squeezed his shoulder. "That's what Sheila needs."

"What do you mean?"

"Sheila needs someone to meet her where she's at. Someone who really understands where she's been and where she is now."

"You're saying that's me."

"Are you?"

He wiped his forehead with his arm. Where did Debbie hide the stupid clicker? "You don't know what you're asking."

She shrugged. "Sheila's gone through a lot these past months, and she is getting better. Post Abortion Stress Syndrome is as real as postpartum depression and post-traumatic stress disorder. Part of Sheila wants to deny her nightmares, the insomnia, and suicidal thoughts have nothing to do with what she did. It's very hard to come to the conclusion you've killed your child."

Or murdered some man's son or daughter. Richard propped his elbows on his knees and rested his head on folded hands.

"Men aren't immune either, by the way. A sure way to make a man feel powerless is by aborting his child."

God, she knows about Marissa. How can she know?

"Think about it. Three of man's basic needs are to procreate, protect, and provide. An abortion robs him of all of those."

He didn't care about any of that. All he wanted was his child. He'd do anything to save someone else from this torture. How could he support someone who condoned and supported the very action he despised?

"What does this have to do with me?"

"Just making conversation."

Right. He stared at the still screen again. "Come on, where did you put the clicker?"

"On your bed table by the window."

He twisted around. Sure enough, there it sat on the wrong table. He stood to retrieve it and held his thumb above *Play*. Yes, Sheila was on the wrong side of the issue. Should he ignore her or meet her there? *God, what do I do?* He'd been asking that question a lot lately. The answer often contradicted what he wanted to do. Still, it was clear what he needed to do.

Just one question had to be asked first. The answer didn't matter, but the truth did. He'd take the truth and support her from there.

"Are you going to hit *play* or not?" Debbie asked.

He looked at her, smiled, and underhanded the remote then picked up his Bible, clutching it tightly. "There's a question I need answered." And it needed to be asked with his full armor intact.

"Ricky, what are you going to do? Please, don't hurt her anymore."

"I don't intend to." He headed for the door and looked back. "I just have to ask a question. When I know the answer, then I can help her, regardless of her response. I promise."

Debbie picked up the remote and aimed it at the television. "Okay, I'm going to trust you."

"I appreciate it." He stepped through the door.

"Oh, and Ricky?"

He turned back. "Yeah?"

"When you're ready to talk, I'll listen."

Maybe someday. "I appreciate it. And say a prayer for me too."

"You know I will."

Yeah, he knew.

It took only ten steps to reach his kitchen. Ten steps closer to the truth.

Sheila still sat at the table, studying the computer, hopefully discovering truth.

He sat across from her, remaining silent until she looked up. "I have a question for you."

She lowered the laptop screen and bit into her lower lip, looking very much like the vulnerable child she was.

"Before I ask though, I want you to know, regardless of your answer, I promise to support you in whatever form that takes."

"Okay ..." she said with a slight hesitation. "I'm listening."

He sucked in a breath and forced it out. In truth, he did want her answer to be "yes" even with all the complications that would follow. As long as he walked with God, he'd make it through. "What I need to know is ..." He glanced up at his ceiling. *God, why is this so hard?* "Sheila, I was wondering ..." He wiped his palms on his jeans. *Just say it!* "Sheila, are you pregnant?"

CHAPTER *forty*

I'm pregnant. Meghan practiced the phrase in her head as she entered the university cafeteria. The stench of the school's processed spaghetti made her stomach lurch. A peanut butter sandwich would have to suffice today, but any food would have to wait. She scanned the rows of tables searching for Doran. He always ate at this time. Once upon a lifetime ago, she used to join him.

She spotted Emily first. Although the girl sat beside Doran, her focus on her plate said Emily was very much alone. Doran's conversation with his buddies indicated his indifference.

Good. She gets what she deserves. Meghan strode to the table. Confronting Doran in front of his friends would be justified payback.

Emily saw her first, and instantly laced her arm around Doran's.

He shrugged her off. "Would you get a life?" He rolled his eyes than connected with Meghan's. A smile hinted on his lips.

"Maybe you need to treat your girlfriends a little better." Meghan watched a glossy-eyed Emily slink away from the table.

"What?" Doran looked at the seat Emily abandoned and waved his arm. "The kid won't leave me alone." He pointed to the open seat and grinned. "Got a minute?"

That smile wasn't going to work on her anymore. She leaned over the table, between two of his friends, and slapped the plastic stick on the table. "That's how I'm doing," she said loud enough for all the surrounding students to hear. "I'm pregnant."

Whew. It's done. Shoot, now she felt like crying. Well, she wasn't going to cry. Not in front of him anyway.

Hoots and whistles sounded from around the room as Doran stared down at the plus sign. "You sure it's mine?" Wide, frightened eyes looked up at her.

She cocked her head to the side and rolled her eyes.

"Yeah, right." He slumped into his chair then looked back up. "Can we talk about this in private?"

She gestured toward the cafeteria door and led the way out the door and down a hall lined with gray lockers, veering off into a janitorial closet reeking of ammonia. Once Doran shut the door behind him, Meghan rested against a shelf filled with bleach and crossed her arms below her chest. Too bad she couldn't remove the consequences of her choices as easy as bleach whitened clothes.

Doran leaned against the same shelf, coiling his thumbs through his belt loops.

Good. Then they didn't have to look at each other.

"What do you plan to do?" he asked.

Meghan laughed. "What choice do I have? I can't raise a baby on my own, and I've just started college." This was where he was supposed to chime in saying, "I'll help you." Give her at least one more option. She could do it with him, but not alone.

He shrugged. "Doesn't leave you much choice then, does it?"

"Us, Doran. This is a two-people problem."

"Okay, whatever." His heal kicked at the linoleum squares.

"Someone could adopt her." Meghan's chin quivered. It wasn't a palatable choice, but better than the final option.

Doran stood up straight.

She didn't look his way but felt his angry glare.

"You think I want some kid of mine being raised by a stranger? Not a chance."

Her arms tightened around her midriff. "Then what?"

"Come on, Meggie, you're not stupid."

A rogue tear fell on her shirt. "I don't know." Her hands glided over her stomach.

"Okay." Doran lifted her chin. "Here's what we'll do."

She closed her eyes and listened to him lay out his solution. Not one she liked, but truthfully, the only logical one.

SHEILA STARED ACROSS THE TABLE, HER MOUTH gaping open.

Richard set his Bible on the table and reached both arms across. "I'm ready to take responsibility."

He was serious!

Laughter escaped her throat. "Sweetheart." She laced her fingers with his. "Let me explain something to you."

He stared back, his brows arched with confusion.

"You see, I learned very long ago that in order to be pregnant, a woman must first have sex." What in the world could he be thinking? She couldn't wait to hear his explanation.

He released her hands and sat back in his chair. "I realize that, but—"

"Dear, I desperately wanted to make love to you that night but my memory, which is quite good yet, tells me it didn't happen. Believe me, I would remember."

He shook his head. "I know, but your nausea, fatigue. I even watched you eat a second piece of cake."

Lucky for her he didn't see her eat the third piece. "Migraines, dear."

"Migraines?" His shoulders slumped.

"I've been having migraines. Probably because I haven't had any sex. The chocolate you can blame on your sister."

Richard's cheeks burned crimson. "Man, do I feel stupid."

Goodness, he was cute right now. She couldn't wait to hear the rest of his explanation and watch him blush his way through. "If you can explain to me how I could become pregnant without sex, I might just elevate you from stupid."

He folded his hands on the table and bowed his head, but his eyes peeked up. "I thought you, uh." He cleared his throat. "I thought there was some other guy."

Another guy? That hadn't been a thought for months. "I haven't been on a date for weeks. As for having sex? The last person was Joe, and he was very, very long ago. To be honest, there's only one person I would consider sharing myself with anymore." It was her turn to look down.

"What about Jamaica?"

Jamaica? Oh, that's right. "I went with a *girl* friend."

"Oh, man, Sheila. I'm sorry. Really sorry. It's just, everything pointed …" He chuckled. "To be honest, I wanted it to be true. I wanted to have a reason to marry you."

"Marry me?" Her heart jumped.

"But, I can't." He reached for his Bible gripping it with both hands. "I know you don't understand."

It felt like her heart stopped completely. She'd never understand.

"There is something I would like to do for you, though. As a friend."

Friend. That horrid word again. Muscles tightened in her cheeks as she attempted to reign in her emotions.

"If you'll allow me, I'd like to come with you to Madison, listen to what you have to say. Today, you listened to me. Maybe it's time for me to understand where you're coming from."

She thumbed her tears. "You'd do that for me?"

"You did it for me." A smile lit his eyes. "Of course, we'll need separate rooms."

"I'll even stay in a separate hotel, if that's what it takes."

His grin grew. "You never know. That might be a good idea."

Sheila stared at the man sitting across from her. A man ready to be a father to another man's child. A man offering friendship to a woman he shouldn't trust. A man willing to follow her to a place he despised. Maybe, just maybe, his religion wasn't so bad after all.

"I'd love to have you with me. There's just one little stipulation."

"Oh?"

"I'd like to borrow your Bible."

CHAPTER *forty one*

Richard itched his whiskered chin as he steered his Audi through the heart of Madison, Wisconsin. Just another thirty-some hours, then the beard could go. It may be foolish for him to hide behind facial hair tinted with more salt than pepper, enough to age him ten years, but the thought of being identified entering an abortion clinic was one he couldn't stomach. The fact that Sheila didn't instantly recognize him this morning when he picked her up, proved his disguise was a success. Considering they would be sleeping only rooms apart this evening, it didn't hurt that she said it looked awful on him. Anything to lessen the temptation.

He wasn't thrilled, either, with the idea of Sheila meeting with the Roe v. Wade Rally coordinator at the abortion clinic, but he'd made a promise to her, and to Debbie, that he'd be supportive. Besides, wasn't this the very place Jesus would go to meet the sinner?

"Take a left at the light." Sheila pointed at the upcoming intersection.

He steered left onto a four-lane street that seemed to take him back in time. It was probably one of the original business districts in town. The buildings' facades were covered in old brick, but appeared to be well maintained or recently renovated. Mosaic planters, filled with snow-flocked pine tops, sat next to each business entry. Naked ornamental trees grew up out of the concrete sidewalks. In a few months, the trees would flower then leaf-out to provide beauty and needed summer shade. The ambiance created, even in winter, was welcoming.

He steered into a parking space opposite Rivers Clinic for Women. Such a benign title for a place selling abortion. As he parked, he surveyed the other businesses on the street. A typical college hangout. There were a couple of bars, an espresso/internet café, a used bookstore and, at the far end, a place called Vivant Family Services—Support for Unplanned Pregnancies. Now there was a place he'd like to check out.

"This is it." He turned to Sheila. Her face was pale, and tears trailed down her cheeks. *What now?* "Sheila, what's wrong?"

A light chuckle came from her throat. "I thought I could handle seeing this place again."

"Again?"

She nodded toward Rivers Clinic. "There. It's where Mother brought me."

When she grew up in Minneapolis? "I don't understand."

Sheila peered at her lap. "My mother was too proud to bring me to a clinic in Minneapolis. Someone might see her. I would have embarrassed her again. Mother was all about appearances, you know. For her, it only made sense to drive a few hundred miles to avoid being seen."

She looked up and stared at the clinic.

"They harassed me." Her voice remained low.

"Who?"

"The demonstrators. Some sang of *Amazing Grace* while others tugged at my arms, my shoulders, my clothes, trying to stop us from going in. When I came out they called me a murderer, a baby killer."

God, how can we overcome the damage done in your name?

Meet Sheila where she's at. Debbie's advice echoed in his brain. Which was precisely why he was here, like it or not. "Are you ready to go in?" He was ready to follow.

Sheila wrapped her fingers around the car door's handle and breathed deeply. "Let's go."

God, please come with us.

SHEILA GLANCED AROUND THE SMALL WAITING room, recognizing little of it. Of course, it had been over eighteen years since her mother dragged her here. Walls painted pastel green were lined with soothing pictures of waterfalls, rivers, and sunsets, all chosen specifically to calm the patient. Eighteen years ago, it hadn't done its job. Why would it help anyone today?

Richard touched her arm as she aimed for the receptionist. "I'll wait here."

She nodded and watched him fill one of the ten seats in the room. All empty yet. Richard was probably quite happy about that. To think he came in spite of his adverse feelings, gave her a new appreciation for the man she still loved.

"May I help you?"

Sheila turned to face the receptionist. "Yes, I have an appointment with Carolyn Rivers. I'm Sheila Peterson."

"I'll let Carolyn know you're here." The young woman was probably an idealistic college activist working here out of a moral duty to keep choice legal. A perfectly good intention, but did the student know the downside of the issue? By the time Sheila completed her speech tomorrow, the town would know the complete story. Maybe even Richard would experience a change in heart.

If only that were possible. She watched him as she waited. With the navy Twins baseball cap covering his hair, and the grey whiskers coating his chin and circling his mouth, the man appeared unkempt. No one would recognize him. Still, he was one beautiful specimen.

"Ms. Peterson?"

"Yes." Sheila turned to the voice.

"Carolyn Rivers." The doctor's wife, the organizer of the rally tomorrow, offered a limp hand, her fingers ornamented with gem-studded rings. Bought and paid for out of women's misery.

"I'm pleased to meet you." Well, maybe not …

"I'll show you to my office."

Sheila walked side by side with a woman she knew to be in her sixties, but the lack of wrinkles showed money clearly attempted to purchase youth. A plastic surgeon also benefiting from a woman's difficult choice. Too many people profited from this life-altering procedure.

Tomorrow, Sheila would do what she could to truly make it rare. And maybe she'd win Richard back in the process.

THE CLINIC DOOR OPENED, DRAWING RICHARD'S attention away from his book. A young couple entered. About to make the worst mistake of their lives. If only there was something he could do or say to stop them.

The girl sat as the young man swaggered to the receptionist desk. When he returned, he sat next to her and slumped in his chair. She held her head down and directed her eyes toward her lap. The young man picked up a magazine and opened it, then closed his eyes.

Richard couldn't pry his gaze from them. Something about the girl was familiar. But, he didn't know anyone in Madison.

Still, a whispered voice blew through his thoughts. *Go talk to them.*

That wasn't happening.

Go. Speak with them.

No way. What would he possibly have to say to a couple of strangers?

Trust me.

Why him? He hadn't been able to convince Marissa to keep *his* baby. His words certainly would have no effect on an unfamiliar couple.

Go.

Okay. Fine. *Lord, give me the words.* Grasping his book, he looked toward the couple and forced a smile. "Good morning." Uncertainty crackled through his voice. The young woman peered up at him? Why did she look so familiar?

MEGHAN STARED AT THE STRANGER THROUGH her bangs. He was watching her. Smiling. She shivered. This place probably attracted all kinds of weirdoes.

So, why was she here?

"Are you having a baby?" the stranger asked.

Well, duh!

"Not after today." Doran sat up straight and glared.

Not after today. That meant right now, she still was pregnant. Right now, a baby still grew inside her. A baby Doran didn't want.

One she couldn't care for.

In just a short time, it would all be over. Next time she wouldn't make the same mistakes.

WHERE HAVE I SEEN HER ...? WHY COULDN'T HE place the face? *Okay, God, where is this going? What am I doing here?* He listened to silence then looked at the girl again. She wasn't much more than a girl either. Maybe eighteen? Nineteen? Strawberry-blonde hair. Sad eyes.

No! It couldn't be, could it?

The sad eyes from the girl's graduation picture, those same eyes that had stared at him with contempt during the confrontation at her house. It was her. *God, I don't understand.* Richard almost felt like Lady MacBeth, vainly trying to blot out the stain of sin that would never go away.

Clutching at the key bearing his stain, he moved, taking the seat opposite the couple, silently asking for the right words. God had brought him here for this.

Meghan shifted in her seat, clearly uncomfortable with his close proximity, but this had to be done.

The young man glared, warning him to move away.

Richard didn't know the young man, but he recognized the type. He saw an image of himself eighteen, twenty years ago, right down to the cheap cologne. This boy carried an arrogant expression of intelligence Richard himself had worn back in college. Self-assured, controlling, and, underneath that cocky veneer, scared to death. If Richard had faced the same dilemma years ago, his solution would have been no different.

If he was to have any hope of getting Meghan out of here without her doing something tragic, he had to appeal to the girl. This boy wouldn't be the type to listen.

"Meghan?"

She squinted at him. "Do I know you?"

"Richard Brooks."

Her eyes grew wide and blazed fire. There was the hatred he'd seen before. Her head turned toward her boyfriend, and she grabbed his arm. "Doran, make him go away."

Doran glanced from Meghan to Richard. "Meggie? Who?"

She inhaled a deep breath. "It's the man—" Her voice remained low, crackling. "It's the slime who killed Justin."

Killed Justin. Richard sighed. He'd never get used to that truth. He'd been responsible for too much death over the past two years: the death of his baby, the death of Justin, the break-up of the boy's family. Now, unless he could come up with something brilliant, he'd be responsible for the death of another child.

Words burned in his heart. He didn't understand how they would help, but he was convicted to say them. "Meghan, I understand how you must feel about me. I know I earned it. Every day I live knowing *I'm* responsible for your brother's death, it was caused by *my* irresponsible actions."

"Listen, dude, you're upsetting my girlfriend. Leave us alone."

"No." Meghan touched the boy's arm. "I want to hear this."

Hope sparked in his heart, and he focused directly on Meghan. "I realize the person you saw back then showed little remorse, but I was sorry, even though I never said it. Meghan, I am sincerely sorry for what happened. I'm sorry for what I've put your family through, what I've put you through. I wish I could take it all back." Oh, how he wished that. The penalty of his sin seemed to be never ending.

The girl remained quiet, breathing rapidly.

"That night ..." He turned his attention to Doran. "The night of the accident, I found out my girlfriend was aborting our child. *My* child. Don't think this won't hurt you." No one, male or female, deserved to suffer through this personal hell. "Don't think it will solve all your problems. It only made mine worse.

"But, now." He softened his tone and spoke to them both. "I've turned my life back to Jesus. He's forgiven me. I pray you can find it in your heart to do so as well."

Richard stood and turned to leave, but the couple's silence beckoned him. "Your parents love you, Meghan. Call them. They'll forgive you."

He rushed out of the clinic and slumped against the outside wall. Had he done the right thing, or did he mess things up even more?

MEGHAN'S GAZE FOLLOWED RICHARD OUT THE door, a woman hurrying behind. It seemed to take forever for him to disappear—hopefully out of her life forever. Her hands shook, and she clasped them together, but the shaking didn't stop.

"Can you believe the nerve of that guy?" Doran reopened his magazine, as if unaffected by Richard's apology.

She wished that were true for her, but Richard's words wouldn't leave her thoughts. Who was he to say her parents loved her? What right did he have to preach about responsibility? Forgiveness? The man who took no responsibility? Who didn't deserve forgiveness?

Darn right, he was responsible for Justin's death. She pinned her trembling hands between her knees. At least he finally admitted it. The guilt would plague him for forever. Maybe that was a worse sentence than jail time.

#

Sheila found Richard slumped against the brick, hands holding his head down. She'd heard every word he'd spoken to that young couple. At last, she understood his anger and his passion. Ignoring the freezing concrete, she crouched down in front of him. "Why didn't you tell me?"

"Tell you what?" He spoke to the sidewalk.

"I heard what you said to that couple. I know she's the sister of the boy killed in your car accident."

He crossed his arms and tucked gloved hands beneath his arms.

"I know what your old girlfriend did to you." She removed her glove and tilted his chin up, making him look at her. "Richard, I know she killed your baby."

Her hand flew to her mouth as truth slammed into her conscience.

That's exactly what she did to Joe.

"MEGHAN KEENE."

Doran's hand touched her arm. "You ready?" He was obviously eager to get this over with, to abdicate himself from all responsibility and move on as if nothing had happened. Clearly, Richard's words of warning had no effect on him.

Unfortunately, the man's words were getting to her. She sucked in a deep breath and looked down at her stomach. Was she ready? Could she be responsible for concluding this little life?

"Meggie, come on."

She ignored him. If she went through with this, how would she be any different from Justin's killer? She laughed. There would be no difference. She wouldn't be any better than him. Her life sentence of guilt would be as great. She couldn't live with that.

God, help me. The prayer was a simple one—the first she'd purposely uttered in months. Still, she felt God pointing her in a new direction. She had to leave.

Call Mom and Dad. It was a scary thought. They would be shocked. Disappointed. Angry. But, that was infinitely better than living with what she'd almost done.

"Doran, I can't." She stood and ran from the clinic. It didn't matter if he was behind her or not. All that mattered was calling her mom and dad. With tears blurring her vision, she glanced left and right, then stepped into the street.

Tires screeched. She turned, and a car barreled toward her. Time slowed as she heard voices shouting, brakes squealing, and horns honking before her body hurtled through the air.

RICHARD REACHED OUT TO STOP MEGHAN FROM stepping into the street, but was too late. The car's brakes screeched as it rammed into her, flinging her back onto the sidewalk. He knelt next to Meghan, and Sheila dialed 911. The girl was unconscious, but had a pulse and was breathing, thank God. Her left leg was bent back unnaturally, bleeding. *Please God, help her.*

"Meghan?" Doran squatted next to Richard.

A bystander yelled into the clinic, asking for a doctor.

"I didn't mean to hit her." A college-aged woman stood by the dented hood of the offending car, arms hugging herself. "She just stepped out in front of me."

"I know." Sheila was right there, offering a hug. "We saw the whole thing. It was an accident."

A grey-haired man in a white lab coat jogged from the clinic and knelt across from Richard.

"Please, everyone step back." The doctor checked Meghan's pulse.

Richard stood and backed away, pulling Doran along with him while Sheila sat and held Meghan's hand.

"Is she going to be all right?" Doran's voice quivered.

"Pray." Richard backed into the wall, closed his eyes and steepled his hands over his face. Seconds later he felt someone next to him, cheap cologne wafted through the air. Richard braced his hand on Doran's shoulder and whispered a prayer.

A distant siren whined over the plea. Richard's petitions swelled as the siren grew louder and its vibrations shook the sidewalk, then faded to eerie silence. Meghan had to be all right. The Keenes couldn't bear another loss. *The Keenes!* He rubbed his temples. He needed to be the one to place this devastating phone call.

CHAPTER *forty two*

Sheila gripped Richard's trembling hand as they entered Meghan's hospital room together, hours after the accident. To have this young woman ask for him was a true miracle.

They stopped beside her bed. Richard released Sheila's hold and stuck both hands in his pockets. "Your dad says you're doing well."

Meghan held up an ultrasound picture. "I'm about ten weeks along. I even heard her heartbeat. Amazing, isn't it?"

Richard stared at the picture. "Incredible."

"May I?" Sheila reached for the child's first portrait and studied it. Already the head and limbs were apparent. "Beautiful."

"She is, isn't she?"

"She?" Sheila jerked her gaze from the photo toward Meghan.

"Well, they can't tell yet, but I don't like saying 'it.'"

"I understand." How often had Sheila said 'it' when referring to her pregnancies? This child was real. Not just some nameless blob on a medical website. Not a clump of tissue. Not an 'it.' Suppressing tears, Sheila handed back the photo. "A miracle."

"I know. It's hard to believe I almost …" Meghan sniffled.

"Shhh." Sheila handed Meghan a tissue, and used one herself. "I've been in your shoes. You don't need to offer any excuses."

"Really?"

Sheila nodded. "I'll give my card to your parents. Call me anytime if you need to talk."

Richard circled his arm around her waist, sending warmth throughout her body. "Believe me, she's a good listener."

Meghan bit into her lip. "Would you mind listening now?"

"I'd love to." What Sheila would have given to have someone

329

listen to her all those years ago.

"Thank you."

Richard carried two chairs to Meghan's bedside.

They sat, and Meghan slowly raised her gaze to Richard. "I need to thank you for talking with me back at the clinic. You saved me." She patted her stomach. "You saved us."

Sheila wrapped her arm through his. The poor man still shook.

"I didn't do anything, really."

He did more today than he realizes.

"If you hadn't been at the clinic …" Meghan wiped her eyes. "Mom said you two stayed with me all day."

Sheila clasped Meghan's hand in hers. "It was the least we could do. It took your parents a while to get here. We wouldn't have left you alone."

Meghan peered up at Richard. "Even after how I treated you?"

"You had good reason." Richard's hands fisted on his thighs.

"Maybe, but you're not the person I always believed you to be."

"Your beliefs were justified."

"I don't know about that anymore. What I do know is, I need to make it right. Back at the clinic, you asked for forgiveness … I do forgive you."

Richard pinched the bridge of his nose. "You don't have—"

Sheila lightly elbowed his side. The man wouldn't let go of his guilt.

He reached behind his neck, grasping at the chain. "Thank you."

Meghan leaned back into the pillows stacked behind her. "It wasn't your fault."

He released the chain. "What wasn't…?"

Tears caressed the poor girl's cheeks. "Justin's death … It was my fault."

Richard shook his head. "No. You weren't anywhere near—"

"He shouldn't have been on that road. He was going to protect my honor."

"Meghan, please," Richard said. "You don't have to—"

"Please, let me say this."

Richard nodded.

"You see, at one of the graduation parties Justin went to, he overheard some guys bragging about how the night before, this guy …" Meghan blinked.

"Honey, it's okay. You don't have to say anymore." Anger boiled in Sheila's gut. She gave Meghan's hand a gentle squeeze.

"But, nothing happened. The guy wanted to, and even tried … but his parents drove up. I was able to get away."

Richard's knuckles whitened. "And you never told anyone."

Meghan shook her head. "I wasn't supposed to go out with him in the first place. How could I say anything? And then Justin …" Meghan's jaw trembled.

"Oh, honey. It wasn't your fault. None of this was your fault."

"But I feel … if it weren't for me …"

Richard touched Meghan's arm. "Justin still made the choice to drive, Meghan. It wasn't your fault."

"But—"

"But, right now you need to focus on the future." Sheila pointed to the ultrasound. "Let beauty grow from the tragedy."

Meghan stared at the picture, and a smile bloomed on her face. "Justin would call this a miracle."

In more ways than one.

"Good evening, Meghan."

Sheila turned toward the male voice, and a doctor walked toward them.

"If you'll excuse me, folks."

"Certainly, doctor." Richard embraced Meghan's hand between both of his. "Thank you."

Sheila kissed Meghan's cheek and whispered so only Meghan could hear. "I don't think we're done seeing miracles."

CHAPTER *forty three*

Richard ran a hand over his whiskered chin and knelt at the railing in the hospital chapel. Sunlight no longer filtered through the stained glass panels lining the walls. Thankfully, it had shone on Meghan earlier in the day. That she'd survived the accident, sporting only a broken leg, was a true miracle. Add to that a healthy baby and the arrival of Meghan's parents, not even Sheila disputed God's presence. It was fitting he spend time giving thanks for prayers answered.

A hand embraced his shoulder as he prayed, then the cushion sank below his knees. He opened his eyes and peeked over. "Sheila," he whispered.

"Hi. Would you mind if we talked for a second?"

"Sure." Richard took her hand and led her to a cushioned pew.

"Can we talk in here?"

"Can't think of a better place." He squeezed her hand and held on. "What do you need to talk about?"

Her eyes rose to his. "About earlier today. About what you told Meghan and Doran."

He looked down. How those words about Marissa's abortion had spilled out earlier in the day, he'd never understand. He'd never told anyone and planned to keep it that way for forever.

"Please. You can tell me."

"You wouldn't understand." Sheila was the last person he wanted to confide in.

"Try me."

Richard released her hand, folded his arms on the back of the pew in front of him, and stared at the crucifix hanging above the altar.

A loving father's sacrifice.

Maybe it was time Sheila heard the father's side of the story. "I never told you about the disagreement I had the night of the accident, did I?"

"You said you had a nasty encounter, but never explained. I never thought to ask. I assumed it was business related."

He shook his head, and relayed the events of that night, reliving it once again. Once the story was told, he dried his eyes and glared at Sheila. "What kind of man does that make me? I couldn't even protect my own child!"

"You're certain she went through with it?"

"Absolutely. Marissa called me afterward to rub it in. Said she was glad she wouldn't have to raise a child of a killer."

Her hand rested between his shoulder blades. "I'm so sorry."

Sorry didn't bring aborted baby's back. *Sorry* couldn't bring Justin back. *Sorry* couldn't undo anything he'd done. "I lost a lot that week, all due to my own selfishness. Nothing happened I hadn't begged for." He gazed at the cross where Jesus still hung. Richard's vices had nailed him there. "At least I've got Jesus to turn to now. Without him, I'm scared to think of where I'd be."

"Have you told anyone else?"

"No. My family knew I'd been dating Marissa. I told them we had an argument and broke things off that night. I never explained what the argument was about."

"Why not? It's obviously wearing on you."

"One tragedy per night is enough to burden people with. Can you imagine how my mom would feel if I told her she should have another grandchild, but that grandchild had been ripped from the womb courtesy of its own mother? That would kill my mom. She doesn't need to know. No one else ever needs to know. God knows. You know. Marissa knows. That's enough."

Sheila draped her arms over the pew and nodded toward the front of the chapel. "I thought Christian beliefs were based on an empty cross."

His gaze shifted toward her and then upward to the cross. The change of subject was appreciated. And, the topic she brought up was one he'd gladly talk about. "Yes, an empty cross, but more importantly, an empty tomb."

"Debbie says the empty cross is a reminder to Christians of

Jesus' resurrection." Sheila pointed to the crucifix. "Why is he still hung here?"

"Sometimes, when we see pristine crosses made of gold, silver, stained glass, it's easy to forget Jesus' sacrifice. The crucifix reminds us of his pain and suffering, of the blood he shed just for us. He was perfection, taking on all our sins."

She sat back in the pew.

He joined her and continued to stare forward.

"Do you think—" Sheila turned to him and dragged his chain and key from its hiding place. "—the reason Jesus is still on the cross is because you won't let him down?"

Richard opened his mouth, but nothing came out. He glanced down at the key, at the sin he refused to relinquish.

For someone disdaining Christianity, Sheila was far too wise.

CHAPTER *forty four*

God, what am I doing here? Richard had hoped, he'd prayed for another miracle. Apparently, the answer was no as here he stood freezing next to a makeshift stage fronting a crowd of abortion supporters, listening to Carolyn Rivers make Sheila's introduction.

"I'd like you all to welcome Sheila Peterson, a University of Wisconsin at Madison alumnus who made a name for herself on campus representing women's reproductive rights in the late eighties and early nineties. Currently she holds an esteemed position as Executive Sales Director for Wharton Sports out of Minneapolis. Please welcome her back."

Sheila strode to the Plexiglas lectern amidst vigorous applause.

He couldn't clap. If anything could have changed Sheila's mind, it would have been yesterday's events. But no, she asserted yesterday's wonders solidified her grounds for speaking today. Therefore, he was here providing the support he promised.

Why did he have to fall in love with someone he could never marry? After today, it would be time to move on, leave her entirely in God's hands, no matter what Debbie said. If that meant living alone for the rest of his life, then so be it.

Sheila glanced over at him.

Without smiling, he gave a short wave then planted his gloved hands into his jacket pockets as she raised the microphone to her height.

"Thank you for welcoming me back to your lovely city." Her words froze into white clouds. "My time in Madison was very memorable. I am thrilled to be asked back to talk about an issue that is very near to my heart, one that has had a profound effect on my life."

And mine. Richard stared at his boots, clenching his teeth.

"Carolyn's introduction was quite correct. When I attended college here in the early nineties, I was an outspoken campaigner for the women's Right to Choose movement, for a woman's constitutional right to privacy."

For denying father's rights.

"At that time I stood where many of you now stand, or may have stood. Some of you may be confronted with the same decision I faced before entering college. You see, when I was sixteen, I was the victim of date rape."

A murmur whispered through the audience.

"And, yes, I became pregnant." Sheila looked down briefly. Her chest rose and fell before she glanced back up. "There was no way I was bringing a baby into the world under those circumstances. And, who could argue with me? Plus, I was an honors student working diligently to earn scholarships for college. A pregnancy would eliminate all hope of that. I knew I couldn't remain pregnant. My mother agreed."

Right. She forced you.

"I had an abortion."

Richard's stomach seized. *God, I hate this!*

"Dr. Rivers was the doctor, the same doctor providing the service for many of you today." Sheila turned and gestured to the white-haired physician seated between his wife and a state senator. Dr. Rivers stood and waved, responding to generous applause. Seated next to the senator was a woman Carolyn Rivers had introduced as a representative of the local Planned Parenthood health center.

Planned Parenthood health center. There was an oxymoron if he ever heard one.

"Dr. Rivers was gentle and carefully explained what was happening. My mother stood by me, supporting my choice wholeheartedly. I firmly believed I had made the right decision, it was the *only* choice to make."

That's such a lie. He wished he could scream it out to the crowd.

"Several years later I became pregnant again. This time the father was someone I didn't love, someone whom I had no

338

intention of marrying. I had my career to think of. I had worked too hard to achieve my goals, and a baby would only complicate matters. I wasn't about to forfeit my career as I had seen so many other women do when faced with an unintended or unwanted pregnancy. Again, there was only one viable option for me."

For you? What about Joe? God, why did I come? What possible purpose did he serve by being here?

"Admittedly, I underwent the procedures with a great deal of naiveté. That's what truly encouraged me to return today."

His head jerked up, and his gaze briefly met hers before she focused back on her captive audience. One that now included him.

"Controversy has plagued a woman's right to know. What I have gone through during the past several months has convinced me women *want* to know. We want and deserve to be educated on all the consequences of abortion. The good and the bad."

Richard eyed the four-dignitary panel on the stage and felt a smile pull at his lips. So, they weren't aware of Sheila's intentions either. Her subterfuge had them squirming in their frozen chairs, and it clearly wasn't from the below zero temperatures.

"I discovered Post Abortion Stress Syndrome is more than just a medical term meant to frighten us away from the abortion clinics. Pain, nightmares, a longing to cradle my baby, the desire to permanently terminate my inner pain, were all very real, and that is just a brief detailing of the possible symptoms."

The panel muttered amongst themselves. An agitated crowd echoed the sentiments.

If they were worried, maybe he should be rejoicing.

"Now, when I look back on my choice to have the abortions, to be free to go on with the life I had perfectly landscaped for myself …"

Her shoulders rose and fell as she looked out at the audience. She turned and peered at those behind her. Carolyn Rivers sat on the edge of her chair as if preparing to stand. Then Sheila locked smiling eyes with him.

This time he smiled, pulled his hands from his pockets, and gave her a thumbs up.

She turned back to the microphone, shoulders squared, chin

raised. "I realize both times … I made the wrong choice."

Yes! He pumped his fists. *God, she does understand.*

She looked over at him and winked, ignoring the angry voices jeering through the crowd, and Carolyn Rivers hustling toward the lectern.

"Those babies …" Sheila looked at him and smiled her deepest dimpled smile, keeping her focus on him as her voice carried over the loudspeakers. "They were real. Babies who, I believe, are now resting in God's arms."

Richard's jaw dropped. He ran up the stage steps, two at a time, placing himself between a stunned mob and Sheila.

"We need to get out of here." He tugged her away from the lectern, and pushed her to the steps. Her bracelet caught on the stair railing, slid from her arm, and fell between the metal steps. She froze for a millisecond and stared, but then she smiled and ran alongside Richard to his pickup. Only once they were safely on the road, did they start laughing.

Maybe he was going to get his miracle after all.

CHAPTER *forty five*

Sheila opened her condominium door before turning back and accepting her luggage from Richard. "You sure you won't come in?"

He shook his head. "No way I'm crossing that threshold without a crowd of people."

With her finger, she drew an "X" over her heart. "I promise, no games."

Smirking, he pocketed his hands in his jacket. "Like that would matter."

"Okay." She placed her suitcase, only one this time, inside her home then stepped out and shut the door. "I guess we'll have to talk out here." The temperature had risen to a near-balmy ten degrees above zero. With no wind, it actually felt good.

Grinning, he leaned his shoulder into the side of her building. "Haven't we just spent the last five hours talking?"

How she loved his smile. She'd missed it the last few days hidden beneath that hideous beard. Those whiskers said their farewell at a truck stop along the way home, thank goodness.

"Perhaps. But, that was car talk. This is serious." She walked past him down her steps.

"Uh-oh."

She turned around and glanced up. "Maybe you should reserve judgment."

He nodded and jogged down the steps. "After your speech this afternoon, I guess you're right."

When Richard tucked her arm around his, she was surprised, but said nothing, pretending it was the most natural thing for him to do.

Perhaps it was. It had been that way since the very first date.

Without speaking, she led him down the sidewalk toward the Mississippi, a river brimming with character. To judge this wide, wild river by its humble beginnings at Lake Itasca, Minnesota, where even the youngest child could walk across its flow, would clearly ignore its true character.

She swallowed hard. Was that what she'd done with Jesus? Judging him and stereotyping all Christians because of her singular experience rather than view the complete picture? Until she met Richard's family, she'd been unwilling to take another look. They aroused her curiosity with their acceptance. Debbie answered questions with her friendship. Richard convinced her through his willingness to love her even when she dragged him back through his nightmares. Perhaps it was time to view the truth.

"I'd like to go closer." She nodded toward the river.

"Lead the way."

She pulled him across the asphalt parkway. and plowed through knee-deep snow toward the icy water. The Mississippi had nearly surrendered to winter's onset. It would never completely submit. To give up its fight would mean its death.

Maybe that was what she'd been thinking these past months. To surrender to Richard's and Debbie's God, would ultimately end her life. Considering the direction her life was heading, that may not be so bad.

In a few months, the great river would experience a rebirth and rush unhindered toward the goal it was created for. Sheila didn't want to wait until spring. She didn't want to wait another minute.

She quickened her steps, pulling Richard down a recently cleared walking/biking path to a concrete bench hiding beneath a two-inch snowfall. Together, they pushed the snow to the ground then sat side by side. His arm didn't return to hers. Truthfully, it didn't matter anymore. Other issues now took precedence.

"Thank you, again, for supporting me these past couple days. It meant more to me than you can imagine."

"You don't know how many times I wanted to call and back out. But if I had …" He shook his head. "I would never have seen God's hand so clearly at work."

"Me neither." She stared out at the frozen water.

"Excuse me?"

In her peripheral vision, she saw him turn toward her. "That's what I want to talk to you about." Slowly, she pivoted her body until her knees grazed against his. "These last forty-eight hours were about seeing the big picture and admitting the truth. To deny God would be like denying winter's here. I can't do it anymore."

With her gloved hand, she wiped a tear from his cheek. "You're an old softy." Her hands covered his and pulled them down so her gaze could meet his. "I need your help. What do I do now?"

"You say 'yes.'"

"Yes?"

He nodded, his eyes ablaze with sincerity. "Say 'yes' to letting Jesus in. He's waiting for you. He waited for me a very long time."

"Will you help me?"

A grin shimmered on his face, and his hands surrounded hers as he bowed his head and led her in prayer.

She kept her head down instructing herself to breathe. She hadn't expected to feel anything, but a swell of emotions rushed over her. Like the mighty Mississippi surging from Lake Itasca down to the Gulf of Mexico, her body tingled and warmed as if she was being renewed from head to toe.

Reborn.

RICHARD RELEASED SHEILA'S GLOVED HANDS and stared up at a full moon with one thing on his mind. *Can I?* A lone cloud hid the moon then revealed it, winking the answer Richard knew was right. So, he wasn't totally prepared; Sheila would forgive him.

He covered Sheila's hands with his. "How are you doing?"

Her eyes flickered open and she smiled, illuminating her eyes with a depth he hadn't seen before. "I'm sorry I waited so long."

"You and me both." He squeezed her hands. "There's something I'd like to tell you."

"I'm listening."

He cleared his throat and stretched his neck from side to side summoning the courage to speak his next words, words he'd rehearsed more out of wishful thinking than belief he'd ever utter them. "Nine months ago, I was a man who merely existed from day to day, unsure of what the future held for me. Then you smiled at me and found your way into a closed heart."

Just as she was smiling now. No, now was even better. This smile held love and sincerity, not ulterior motives. "You gave me something to look forward to each day. You made me smile again—laugh again. You challenged me. You made me think of someone other than myself for once. I really believe if I hadn't met you, I would still be that brooding, unhappy man. I know God placed you in my path that day, and I've thanked him every day for you, even when I didn't believe we could be together. Admittedly, the thought of living without you has been unbearable."

"Richard?" Her hands quivered beneath his.

"Shh. I'm on a roll, here."

She bit into her lower lip, but a coy smile remained.

He removed a glove and traced the outline of her face. "I want to be there for you when you're happy, when you're hurting, and for all the everyday moments in between. I hope you feel the same way."

Her hand covered her mouth, and she nodded.

Yes! That was his signal. Without releasing her hand, he rose from the bench. He knelt one knee in the snow, keeping his eyes locked with hers. "I know I'm not prepared for this, and I'm hoping you'll forgive me, but I don't want to wait another second."

"Don't," she whispered with tears freezing on her cheeks.

His thumb caressed her ring finger. "Sheila Marie Peterson, I love you more than I believed I could love someone else. I have for a very long time." He swallowed the knot in his throat. Once released, his next words couldn't be recanted. "I'd be honored if you would choose to spend the rest of your life with me."

He raised her hand, removed her glove and kissed her empty ring finger before peering up. "Sheila, will you marry me?"

She reached over and started unzipping his winter coat.

"Hey, hey." His hand covered hers. "First you've got to say yes, then we both have to say I do."

With a smirk, she shook his hand off. "I have one condition before I give you an answer."

"Oh?" *God, I thought you said yes.*

She reached inside his jacket, inside his sweatshirt, and pulled on the chain, dragging the key against his chest before it broke free from the beneath his shirt. "There's something you need to get rid of first."

Richard stared down at the key now resting in her hand. Funny how a person gets accustomed to hauling around an anchor. His hand covered the key as his gaze rose to meet hers. "Is that a yes?"

She leaned over and touched her lips to his. "Definitely a yes."

CHAPTER *forty six*

Richard parked the rental sedan short of the intersection, just as he had about four months earlier. Little had changed in that time, although the snow floating lazily from the sky spread a clean, sparkling white blanket over the ground. The stoplights were still easily seen, and the cross still pointed heavenward.

No figure hung from the cross.

Remnants of any bloodshed were washed away.

Sheila was right. It was time to die to his old life. God had forgotten it. Now it was time for Richard to do the same.

He unbuckled his seat belt and opened the car door. As he put one foot on the snow-covered ground, he felt Sheila's hand on his arm.

"Are you sure you don't want me to come?"

He looked back at his fiancée—two long months stood between now and their wedding day—and smiled. "I'm certain. This is something I need to do on my own." Although, it would be easier with her beside him.

Nerves rattled his body as he tread through the snow to the place where his life changed forever. Why was it so hard to let go?

He knelt in front of the cross and read the tributes. This time Richard smiled. He'd meet this young man in heaven.

Breathing deeply, he reached up behind his neck. Both hands grasped at the chain and lifted. As the shackle rose above his head, the key appeared from beneath his shirt. His neck felt naked, but strong. He fisted his hands around the chain and pulled at the links. The chain was stronger than expected, but he wasn't going to give up.

At last, a link weakened and broke.

His breath quickening, he dropped the chain and key into his hand. He stared at them then closed his fist.

At the base of the cross, he dug into the snow and then opened his fist. The sun's light reflected off the key, momentarily blinding him.

Ah, there was one difference in the visit to this cross. One very important difference. This time, he wasn't surrounded with darkness. For the first time ever, he was here in the day's glorious light. And that light shined brightly on him, warming him outside and in.

He turned his hand over and let it all fall, leaving his broken chains at the foot of the cross.

He was free.

> *"Then they cried to the Lord in their trouble, and he saved them from their distress. He brought them out of darkness and the deepest gloom and broke away their chains."*
> Psalm 107:13-14

EPILOGUE

You're gonna flip when you see Sheila."

Richard pulled his gaze from the mirror and glanced over at Marcus who had just entered the small Sunday school room.

"You've seen her?" Richard turned back to the mirror and attempted to loop his bow tie.

"Pictures. Remember? I like that you two decided to wait until the ceremony to see each other. It's the way it should be."

"The photographer didn't think so, but I don't care. We'll have plenty of time after the ceremony for the rest. We've got a string quartet and *hors d' oeuvres* at the hall to tide guests over till we arrive." He studied his full-length reflection, turning slightly to check his back. "Everything straight?"

Marcus stood behind him and tugged on the tuxedo. "Looks good, but you can't hold a candle to Sheila. She looks amazing, Ricky."

"You finally approve?"

"We all do. It just took awhile to get it through this thick skull that she's been good for you."

Richard yanked at the lopsided bow and huffed out a breath. His fingers weren't working right today. "How much time is left?"

Marcus tapped Richard's watch, smirking. "You've got ten more minutes to skip out. But, if you do, you can count on never speaking to us again." Marcus adjusted his own tie while Richard fumbled with his. The smirk remained on Marcus' face. "Why don't I give you a hand?"

Moaning, Richard pulled out the tie again. "Be my guest."

Marcus stood in front of him. The grin turned serious as Marcus easily formed the loops. "Did I ever apologize for not having you in our wedding?"

"No. I was angry then. If it wouldn't have tainted the rest of the family, I wouldn't have come. As it was, I heard all the whispers about me that day." He sighed, recalling his boorish behavior. "But, if you had asked, I would have said no anyway. I'd already decided that when you told me you were engaged."

"I figured so, but I'm sorry anyway. I'm as responsible for the rift between us as you were, and I'm honored you'd even ask me to stand up for you." Marcus finished the loops and stepped back. "Perfect, just like you'd do it yourself."

Richard lifted his chin eyeing the tie in the mirror and nodded. "You were also responsible for helping pull me back to the straight and narrow. Believe it or not, I heard every word you ever said to me. Some of them even sunk in." His gaze remained forward. Everything was straight, perfectly tucked, each hair in place. "You've got the ring?"

"Absolutely safe." Marcus pulled the ring from his pocket.

Richard took the ring and studied the band woven with three strands—two polished yellow gold and one white gold, with small diamonds inserted among the weave. The jeweler had outdone himself. He handed the ring back to Marcus, but it slipped from his fingers and rolled on the linoleum.

Marcus leaned down and snatched it. "I swear, you're the jitteriest groom I've ever seen." He stood, secured the ring in his pocket, gave it a reassuring tap, and laid his arm across Richard's shoulder. "If anyone should be ready it's you."

"Well, I've never gotten married before. I've never had a wedding night before."

Marcus laughed. "You're the last person who should be nervous about that."

"We waited."

Richard loved the wide-eyed expression on Marcus' face. The news actually silenced his brother. Richard wasn't going to mention how close he'd come to blowing it. Even the two-month engagement period had almost been too long.

A lopsided smile crept to Marcus' lips as if reading Richard's mind. "I'm sure it'll all come back to you."

"No doubt." Richard echoed the smile. Tonight couldn't come quick enough.

A knock on the door drew his thoughts from the wedding night back to the present. The pastor stuck his head in. "It's time, boys."

"I'm happy for you Ricky." Marcus patted his shoulder.

"I'm glad you're here for me."

BERNARD BROOKS' BASS VOICE SOUNDED through the door. "They're ready, ladies."

Sheila turned to face her reflection one more time. She was ready and excited, but that didn't take away her anxiety. She always loved capturing people's stares, but today was different. There was only one person she wanted to impress, and for him she needed to be perfect.

"You're already going to leave him speechless, Sheila. Personally, I can't wait to see the look on Ricky's face when he sees you." Debbie patted her ballooning stomach. "I'm another story. Why you ever asked me to be your Matron of Honor when I look like this, I'll never know."

Sheila returned Debbie's gaze. "You know you're radiant."

"Please." Debbie rolled her eyes and grinned. "I admit I'm trying to enjoy this pregnancy more than the others, since it's definitely going to be the last."

Sheila looked back in the mirror at the flat stomach she worked so hard at maintaining, and tried to imagine being pregnant. Maybe, she too would soon wear that same radiant glow. Both she and Richard longed for parenthood.

"Ladies?" Bernie tapped on the door. "Are you ready?"

First, she had to get through the wedding.

Debbie laid her hand on Sheila's arm. "Ready?"

Sheila inhaled a deep breath and nodded. She couldn't speak, afraid her voice would expose her tousled nerves.

They walked from the room led by Kaitlynn, Lilly, and Jaclyn, who couldn't wait to play the roles they had rehearsed so hard the night before. Bernie tucked Sheila's arm into his as they lined up behind the closed doors leading into the sanctuary.

There was no turning back now.

RICHARD FOLLOWED MARCUS TO THEIR PLACE IN front of their parent's church. The pews were full. It seemed everyone wanted to see for themselves that the wayward son had decided to settle down. He caught his mother's eyes, moist with joy, and smiled. Janet and Jerry sat alongside, returning his smile. Nathan and Joshua stood as silent sentinels in the back, dressed handsomely in their black tuxes, prepared to open the doors.

The organ processional began, and he scanned the rest of the faces. Relatives, family friends, Wharton employees, and his secretary occupied the pews. With the exception of Ethan, no one from ACM Technologies—not another person had even been invited from the place where he'd spent nearly his entire grownup life.

Then he spotted the Keenes. Vernon, Mary, and Meghan, seated near the back, smiled when Richard found them. No other guest made him feel this way—humbled that they had not only found it in their hearts to forgive him, for what he'd deemed an unforgivable sin, but that they would also honor him by witnessing his marriage vows. He gazed up at the arched ceiling, squeezed his eyes and swallowed. *Thank you, Lord.*

"YOU LOOK LOVELY TODAY, SHEILA." RICHARD'S father tapped her hand as the processional played in the background. The girls began their walk up the short aisle, baskets in hand, dropping orange petals a handful at a time on the white runner. "We're all delighted that you're joining our family."

Sheila shut her eyelids and held them closed. She almost wished he'd be quiet. With her voice shaking, she gave a short response. "Thank you, Bernie." Her full feelings would be expressed later when she was less emotional, but his next words dug deeper, and it was all she could do to keep from bawling.

"Call me Dad, please," her soon-to-be father-in-law said as Debbie disappeared through the door. "You're part of our family now. I hope you feel welcome."

Sheila squeezed his arm, grateful beyond words that God was blessing her not only with an adoring husband, but with a family who graciously accepted her as sister and daughter.

GRINNING, RICHARD WATCHED HIS NIECES, CLAD in long orange dresses, walk over the white runner, sprinkling it with orange petals. After they reached the final pew, Kaitlynn grabbed Lilly's hand and led her to their daddy before walking to her designated spot. She stood not an inch away from where she practiced the night before. That was his Katydid, all right.

Debbie and Jerry had done a marvelous job of parenting their girls. Richard hoped he'd be half as good a father. His gaze turned back to Jaclyn as she passed the front pew.

She looked up and spotted him. "Uncle Ricky." She ran to him, the remaining petals flying from the basket.

He boosted her up and kissed her forehead with guests giggling in the background.

"Did I do good?" Jaclyn asked.

"Absolutely perfect, Princess," he whispered, rubbing his nose against hers. "Now go see your mommy." He put her down in the direction of her mother and patted her bottom.

Marcus leaned in. "She doesn't even care about her daddy."

Richard grinned and redirected his gaze to the back of the sanctuary where Debbie appeared.

Marcus leaned in again, whispering, "Our sister sure cleans up nice."

But, Richard looked past Debbie, eager to see his bride.

Debbie finished her ascent up the short aisle and Marcus left his side. The music flowed into a change and Sheila stepped up.

"Wow." His lips quietly formed the exclamation and his knees nearly buckled.

Sheila's hair fell in loose curls behind her neck accenting its long and slender line. The dress was simple, really: all satin, no lace, and a hint of orange. Its neckline formed a wide "V" from off the shoulders, and the sleeves hugged her arms, reaching to her hands. Its A-line silhouette complimented her body.

She carried a single, orange rose, the flower of fascination.

And passion.

Sheila's quick smile indicated she caught his look, and she seemed to flow up the remainder of the aisle. His father hugged and kissed her as he passed her off to his son. A simple pat on the back was all Richard needed to know that his father was proud of him.

DISCUSSION QUESTIONS

1.) Did you enjoy the novel overall? What was your favorite scene?

2.) Who was your favorite character? Your least favorite? Did your feelings toward them change as the novel progressed? Did you identify with any of the characters? Why or why not?

3.) *Chain of Mercy* is a story of forgiveness, not solely in forgiving those who've wronged you, but also learning to receive forgiveness—sometimes a more difficult task. Can you think of a time you've needed to forgive, but found it difficult? Or have you been forgiven for something, but felt you didn't deserve it?

4.) Richard Brooks is an unlikely hero for a novel in that he's responsible for a young man's death. Did you find him a likable character? What did you think of him after learning about his role in Justin Keene's death?

5.) Each of the main characters (Richard Brooks, Sheila Peterson, Meghan Keene) has a literal and a figurative chain. Can you identify each chain? Has there ever been a time in your life when you've felt chained by something you've done or something that's happened to you?

6.) Prior to moving to Minnesota, Richard Brooks was a successful businessman in New York. Why do you think he took a job as a janitor when he could have had his choice of executive positions?

7.) Abortion is viewed from several different perspectives: from the father who had no say, a outspoken proponent of Roe v. Wade, and a teen who feels she has no choice. Were you surprised by their struggles? Could you empathize with them?

8.) Why didn't Richard want to tell anyone about his aborted child? What do you think his family's reaction would have been had he told them?

9.) The farm is a place of tranquility for Richard. Why do you think he avoided it for so long?

10.) Family plays an integral role in the main characters' lives. How did family affect Richard's behavior? Sheila's? Meghan's?

ACKNOWLEDGEMENTS

During this hilly journey of bringing *Chain of Mercy* to print, I discovered that writing a novel is far from a solitary effort. There are several people w ho deserve to share in the credit for making this dream a reality:

To my very first readers Lisa Laudenslager, Debbie Berglund, Sandy Pippo, and Pr. Steve Perkins who courageously read through a very early draft of *Chain of Mercy* before I even dreamed it could be published. I appreciate all your encouragement, helpful comments, and prayers. It was your initial support that gave this story wings.

To my first editors Jill Alton, Lori Welle, and Beth Erdahl for helping polish those early drafts.

To Dr. Connie Carleen who graciously read through an early draft and provided additional insight into medical situations and fetal development.

To Bob Everhart who guided me through legal situations.

To my critique partners:

~My first critique group—Lorna Seilstad, Shannon Vannatter, and Jerri Ledford. I think I've learned more about writing from the three of you than from writing courses and books combined. You took this rookie writer and made my stories shine! Not only did God bless me with fabulous critique partners, he blessed me with lifelong friends!

~Stephanie Prichard, my hawk-eyed, grammar-guru critique partner. You never let me get away with anything! Thank you for that!

~Stacy Monson—critique partner, sounding board … friend. I'm so very glad we're on this journey together!

~Monday writing group: Sharon, Chawna, Carol, John, Michelle, and Stacy. I'm in awe of the skill in this group! And to think you welcomed me in! Thank you for sharing your expertise with me.

To the Inkspers at Inkspirational Messages. I love blogging with you ladies!

To Nicole Petrino-Salter. I'm thrilled to have found someone who enjoys the same stories as I do! Thank you for being a great listener and for your constant encouragement and prayers.

To the American Christian Fiction Writers (ACFW) Minnesota Chapter, ACFW MN NICE. Thank you for your support and your excitement for teaching and nurturing fellow writers. You really are Minnesota Nice!

To Winslet Press for taking a chance on me! I love the personal attention you give your authors!

Special thank you to my sister, Gayle Balster, who read through my initial outline and then several drafts, always without complaint. I'm blessed to have you for a sister!

Hugs to my children Sarah, Bryan, and Brandon, my biggest cheerleaders, who have endured my hours of disappearing into the office whenever inspiration hits. You three are true blessings from God!

A loving thank you to my husband Marvin, my head cheerleader, sounding board, first reader, encourager. I'll never forget your response when I told you I was finally writing a book. You said, "It's about time!" Now that's love!

And finally, to my Lord Jesus Christ who provided the inspiration, who gave me this dream and encouraged me to follow through, who took my ideas and molded something new and wonderful out of them. All glory goes to You.